THESE
SORROWS
WE SEE

TAMSEN SCHULTZ

*everafter*ROMANCE

EverAfter Romance
A Division of Diversion Publishing Corp.
443 Park Avenue South, Suite 1008
New York, New York 10016
www.EverAfterRomance.com

Cover Design by Sian Foulkes
Edited by Julie Molinari

This is a work of fiction. Names, characters, places and incidents either are the
product of the author's imagination or are used fictitiously. Any resemblance to
actual persons, living or dead, events or locales is entirely coincidental.

For more information, email info@everafterromance.com

First EverAfter Romance edition March 2017.
Print ISBN: 978-1-63576-036-1

To Nav, because you're making the most of this brave, new world.

And the boys because you're the best ten-
and twelve-year-old marketing team a mom could hope for.

CHAPTER 1

MATTY BROOKS LET OUT A long-suffering sigh. It was loud enough for her friend on the other end of the cell phone to hear over the wind and noise created by Matty's new, sleek convertible. She was driving north on the Taconic State Parkway toward a small town called Windsor, a few hours upstate from New York City. She should have stayed in the city. Having been born and raised in urban areas—first New York, then DC—she was a city girl, by birth *and* by preference. But she hadn't stayed and she knew why—even if she didn't want to share that reason with her best friend. And so, opting to be obtuse, Matty answered the question Charlotte posed, if not the one she'd really been asking.

"I desperately need an expert in modern Chinese political history, Charlotte. That's the only reason I agreed to come up here, to the middle of nowhere, and dog-sit Brad's brood for a few weeks."

"Bull," came her friend's answer. "There's something bothering you. Are you having problems writing? Is your mom okay? Did Brad say something to get you to drive all the way up there?"

Her writing wasn't going as well as it usually was at this stage; she had a draft of her fifth book due to the editor in four weeks and she was behind schedule. Her mom had made no attempt to hide what she thought of Matty house-sitting for Brad. But it was the last question Charlotte asked that made Matty most uncomfortable.

Brad, her half brother, hadn't really said anything persuasive to get her to come up. Under normal circumstances, if they had been a normal family, that might not be so unusual. But she and Brad had spoken exactly three times in her life—once when she was seventeen, once at their grandmother's funeral, and once, this last time, when he'd called to ask her if she would come dog-sit for him while he was away for three weeks. He had called her several times in the past few years, but she hadn't answered. Why she had picked up the phone yesterday she didn't know, and why she had even entertained the idea of house- and dog-sitting for him, let alone agreed to it, she could no more explain than quantum physics.

But he *had* promised her an expert on modern Chinese political history—something she needed in order to finish the research for her next book. She'd tossed the request out more like a challenge than anything else when he'd asked what he could do to get her to agree to come up. Of course, Brad, with his family connections, knew someone. A classmate of his from Princeton, now the head of the Chinese department at one of the universities in Boston, was a friend and had a house in the Hudson Valley too. He'd be happy to make the introduction.

Matty didn't *really* need Brad to find an expert for her. She had enough of her own connections—especially at this point in her career—to find an expert in DC herself. But he had given her a reason, if a flimsy one, to say yes. And so she had. Though she still wasn't sure why.

"Everything is fine, Charlotte. I promise. You can imagine my mom isn't too happy, but she'll get over it. And it's not like Brad is going to be there or I'll be spending any time with him. I'm just staying at his house and watching the dogs. Besides, it's kind of pretty up here, in a bucolic kind of way," she added, taking in the view of a lush, green valley as she rounded a bend in the road. "It will be good for me to be up here, away from everything, while I finish this draft."

Charlotte made a noise and Matty knew that, although her friend wasn't buying it, she had decided not to press the issue right now. "Just be sure to wear bug spray," Charlotte said—her way of conceding, if only for the moment. "They have a lot of ticks up there. The kind that carry Lyme disease," she added. "And it's supposed to be hotter up there this week than it is down here, so be careful."

Matty smiled. No doubt Charlotte had researched everything there was to know about Windsor the moment Matty had told her she was going.

"Yes, Mom."

"And call me—or your mom—every day. I don't like the idea of you staying in a country house in the middle of nowhere all by yourself."

"But you don't mind that I stay in a city mansion in the middle of one of the most dangerous cities in the US all by myself?" Matty teased.

"You're city wise, Ms. Brooks, not country wise. Besides, they had some trouble up there a few months ago, caught some serial killer. He ended up shooting himself before they could arrest him."

Matty frowned; Brad hadn't mentioned that. Not that it changed things all that much. "People get killed in DC every day. I'm sure the serial killer was just one of those fluke things. Did he kill a lot of people?" she couldn't help but ask.

"They think about twenty-one women, but only two bodies were found in Windsor. The rest were all over the country."

"And the small-town police force caught him," Matty pointed out; it was an assumption, but a fair one, she thought. "I'll be fine."

"Just call me," Charlotte issued the order before hanging up. Matty smiled, thinking of her over-protective friend. Charlotte's reasoning wasn't always logical, but the two of them had known each other practically since birth and had been looking out for each other almost as long.

Matty pulled off the Taconic, turned left, then made an immediate right, following the directions Brad had e-mailed her. Based on the road sign she saw, she was heading away from the town itself, but her half brother had assured her that, while it might look as though the roads could wind to nowhere, it was, in fact, the right way.

But before driving too far, she was forced to stop behind a

truck and trailer waiting to make a left turn into a gas station. Noting that the station had a mini-mart—always a good thing to know—she let her eyes wander to two men who were talking out front. One wore a beige uniform of some sort and was leaning against a huge SUV that had lights on top and the head of a goofy-looking dog hanging out the window. The other man, with his hip hitched against a massive blue diesel pickup, was clad in boots, jeans, and, despite the August heat, a long-sleeved shirt that was rolled midway up his forearms. Matty let out a little laugh; she definitely wasn't in Kansas anymore—or the city, to be more precise. Maybe it was the size of the two trucks flanking the men or the fact that the man not in uniform wore clothes that were utilitarian rather than stylish, but there was no doubt in her mind that the next few weeks would be very different from her urban life. She just hoped it was in a good way.

Following Brad's directions over a railroad bridge and along a road that, on a good day, could be called one and a half lanes, she passed farmhouse after farmhouse. It all looked like something out of a Norman Rockwell painting to her—too wholesome, too quaint to be real. In fact, it was so charming she actually reminded herself of the recent serial-killer incident Charlotte had mentioned just to make the place seem a little less perfect. A little more accessible.

Quelling her rising doubts about the wisdom of her decision to come here, she passed through what Brad called Old Windsor, a "town" that consisted of Anderson's Bar and Restaurant, a post office, and a general store. Exactly another seven-tenths of a mile down the lane, she turned left onto a dirt road. There she paused for a moment and consulted the directions for the umpteenth time. According to her half brother's e-mail, the road was shared with his neighbor and Brad's house was located at the end. An end she couldn't see from where she sat, though if she craned her neck, she could make out a weathervane and what looked like the top of a barn.

Two mailboxes were perched at the side of the road—a simple black box and, next to it, a rather more colorful one. Painted hot pink with a white roof, the second box resembled an old school-house, complete with a tiny chimney. Matty assumed the pink one was the neighbor's. Brad hadn't said anything about his neighbor, but if the mailbox was anything she could go by, she guessed its owner was decidedly un-Brad-like and therefore someone she needed to meet.

The undeniable beauty of the place, the clean and quiet air, and the interesting mailbox all served to quash the remaining doubts she harbored about making the trip. In fact, as she made her way slowly up the road, she was actually beginning to think this little journey had been a good decision, albeit an out-of-character one for her. And then, as she came around a slight bend and Brad's property came into view, her heart actually fluttered a little bit. She might not care much about her half brother, or even know him well enough to know if she cared, but his home made her feel like she was stepping back into the warm embrace of history.

Continuing up the drive, she came alongside an enormous red barn on her right. She had no problem envisioning generations of farmers moving in and out of the structure, tending to livestock, storing hay, and doing all sorts of other things farmers did. She braked for a moment beside the building and took it in. She'd never seen a barn of this size before. Scratch that, she'd seen polo barns and more modern barns of this size, but she'd never seen a historical barn of such stature. And it *was* old—she could tell from the wood siding, which was well tended but weathered, and the slight tilt to the entire building.

Unbidden, a smile touched her lips, and what little tension was left in her since she'd agreed to come to Windsor slipped away. She eased her foot off the brake and continued up the road. Also on the right, the house was positioned so that the drive came up parallel to the entrance rather than straight on. The two-story wooden farmhouse was built on a hill with what looked like a stone foundation. It appeared that the view from the other side was of a vibrant, sweeping, green pasture that seemed, from her perspective, to go on for miles.

The house itself was built in the Greek Revival style. Clean lines dominated the exterior and the big, paned windows were lined with shutters. There was enough architectural detail to provide some depth and the soft cream color, highlighted with earthy tones, made it inviting as well as stunning. There was also a free-standing garage facing the gravel parking area in front of the main house. Though built in the same style as the house, judging by the materials, it was probably the newest building on Brad's property.

But the beauty of the architecture aside, it was the gardens that made the place seem magical. Lush, green fields surrounded the property, but well-tended planting beds and paths had been created, and they meandered around the land closest to the house. In those beds and along those paths were flowers of every color, style, and height that she could imagine. Inhaling a deep breath scented with fresh-cut grass, humid air, and roses, Matty acknowledged that never in her life had she seen such spectacular gardens outside of an arboretum. Not even in her own yard.

From Brad's e-mail, she knew that the main entrance to the house was actually a small door that led into the kitchen—toward the left side of the house—even though a more traditional grand entry graced the center of the building. And as she pulled to a stop by this side entry, she could hear the cacophony of Brad's dogs inside. She'd been told there were five and, by the sound of it, they were a vocal five.

She stepped onto the small flagstone patio in front of the door and found the key under a pot of dahlias where Brad had said he'd leave it. She would have taken a moment to appreciate the sweet little café table and chairs set up on the patio, a perfect place for an early morning cup of coffee, if it hadn't been for the melee she heard inside. With a small laugh at the big noise, she opened the screen and unlocked the door. When it swung open, she was immediately accosted by noses, tails, and furry bodies.

Laughing aloud at the chaos, she managed to push her way inside to the kitchen. Not pausing to look at her surroundings just yet, she dumped her purse on a table and went down on her knees to greet the dogs. Not surprisingly, the yellow Lab, Bob, was right in her face. Rufus, the Great Dane, was nosing her head while Lucy, a wiry little mutt, was springing up and down from all four of her short, dainty legs. Roger, the Newfoundland mix, was gently sniffing Matty in curiosity, and Isis, the gorgeous Ridgeback, was standing back, assessing the situation. It was a motley crew, but she knew from Brad that all of them were rescue dogs and had come to him in various ways over the past two years.

She stayed low to the ground, petting all of them and letting them check her out until, with the exception of Lucy who seemed in a perpetual state of wiggliness, they all quieted down. Rising, Matty glanced at the water bowls lined up against one of the walls and was pleased to see the dogs hadn't run out of water while waiting for her. She was about to take a closer look at the house when the dogs suddenly burst into renewed chaos and all ran to the door. The noise caught her off guard and her heart rate leapt in response. She didn't know what they were barking at but figured that with five dogs, sudden chaos was probably something she was going to have to get used to. At least she'd get some cardio workouts in without actually having to exercise.

When she opened the screen door to let the animals out, all but Isis went tearing down the driveway. In the quiet of their absence, she could hear what had set them off—the telltale sound of a diesel pickup truck. And judging by the increasing volume, it was headed up the drive in her direction.

Frowning to herself, Matty walked out onto the patio as the truck she'd seen at the gas station on her drive in pulled into a small parking area by the barn. The dogs surrounded the driver's door and, when the lanky man in the long-sleeved shirt and jeans stepped out, the barking stopped—even if the body wags continued. She had no idea who he was, but at least it looked like the dogs knew him and, judging by the way the man rubbed heads, scratched ears, and patted shoulders, he knew the dogs.

When she stepped from the shadows and into view, the man's head came up and in that instant she experienced something she never had before. The moment slowed and everything around her faded into a dull presence. She recognized the sound of birds and sensed a breeze against her bare throat, but she didn't really hear or feel them. Everything inside her, for one brief moment, stilled and focused only on this man in front of her—on his eyes that were locked on hers.

And then Isis pressed her cold nose to Matty's bare thigh and the world fell back into place.

With a little shake of her head, she moved off the patio; the man straightened away from the dogs as she walked toward him. She'd already noticed his form, but hadn't realized how tall he was—two or three inches over six feet, if she had to guess. She'd place him in his early- to mid-thirties and, given his wiry build, which she thought suited a man, she'd bet he had been a very skinny kid. But it was his eyes that caught and held her attention, eyes that didn't stray from hers as she made her way toward his truck. They weren't an unusual shade or anything like that, but they were a rich, dark—very dark—brown that matched his hair almost exactly. Hair that was a little longer than was fashionable, at least in the city, and that curled over the tops of his ears.

"I'm Dr. Dashiell Kent, Brad's vet. I'm here about the cows," he said, holding out his hand. Matty took it in hers and immediately noticed not just the rough texture but the dry heat of his palm.

"Hi, I'm—wait, did you just say *cows*?" she repeated, dropping his hand and looking around. She hadn't seen any on her drive up and Brad had most definitely not mentioned any cows.

He inclined his head. "Yes, six of them. Brad probably put them in the barn."

Her stomach dropped. Dogs she could handle, but cows?

"Is Brad here?" Dr. Kent asked, moving to the back of his pickup. He let the tailgate down and began pulling out supplies of some sort.

Matty shook her head. "No. I'm Matty Brooks. I'm Brad's half sister. The more honest and forthcoming half, obviously. He asked me to dog-sit for him but sure as hell didn't say anything about cows." It dawned on her that she didn't know this man from Adam and perhaps she should watch her language. He didn't look like a prude, in fact, if the vibes she was picking up from him were anything to go on, he was probably about as nonprudish as she was, but still.

He smiled as he reached for a wicked-looking needle. "Well the good news is, especially this time of year, the cows are easy to take care of. I just need to give them a vaccination, and then I'll turn them out into the pasture. They don't need to be fed since the grass is good, but you may want to keep an eye on their water. It will refill automatically, but in this heat it's always good to check it occasionally to make sure the refill mechanism hasn't broken."

His words were meant to be comforting but somehow they weren't—what if something happened to one of the cows? She would never be able to tell if one was sick or hurt unless it was actually hobbling on three legs—or dead.

"Wait," she said as his words sunk in. "You said the good news is the cows are easy to take care of. Does that mean there's bad news, Dr. Kent?"

"Call me Dash," he answered. "I don't know if I'd call it bad news, but I'd guess if he didn't tell you about the cows, he probably also didn't tell you about the cats, rabbits, and chickens," he continued.

Matty stared at the man for a long moment, waiting for him to laugh and say something like "gotcha!" But he didn't.

"That son of a bitch," she muttered then cast a look at Dash to make sure she hadn't offended him.

He laughed even as he continued prepping his shots. "I've heard worse, believe me. Brad really didn't tell you about the other animals? That's not like him," he continued, not waiting for her reply, "he's pretty meticulous about their care."

Matty shook her head. Mostly in dismay.

"And he didn't leave you any directions or instructions or anything?"

She started to shake her head again then stopped. "Actually,

I just arrived a few minutes before you did. He might have left something for me, but I haven't had a chance to take a look."

Dash held up a second mean-looking needle and tapped the container of liquid with a free finger. "Why don't you go inside and see if he left anything for you. I'll take care of the cows, let them out, then stop by. If he didn't leave anything for you, we can walk through what you'll need to do. If he did leave something, have a look and if you have any questions we can go over them."

It seemed wrong to leave him to handle six cows on his own, but as he filled a bucket with water from some tank on his truck and then arranged his supplies in a tidy box, he looked like a man who knew what he was doing.

"Are you sure?" she asked, still feeling a little guilty about leaving him to his own devices.

He smiled and she noticed he had a dimple in his left cheek. "Yeah, I got it. Brad's cows are pretty docile and the shots are quick. You go on and I'll be up in about ten minutes."

She gave him one last look before nodding and turning back toward the house. Isis and Bob trotted after her while Lucy stayed behind. Roger and Rufus, having assessed the situation and moved on several minutes earlier, were already crashed out on the patio; neither even bothered to raise their heads when she walked by.

Fifteen minutes later, Matty looked up from where she sat at the kitchen island to see Dash at the screen door.

"Come in," she waved him in.

"My boots are filthy."

"I'm not feeling so inclined to care much about Brad's floors these days."

Dash let out a little chuckle as he stepped into the room. "Those the directions?" he asked, nodding toward the paper in her hands.

"All four pages of them," she answered.

"*That* sounds more like Brad. Do you have any questions? Anything I can help with?"

She took one last look at the typed, single-spaced text. "I tried to call him but I'm sure it won't surprise you to hear he didn't answer," she said, not without a bit of wry sarcasm. Then she shook her head and set the pages down. "And why on earth would anyone want rabbits? I mean they're cute and all, but you can't cuddle them and he only has two, so it's not like he's collecting angora or anything."

"Brad's an interesting guy," Dash said, crossing the room and coming to a stop a few feet from her.

Matty arched a brow. "That's an interesting comment."

"It's not a commentary, just an observation. Where is he, by the way?" Dash asked, his eyes not leaving hers.

"I don't actually know," she frowned. And thinking back to the conversation she'd had with him, Brad hadn't really left her an opening to ask. "He didn't say and didn't really give me the opportunity to bring it up. He just asked me to come up for a few weeks and watch the dogs."

"From where?" he asked, leaning his hip against the island and crossing his arms.

"DC," she answered. "I'm a city girl. Dogs I can do, and the cats won't be too bad, but cows, chickens, and rabbits will be a new one for me."

"Well, here," he pulled a card out of his shirt pocket. Reaching for a pen on the counter, he scribbled on the back. "If you have any questions, just call me. Brad takes good care of his animals. My guess is that the biggest problem you'll have with them is what to do with all the eggs his chickens are producing this time of year."

"I should be so lucky," Matty said, taking the card and noting the cell number he'd added.

"You'll be fine. Once the surprise of it all has worn off, you'll be able to kick back, relax, and enjoy the country, cows and all."

"I think I'm going to start now. Brad says I'm welcome to any of his liquor," she said, holding up the last sheet of paper. It was a weird thing for him to write, he didn't even know if she drank. "A gin and tonic and a cool bath sounds just about perfect after my long drive. Care to join me?" She meant in the drink, but the side of his mouth ticked up and she realized how ambiguous her question sounded.

"I'd love to, but I have a few other calls I have to make. I'll take a rain check, though."

And she knew he wasn't just referring to the drink. It hadn't been her intention to suggest they share a bath, but now that it was out there, albeit only playfully so, she couldn't bring herself to think it would be a bad idea. But rather than comment, she simply inclined her head and rose from her seat to walk him out. He offered again to be a resource for her should she need it and, a few minutes later, was climbing into his truck and heading back down the road. Matty, deciding to skip the drink, stood on the patio for a few minutes listening to the sounds of the country around her. There was a sense of peace and calm about the place.

She just hoped she didn't ruin it by accidentally killing one of Brad's animals.

• • •

Dash eased his truck to a stop at the end of the dirt road that Brad's house shared. Pulling out his phone, he dialed a familiar number.

"Hey," his sister Jane answered.

"I just met her," he said without preamble.

"Met who? Oh!" she said, the realization dawning. "Really? You met her?" she repeated, beginning to laugh.

"Yes and it's not funny."

"Yeah it is. After all those years of you saying it was never going to hit you, it's kind of funny. I'm looking forward to the next month or so, it's going to be so interesting," she added, not bothering to hide her enthusiasm.

"Nice, thanks for the support. I'm a little freaked out."

"Yeah, it's like that. So, what are you going to do about it?" she asked.

"Avoid her," he answered even as he thought of the cell number—his personal cell number—he'd added to his card.

"Like that's going to work," she retorted.

"I know, but at least it might buy me some time to get used to the idea. I feel like I can't breathe."

"Oh, you're such a drama king. It might be scary as shit when it hits, but it works out fine. That's the way it's always been," he sister responded, none too helpfully. "What's she like?" she added.

Dash thought about Matty, about how concerned she was about doing the right thing for the animals and how relatively in stride she took the shit her half brother had dumped on her. Which, if he let himself think about *that* particular turn of events, was unusual too. Brad wasn't usually a "shit- dumping" kind of guy. Usually, Brad was the exact opposite. He frowned.

"Well?" his sister pressed, bringing his mind back to Matty.

He thought of the way she'd looked with her long, black hair, light brown eyes, and a face and complexion that hinted at a Latina heritage somewhere in her genealogy. And her curves—it would have been hard to miss those as she'd stood in front of him wearing a pair of short shorts and a tank top. Matty Brooks was not a waif and for that he was truly grateful.

"I'm not talking about it," he answered.

"Because that will make it more real," she taunted.

"You don't have to sound so gleeful."

"I'm your sister, of course I do. I can't wait for Mom to find out."

"But she won't find out from you, Jane," Dash warned. Lord knew what would happen if, or when, his mom found out about Matty.

"Oh please, Dash," Jane brushed him off. "You know how it works. It's the same for *everyone* in the family, and you've just acknowledged you're no different. You and this woman, whose name I don't even know, will be married within a month. I guarantee it. It's our family curse, or blessing, depending on how you look at it, so you may as well just embrace it and tell the parents. It's not like you'll be able to keep it a secret for long."

And that's what he was afraid of—because Jane was right. For as many generations as they could go back in their family, not a single person had had a period of more than a month between meeting the person they would spend the rest of their life with and marrying them. He'd always chalked it up, back in the early days, to arranged marriages and just a different kind of lifestyle. And then, with the more modern generations, he'd just thought the family promulgated the tradition because it was kind of fun and quirky. But after what had just happened to him when he'd met Matty Brooks, he wasn't so sure anything was made up. Because the feelings that had overloaded every one of his senses had been very, very real.

"Fuck," he muttered.

"You'll get there."

"I'm hanging up, Jane."

"Okay. I'll be up for the pancake breakfast in a couple of weeks. I look forward to meeting my new sister-in-law."

"You suck, you know."

"You love me. Good-bye." And she hung up.

He'd been hoping for some sympathy. He should have known better. And, unfortunately, the one thing he could agree with his sister on was that it was most definitely going to be an interesting month.

CHAPTER 2

THE NEXT DAY DAWNED CLEAR and beautiful. Matty attributed the lower temperatures to the fact that she was surrounded by open land rather than the concrete jungle of DC and took her coffee out to the back porch to enjoy the cool morning before the day got too hot. She'd explored the house the night before and had quickly realized that the north side of the building, the side that held the kitchen with its huge slate island and large French country–style table, was going to be her primary domain. From the kitchen she could easily access both an office, with windows that looked out across the fields from the back the house, and the upstairs bedrooms, through a passageway to the center hall staircase. The center hall itself, anchored at the front of the house by the formal entry, ran the length of the building, effectively dividing the house into the north and south sides. The office and the kitchen were on one side and a study and large sitting room, both of which Matty had determined to be too formal for her tastes, were on the other.

Her favorite discovery, also off the kitchen, was the screened-in porch at the back of the house. She adored its sweet little love-seat and chairs that gave her a sweeping view of the gardens that wrapped around from the sides of the house and the countryside before her. And the cows.

She eyed them from her perch and spotted all six lazily grazing not far from the house. Isis and Bob were with her on the porch while Roger and Rufus opted to stay inside. Lucy was chasing a butterfly on the lawn. The four cats had made a brief appearance to be fed, and Matty had managed to locate and care for the two rabbits and the six chickens. She still questioned Brad's interest in the rabbits, but when she collected five fresh eggs from the chicken coop, she kind of understood the appeal of the less than cuddly birds.

She was settling into the new sounds—crickets, frogs, and the occasional chicken cluck—and smells—fresh cut grass and clean air—when her phone interrupted her peaceful musings. She didn't have to look at the name on the display when it rang. It was seven o'clock, only Charlotte would call her this early.

"Yo," Matty said, answering.

"You didn't call last night. You were supposed to call when you got there."

"I am supposed to call every day. It's been less than twenty-four hours since we last spoke."

"Hours in which you could have been attacked by a serial killer or died of Lyme disease or been accosted by a ghost."

"A ghost," Matty repeated. "That's a new one." No doubt a well-researched new one.

"I was online last night and I looked up the area. Do you know they did a television special on the ghosts up there? There were a lot of Revolutionary War skirmishes in the valley and it was part of the Underground Railroad. Lots of people have died violent deaths there."

"But not in the last hundred and fifty years or so, right? And don't mention the serial killer again. He's dead already."

On the other end of the line, Matty heard Charlotte let out a long sigh. She knew her friend well and knew that Charlotte was, simply put, a worrier. But she also knew why; they'd shared many of the same early childhood experiences, experiences that had made Charlotte the way she was. And, because she understood Charlotte so well, Matty knew to let her friend do her thing. Once Charlotte got it off her chest, she wouldn't exactly stop worrying, but she would start to act like the *mostly* normal person she was.

"Thank you," Charlotte said.

"You're welcome. Feel better?"

"I'd feel much better if you were back in DC or traveling with someone. But all things considered, I'm fine."

"Good, because you're never going to guess what Brad did," Matty said then proceeded to tell her friend everything about every one of the many animals. Charlotte could always be counted on to provide sympathetic outrage on Matty's behalf and it was no different, and no less gratifying, now. They then spent a few minutes railing against Brad and his family and their lack of consideration and general uselessness. When she felt thoroughly vindicated for being tasked with such a different job than the one she'd signed up for, she ended the call by reiterating her agreement to call Charlotte or Carmen, Matty's mom, every day. The only catch was that Charlotte was off to Greece in a few days for business. And it wasn't that she didn't want to talk to her mom, they were close and talked often, but they rarely talked every day—not even when they were both in the city at the same time—and given the situation, she had rather hoped to avoid her mom, for the most part.

Still, she knew Charlotte was right; staying in touch with someone from "the outside" was probably the smart thing to do. She took a sip of coffee and stared out across the valley as she thought about her mom. A familiar wave of sorrow swept over her as she did. Her mother had risked and lost so much in her relatively short life. Abandoned by the man who had taken advantage of her and fathered her child, Carmen Viega had tried her best to make a life for herself and her daughter.

But the brutal truth was, Matty's father—Brad's father—had left them to a life Matty tried her best not to remember. Despite everything her mother had tried to do to make it better. And she couldn't imagine her mother felt any differently.

With these thoughts and memories bouncing around in her head, Matty knew she needed to be sensitive to what her mother might be feeling or thinking—for most of their lives, they were all each other had had. So she decided not to wait but to make a quick call to check in. The conversation was a bit stilted, but in the end she was glad she had made it. There was no way Matty was ever going to convince her mom that coming to Windsor was a good idea, but the call was more about showing, if not actually speaking, her loyalty to her mom.

After finishing her coffee and making sure the cows were still alive, Matty trotted back upstairs to shower and prep in the massive master suite that took up one entire side of the second floor. She was fairly sure Brad had intended for her to take one of the guest rooms down the hall, but there was no way she was going to pass up the master suite's jetted tub and king-size bed, not to mention the spectacular view from its huge windows.

Dressed in shorts and a t-shirt, her long black hair pulled back, she returned to the kitchen and opened the fridge. She had five fresh eggs, but she didn't have much of anything else for breakfast. Or any other meal. Closing the fridge, she drummed her fingers on the kitchen island and debated. She could stick with eggs all day, not make a store run, and just focus on writing. She did have a looming deadline; she did need to write.

Turning toward the door instead, she grabbed her keys as she ruthlessly replaced the words "procrastination" and "avoidance" that were floating in her head, with words like "justified" and "food is necessary." Anticipating escape, all five dogs suddenly decided to race her to the door and in the scuffle of pushing them aside she bumped into an outbound mail cubby hanging on the wall. A couple items fell out and, as she picked them up, Matty noticed that the topmost envelope was addressed to the telephone company, stamped and ready to go.

Pausing, she looked at all three of the envelopes. The second was addressed to the power company and the third to someone in DC. None of them had return labels, but reasoning that it would be a bad thing to run out of power or lose access to a landline, she shoved all three into her purse, just in case, pushed her way past the dogs, and locked the door behind her.

Twenty minutes later, she pulled into the town of Windsor. Making her way around what was perhaps the most backward, wayward roundabout she'd ever driven through, she slowed down as she traveled down Main Street. She passed a number of quaint-looking stores including an ice cream shop, a quilt shop, and a gift boutique. She also couldn't help but notice that there were two bookstores, one new and one used, on the few short blocks. Pulling into an empty parking spot across from the one selling used books, she acknowledged that the town might actually have something in its favor—with two bookstores, how bad could it be?

She hadn't seen a real grocery store on her short trip through town, but she stepped into a small health food store she'd spotted and found most of what she needed. The man behind the counter was nice enough to give her directions to a farm stand that carried both fresh vegetables and local meats, which was all she needed to round out her pantry for a week or so. Also at the recommendation of the clerk, she crossed the street to Frank's Fed Up and Fulfilled Café to grab a mocha before heading out to the farm.

She eyed the menu hanging from the wall behind the register as she stood in line. Much to her mother's chagrin, Matty didn't often eat breakfast; she wasn't interested in having it now, either, but figured it was always good to know what was available.

Stepping up to the counter she looked at the man on the other side. He certainly wasn't going to win any fashion awards any time soon, but it was the fleece vest he was wearing over his shirt that caught her eye. It was already pushing eighty-five degrees with about the same amount of humidity and in deference to economics, she assumed, the air conditioning wasn't exactly cranking.

"Aren't you hot?" she asked.

He looked at her, hovering a pen over an order pad. "What do you want?" he answered.

She almost laughed. He stared back at her, an eyebrow raised, daring her to take up more of his time. Whoever he was, he was throwing down the gauntlet. But she was pretty sure he'd never encountered a Puerto Rican girl from the Bronx with a heavy DC influence before. Matty leaned against the counter and smiled.

"I'd like an iced mocha, please."

"We don't make iced drinks," he responded.

"You do now. You know, it's not that hard. Just the mocha and a little ice."

"We don't make iced drinks," he repeated.

"I understand. It *is* hard; you have to have the right mix of drink to ice so that it doesn't get too watered down and all that. How about this," she continued, placing her hands on the counter and leaning toward him. "You make me a nice little mocha and then hand me a big ol' cup of ice and I'll take care of it. That way, if it doesn't live up to your obviously high," she paused and let her eyes drift over his clothing, "standards, I'll have no one to blame but myself."

She saw his jaw tighten as his eyes narrowed on her. She continued to smile but it was fifty/fifty whether he would actually make her what she'd asked for or kick her out. But if there was one thing she'd learned in life, it was to never let them see you sweat.

She raised a brow at him, issuing a silent challenge.

After what seemed like hours—silent, still hours—but what was probably closer to ten seconds, the man threw his pen down and began muttering to himself as he stabbed buttons on the register.

"That'll be three-fifty."

She knew better than to gloat, so she silently pulled the money out of her purse and handed it to him. Then she dropped a generous tip in the tip jar and stepped aside to wait for her beverage. A few minutes later, she walked out, iced mocha in hand. The man's attitude didn't bother her; in fact, she kind of liked it. At the very least, it showed that some people in this town had character. She might not love that character, but in her opinion, it was always better to have it than not.

After swinging by the local farm stand to pick up some veggies and meats, she made her way back to Brad's. Taking more time than was reasonable to put the groceries away, she made an early lunch, cleaned up, brushed the dogs, and washed the cat bowls before finally admitting to herself that what she was doing was procrastinating.

Once she acknowledged it, the type-A part of her insisted she "beat" her inclination, buckle down, and start writing. But another part suggested that it wouldn't be such a big deal to explore Brad's gardens—that it might even be inspirational if she did. Of course, standing in the kitchen experiencing an acute case of analysis paralysis, she knew the former wasn't as easy as it sounded or the latter as helpful as it could be given that it was unlikely Brad's beautiful New England garden would do much to inspire her modern-day political thriller set in Beijing and New York City.

And because she couldn't quite bring herself to make a decision either way, she started to clean some more. She was tidying up Brad's already tidy shelves in the office off of the kitchen when she took a moment to look out the big picture window onto the cow pasture.

It was a picturesque view of a gently rolling field. Green grass grew to knee height and the light brown cows, reminiscent of Norman from the movie *City Slickers*, dotted the landscape. Only they weren't grazing.

She frowned and walked over to the window to get a closer look. When she had a better view of the six bovines, her head, of its own accord, cocked to the side. Scattered near a few of the large maple trees that grew along the edge of the field, the cows were lying down. All of them.

Was this normal? She had no idea. Her mind flittered to the card Dash Kent had left the day before and his offer of help if she had any questions. But it seemed ridiculous to call a vet and ask if it was normal for cows to be lying down. Opting for the next best thing, or what she thought might be the next best thing, she flipped open the laptop she'd set up earlier, logged into the wireless account using the credentials Brad had included in his directions, and began to research.

But several sites later, Matty wasn't reassured. All the articles she found said that it was normal for cows to lie down, but they also said that lying down could be a sign of illness. Cursing her half brother to hell and back while simultaneously preparing her excuses to him should one of his cows die, she dug out Dash's card and placed the call.

"Dr. Kent," he answered.

"Hi, um, Dash," she hesitated, wondering if he would remember her. "It's Matty Brooks, Brad Brooks's sister. We met yesterday."

"Of course. Is everything all right?"

She paused and in that brief moment of silence the dogs erupted with barks, startling the crap out of her.

"Matty?" Dash asked. "Is everything okay?" he repeated.

She shook her head at herself, "Yes, everything is fine. Well, at least I think it is." The dogs were pawing at the door so she shoved them aside and opened it. They all went barreling out, leaving a sudden quiet.

"Matty?"

"Sorry, I got distracted for a moment. I think someone is coming up the drive, but that's not why I called."

"Can I help you with something?" he asked.

She walked out onto the patio and watched as a sleek, black Porsche made its way up Brad's driveway. She had no idea who might be visiting, but she pulled her attention back to Dash even as she kept a wary eye on the car.

"Yes, sorry, someone *is* pulling up the drive and the dogs went a little crazy. But the reason I'm calling is because the cows are lying down. All of them. And before you think I'm totally useless or crazy, I did look it up online. The problem is that everything I looked at said it was both normal *and* could be a sign of illness. So I'm calling you."

A moment went by before he answered—a moment in which she was certain he was calculating her intelligence.

"I'm sure they're fine," he said. "In the kind of heat we're having, it's not unusual for them to take a break, kind of like we do. Just keep an eye on them. If they seem really uncomfortable, give me a call back and I can swing by."

"Uncomfortable how?"

"Biting their stomachs, coughing, rolling, that sort of thing. Or if they haven't gotten up in the next few hours, definitely give me a call."

"Hmm, okay," she said. She heard him and she even understood. But the Porsche had parked and a man was unfolding himself from the driver's side door. He was much taller than the majority of Asian men she knew, but he had the same lean figure shared by many Chinese. His features were angular and it was clear from his impeccable suit and the form underneath it that he took care of himself.

This, she thought, must be the expert Brad promised her.

"Mr. Zheng?" she asked as he walked toward her.

"Call me Chen, please. You must be Matty Brooks, Brad's sister," he said, extending his hand.

"Matty?" Dash's voice cut into her mind. She'd forgotten she was on the phone. She held up a finger asking Chen to wait a moment. He nodded and turned his attention to the field behind the house.

"I'm sorry, Dash. I got distracted. Again," she said, returning to the phone. "A friend of Brad's just showed up. Thank you for taking my call and I'll let you know if the cows seem to be having more trouble."

"Matty, are you sure it's a friend of Brad's?"

"What? Yes, I'm sure." It was an odd question and it brought her up short.

"Okay, as long as you're sure," his voice held a tone she couldn't quite place.

"I am. Thank you, again. Hopefully, I won't have to call again, but I appreciate your help, really, I do. I'm sorry to call and run, but I do need to go."

He mumbled something as she hung up. It didn't sound like an indictment of her intelligence but it was just gruff enough that she was pretty sure she was glad she didn't hear it.

"Everything all right?" Chen asked.

"Everything is fine. I trust Brad told you what I'm looking for?"

"An expert in modern Chinese political history to help set the backdrop for your next *New York Times* bestseller? Yes, he might have mentioned it. And I'm happy to oblige."

She smiled. "You have no idea how happy I am to hear that. Now, can I get you a drink while I interrogate you, Chen?"

CHAPTER 3

DASH PULLED INTO BRAD'S DRIVE wishing he could say he didn't know what he was doing or why he felt the need to stop by. But much to his disgruntlement, he knew exactly why. Matty had called and he'd heard her voice. And then he had heard a man pull up. Jealousy didn't quite define what he felt, but it was definitely a close kin.

The woman in question was standing in the garden with a tall, dark-haired man and they were watching Dash as he pulled his truck to a stop. Neither walked to greet him and they were each holding a glass of wine. His day hadn't been all that great, a horse had colicked and nearly died and he'd spent a good chunk of his afternoon putting a dog's hip back together after it had been hit by a car. And at this point, it didn't look like the day was going to get any better.

"Matty," he said, walking toward her.

"Dash," she responded. "What are you doing here?" she added.

He tilted his head toward the pasture. "Thought I would stop by and see the cows."

"That's nice of you," she smiled. "This is Dr. Chen Zheng," she said, gesturing to the man at her side. "Chen, this is Dr. Dash Kent."

"I should be going," Zheng said after Dash shook his hand. "I didn't realize how late it was and I have a dinner appointment up in Albany."

Dash watched as Matty's eyes darted between him and Zheng; she was obviously trying to get a read on the situation. After a moment, she turned to Zheng and held out her hand to take his wineglass.

"Thank you so much for coming out today, Chen. Talking with you has helped me more than you can imagine."

Zheng smiled back and Dash looked away. "You're very welcome. I'll be up here for the next two weeks preparing for the next semester. You have my contact information; please call at any time. And these," he said, holding up his empty glass and taking hers, "I can drop off myself. You can stay out here and check out the cows."

Dash said nothing as the two said good-bye and stayed silent until Zheng had climbed into his Porsche and started down the driveway.

"You didn't need to stop by, you know," Matty said. It was a hell of a way to start the conversation. Nice and inviting.

"I was in the area." He could feel her eyes on him, but he stayed focused on the field where the six cows grazed peacefully.

"I think they're fine," she said. "They were lying down by the trees over there." She pointed to a line of big maples along the fence. "But when that quick summer storm came in, they all got up and moved under the trees out of the rain. Once it stopped, they started grazing and have been ever since." She paused then added, "I'm sorry I bothered you."

"Better to be safe than sorry," Dash answered. "How are you getting along with the rest of the animals?"

"The dogs are great, the cats are cats, and I still don't get having rabbits as pets, but I haven't done anything dumb yet that might result in their demise—and the chickens, well, I have to admit, I kind of like them," she said with a smile.

"The chickens?"

"I know," she shrugged. "Seems like I should like the rabbits because they are pretty cute, right? But the chickens all seem to have personalities *and* they had fresh eggs waiting for me this morning. Can't complain about that."

"That is one of the benefits."

"Although, like you said," she continued, "if they keep giving me five eggs a day, I'm going to have so many I'm not sure I'll be able to do anything with them. Don't get me wrong, I can use them in baking, and I love them as a meal, but thirty-five eggs a week is a lot to go through, especially if I don't have people around to share the baking with."

"There's a pancake breakfast in a few weeks. I'm sure they could use them if you have extras," Dash suggested as they began to move through the garden. The storm Matty had mentioned had left the air feeling a little bit cooler and the smells of the garden were fresher, less dense, than they would be in high humidity.

"A pancake breakfast?" she asked.

"To support the volunteer fire department."

She stopped and smiled. "That's sweet."

"That's condescending," he responded.

Matty laughed. "I know, you're right. Even as I said it, it sounded that way. But I promise you that's not the way I meant it. I mean, it really is nice. I'm used to black-tie fundraisers where all people care about is either getting their picture in the paper, getting something they want from someone else, or, better yet, meeting people who want something from them." They stopped at the vegetable part of Brad's garden. Dash could smell the tomatoes and fresh herbs, which prompted his stomach to remind him that he hadn't eaten since breakfast.

"I think it's nice that everyone comes together to support something that really does benefit the community," she continued. "And I don't assume everyone likes each other, but my guess is people probably come to catch up with friends and neighbors, too. I think it sounds fun."

'Fun' isn't exactly what Dash would call it, but that was mostly because his mother, who was one of the head organizers of the breakfast and had been for years, usually had him manning the griddle for four hours—inevitably after a night spent out on emergency calls. But it *was* nice, and he said so.

"This garden is amazing," she said, changing the subject. "I think I'm going to make something Italian tonight with these tomatoes and the basil over there," she pointed to her left as she bent over to check a couple of the bright red fruits. "I don't know if you have any plans, but you're welcome to join me."

He heard the words. They even registered. But his mind was on one track at that particular moment, focused as he was on Matty's well-rounded behind, which was being presented to him as she hunted for ripe tomatoes.

"Dash?" she said, turning to look at him over her shoulder.

"No." His voice was abrupt and he knew, though she didn't, that the force of his refusal had more to do with his family tradition than dinner.

Her eyebrows went up. "Uh, okay."

He took a deep breath and very conscientiously pulled his mind back to the conversation. "Sorry, I didn't mean to sound rude. It's been a long day and I still have two more calls to make."

She straightened and faced him, looking unsure about whether or not to believe his excuse. Her hair was down and looked thick lying across her shoulders and down her back. He wondered what she would do if he just slipped a hand behind the nape her neck, pulled her toward him, and kissed her.

"Dash?" A look glinted in her eye and he knew in that moment that if he did kiss her, she wouldn't object in the slightest.

"I need to go," he said, stepping back.

"Okay," she said after a moment.

"I mean, I really," he took another few steps back. "I really need to go. Please don't hesitate to call again if you have any questions about the animals. I really don't mind at all."

She stood there cradling four tomatoes in her arms, watching him. "Okay. Thanks?"

"Not a problem." And he turned and walked away. He didn't look back but knew she'd stayed where he'd left her, watching him leave. He had no doubt she thought him a little unusual, maybe even a bit wacky, but there wasn't much he could do about that now. Now he just needed to get away and breathe. This family curse was going to be a bitch.

• • •

As the sound of Dash's truck faded away, Matty stood in the garden. Not sure what to think about what had just happened, her mind was blank. Then Isis nudged her little red Ridgeback nose against her thigh and Matty shook off the confusion.

For a moment there she would have sworn Dash was going to kiss her. His eyes had dropped to her lips and he'd gotten that distant but focused look that guys get when they see something they want and have every intention of getting. But then he'd gone cold and left faster than a clown at a funeral.

With a shrug, she turned and started toward the house. After leaving the tomatoes on the patio table, she went to make sure the chickens were in their coop for the night, then headed inside to make dinner and mull over everything she and Chen had talked about.

Two more eggs were waiting for her, which reminded her of Dash's suggestion to donate them to the pancake breakfast. There hadn't been any eggs in the fridge when she'd arrived, so she figured Brad must have some way of dealing with the extras. But since she didn't know what that was, Dash's idea seemed like a good one. At this rate, she was going to have over a hundred and fifty eggs; she was good with the ingredient, but she wasn't that good.

Once she'd put the eggs in the fridge and washed the tomatoes, she reread Brad's notes for the fourth time then picked up her phone to call him. His voice mail answered and she left him a message asking him to call or e-mail her if he had any suggestions for the excess eggs and letting him know that, if he didn't, she was going to give them to the pancake people.

Looking at the tomatoes on the counter, she sighed. It would have been much nicer to have company for dinner. Well, it would have been nice if *Dash* had agreed to stay for dinner. She didn't know him at all, but she felt a little greedy for his company. Not in an obsessive way, but more like she just knew they would get along and have a good time together. There was an attraction, yes, but there was also something more—something telling her that they might actually *like* each other, too. And it would be nice to have a friend around.

Not wanting to slip into maudlin thoughts about how she had no friends and no one to keep her company, she opted to make a fresh salad rather than the more elaborate pasta and chicken she would have made had Dash agreed to stay. And when she finished her utilitarian meal, she finally sat down to do what she had come up there to do in the first place. She started writing.

CHAPTER 4

MATTY DREAMED THAT HER BARE arms were being hit by little pieces of ice over and over again. Even in sleep, she knew that didn't make much sense. But the cold and wet sensations kept assaulting her like little sharp daggers. Finally, in half-awake, half-asleep frustration, she flung her arm up over her head, only to be fully awakened by a yelp from Bob as her elbow met his snout in the process.

She opened her eyes to find the yellow Lab staring at her, smiling with a lolling tongue. Isis stood behind him while Rufus and Roger leaned their bodies against the wall. Rolling her head to the other side, Matty found Lucy standing on the bed next to her. It wasn't ice; it was little doggy noses. Wet doggy noses. Maybe this was the reason Brad had lined up all the dog beds in the kitchen downstairs.

Still, despite the morning greeting, she was hard pressed to feel bad about having moved all those beds up to the room in which she slept when she turned to her side and reached for Bob. His smile grew bigger, if possible, and his tail started to wag in circles as she rubbed his nose and apologized for accidentally whacking him. Like most Labs, he didn't seem to mind and he leaned forward trying to lick her. She drew her head back—she didn't mind the love, but licks weren't her favorite—and caught sight of the clock. Ah, that would explain why all five of them were staring at her. It was thirty minutes past their allotted breakfast time, as dictated by Brad.

Mumbling her apologies to the dogs, she climbed out of bed

and before she was even at the bedroom door, five sets of paws were clamoring down the stairs, toenails clicking on the hardwoods. It was a cacophony and the chaos made her laugh. Maybe Brad wasn't so strange after all to have five dogs—waking up laughing was not a bad way to start the day.

She watched the five of them absentmindedly as they ate. Judging by the thermometer outside the kitchen window, it was already hot and no doubt going to get much hotter. She thought about making coffee, but decided if she was going to get outside at all today, she should do it now. So, after letting the dogs out to do their thing, she changed into her summer uniform of shorts and a tank top, brushed her teeth, combed her hair, and slipped on her flip flops. By the time she was back downstairs, all five dogs were ready to come in.

She checked their water, and the cats' food and water, and made to head out. She paused at the door and glanced at a set of keys hanging on a small hook. She had seen Brad's big fancy truck in the carriage house garage but hadn't felt the need to drive it. Her little convertible was comfortable and easy to maneuver on the country roads, but it was also black on the inside. The interior of Brad's truck was beige, a much better choice in the heat. Not to mention that it was parked in the garage and hadn't already spent the morning baking in the sun, unlike her little coupe.

Making her decision, she slipped the keys off the hook. She hadn't driven a truck in a long time and it would be fun to cruise the backcountry roads in such a big vehicle. She might even roll the windows down and put on some country music—wouldn't Charlotte love to see that.

Which reminded her of her promise. She dialed her friend and they caught each other up while Matty checked on the other animals. As she chatted with Charlotte about the progress she'd made on her book the night before and filled the rabbits' water, she made mental a note to herself to put the cooler Brad had left for them in their cage when she returned from town. Apparently, rabbits didn't do well in the heat, another ding against them in her mind, so Brad had a special air-conditioner type device made for them.

She also knew she needed to collect the chickens' eggs, fill their feeder, and clean their water dish, but for now she simply let them out to wander their enclosed garden. Ending her call, she popped back in the house to wash her hands and as the cool inside air hit her, she broke out in goose bumps, her skin already damp from the heat despite the early hour. She was glad that the dogs and cats didn't mind staying inside because she was pretty sure that the phrase "dog days of summer" was coined on a day like this one.

After climbing into Brad's truck, adjusting the seats and mirrors, and getting a sense of the massive machine around her, she cruised into town with the windows down and the country station turned up a little too loud. From talking with Chen, she knew now that the man she'd met behind the counter at Frank's Café the day before was indeed the curmudgeonly Frank. And so, after finding a parking spot in front of the café and heading inside, she gleefully introduced herself to him, much to his dismay, when she ordered her iced mocha and, at Chen's recommendation, an egg, bacon, and cheese bagel.

She took a corner seat at a table for two and watched customers come and go. Two police officers arrived and ordered lattes, and an older woman greeted them by name, Marcus and Carly; the three chatted as they waited for their drinks. Two young women, maybe high school aged, sat in another corner leaning over breakfast plates, engrossed in their conversation. Judging by the looks on their faces, Matty was pretty sure they were talking boys. Other people came and went and by the time she finished her breakfast, she felt that she had a slightly better sense of the town.

She swung back by the health food store to pick up some baking supplies and it was close to eleven by the time she headed home. She had her windows rolled down again and the music playing as she plotted her day. She knew from experience that the outlining and drafting she'd done the night before, as well as her energy this morning, meant she was in for a productive day. She would work for several hours, take a break in the afternoon for some food, then work for several more before nighttime. Once she was at a good place to stop, she'd pour herself a glass of wine, make a leisurely dinner, and wind her brain down before going to bed.

She was debating the benefits of a bath in the evening as she rounded a corner a few miles away from Brad's. She slowed for a moment to take in the scene before her—an old, stone farm-house surrounded by white-fenced fields filled with quietly grazing horses. She half expected a man riding a horse with a pack of hounds to come into view. Windsor, and the surrounding area, really was quite beautiful, she acknowledged to herself.

She was savoring the rare moment of complete contented-ness—enjoying the smells of a country summer, the feel of the clean, humid air on her skin, and the wind blowing her hair. A smile formed on her lips, but just as it did, something came crash-ing down into the bed of Brad's truck.

"Holy shit!" Matty cried as she slammed on the brakes. The truck came to a screeching halt, and having ducked on instinct, she sat hunched in the driver's seat. Her heart was racing and she had no idea what could have made that kind of noise or had that kind of impact on the truck—enough of an impact that she had not only heard whatever it was hit the truck bed but had actually felt the weight of it depress the back end of the huge vehicle. Completely at a loss, she stayed hunched down, waiting. She heard nothing but a song about riding a cowboy still playing on her radio. She felt nothing moving in the back.

Her stomach was tied in knots, but after a few moments, she knew she needed to get out and check the truck. She gave a fleeting thought to driving to the shoulder, since she was stopped in the middle of the lane, but decided it was more important to find out what exactly it was that had landed in the truck before she moved anything.

Putting the truck in park and turning the ignition and music off, Matty congratulated herself on at least having the presence of mind to put the emergency flashers on. Tentatively, she craned her neck to see if she could see anything through the back window, but all she saw was the inside of the tailgate. Taking a deep breath, she opened the door and peeked around the side. She couldn't see anything from where she sat, so she slowly exited the truck and inched her way toward the back, keeping as much distance as she'd need to jump out of reach should something leap out at her, while staying close enough to see inside the truck bed.

She had just passed the rear passenger door of the extended cab when something came into view. She paused and stared. She took another bigger step toward the bed of the truck, then frowned. Finally, she approached the side and took it all in. She wasn't sure what she had expected; really, she'd had no idea. But never in a million years would she have thought to find this. As she stood in the middle of the lane, the sounds of cows lowing in the distance and tractors at work in nearby fields filtering into her brain, Matty stared at what was, undoubtedly, the decomposing body of a man.

CHAPTER 5

MATTY FOUND HERSELF GAWKING IN shock until the sound of another vehicle snapped her back into action. Not wanting an unsuspecting driver to come upon her parked in the middle of the road, she walked away from her truck, and the body inside it, to flag the driver down. She needed to call the police and she needed to set up some flares to warn other cars. She hoped the driver of the approaching vehicle could help with at least one of these two things.

She breathed a sigh of relief when she recognized the grill of the massive diesel truck slowing down as it approached her. She watched as Dash pulled to the side of the road behind her.

"Everything okay, Matty?" he asked as he climbed from the cab of his truck and came toward her.

"Um." She hadn't really thought this through, how to explain the situation. *She* was fine, but the situation was not.

"Matty?"

She saw a look of genuine concern in his expression and his hand came up to her shoulder.

"Are you okay?" he asked again.

She focused on his eyes. "I'm okay, but there's a problem with my truck and I could use some help."

She saw a look of relief flash in his eyes. "What is it? A tire? The engine?"

"Um, not quite. There's a—" she paused then stuttered out the rest of the sentence, "a body in the bed of my truck. A human body. A dead human body," she added, noting that her hands were a little shaky when she waved in the direction of the truck bed.

Dash blinked. "A body?"

She nodded. "It fell."

"Fell?"

She nodded again then looked up. "I think from there," she said, pointing to a tree not far from where they stood. His eyes followed her wobbly finger and he looked up, too.

"A body?" he repeated.

She nodded again. "And I need to call the police and set up some flares to warn anyone else who might come along." That sounded reasonable.

"Why do you think it fell from there?" he asked. It wasn't the most important question she thought he might ask, but somehow, in the way that people deal with stressful situations, it made sense.

"Because it looks like there's a red sock on the branch about two-thirds of the way up and the body is wearing one the same color."

Dash looked at her and for a second, she wondered if he thought she was crazy. But then he nodded and walked back to his truck. He was making a call and carrying flares when he came back.

"Here," he said, handing her two of them. "I'm trying to reach Ian, the county sheriff."

"Not the police?"

"We're in an unincorporated part of the county, Ian's team has jurisdiction here, but I'm sure he'll call in the police."

Matty didn't really know what that meant; well, she knew what jurisdiction was, but it was safe to say that who had it in which parts of the county was a bit of knowledge she never thought she'd need to know. Dash walked ahead of her, away from their trucks, gesturing that he'd lay the flares furthest away. She nodded and lit and laid the other two closest to where they were parked.

When the flares were all lit, they met at the front of his vehicle. She went to lean against it then jumped as the heat of the metal made contact with her bare skin.

"You okay?" he asked. "Can I get you anything? I have some water and soda in the cab. It will be cold," he offered.

She shook her head, though distantly she remembered sugar being good for shock victims. Not that she was actually going into shock, but it wasn't every day that a body fell from the sky into her vehicle.

"Ian MacAllister is on his way. He should be here in about ten minutes," Dash said.

"The sheriff?"

Dash nodded. "Used to be the deputy chief of police but the last sheriff just retired and Ian was asked to run and was voted into the position. He's a good guy, good at what he does."

Absentmindedly, Matty nodded. They stood in silence waiting for him to show up. The heat from the road snaked up her legs and curled around her body; she began to feel sweat beading on her skin. Remembering the hair band on her wrist, she swept her hair up into a ponytail and tied it up off her neck. Dash moved toward his cab, came back with a cold bottle of soda, and handed it to her.

"Thank you." She wasn't much of a soda drinker, but now that it was in front of her, the thought of the cold, sweet drink made her mouth water.

"You're welcome. I'm going to have a look," he said, taking a step forward.

"Dash," she put a hand on his arm, stopping him, "I wouldn't recommend it. Between the heat, the rain, and the bugs, he's not a pretty sight."

"How do you know it's a he?" he asked with a small frown.

Involuntarily, her lips twitched in morbid humor. "That red sock I mentioned earlier?"

He nodded.

"It's all he's wearing."

Dash looked at her for a long moment, then, without a word, walked to her truck, leaned over the tailgate for a few seconds, then walked back.

"An interesting getup for a walk in the woods," he said, returning to her side. "You seem to be doing okay with all this though?"

His question was part concern and part curiosity. Matty let out a little huff of air; it was a sad commentary on her life that the sight of a dead body didn't upset her more. That's not to say she was completely okay with it, but it didn't send her screaming into the hills.

"Yeah, well it's not the first dead body I've seen," she answered. "You?"

"Not mine either. I was in the military right after college; they paid for vet school. You?"

"I grew up in the projects of New York City. It was a violent area. And now, because of what I do, I have a lot of friends with interesting jobs that let me tag along every now and then."

She felt his eyes on her.

"I thought Brad grew up in Greenwich?"

"Brad did grow up in Greenwich. I grew up, with my mom-who-used-to-be-the-Brooks'-housekeeper-until-I-came-along, in the Bronx." Her voice was more caustic than she'd intended. On the rare occasions she talked about her father's family, she was always careful to keep her tone neutral, void of any emotion.

"I see," he said. "I was wondering why Brad never mentioned you. I take it you aren't close?"

"I've spoken to him three times in my life, and two of those conversations weren't good," she responded, intentionally lightening her tone.

Dash stared at her for another moment, then walked to the cab of his truck and returned with his own half–finished bottle of soda. Twisting the top off, he took a long sip.

"If you don't mind my asking, if you and Brad aren't close, how did you end up here?" he asked, closing his drink.

She thought about saying that she did mind him asking; she wasn't used to talking about herself, not on this topic of family. But instead, she found herself shrugging and answering.

"I'm up here mostly because of what I do for a living," she

said, starting to explain. "I'm a writer and I think I was feeling a bit listless and stuck working at home in DC. We moved to DC when I was twelve," she added as an aside, remembering she'd told him she'd grown up in the Bronx. "I think I was already thinking about a change in scenery when Brad called. For some reason I have yet to understand, I actually answered the phone when I saw his number. We talked a bit, he asked me to come up, and I agreed." She went on to tell Dash about Brad's additional incentive of introducing her to Chen in exchange for watching the dogs.

"But you have no idea where he went?" Dash asked when she finished.

She shook her head as they heard the sound of a car in the distance. "Since we didn't talk much, I didn't think much of it. But given that he left me more than I bargained for, I think it's strange. But then again, maybe he just wanted to be sure I couldn't reach him once I realized what I'd walked into."

As she finished talking, a big SUV pulled up and, right behind it, a police car. A brown-haired man exited the first car; Matty recognized him as the man Dash had been talking to outside the gas station on the day she'd arrived. Behind him, the two police officers she recognized from Frank's—Marcus and Carly—followed.

"Ian, this is Matty Brooks, Brad Brooks's half sister. Matty, this is Sheriff Ian MacAllister and the new Deputy Chief of Police, Marcus Brown, and Officer Carly Drummond," he said, introducing the officers respectively.

They all shook hands and the three law enforcement officers walked over to have a look in the truck. Matty watched as they talked amongst themselves, their voices too quiet to be heard from where she and Dash stood. The three gestured and pointed in various directions quite a bit before walking back.

"That must have been quite a shock," the sheriff said as he stopped right in front of her.

"Yes, it scared the shit out of me when it hit the truck bed, Sheriff." She caught her language a moment too late—it happened to her often. But at least she could blame shock this time around.

And the sheriff's strikingly unusual shade of green eyes that had caught her attention. She filed away the color in her brain—something she often did—to give to one of her characters at some point.

He smiled and even let out a little male chuckle. "I bet," he said. "And call me Ian, everyone does. Vivienne is on her way," he said, turning to Dash. "My fiancée is a medical examiner," he said, shifting his attention back to Matty. "She was just coming back into town from Boston when I called her and will be here shortly. In the meantime, do you want to tell me what happened?"

And so she did. And it took approximately thirty seconds. Ian asked a few follow-up questions, questions she didn't have any answers to, and just as she was thinking that they were going to be forced to move on to idle chitchat if they wanted to keep talking, a third car pulled up.

She saw the smile in Ian's eyes, if not his face, as he moved toward it.

"The fiancée?" she asked Dash. He nodded.

She watched as an athletic-looking woman with a long brown ponytail exited the car. Pausing beside her car, the woman smiled as her fiancé came toward her. Ian stopped just inches from her and said a few quiet words, making her smile even more, then dipped his head and gave her a sweet kiss. Together, they walked back to the gathered group.

"Ms. Brooks, this is my fiancée, Dr. Vivienne DeMarco."

"Holy shit," Matty said, smiling in surprise. She quickly continued when she realized that, yet again, her mother would be ashamed of her language. Not to mention that everyone was looking at her with open curiosity. "I've heard all about you, Dr. DeMarco," Matty gushed as she took the woman's hand. "Pinky Patterson is one of my really good friends. She talks about you all the time. I always seem to be traveling whenever you come to town but Pinky is *always* telling me I need to meet you," she explained. She knew she was babbling, but on top of the surprise in the truck, to meet a woman out here in the middle of nowhere that one of her closest friends had been telling her about for years was almost too much.

"And call me Matty," she added with a look at everyone else, including Ian.

Dr. DeMarco laughed as she shot Ian a reassuring look; apparently he was the protective type. "I love Pinky," she said. "You must be the famous Hilde Brooks she's always telling *me* about. And, please, call me Vivi."

Matty smiled. "I'm not sure if famous is the right word, I'm pretty sure Pinky would be more likely to call me infamous, but yes, that's me. It's so nice to finally meet you," she paused then frowned. "Albeit under very bizarre circumstances."

Vivi inclined her head. "So Ian told me. Of course, when I first came into town, I found a dead body, too. It's how I ended up staying here and meeting Ian. Maybe it's just the town's way of greeting people it likes."

"Good god, I hope not, Vivienne," Ian muttered and she gave him a bump with her hip to make him smile. He shook his head at her, but an unmistakable look of affection passed between the two of them.

"Something good came of it all, we *are* getting married," Vivi rejoined. "Maybe the town has plans for you, too," she added with a look and a grin directed at Matty.

Matty recalled the serial killer Charlotte had told her about and wondered if that incident had anything to do with what Vivi was referring to, but it didn't seem the time or place to bring it up, so she went in a different direction.

"As attractive as you three are," she said, looking at Carly, Marcus, and Dash, "And statistically unrealistically so, I might add, I have no intention of getting married, so I'm hoping it's just a weird fluke thing that's happened and not some strange town portent of things to come."

Vivi laughed. "Well," she said, pulling a pair of latex gloves from her pocket. "Only one way to find out. We'll be back in a minute."

The four walked to the truck, leaving Matty and Dash again. "I promise I don't have cooties," she said, offering Dash a sip of the soda he'd given her. His was long gone in the heat of the August day. He gave her a look before reaching for the bottle and a taking a sip.

"Hilde Brooks?" he asked. "The writer?"

She nodded. "My full name is Mathilde. My friends call me Matty, the rest of the world, or at least those that read me, know me as Hilde."

"I don't read a lot of fiction, but even I've read you."

She laughed at the disbelief in his voice.

"You're famous," he said.

"My books are popular, there's a difference."

He tilted his head as if he wasn't sure whether or not he believed her, but in Matty's mind there was a big difference. Her books were her books, things she made up and created. Sure they were a part of her, but not as much as some people thought. She was simply someone who had a job she loved and happened to be good at. She wasn't all that different from most successful professionals—within the world of her genre's readers, her name was well known; outside of it, she was virtually unknown.

"Well," Vivi said, walking back with Ian after leaving the other two officers at Brad's truck, "The good news is your truck isn't a crime scene." She removed her gloves and slipped them into a small evidence bag Ian held. "The bad news is it's definitely not a natural death and Ian is still going to have to requisition your vehicle until we move the body and any evidence it leaves behind."

"Murder?" Dash said.

"I fucking hope not," Ian said with a look heavenward. "Sorry," he added when Vivi nudged him. "It's just that we've had enough of that recently." A pained expression crossed Ian's face and he cast a worried look in Vivi's direction.

Vivi's expression turned sympathetic. "It might not be murder. The cause of death appears to be, from what I can tell, a gunshot wound. We won't know for sure until we get the body up to the lab. But even if it is a gunshot wound, that doesn't mean it was intentional. As we all know, people hunt around here all the time."

"But what was he doing up in the tree?" Matty asked.

Ian shrugged. "Who knows? We'll have to identify him and then see what we can find from there."

Matty was curious and wanted to ask more, but she had enough cop friends to know that at this point very little could or would be shared. So she simply nodded.

"Do you have a ride home?" Vivi asked. "I can take you if you like."

"I'll take her," Dash interjected before Matty could answer. Vivi's eyes went from Matty's face to Dash's then back again. Matty recognized the silent, female language and gave a small nod to Vivi's silent question of whether or not Dash's proclamation was okay with her.

"Thanks, Dash. That way I can stay here with Ian and the team," Vivi responded.

"I can't tell you how long it will be before you get your truck back, though," Ian said.

She shrugged. "It's fine. It's Brad's truck. I have my own car back at his house. I'll just need my purse from the cab and I have some grocery bags in the back seat that I'd like."

Ian called to Deputy Chief Brown asking him to grab the items and in short order she was seated in Dash's truck, headed home.

"Thanks for the ride," she said.

"No problem. Are you sure you're okay?"

"A little shaken, nothing I can't handle."

He glanced at her. "Is there anything I can do to help?"

Get drunk and go to bed with me popped into Matty's head. "Thank you, but I'm fine. I'll probably bake today," she said instead.

"Bake?" She saw his lips tilt into a smile.

"It's a great reliever of stress and has the secondary benefit of using some of those eggs."

He opened his mouth to say something then closed it.

A moment later he asked, "What will you bake?"

"Cookies, brownies, that sort of thing."

"Sounds good."

"Feel free to come and pick some up. I almost never eat what I make, or at least I almost never eat *all* of what I make."

He laughed as they pulled onto Brad's driveway.

When they reached the house, she thought about asking him in for lunch. She wasn't all that hungry and hadn't left town all that long ago, even if it felt like hours had passed. But she had asked him twice before, once for drinks and once for dinner, and twice he'd declined. He may be attracted to her, but something was holding him back. It was possible he was married or had a girlfriend, in which case, she didn't want to make things awkward for him.

"Thank you again," she said, sliding out of his truck and reaching for her bags in the back.

"I'll help you with those," he said, moving to unbuckle his seat belt.

"Too late, I got it." She pulled the last bag out and shut the door with a bump of her hip.

Ignoring her, Dash got out, rounded his truck, and took the bags from her hands. He followed her to the door and as she unlocked it they were greeted by the barks and yips of the dogs, which turned into jumps, doggy head butts, and tail wags when the door swung open. She knew Dash wouldn't stay, but she knew the dogs, particularly the Ridgeback, Isis, would be there to keep her company. And for that she was glad.

She set her purse down then took the bags from Dash. "Thanks again, I appreciate it."

He shoved his hands into his jeans pockets and rocked back on his heels, looking uncomfortable. The thought that he might have a wife or girlfriend entered her mind again.

"Look, Dash. I'm fine, really. I have some things to do today and I'll just focus on them. I've got the dogs for company and maybe I'll go for a walk later—maybe even down to that restaurant in Old Windsor for dinner, or an after-dinner drink if it doesn't cool down early enough. I'll be fine. I'm sure you have places you need to be today." And maybe people he needed to see, but she didn't add that.

He didn't look any more reassured, but he took a step toward the door. "Call me if you need anything. You have my number."

"I do, but really, I'll be fine. Vivi also gave me her cell and home numbers, so I'm well connected. Now, I actually do have some things I need to do today, so…" She let the end of her sentence hang. She didn't really have all that much to do, but if thinking she did gave him a reason to leave, then so be it.

"Right, of course."

She walked Dash to the door and watched him climb into his truck. He gave her one more wave before turning the truck around and heading down the drive. She let out a deep sigh that held some emotion, or, probably more likely, lots of emotion, and looked down at Isis at her side.

"We have chickens to feed, eggs to collect, and rabbits to cool down, Isis. And then maybe we'll bake some cookies. How does that sound, girl?" She reached down and scratched the dog's smooth red fur. Isis's tail wagged slowly from side to side, she wasn't one to show much emotion. Maybe that's why Matty felt such a kinship with her.

• • •

Dash drove to his next call, preoccupied with thoughts of Matty. She'd handled the situation well, probably better than he would have, had a body landed in the back of his truck. But still, when she'd all but pushed him out of Brad's house, he didn't miss the look of forced "fineness" on her face. She had told him more than once that she was fine. He knew she wasn't.

But he'd driven away anyway. God, he was an ass. He hit the call button on his Bluetooth and dialed Jane because, despite being his annoying know-it-all older sister, she was still the only person who might understand what was going through his head. He sure as shit didn't.

"Dash?" she answered.

"Yeah, it's me."

"And don't you sound cheery?" she responded. "What happened?"

And so he told her. Everything. He told her about Chen Zheng, turning Matty down for dinner, the body in the truck, and subsequently being hustled out of Brad's house.

"A body? A real, live, dead body fell into her truck?" Jane repeated when he'd finished talking.

He turned onto one of the many dirt roads that cut through the county. It was a more direct route to where he was going, if not a faster one. If he were honest with himself, which he was trying not to be, he was mostly just buying himself some time before having to be "Dr. Kent" again. "No, a real, *dead*, dead body," he responded.

His sister told him exactly what he could do with himself, then was quiet for a moment. "Wow, that sucks," she finally said. "Everyone in town is going to hear about it. And right on top of what happened just a few months ago. I'd be surprised if the mayor is re-elected next year," his sister reflected.

"Jane."

"Right, you don't care whether the mayor gets re-elected or not. But honestly, Dash, I'm not sure what you want me to say. Given what she does and the fact that she appeals to you, I'm assuming she has a brain in her head. And you've turned her down twice, if I've heard you correctly. She probably thinks you're not interested and were just offering to stick around to be nice. And since you can't even admit to yourself whether you're interested or not, can you blame her for kicking you out?"

"It's not like I wanted to stay and seduce her. I just wanted to stay to make sure she was okay, and she wouldn't let me do that," Dash pointed out.

Jane snorted. "Yeah, sure, whatever, Dash. You want to know what I think?"

"Probably not."

"Of course you do, that's why you called me. I think you're being an ass. I think you want to know that she wants you as much as you want her because that would be the only thing that would make any sense."

"You're not making sense, Jane."

"Only because you're being an ass. You can't explain or understand what's going on between the two of you and it's making you feel insecure because you don't have *the answer*. And so, when she pushes you out the door telling you she can take care of herself, that she doesn't need you, your little male ego can't handle it and you're kind of freaking out."

"I'm hardly freaking out, Jane," he pointed out as he made a turn onto County Road 7—a very controlled turn onto County Road 7, as if he were making a point.

"You are."

"I'm not."

"Then why did you call me?"

Sometimes Dash hated his sister. "Because I'm not sure what I should do."

"And you want to do something because, whether you like it or not, it kind of feels like a biological imperative that you do something, doesn't it?"

And strangely enough, that summed it up. He physically felt that he needed to be with Matty, that he needed to make her feel better, make her laugh, make sure she didn't feel worried or scared after what had happened that morning. It wasn't just the good manners his mother had taught him, or even common sense. It was something more primal than that. And he didn't often, if ever, think of himself as a primal kind of guy.

He grunted.

"It will get better when you just accept it."

"I'm not ready for that."

"Clearly," Jane shot back. "And not to mention the fact that the way you've treated her certainly isn't going to make *her* acceptance any easier."

He had a fleeting image enter his mind, an image of him telling Matty about his family history. She was a city girl, raised in the projects. He didn't know about her transformation from a girl in the Bronx to a famous author in DC—something he hadn't mentioned to Jane—but he didn't doubt that it took a lot of courage, confidence, and intelligence.

Matty would laugh at him if he told her.

"Dash?"

"I'm at my next call, I need to go," he said, bringing his truck to a stop beside the barn of a longtime client.

"You're avoiding me."

"For the moment," he responded.

"Just don't avoid *it*," she said, not needing to clarify what *it* was. "This thing that runs in the family, when it hits, it hits, Dash. There is nothing we can do to avoid it. And believe me, because I am speaking from experience; if you try to ignore it, it will only get worse."

"Sounds fun," he grumbled.

"It is, once this part is over. Trust me, it can be really fun."

Dash knew his sister believed what she was saying. He just wasn't there yet. He thanked her and made a mental note not to call her again until he'd sorted this all out on his own, because she had done nothing to make him feel better.

But several hours later, when Dash pulled up to his own house, he felt even worse. He was nowhere near sorting it out on his own. Sure, he'd put in a good day's work, but every chance he'd gotten, he'd let his mind wander back to Matty and how she was coping with the events of the day.

His house, steeped in darkness and shadows, did nothing to lift his spirits. Neither did the warm, stuffy air that hit him when he walked through the door. He didn't tend to keep the air-conditioning on when he left for the day, but the fact that he'd also forgotten to open any windows that morning served to make him even grumpier.

Stepping out of the shower a few minutes later, he stood naked in his closet staring at his clothes, neatly stacked on a few shelves. He could crawl into bed, he was that tired, or he could pull on a pair of boxers, jeans, and a t-shirt and head out to Anderson's, the restaurant Matty had said she might walk to for dinner or a late evening drink.

He didn't even know if she would be there if he made the trip.

Which wasn't all that far.

He ran a hand over his face and through his damp hair. Letting out a deep breath, he grabbed a pair of boxers. Maybe his sister had a point; maybe he should just stop fighting it.

Walking into Anderson's twenty minutes later, his eyes immediately found her sitting at the bar, sipping what looked like whiskey and chatting with the bartender, Amy. He'd only ever seen Matty in shorts and tank tops but tonight she wore a summer dress. A dress that rode up her thigh as she perched on the bar stool.

"Mind some company?" he asked as he came to her side.

She looked up with a surprised expression that was followed by a brief furrowing of her brow and a small frown. She seemed a little confused and he couldn't blame her. But he had to give her credit, the expression was fleeting and she gestured her acceptance with a nod at the stool beside her.

"I was hoping you'd be here," he said as he signaled to Amy.

"Drinking the horrors away?" she said, her tone sardonic.

"So I could see how you are doing," he clarified.

"I'm fine, but if you were that concerned, you could have stopped by the house. Or called."

He ignored her very rational response and ordered the same thing she was drinking, which turned out to be Lagavulin with one ice cube. "Have you eaten?" he asked.

Matty looked at him for a moment then turned her gaze back to the space behind the bar. "I just ordered a burger about five minutes ago. Amy said they were good."

"They are," he confirmed then placed an order for the same thing. "Want to move to a table?"

Dash knew, by the look on her face, that she was trying to

figure him out, but not succeeding. She didn't look like she was going to tell him to go to hell, but it was a close call.

"There's a storm coming in tonight and we'll have a good view," he said, picking up her drink and making the decision for her.

"Are you married?" she asked once they'd sat down. He choked on his drink.

When his throat cleared, he replied, "No, why would you ask that?"

"Dating someone?"

"No."

"Are you sure?" she pressed.

"Very," he answered.

Her light brown eyes searched his for a long moment before she finally seemed to come to some decision and she sat back and took a sip of her drink.

"Why do you ask?" he asked again.

"I can't get a read on you, Dash. It bothers me. One minute you look like you want to kiss me, at the very least, and the next you're bolting in the opposite direction. I'd say that's common behavior for someone with commitment issues, but we don't even know each other well enough to reach that stage, so it doesn't make any sense to me."

She'd certainly called a spade a spade, but he wasn't ready to talk about it yet. "It's complicated. I'll tell you about it one day. In the meantime, why don't you tell me how you went from the Bronx to being Hilde Brooks, bestselling author?"

She drummed her fingers on her glass, very clearly debating whether or not to answer.

"I know you have no reason to trust me," he continued, "but things are a little complicated in my life right now." Since she came to town, more precisely, but he didn't say that. "I'm sorting it out, but I can promise you, and you can ask anyone here, I'm not married, never have been, nor am I dating anyone, seriously or otherwise."

She actually snorted at that. "Forgive me, but I have a hard time believing that."

"Right now," he clarified. "I'm not seeing anyone seriously or otherwise, *right now*," he repeated, feeling his past creeping up on him. He wasn't a cad by any means, but when he felt the need for female company, he generally hadn't had a hard time finding it. Not something he thought Matty would appreciate hearing even if she already thought it.

"And as for wanting to kiss you, at the very least," he continued, using her words, "I'm not going to deny that, but what I would really like, right now, is to just have some dinner, talk a little, and make sure you actually are okay, rather than you just telling me you are."

When he finished talking, her eyes searched his for just a few seconds before she turned her head, and her gaze, toward the window. He studied her profile as the first gusts of wind heralded the coming storm. He knew her to be up-front and figured, given what little he knew of her life, she must be strong. And her personality fit that assumption, too. She was confident, didn't get easily flustered, but was also quick to laugh and definitely didn't mince her words. But she had a delicate profile. Her eyes were more oval than round and her nose had a little upward tilt to it. Her lips were full, but not synthetically so, and her chin was in proportion to everything else.

"So you want to know about Hilde Brooks?" she asked, turning back to him.

"I'm more interested in how you got to where you are than in hearing about where you are."

"The life story." Her lips tilted up into a small smile.

"It's bound to be more interesting than mine," he offered.

She inclined her head. "We'll see, maybe not. But if I share, you have to share, too."

His life was an open book; he had no problem sharing and said so. "So, tell me how it all started," he prompted.

And for the next thirty minutes, she did. She talked, he asked questions, they laughed, food arrived, they ate, and he asked more questions. He learned from her that her mother had been the housekeeper in Brad's Greenwich home when she caught the eye of the elder Brooks, a man very much under the thumb of his society wife.

Carmen, Matty's mother, was wise enough to know that she and Douglas Brooks weren't in love, but she wasn't worldly enough to know how to stop the affair. And when she became pregnant and Sandra Brooks found out, Brad's mom threatened to have Carmen deported if she told anyone or demanded any support. And again, Carmen wasn't experienced enough to know whether it was even possible for Sandra to follow through on her threats; all she sensed was a threat to her life in the United States and the life of her unborn child. So she'd left the Brooks' home in the dark of night and went to the only place she could afford, the projects outside Manhattan.

"And you were born there?" Dash asked, taking a sip of the beer he'd ordered when the whiskey in his glass had run dry.

"I was, and my mother's biggest rebellion against Sandra was to give me the Brooks name."

"And how long did you live there? Until you were twelve, right?" he asked, remembering she had mentioned a move to DC when they'd been waiting for Ian.

She nodded as a crash of thunder rolled by. Both of them turned to see the storm, in all its force, outside their cozy little window.

"Yes," she continued, her voice low. "My mother got really sick when I was twelve. She wasn't sure if she was going to live or not, so she wrote to Douglas, my dad, and asked for help. My grandmother, Douglas's mom, intercepted the letter and took control of everything."

"Meaning?" he prompted, fighting the urge to reach across and run a finger down the bare skin of her arm.

"Meaning she rode in on her metaphorical white horse and rescued us. The Brooks family is an old family and a loaded one, too. Historically, they've always been more aligned with the social democrat types, although Sandra definitely turned Douglas way more conservative than his mother."

"Which means?"

"Gran was horrified when she heard the story, and so embarrassed by her son's behavior, by his disregard for his child—that would be me," she added, pointing to herself with a smile, trying to make light of what couldn't have been a very good period in her life, "that she swept us off to her DC estate where I was properly schooled, dressed, fed, and very much loved. She also took care of my mother, who recovered from what ended up being a form of thyroid cancer."

"And Brad's family, his mom and dad, what did they do?"

Matty laughed. "I knew of them, of course. And I'd even seen pictures of them, but Sandra and Gran feuded over the *incident* for years, and I'm pretty sure they all actually stopped talking for a long time. I don't really know what went on. To be honest, all I cared about was that my mom didn't have to work so hard, or at all, and that she wasn't going to die. It was icing on the cake when Gran hired my mom's best friend Nanette to come be her cook so that Nanette and her daughter, my best friend Charlotte, could both move into the carriage house and be nearby."

"She sounds like a force of nature, your grandmother."

Matty smiled again. "She was." She paused and looked away again. Given her use of the past tense, Dash figured the woman must have died. And that Matty was still dealing with the loss.

"When did she pass away?" he asked.

"Believe it or not, five years ago." She gave a small shrug. "She was such an amazing person that both my mom and I still miss her. And it wasn't just the money. Yes, she completely changed our lives in that respect, but more to the point, she was just a woman who loved life. She was kind and funny and always, always game for something new. She showed us kindness, and in doing so, she let us see kindness in the world in a way we hadn't been able to before. She was a remarkable woman."

Not unlike her granddaughter, Dash thought to himself.

She gave him a smile, the kind that said it was time to change the subject. "So, enough about me, what about—" she cut herself off as her eyes went over his shoulder. Her smile widened and she waved. He turned in the same direction to see Carly and Marcus walking in, out of uniform and looking off duty.

"Deputy Chief Brown, Officer Drummond," Matty said as the two approached the table. "How did the rest of your day go? Join us for a drink?"

Marcus cast Carly a look and she responded with a small nod. "Please, call us Marcus and Carly. You don't mind?" Marcus asked, looking more at Dash than Matty. In truth, Dash was kind of glad to have the distraction. Not because he wanted to avoid talking about himself, he didn't have much to hide, but because he was still processing what Matty had just told him. And what she hadn't. A little buffer between him and what she was making him think and feel might not be such a bad thing.

"Please," he said, gesturing with his hand for them to sit. Amy came over and the two placed their drink orders.

"So, what can you tell us?" Matty asked, not needing to elaborate further.

"Not much," Carly answered. "Vivi took the body up to the state lab in Albany and I'm not sure when they scheduled the autopsy. But the good news is I think they processed most of the truck this afternoon—Ian thinks you might have it back by tomorrow afternoon."

"I don't really need it but that's good to know," Matty said then hesitated before continuing. "But I was sort of wondering about the cleaning part of it. I mean, I'm not all that squeamish or anything, as I'm sure you could tell this afternoon, but cleaning human remains out of a truck bed might be a bit much for me."

Marcus and Carly laughed. Dash tried to join in but couldn't quite bring himself to. Matty had glossed over her years in the projects saying nothing more than that they'd been violent. He didn't like the idea of her having to come face-to-face with even more violence now.

"I can clean it," he offered.

"There's no need," Marcus said. "Even if Ian were inclined to let it come back to you in the state it was in this afternoon, Vivi would never let him. Don't worry about it, I promise you Ian will have it as clean as a whistle when the tow truck drops it tomorrow."

Matty smiled. "I don't know them at all, but they seem like good people."

"Yeah, they are," Carly smiled. "Between the two of them, they have more experience in our line of work than probably everyone else in the county put together. But they like it here. Even though we don't usually keep Vivi that busy, the state lab is close, and she still consults with the FBI. We're lucky they stayed."

"Were they thinking about leaving?" Dash found himself asking. He and Ian had known each other in high school and were pretty close then. But they'd both headed off to college then joined different branches of the military. Dash had been back in the area for five years, but Ian had just come back a little less than a year ago and they hadn't really reconnected much except over Ian's dog, Rooster.

Marcus gave them a "who-knows?" look before speaking. "I don't think they really considered it, but given what happened earlier this summer, and then Ian and Vic not getting along, it wouldn't have surprised me."

"Vic?" Matty asked.

"Our chief of police. He's not a bad guy, but he and Ian never got along. I think he felt threatened by Ian, especially when Ian stepped right into the deputy chief position. It was touch and go for a while."

"But now he's the sheriff, right?" she asked.

Marcus and Carly nodded.

"And you're the new deputy chief?"

Carly gave a little knowing laugh and Marcus rolled his eyes upward, "Apparently."

"I'd say congratulations, but somehow it doesn't seem you're all that excited about it?" Matty prompted.

"Vic convinced me, as did the mayor. It wasn't something I was looking for or even something I think I'm ready for, but they don't want to bring in anyone new. Still, it feels a little sleazy," Marcus said.

"Sleazy?" Matty asked.

"Yeah." His shrug was nonchalant, but even Dash could tell Marcus was uncomfortable. "We had a killer up here," Marcus continued then paused to share a look with Carly. Dash knew all about the killer, everyone did. It had been the talk of the county, of the state, for a good long while.

"He came after Vivi and it was ugly," Carly picked up where Marcus had stopped. "You might have read about it in the news, but the long and short of it is he'd killed twenty-one women before we tracked him down here in Windsor, and then he killed himself."

For a moment, Dash's mind flashed back to earlier in the summer. Everyone had known about the two bodies Vivi and Ian had found and the subsequent attack on the young owner of the ice cream store in town. And though the attack on Meghan, the store owner, was later found to be unrelated, the violence and the presence of a killer in their midst had shaken the small community. He glanced at Matty and wondered how Ian had coped with knowing the killer was ultimately after Vivi. He thought about the violence that had touched Matty's life as a young girl and the violence she'd seen today. It was more than a person should experience in one lifetime as far as he was concerned. He took another sip of his beer and remained quiet as Matty continued her conversation with Marcus and Carly.

"And that has to do with your promotion how?" she pressed Marcus as she picked up the last French fry on her plate and popped it into her mouth. Dash watched as Carly leaned forward and answered.

"Well, Ian became sheriff, Wyatt, one of our other officers, was recommended by Vivi to participate in a highly competitive one-year training program with the FBI, and Marcus was promoted to deputy chief."

"And it feels like people ended up benefiting from a horrible tragedy," Matty finished. Both Marcus and Carly nodded.

"Well, not to point out the obvious," Matty started, "but no one asked for such a publicized case to land on your doorstep and it sounds like no one really sought to use it to their advantage. It sounds like stuff just happened—new jobs, new relationships—and you had to learn to take the good with the bad. If you like your job, and you're good at it, no one can blame you for trying to branch out and do more. I'm sure you'll be a great deputy chief, Marcus," she added.

"He'll be fine, it's just something he has to get used to," Carly answered.

"I'll drink to that," Marcus said, raising his glass. They clinked and drank and though Dash joined in, he was thinking of Matty as a little girl in the projects, what it must have been like to have been uprooted to DC so suddenly, and the path she took to being here now, in Windsor—taking care of animals she'd never been around before, chatting easily with the locals, even cheering them on. There was no doubt she was a remarkable woman and he didn't want to do a thing to change that.

"Excuse me for a moment," Matty said, rising from the table and gesturing toward the restrooms in the back. Dash watched her walk away and wondered if she would want to uproot again. Her friends and what family she had were in DC. The ties to her grandmother were in DC. Would she ever consider moving? If not, did that mean he would have to move if the family curse proved to be real?

"I'm not sure you two could be any more obvious," Carly said with a laugh that brought Dash back to the present.

Apparently, he hadn't been the only one to enjoy the spectacle of Matty leaving the room. He cast a glance at Marcus who looked unapologetic in his admiration of Matty's assets.

"Hard not to appreciate the view," Marcus responded with a half smile. Carly rolled her eyes.

"Would you guys mind giving Matty a ride home?" Dash asked, the need for space having suddenly swamped him. Again.

"Didn't she come with you?" Marcus asked.

Dash shook his head. "She walked and I was going to give her a ride home because of the time and the storm, but I need to get home. Would you mind?"

Carly frowned. "Of course not."

After thanking them and ignoring the curious looks they both shot him, he walked to the bar to pay the tab he and Matty had raked up. He was just signing the credit card slip when she walked up to him on her way back to the table.

"You're leaving," she said. He saw disappointment flash in her eyes but what really cut him was the look on her face that said she should have known better than to think he would stay.

"Marcus and Carly will give you a ride home."

For a moment she simply stared at him. And then, without a word, she started walking away.

"Wait, Matty," he said, putting a hand on her arm to stop her. He looked into her faded brown eyes and let out a long breath. "Look, like I said, it's complicated. It's a family thing I can't really explain right now. You'll think I'm crazy and I'm not sure I'm ready for it anyway. And I'm pretty sure you aren't."

"You aren't making any sense, Dash," she answered.

"I know. Believe me, I know. But I will explain it all. I just can't do it now."

Her eyes searched his, looking for something he knew she wouldn't find. And though he didn't expect anything else, it still didn't sit well when she gave a dismissive "whatever" gesture with her hands.

"Thanks for joining me for dinner, Dash. I'm going to sit back down now." And she walked away. And he let her.

He took his time signing off on the bill and when he passed the table on his way out Marcus raised a hand in farewell and Carly gave him a nod, but Matty just watched him leave.

CHAPTER 6

AFTER ANOTHER HOUR AT ANDERSON'S that Matty spent getting to know Marcus and Carly—after all, a thriller writer could never know too many cops—the pair dropped her off at home. She'd thought about making her way home on her own, but the storm had cooled the air down and the roads were wet, making a walk in flip-flops less than appealing. Again, she was thankful for the dogs when the taillights disappeared down the drive and darkness engulfed her. Entering the house, she greeted the pups and then pulled her phone out of her purse and dropped it on the kitchen table.

Once the dogs were settled, she dialed Brad's number as she poured herself a glass of water. His voice mail picked up, again, and she left a third annoyed message. In the three days she'd been at his house, she'd had more animals than she knew what to do with, a man who flipped from hot to cold faster than a speeding bullet, and a dead body, literally, fall into her life. And she was beginning to feel a little grumpy. Not that she thought it was all Brad's fault. If she cared to admit it, which she didn't, her agitation had more to do with Dash than the other bizarre things that had happened.

Setting her phone down on the kitchen island and resting her hands on the slate top, she simply stood, waiting for fatigue or something else to propel in her one direction or the other. But nothing came. The silence of the night enveloped her and she realized that, for the first time in her life, a man had made her feel unsettled. And it wasn't a very comfortable feeling.

Even though she'd left Brad a message not ten minutes ago,

she picked up the phone and called him again. Maybe seeing four calls from her would worry him enough that he'd call back. Because at the moment she wanted an excuse to leave—an excuse to avoid dealing with Dash and an excuse to go back to something familiar.

Isis nudged her hand and Matty looked down at the beautiful red dog. And let herself smile a bit at what Isis seemed to be saying to her. All she really needed to do while she was here was take care of the animals and write. If she cut out all the rest, all of the noise, and focused on those two things, she'd be just fine.

She knelt down and nuzzled the dog, "Thank you for reminding me, girl. Life doesn't have to be so complicated, does it? Dash may think it does, but that doesn't mean I have to let him complicate my life, right?"

Isis bumped her forehead against Matty's chin. "You think it's bed time?" At those magic words, all the dogs were on their feet waiting for her to lead them upstairs. She laughed and started toward the stairs. As she walked by the refrigerator, an old newspaper on the counter caught her eye. She paused and picked it up. It had fallen out of the liquor cabinet earlier in the afternoon when she'd made herself a much-needed gin and tonic after kicking Dash out. Of course she had told him she was fine, and really she was. But the gin and tonic had definitely helped smooth some of the ruffled edges.

Taking a closer look, she realized it wasn't actually a newspaper, but rather a racing form, and that there were odd bumps running over the name of one of the horses. The form was dated about a year ago and provided information from one of the local, though nationally known, tracks up near Albany. Matty knew very little about horse racing, but thought it a strange thing to find in the cabinet. It was possible it had been put in there to prevent a bottle from leaking onto the bottom of the cabinet. She could see Brad doing that; his house was meticulously clean. But it was the raised dots that caught her attention.

She traced her finger lightly along the bumps. They didn't mean anything to her, but they looked intentional. Frowning, she held the form up to the light to see if the bumps spelled anything or highlighted anything in particular on the form but found nothing. Not knowing what else she could do with it, certainly not this late at night, she put the racing form back down on the counter and, after one last glance at it, headed off to bed.

• • •

Matty stretched in bed then winced. The morning light shone brightly through the window. Really bright. She hadn't had that much to drink the night before, a whiskey and two beers over the course of four hours, and a gin and tonic several hours before that, but it was more than what she was used to and her head wasn't being shy about telling her so.

Raising herself up on her elbows, she blinked. Of course, Bob was beside her. Lucy the mutt was at the end of the bed, Isis was on her dog bed in the corner, Rufus was stretched out in all his Great Dane glory on the rug under the window, and Roger's big Newfie-mix body was taking up the doorway. And every set of eyes was staring at her. She glanced at the clock and saw it was close to nine. It was two hours past their breakfast time; apparently they were more flexible than her half brother gave them credit for. Or maybe they were just getting used to her.

Still, feeling guilty, she rose quickly, fed the patient animals, and let them out before getting dressed and getting herself ready for the day. She didn't have much planned, except for writing, so it didn't take long. Heading back downstairs, she let the dogs in that wanted in and then went out to check on the other animals and collect the fresh eggs. She wasn't hungry yet, so she just made coffee, sat down at her computer, and got to work.

At around two o'clock, Matty sat back and stretched her back. Her stomach grumbled in protest when she realized she hadn't yet eaten. But it was a small price to pay. She'd done a lot of good work in four hours, and thanks to the insight Chen had shared with her, she was starting to feel that this story was actually coming together.

She was making a salad when she heard a car drive up. She didn't deny the relief that swept through when she realized it wasn't a diesel and so unlikely to be Dash. Her day was going just as planned so far, and it was a balance she wanted to keep. She opened the patio door just as Vivi and another woman were closing their car doors.

"Matty, hi!" Vivi said, walking toward her.

"Vivi, how nice to see you," she responded, smiling at the two women.

Vivi gestured to the other woman. "This is Kit Forrester, another local—"

"Oh my god, *the* Kit Forrester?" Matty cut Vivi off. The woman looked a little sheepish, but there was no denying it was the very one. Her distinct golden eyes gave her away. "Oh, wow. I had no idea you lived up here, too," Matty said, holding out her hand.

Kit smiled and shook Matty's hand. "I moved up here five years ago and love it. Vivi thought you might like meeting another local writer."

"You're one of my favorites and I'm not just saying that because you're here," Matty was gushing. Again. But, like when she met Vivi, she couldn't have been more surprised to see one of the country's most prominent, and highly awarded, young writers standing in her driveway. She knew Kit was only a few years younger than she was, but the novels Kit had written had won critical acclaim both nationally and abroad and she was already considered one of the country's literary vanguards.

"I'll say the same to you, and also not just because you're standing right in front of me. I loved your last book, *The Solace*, it was amazing," Kit responded.

Matty laughed. "What I write is pure escapist entertainment. Don't get me wrong, I love it, but it's nothing compared to your talent. Now," she said, cutting off Kit's protest, "before we start comparing ourselves even more, why don't you come inside for a drink? I was just about to make myself some lunch, would you guys like to join me?" Both women had eaten, but they joined her in a glass of iced tea as they all sat.

"I just wanted to stop by, say hi, introduce you to Kit, and let you know that Ian will have your truck delivered by four or five this evening. Clean," Vivi added with a smile.

"You ran into Marcus or Carly, I take it?" Matty asked, taking a bite of the salad she'd thrown together.

"This morning at the lab. They said they saw you and Dash Kent at Anderson's last night."

She heard the question in Vivi's voice and laughed. "You're not very subtle, you know," she said.

Vivi made a face. "I know, you'd think I'd be better at it considering what I do for a living, catching bad people who do bad things, but I suck at subterfuge and subtext myself."

"And besides, everyone is curious when Dash is seen out with a woman since it doesn't happen that often," Kit added. "Don't get me wrong, he's far from a monk if the rumors are anything to go by, but he's usually discreet. It's the *being out in public* with a woman that tends to catch people's attention. And you can imagine that, looking the way he does, he's a bit of a hot topic of conversation among the ladies."

"Yourself included?" Matty asked Kit.

Kit laughed and shook her head. "Nope. As fine as he is to look at, he's a bit too standoffish for my taste. Nice guy and all, but just not my type."

"He does run hot and cold," Matty conceded.

"Meaning?" Vivi pressed.

"Nosy much?" Matty rejoined, laughing at her new friend.

"I saw the way he was looking at you yesterday. There was nothing standoffish about it," Vivi answered.

Matty shrugged. "He stopped by Anderson's last night to check in on me. I walked down on my own and we ended up having dinner together. Marcus and Carly drove me home. Nothing too exciting to report, I'm afraid."

"Not your taste either?" Kit asked.

"When I date a man, I prefer that he be certain that he also wants to date me. Not for forever, but for the time we're together. Dash can't even be sure, one way or the other, over the course of a dinner. It's too much drama for me," Matty answered.

"He looked pretty certain when I saw you two together yesterday," Vivi said.

"And fifteen minutes later he was running for the hills," Matty responded. "He's, well, I can't quite figure him out. And then he said the strangest thing to me last night," she said, pausing with her fork in midair as she remembered. "He said something about it being a family thing and that it was complicated and that someday he'd tell me but he wasn't ready and neither was I."

"That does sound weird," Kit said.

Matty's brow furrowed. "I know, I can't for the life of me figure out what he meant. And now I find myself wondering if I should even care. All I really want to do while I'm up here is write. And take care of the animals," she added.

"I can't blame you there; there is something about this area that's conducive to creativity," Kit said. Matty nodded her agreement as she rose to take her plate to the sink.

"Dash is usually pretty straightforward and that doesn't sound—oh!" The surprise in Vivi's voice made Matty turn.

"Oh," Vivi said again. "I think I know what he meant." The grin that spread across her face wasn't comforting.

"Do I want to know?" Matty asked, returning to the table with the pitcher of iced tea.

"Uh, I'm *not* actually sure you'll want to know," Vivi answered.

"Well, *I* want to know," Kit interjected. Vivi looked at Matty to get her opinion on the matter. Matty shrugged, how bad could it be?

Bad, Matty thought after Vivi recalled a conversation she'd had with Dash's older sister several weeks ago about the family *tradition*. They'd been at a wedding and Vivi was planning hers so, naturally, the topic came up. And Jane Kent had told Vivi all about the lightning speed at which the Kent family married.

Well, maybe *bad* wasn't the right word, but it did sound crazy.

"I think you're it for Dash and it's freaking him out," Vivi concluded.

"Uh, yeah, it would kind of freak me out, too," she said. "But that's crazy. It takes two to tango and, even if he does think that I'm that person, which I don't think I am, I would have to be prepared for that kind of relationship, which I'm not."

"I think it's kind of sweet," Kit said. Both women looked at her. "Don't get me wrong, in the real world, I think it's insane, but in some other reality—"

"Like one of our books?" Matty interjected.

"It could be kind of sweet," Kit finished.

Matty took a deep breath and then let it out. "Well, I just think that if this is what is bothering Dash, the fact that it's bothering him at all is ridiculous. I'm not interested in getting married, at least not yet, and I'm certainly not the type to get married in six weeks. Believe me, I have way too many issues for that."

"Then maybe you should mention that to Dash," Kit suggested.

She shook her head. "I just want to write and take care of the animals," she repeated. "I'm not planning on seeing him again unless, god forbid, something happens to one of the animals."

"Famous last words," Vivi said.

Matty shot her a look. The whole thing was just too wild to contemplate seriously. "Anyway," Matty said, changing the subject. "Did you figure out who the guy from yesterday is?"

Vivi shook her head. "No, not yet. We put his time of death about three to four days ago. We're running some more tests to narrow down the timeline but we did a facial reconstruction and are running it through the databases along with his DNA. His fingers were too degraded to get good prints."

"That's gross," Kit said, making a face.

"But you don't think it's someone local?" Matty pressed.

Vivi lifted a shoulder. "We don't have any reported missing persons up here, but we can't say anything for certain yet. The property where he was abuts Brad's property on the other side of that hill," Vivi said, pointing to the hill on the other side of the drive. "Did he say anything about seeing anyone around lately?"

She shook her head. "Brad hasn't said anything. I haven't been able to reach him. I've left four messages, but he hasn't returned any of my calls."

"Is that unusual?" Vivi asked with a small frown.

"We're not close and have barely spoken to each other at all, so it's hard to say what's normal and what's not. Until he called me the other day to ask me to come dog-sit, I hadn't spoken to him in five years. When I arrived, I found a four-page set of directions for me, but no information about where he was going." Which reminded her; rising from her seat she went to collect the racing form and brought it back to the table.

"What's this?" Vivi asked.

"It's a racing form. Almost a year old, as you can see. But feel the paper," she directed. Both Kit and Vivi did so.

"There're bumps," Kit said.

Matty nodded. "I know, weird, right? Brad said to help myself to anything in his liquor cabinet in the note he left. I thought *that* was strange since he doesn't even know if I drink, but then yesterday, when I felt I deserved a gin and tonic after the morning I'd had, I opened the cabinet and this fell out."

"Strange," Vivi said, holding the form up so she could look at it from different angles. "I don't know what the bumps are, but I can take a picture and send it to my cousins, Naomi and Brian, to have a look," she offered.

"And you think they'll know?" Matty asked.

"If they don't know, I promise you they can find out. They're kind of scary like that," Vivi rejoined.

Matty laughed and then agreed; she wasn't sure the form meant anything, but it couldn't hurt to have someone look into it. Vivi snapped a picture with her cell phone and sent it off to her cousins.

"I'll let you know as soon as I hear from them," Vivi said, slipping her phone into her purse. "In the meantime, feel free to call me if you have any questions or just want some company, anytime. I'm kind of new to the area, too, so I know what it's like."

Matty thanked her and they all rose. A few minutes later she was alone again in her kitchen. Her mind floated to the crazy things Vivi had said about Dash. The more she thought about it, the more she felt he was simply overreacting. She didn't believe in love at first sight or soul mates or anything like that, and she'd have to if she were going to be a part of whatever was going on in his head. So, as far as she was concerned, he should just chill about the whole thing. And she could make that easier for him by avoiding him in what was left of her time here in the Hudson Valley. And what better way to avoid him than to do what she came here to do.

Feeling pretty good about herself, she took a deep breath, headed back into the office, and tackled her story like a linebacker.

CHAPTER 7

AFTER AN EXTREMELY PRODUCTIVE DAY of writing and a not-so-productive night of sleeping, Matty stood on the front patio with her morning coffee. She'd already taken care of the whole menagerie of animals—late, once again—and then spent some time rereading what she'd written the night before. Taking a few minutes to enjoying the late-morning breeze that had moved in to cool things down a bit, she was allowing herself a short break, letting the words she'd written sink in and swirl around in her brain.

She liked the way the story was shaping up, but there was something missing in the relationship between the two main characters—a young, but politically savvy, attaché and a rogue former member of embassy security. She didn't write sex into her books, but she did like to have a backstory in her head that included it. At the end of her books, her readers liked to know that, even if there wasn't a relationship during the story, there was a possibility of one at the end. It was a lesson she'd learned early in her career and one she'd taken to heart. And because she liked the idea of happy endings too, it wasn't hard to leave that option open to interpretation. But she didn't have that backstory for these two characters yet, and it was bugging her.

Somewhere off to her left, she heard the sound of a lawn mower starting. She hadn't seen or heard a peep from Brad's neighbor yet, so, out of curiosity and in a not-so-subtle attempt to put off the nagging question of her characters, she turned her gaze toward what she could see of the lawn next door. The sound of the motor altered, depending on whether it was going uphill or down, or at least that's what Matty imagined accounted for the change in tone. And after a few minutes, when a stronger breeze blew through, it carried the sweet scent of freshly cut grass. Several more minutes passed before she finally saw the riding mower come into view.

Matty straightened off the post she'd been leaning against and stared. She even rubbed her eyes and looked again. Because, from where she was standing, it looked as though an older woman was riding the lawn mower completely naked.

She took several steps toward the neighbor's lawn, as if getting a few feet closer would clear up the matter. It didn't. Not until the mower turned, causing the sun to catch the rider in a different light, and she saw the shadow of a bathing suit strap. Matty smiled. Her neighbor wasn't naked, she was wearing a nude-colored bathing suit. And she looked to be about eighty if she was a day.

Character, Matty thought. She liked seeing people with character. And she liked meeting them even more, so she took a few purposeful steps in the older woman's direction. But she'd only gone about ten feet when a piercing howl froze her in place. Out of the corner of her eye, she caught Rufus and Roger raising their heads from where they'd been lying lazily on the patio nearby; Isis was immediately at her feet. When a second howl came echoing down the hill a few seconds later, Lucy came bounding around the other side of the house to investigate.

Matty looked around, realizing that Bob was missing just as a third howl came to a crescendo. Suddenly, the yellow Lab came tearing down the hill toward the house, running with his tail tucked between his hind legs and going as fast as he could on three legs—he kept his right front paw held high, only occasionally letting it touch the ground and emitting a yelp every time it did. She stared in horror as Bob came barreling toward her and she saw the blood pouring from his injured foot. Dimly, she was aware of the lawn mower engine going off, but her eyes were fixed on Bob as he made a beeline for the safety of the house.

She met him at the edge of the patio and reached down to grab his collar. She meant to soothe him, steady him, but she only succeeded in frightening him. He turned and snapped at her, nipping her in the arm. She jerked back with a cry of surprise and pain, and Bob, perhaps realizing what he'd done, became even more frantic, backing himself into a corner and whimpering.

"Once we get him taken care of, you're going to need to see a doctor about that arm."

Matty whipped around at the voice behind her and found Brad's neighbor not four feet away. The authoritative tone in her voice brokered no argument despite the fact she stood there in her beige bathing suit and flip-flops and weighed in at about ninety pounds, max.

"I'll get to that, but right now I'm more worried about him," Matty answered.

"Do you have keys to that big truck?" the neighbor asked.

"I do, hanging on the door just inside the house," she responded. As promised, Ian had had the truck delivered, clean and all, the night before. She hadn't moved it back into the garage, even though she had no intention of driving it again.

"You work on calming him down and getting something around that foot. I'll back the truck up and, once he's feeling a bit more reasonable, we'll load him up and take him to Dr. Hubba Hubba."

Matty's brows went up. "Dr. Hubba Hubba?"

"Dash Kent, the vet," the woman said, already striding to the door.

Matty let out a little huff of a laugh; it was actually a perfect name for him. But her attention came back to Bob when he sank to the ground, whimpered, and began trying to lick his bleeding paw. She hadn't ever dealt with such an injured animal, but going on instinct, she lowered her voice and talked to him in as reassuring a tone as she could manage. Inch by inch, she made her way closer until she was able to touch his head. And when he looked at her with his big, brown eyes, filled with confusion and pain, she knew she was going to have to make it all better for him as soon as possible.

When she felt pretty sure he wasn't going to snap at her again, she removed the oxford shirt she'd slipped on over her tank top, kept one hand on Bob's head to soothe him, and very gently reached for his paw. When he didn't panic or retreat further, she slowly wrapped her shirt around the paw and applied a firm but gentle pressure, as she would with a human. She didn't know if that was the right thing to do for a dog, but it was all she knew.

"Do you think he's ready?" the neighbor asked, having backed the truck up and let the tailgate down just a few steps away.

"He can't get in there on his own," Matty pointed out.

"Of course not. You're going to have to carry him," the petite old woman in the bathing suit replied.

Matty stared at Bob for a heartbeat, wondering if she could lift a sixty-five pound injured Lab, but quickly realized that, since she didn't have much of a choice in the matter, she'd better get moving. She wiggled next to him, got her arms underneath his body, and stood, lifting them both up. The neighbor stayed beside her, helping to keep her steady while being careful not to interfere.

Together they made it to the bed of the truck and Matty laid Bob down. She made to close the tailgate, but when Bob started pulling at the makeshift wrap on his foot, she knew it wasn't going to work.

"How do you feel about chauffeuring us to the vet?" she asked the neighbor. "I'm Matty Brooks, by the way," she added.

"I'm Elise Rutherford, and I had already planned on it. I've locked up the house so we should be good to go."

"You okay driving such a big truck?" Matty asked, even as she climbed in and secured Bob in her lap in such a way that she could keep her hand wrapped around his injury.

"I've been driving trucks since I was twelve, I'm going to pretend I didn't hear that," Elise said, closing the tailgate.

A few seconds later, they were on their way to Dash's office. So much for avoiding him, but then again, she wondered if he would even be there. He seemed to be out on calls a lot, maybe his clinic was staffed with other vets.

Of course it wasn't.

Elise pulled up behind the clinic like she'd been there a hundred times, told Matty to wait, and disappeared inside. Less than two minutes later she reappeared with Dash and a young woman. Both were dutifully trailing behind Elise.

Dash's eyes sought hers and his stride lengthened until he stopped at the tailgate. "We need to get that washed and looked at, Matty," he said with a gesture to her bleeding arm as he let the back of the truck down.

"I know, Dash. But right now I'm more worried about Bob," she shot back. Bob, who had crawled as far into her lap as he could get, looked up at her and whined. Dash's eyes held hers and she could see his jaw ticking. In annoyance, fear, or frustration, she wasn't sure, but she didn't want to wait to find out.

"Dash, he's bled through my shirt, please," she pleaded.

Dash took in a quick breath then let it out and leaned forward. Scooping Bob up as if he weighed next to nothing, he took the dog from her grip.

"Follow me," he ordered.

"I'll call a friend to come get me. Your keys are in the ignition," Elise said as Matty followed behind Dash. She didn't have much time to do anything other than murmur a quick thank you before Dash motioned her inside the back door of the clinic and into what looked like a supply room.

"Susan," he said, addressing the woman who'd come outside with him. "Make sure Ms. Brooks cleans that wound and then you can dress it while she makes an appointment to have it looked at."

"I'm not going to the doctor, Dash. They'll have to report it and I don't want to get Bob in trouble."

Dash paused and looked at her. "Of course you're going to the doctor. Don't be ridiculous."

"Dash," she warned.

He took another deep breath, no doubt asking for patience, but it hadn't been Bob's fault she'd been bitten and she knew enough to know dog bites generally had to be reported.

"I'll call Dr. Sanger when I'm done taking care of Bob. I'll tell her what happened and she'll take care of you *without* reporting it."

"Promise?"

He gave her a look. "Yes, I promise. Now go take care of that arm. Susan, I'll be in exam two when you have a chance and I'll need some sedative to get started."

Dash didn't wait to see the woman nod before he turned and walked through a door that led to the back halls of the clinic. When they were alone, Matty looked to Susan, who was wearing an interesting expression.

Before the assistant had a chance to say anything, Matty said, "You can point me to the washroom."

Susan opened her mouth, then shut it, and nodded. "This way," she said, gesturing with her hand toward the hall.

A few minutes later, Matty was elbow deep in antiseptic hand wash, scrubbing away for the prescribed ten minutes in the washroom. She'd had to promise Susan that she would stay for the full ten minutes in order for the assistant to feel comfortable enough to leave and bring Dash the sedative he'd asked for. And, like a good girl, she was still scrubbing when Susan returned with a small first aid kit.

"How's Bob?" Matty asked, starting to rinse the soap from her arms.

"He's probably asleep by now," Susan replied, handing her a towel. "What happened?" she asked.

"I'm not really sure," Matty said. "He just came tearing down the hill, bleeding all over the place. I wrapped his paw up but didn't really get a good look at what happened."

"Well, Dr. Kent will take good care of him," Susan said, adding antibiotic cream to some gauze and placing it over the bite on Matty's arm.

Matty didn't doubt he would, so said nothing as she watched Dash's assistant bandage her arm. When she was done, Susan told her she could have a seat in the waiting room, or if she preferred, there was a bench out back. She opted for the waiting room and left Susan to assist Dash in doing whatever he needed to do to help Bob.

As she sat opposite a well-coiffed woman holding her petite white fluff ball of a dog, awareness of just how dirty she was slowly seeped into Matty's consciousness. There was blood on her white tank top and khaki linen shorts. Bob's blond fur clung to her clothes, the dirt he'd had on him seemed to have transferred to her, and there were splotches of mud on her thighs—there was even one across her shoulder, though how it got there she had no idea. The woman seated across from her was staring, but at least she looked more concerned than horrified.

Over forty minutes passed before Dash opened the door to the waiting room. Matty didn't miss the way the—now two—other women in the waiting room sat up when he came in. They'd been offered rescheduled appointments due to the emergency, but both had opted to wait. And she now knew why. If she hadn't been so worried about Bob, she would have laughed at their eagerness to see Dr. Hubba Hubba.

"Matty," he said.

She said nothing but stood and followed him into his office.

"How's Bob?" she asked when he shut the door behind her.

"He's fine," Dash answered, taking her arm in his hand. He had already removed the tape from the bandage before she realized what he was doing. She yanked her arm back. Not missing a beat, he reached for it again and continued to unwrap the material.

"Bob had his toe taken off," Dash said, appeasing her need to know even as he continued what he was doing. "I'm not sure what did it. Normally, I would say it was bitten off." He held her arm up and examined it, turning it at different angles. Gently, he prodded the skin around the punctures. His eyes shot up to meet hers when she let out a little hiss.

"A couple of over the counter pain meds and I'll be fine," she said, moving to take her arm back.

He rewrapped it then moved behind his desk. "Here," he said, handing her a piece of paper. "Dr. Sanger's number and address. She's expecting you in twenty minutes."

Matty frowned but took the paper. Part of her wanted to protest, but another part of her knew how helpful it really was to be hooked up to a local doctor for a non-emergency appointment; most doctors preferred to spend their time with repeat patients.

"Tell me about Bob," she said, sitting down.

"Like I said, normally I would say an animal bit it off. But whatever separated his toe from his foot probably wasn't teeth, the wound was too clean."

"What else would do that? And which toe?"

"The first toe and a knife would do it, but it was probably either an old trap or maybe even some glass?" he answered. She didn't like the hint of doubt she heard in his voice.

"You don't sound certain."

He shrugged. "We may never know what did it, but it's a good thing it was clean since it made it easier to stitch."

"Does that mean I get to take him home with me?"

Dash shook his head. "We don't know what did it, so I'm running some blood tests. I have him on antibiotics, but I want to check for a few other things, too. And I'll want to run the tests again in twenty-four hours."

"Can't I bring him back in?"

"I'd rather keep him here since he's still groggy from the sedative."

Matty felt like she was abandoning Bob, but what else could she do? She knew Dash's reasoning made sense, but she also knew he wouldn't be above keeping Bob if he thought she would spend her time taking care of the injured dog rather than taking care of herself.

"Fine," she said, sounding every bit as disgruntled as she felt.

A small smile touched Dash's lips. "You'll take care of that?" he asked, gesturing with his head to her arm.

"I said I would."

"Promise?" he repeated her earlier demand.

"Yes," she grumbled as they stood. Dash rounded the desk and came to her side. He meant to usher her out, she had no doubt, and she should have gone with it. After all, she was only in Windsor to take care of the animals and write. Flirting with the locals, especially one that unsettled her as much as Dash, wasn't in the cards. But as she took one last look at him with his strictly business attitude, her inner imp, goaded by guilt-induced frustration, decided to make an appearance. She turned toward him, bringing them inches apart, and put her hand on his chest. She felt his skin jump beneath her touch.

"I heard about your little family curse, Dash," she said, looking up at him.

He looked down at her hand resting against his shirt and said nothing.

"If you ask me, it's crazy," she added.

His head tilted and his eyes met her gaze. "Maybe."

"What if it is? Crazy, that is," she clarified. Her fingers had inched up and she brushed them against the skin of his neck.

"And what if it isn't," he countered.

"Do you want to know what I think?" she asked, leaning into him just enough for her body to brush against his button-down shirt.

He gave a tiny, hesitant nod, as if unsure whether or not he *did* want to know. Smart man.

She smiled. "I think it doesn't matter if we think it's crazy or not, but I'd bet we'd have a hell of time finding out."

She brushed a fingertip across his lower lip then went up on her toes and replaced her finger with her lips in a soft, barely there kiss. She held his gaze and felt a flood of heat pouring from his body, enveloping her.

She stepped away, point made. "I'll call tomorrow, about Bob."

CHAPTER 8

AFTER VISITING DOCTOR SANGER'S OFFICE to have her wound checked and cleaned again, Matty stopped at the car wash to rid the truck of the remnants of Bob's blood then headed back to Brad's. She spent the next few hours scrubbing the patio where Bob had huddled with his wound and calming the rest of the dogs who, sensing something was wrong, seemed to keep looking for their missing friend. In their confusion they did nothing but follow her around as if attached to her hip. While she understood, it was more than annoying to be constantly running into Rufus or Roger, or tripping over Lucy every step or two. Isis, in her usual, detached way, sat quietly at the other end of whatever room or space Matty happened to be in and simply watched.

Still the distraction of the dogs and the cleaning was a good antidote to stewing over her annoyance with Brad, who still had yet to call back. Or stewing over the single, barely-a-kiss kiss she had laid on Dash. And so she was grateful when Chen called and invited her to meet him for dinner in Stockbridge, a town about twenty minutes away. She really didn't want to think about much of anything that had happened that day and he was the perfect answer to that. Talking about China would help her disappear into her book, into a world that was interesting and engaging, but not hers.

On the drive to meet Chen, Vivi called and told Matty that her cousins, Naomi and Brian, had figured out that the bumps on the racing form were braille and composed a ten-digit number. Vivi had run it against a phone number database, but it hadn't turned out to be a legitimate one, and other than that, she had no idea what the series of numbers could mean. Matty, not recognizing the numbers either, asked Vivi to text them to her so she could check them out later, when she got home.

"Are you going out to dinner with Dash again?" Vivi half-teased when their conversation about the mysterious numbers had ended.

"Not even close." And Matty filled Vivi in on her day including her rationale for going to dinner with Chen even though she was feeling a bit wrung out from the past few days.

"Distraction isn't a bad thing, but I'm surprised he didn't pick you up. Why are you driving?" Vivi asked.

"He has tickets to a show at Tanglewood later. He's going with his sister and invited me, but I don't want to be out that late, so we're having dinner first and then he's going to the show. I, on the other hand, will be coming home, taking a bath, and having a gin and tonic before hitting the sack."

"Sounds like an exciting night. Then again, after the last few days you've had, it sounds just about right."

"Amen to that," Matty responded. "Look, I'm just pulling up to the restaurant, but will you keep looking into the numbers for me? I'll think about it too, but if you can spare the time, I'd appreciate it. It's probably nothing, but it's just, well…" Her voice trailed off.

"Just one of those curiosities?" Vivi finished. "Of course I will. Ian and I are having dinner with his parents tonight, but I'll look tomorrow. Naomi and Brian—who could probably figure this out in a flash—are mid-flight right now, so unfortunately I can't get their help right away. But, I'll send them an e-mail tonight so they'll have it when they can access their accounts. It may be nothing, but I agree it's definitely curious."

They said good-bye and as she hung up Matty saw Chen approaching her car with a tall attractive woman at his side. He wasn't in a suit this evening; instead, he wore khaki shorts and a button-down shirt with rolled-up sleeves. He looked casual and sophisticated. Like he would fit right into her city life.

Like he wouldn't have a clue what to do with chickens. Or cows.

She sighed to herself as he opened her car door then she smiled. "Chen, how nice to see you. Thank you for calling me tonight and I'm so delighted to meet your sister."

• • •

By the time Matty returned to Brad's, her brain hurt. She had a feeling Chen wouldn't be inviting her out to dinner again, but that was fine with her. She sensed he'd viewed the evening as a quasi-date, despite the presence of his sister, Mai, while Matty had very clearly treated it as an extension of their interview and information exchange of the other day. And with Mai there, it was two for the price of one as his sister, though not the family scholar, was no slouch herself when it came to Chinese political history.

So, on the one hand, she had pages of notes filled with new material—so many that she hadn't even had a chance to let it all soak in yet—but on the other hand, she was exhausted and doubted Chen would be all that keen on spending time with her again should she have any lingering questions.

Even so, he'd been a perfect gentleman, asking after her, knowing what had happened with the body landing in her truck and all; word traveled fast in the small towns of the Hudson Valley when things like that happened. And both he and Mai were even more concerned when she told them about what had happened with Bob. Chen said all the right things and made all the right comments, but in the end, she was glad to be home. Alone. With four dogs, six cows, four cats, six chickens, and two rabbits.

She was lying in a hot bath with a washcloth over her eyes when her phone rang. Hoping it was Brad, she grabbed it and answered, letting the annoyance she felt come through in her voice. "Hello?"

"And it's nice to hear your voice, too," came Dash's response. She let out a little groan.

"And that sounds even better."

"Hi, Dash," she said.

"Hello, Matty. How is your arm?"

"It's fine. Dr. Sanger cleaned it up, gave me a shot, and said she'd talk to you after Bob's blood work comes back to see if she thought I needed anything else."

"Does it hurt?"

"Not now it doesn't. Now that it's elevated on the side of the bathtub."

There was a moment of silence. "You're in the bath."

A man's mind could switch tracks faster than the speed of light when nudity was involved. "Yep, naked as the day I was born. And when I'm done, I'm going to dry off and slip into bed that same way," she said. The "too bad you're so indecisive or you could be here with me" was left unsaid, if not unheard.

"You're not very happy with me, are you?" he half asked.

She sighed. "I'm tired, Dash. I think I just crammed a semester-long Chinese politics course into a dinner that was just under two hours. My head hurts and you confuse me so, no, I'm not that happy with you."

After a long moment she heard a very male chuckle on the other end of the line. "But you wish I were there, don't you?" he pointed out.

He was right, she did. "Good night, Dash."

"Good night, Matty. And take care of that arm."

She hung up the phone and sank her head under the cool water. She wanted this day to be over. She really did.

• • •

Matty perused the myriad of birdhouses hanging along a wall in the gift shop across from Frank's. Having come to some sort of understanding with Frank—he supplied her with iced mochas but preferred she not order them aloud—she was able to examine the merchandise with her *iced* drink of choice in hand. She had thought to get a simple thank you card for Brad's neighbor, for all the help Elise had given her the day before with Bob, but when she saw the whimsical birdhouses, she changed course and looked for the perfect one.

She selected a hot pink one that complemented Elise's mailbox and had it wrapped up. After that, all she wanted to do was pick up Bob, head home, and get back to writing. But she'd been in town a few days and hadn't yet stopped at either bookstore—which, in her mind, was too large a sacrilege to ignore. So, reining in her eagerness to see Bob, she popped into the used bookstore first, browsed the packed and somewhat disorderly shelves, and chatted for a few minutes with the clerk, an older woman with a penchant for religious books. Walking out with an old coffee table book of pictures of China under her arm, she crossed the street to the new, much more orderly bookstore. There she introduced herself to the owners, a nice couple in their mid-forties, who turned out to be big fans of hers, insisting that if she had the time she allow them to set up a signing for her. She hadn't gotten much sleep the night before, but meeting her readers had a way of helping the adrenalin kick in. And leaving the store, she felt a good writing streak coming on.

Still smiling from her bookstore visits, she called the vet clinic when she returned to her car. Susan told her that Dash wasn't around, but Bob would be ready to be picked up in thirty minutes. Remembering that there was a burger and soft-serve ice cream stand at the gas station across from the clinic, Matty finished her mocha as she drove and debated with herself about whether to get a cone or milkshake. Indulgence is what it was, but it was that kind of morning.

Despite all the options, she went old school and ordered a chocolate soft-serve cone. As she waited for the woman in the stand to call her name, Marcus and Carly pulled up.

"We saw you as we were driving by and thought we'd stop

to ask how you were doing," Marcus said, joining her under the canopy.

"I'll be better once I have my ice cream. Can I get you two anything?" Matty asked. They both shook their heads. "I don't really need one either, but I'm waiting to pick up one of the dogs at Dash's clinic."

"Something happen?" Carly asked.

Matty nodded and told them what had happed to Bob. "It's been a packed few days, too packed if you ask me. Especially when all I want to do is stay home and write. I'm close to finishing," she added.

"After everything that's happened, that sounds like a good plan," Marcus responded. "How much longer do you have to wait before you can pick him up?"

"He'll be ready in five minutes." Dash's voice came from behind Matty.

She spun and faced him. "Where did you come from?"

He gave her a funny look. "My clinic. I'm headed out for a call. I just stopped for gas and saw you all."

She narrowed her eyes. "Susan said you weren't at the clinic."

"I think we'll be going now," Carly said, motioning to her partner with her head. Matty thanked them for checking on her and said her good-byes.

"To be clear, Susan tells everyone I'm not available unless I specifically tell her I am. But in this case, she was probably accurate. I was out back restocking supplies. You probably called then."

She eyed him for a moment, then realized she didn't really care all that much if Susan had told the truth or not. It would actually have been easier for her *not* to see Dash today.

"Matty?" he asked.

Her mind must have wandered because he was looking at her, a small frown touching his lips.

"They're calling your name," he pointed out.

She gave herself an internal shake and went over to pick up her ice cream. Just taking a bite seemed to make the day a little better.

"You need to get some sleep," Dash said, surprising her by taking her chin in his fingers and tilting her head up to look at him. "You look exhausted. Great, as always, but exhausted," he added with a quick save.

"I missed Bob last night," she said.

He eyed her. "What's bothering you?"

"It's just been a long few days, Dash," she said, not wanting to rehash everything.

He inclined his head. "Well, Bob will be ready by now. You should go home and maybe the two of you can take a little rest together."

She didn't fight the small smile that tugged at the corners of her mouth. It wasn't every guy who would suggest she cuddle up with a dog and take a nap.

"Yeah, maybe," she said.

"Why don't we go back to the clinic and I'll help you get him into your car. That way you don't have to worry about what to do with your ice cream."

And then she did laugh. "Thanks, Dash. I would appreciate that."

● ● ●

Matty woke with a start and bolted upright. She paused and blinked, letting the hazy daytime sleep clear from her head. Next to her, Bob raised his head and looked at her, as did Isis who was sleeping in her usual spot in the corner of the room on her dog bed. The other dogs were scattered around the house and, judging by the silence, sleeping, too.

She took a few deep breaths trying to recall what had woken her so suddenly. Fragments of thoughts floated in and out of her mind but nothing took hold. She glanced out the window then down at her clock. The late-afternoon sun was muted and a stream of light shone through the back window of the bedroom.

Swinging her legs over the side of the bed, her eyes caught on the book she'd left on the bedside table. A book. She stared at it for a long moment, before picking it up and opening the cover. And then it clicked.

Thumbing through the first few pages, she found the copyright notice and below it, the ISBN number. Ten digits.

Putting the book down, she climbed out of bed in her t-shirt, tugged on a pair of yoga pants, jogged downstairs, and booted up her computer. Pulling up a search engine, she plugged in the numbers Vivi had given her followed by "ISBN." And when the results came up, her stomach shrank to the size of a pea.

The book was one of hers.

She should have known. The main character was blind. Matty had even spent several days with blind "guides," men and women gracious enough to share their time with her to help her experience what it was like to live in DC as a blind person.

But why would Brad make a point of leaving her a trail to one of her own books? Or was it even a trail at all? Maybe the form, and the numbers, hadn't been left for her, but was just something Brad had laying around for another reason altogether.

She had no idea what to think, other than that it was just strange. And something she couldn't dismiss or drop. Pursing her lips, she opened her file manager and scrolled through the list. She didn't have that particular book on her hard drive so she got up to have a look at Brad's bookshelves. He had several in the office, but she had noticed that he also kept books on the shelves in the formal living room and in one of the guest rooms upstairs.

The guest room, the thought clicked into her head. Where she was supposed to have slept. Deciding to start there rather than the living room, she headed back upstairs and entered the large guest suite. Approaching the shelves, she began to run her eyes systematically back and forth. And then, there, on the fourth shelf down, nestled amongst other genre fiction books, was the book she was looking for. As she pulled it off the shelf, the cover flapped opened and several pictures fell from between the pages.

She was definitely getting a bad feeling about all of this. She thought about calling Brad, but for the first time since her arrival, it crossed her mind that perhaps the reason he wasn't calling back was because he couldn't. Yes, they had talked the day before she had arrived, but the fact that he had left some sort of trail of clues for her to follow and had been, for all intents and purposes, unreachable, just wasn't feeling right.

Taking a seat on the floor, she spread the photos out. There were eleven of them, but it became apparent very quickly that there were only three subjects being covered by the collection. The most recognizable pictures were taken in the aftermath of hurricane Katrina, judging from the architecture and destruction. But they were pictures unlike anything Matty had seen on television. Most were of bodies, some bloated and distended, others battered and tangled in fences or against walls. There were pictures of houses and FEMA shelters. And pictures of supplies, presumably flown in to provide relief. There was also a picture of two men she didn't recognize but would peg as either government or big business, judging by their dark suits and ties.

Placing that set of pictures aside, she gathered up the most graphic of the three sets. In these were pictures of children, dead or dying, mostly lying on cots, but some in the street. And it was the street photos that gave her a clue as to what she was looking at. She couldn't say for certain, but if she had to guess, she would wager the photos were from Haiti, taken after the earthquake. And, like the Katrina pictures, one stood out; it was a picture of three people, two men and a woman, dressed in western clothing, khakis and dark t-shirts. They were white but there was no indication of their nationality.

The last set of pictures didn't seem to fit with the other two. The first photo was of a pretty, young woman. She looked petite and had long, blonde hair pulled back out of her face and she was wearing a big smile. It was a posed photo with a generic cloth background that gave Matty no clue as to who she was or where the photo was taken.

The other picture in the set was primarily of two older

white men shaking hands. The only indication Matty had that it belonged with the other photo was the blurry image of the same young woman standing some distance behind the two men.

There were a number of other people in the background of the photo and, judging by the concrete structures she could make out, she would place them at some sort of sporting event. But what kind or where, she hadn't a clue. Then again, as she fingered the picture and thought about how Brad had set things up so she would find all of the photos, maybe the racing form itself, not just the braille, was a clue. She frowned as she looked at the picture. She'd never been to the track up near Albany so nothing in the photo looked familiar. But it would be easy enough to check, if she felt so inclined.

But even if she confirmed that the photo was shot at the track, that wouldn't explain why it was included in a stack of photos with the other, more graphic, images. More confused than before, she flipped through the pictures again. And then again. On the back of the picture of the two men in New Orleans were names, and she found the same on the back of the picture of the three people in Haiti. But there was nothing written on the picture of the woman or the picture of the two men with the same woman.

Matty sat on the floor for a long time trying to figure out not only what the pictures meant but what it meant that Brad appeared to have hidden them for her to find. So intent on the photos, Matty just about jumped out of her skin when her cell rang. But with a glance at the number, she hit ignore and put it back down. She had no interest in talking to Chen at this particular moment.

But the phone must have alerted the dogs to where she was; suddenly they were all standing in the doorway. Even Bob, with this bandaged paw and cone of shame. Looking at the clock on the bedside table, she realized it was doggy dinnertime.

Debating about what to do with the pictures, she finally opted to slide them into a different book, an unused journal with a picture of Venice on the cover. She didn't have a rational reason for doing so, but she felt, in some small way, that she was acknowledging Brad's message by moving the photos somewhere that was her secret. Even if she didn't know what his message was yet.

She fed the dogs then decided to jump in the shower and wash the remains of her afternoon nap off, as well as some of the ickiness she felt after looking at the photos. Refreshed, she pulled on a sundress, brushed on a little makeup and mascara, and headed down the lane to drop off the gift she'd purchased for her neighbor earlier that day.

When Elise didn't answer her door, Matty realized that, yes, she'd wanted to drop the gift off, but that she'd also been hoping the woman would be home to offer her a distraction. With a sigh, she left the package and card on the porch of the house—a house much more traditional than she would have expected given the owner's mailbox—and continued down the driveway toward Anderson's. She wasn't really hungry and hadn't intended to carry on down the road, but it was better than going back to Brad's and sitting alone all night. Thinking about the pictures.

She was just about to cross the street to the restaurant when she heard the rumble of an old engine. Pausing to see where it was coming from, a smile spread across her face when it came into view. A classic red Cadillac convertible—fins and all—pulled to a stop. And perched in the white leather driver's seat was Elise. Wearing more than just a bathing suit this time, she sported a white sundress, a white scarf around her head, and a pair of big Jackie O. sunglasses.

Matty crossed the street and leaned over the passenger door, grinning. "This is quite a car you have, Elise. She's got some attitude, doesn't she?"

"Life is boring without attitude, darling. This is Greta. I've had her for thirty years. More reliable than most people I know."

"More sturdy, too, would be my guess," Matty said, resting her elbows on the open window frame. "I just left you a little package on your porch to say thank you for your help yesterday."

Elise beamed. "Thank you, darling. It's so nice to meet a young person with manners. You're welcome, by the way—and how is the little guy?"

As she was giving Elise a brief report on Bob, the sound of a familiar truck could be heard coming up behind her. Stopping her narrative, she turned to watch it over her shoulder. Dash stopped at the stop sign, paused a little longer than necessary, then turned right. She thought he might be headed out on a call, but then she heard him pull his truck into the back part of Anderson's parking lot, turn the engine off, and, a few seconds later, open and close his truck door. She and Elise were quiet, still listening. After a minute, they saw Dash standing on the roadside, clearly waiting for her.

She turned back to Elise, who was smiling. "The rumors say he's quite a handful, Matty dear."

Matty laughed. "Is that a warning or a challenge, Elise?"

"That, my dear, is up to you."

Matty straightened as Elise pulled back onto the road. She watched the Caddy drive away, then crossed the street and stopped in front of Dash.

"You're a traffic hazard, Matty Brooks," he said.

"You here to cash in on that rain check?" She gestured toward Anderson's with her head. "If I recall, I offered you a drink," she said, harkening back to their conversation the first day she arrived.

He let out a little chuckle. "You can keep the rain check. I'll buy."

They entered and took a seat at the same table by the window where they'd watched the storm a few nights earlier. There was some sort of huge party going on in the back of the restaurant, which accounted for the number of cars in the parking lot, but the front of the restaurant, which was mostly the bar, was fairly empty.

"You look like you got some sleep this afternoon," Dash commented, picking up the menu.

She nodded. "Yes, Bob and I both took your advice. We needed it. How was the rest of your day?"

They spent the next few minutes talking about his day. She didn't know any large animal vets, and being a writer and a naturally inquisitive person, she took the opportunity to learn a little bit about his job. Amy came and took their orders about ten minutes after they'd sat down and explained that, because there was a wedding rehearsal dinner going on in the back, dinner might take a little longer than usual. Matty had no desire to rush back to Brad's house and be alone for the rest of the evening, so she didn't mind at all. She still wasn't certain what to think about the whole thing with Dash—whether she wanted to pursue something or not, or, if she did, whether he would be interested or still freaked out by his crazy family tradition. The only thing she did know was that she didn't want to go back to the house until she was good and tired enough to fall straight into bed.

Dinner came and went while she asked Dash about his family, growing up in Windsor, and his time in the military—the conversation they should have had the first time they were in Anderson's, before Marcus and Carly joined them. Before Dash fled the scene.

And so, for a few hours, she was able to forget the pictures, Bob's toe, and even the looming deadline for her book.

And then the bride and groom walked by. Maybe it was guilt playing in her mind, but when Matty saw the bride, a young woman who so closely resembled the main female character Matty pictured in her head when writing her new book, for a moment, she was speechless.

"Matty? Is everything all right?" Dash asked. "Matty?" he repeated.

She gave herself a little shake as the couple exited the restaurant, followed by several others in the wedding party. "Sorry, I just got distracted. I'm close to being done with my next book, but just a little behind schedule, and that woman reminded me of something."

"Do you really have a schedule?" he asked.

She wagged her head. "I do, and while it isn't set in stone, I do like to stick to it as much as possible."

"So what's causing the delay? Other than all the shit that's been going on, of course," he added with a smile.

"Strangely enough, it's not that. I tend to find that when I have a lot going on, I actually write more, and even better. But this time it's—well, it's hard to explain."

"Try me," he prompted.

She took a moment to gather her thoughts, then leaned forward and ran her fingers over her beer glass as she spoke. "I don't write sex into my books, but there are definitely elements of romance or potential romance in them. It's something that helps a thriller appeal across genders. And I kind of like the idea of people getting a happy ending," she added with a sheepish smile.

"Sounds good to me," he said.

"But the problem is, I haven't been able to figure out *that* connection between my two main characters. Like I said, I don't include the sex scenes in my books, but I do like to write them out so that it's in *my* head when I write their interactions. I find that it brings a sense of realism to their relationship."

"You write sex scenes?"

He was getting that glazed look again. She shook her head and rolled her eyes. "Yes, I do, and no, you cannot read them. And no, they generally aren't based on experience. Besides, what I write is fictional, it's not real sex."

"How can something be 'not real sex?'"

"Because I write what I write to create and capture a feeling, rather than an act. There aren't any awkward moments, there aren't any jeans getting stuck on feet, or unplanned bodily noises. Condoms appear out of nowhere and everything is perfect the first time around. And the second time. It's planned and orchestrated and helps me focus on what my characters feel, emotionally, so I can leverage that throughout the book. Real sex isn't so constructed."

"And why don't you write real sex?"

"Because people *have* real sex. Like I said, writing fictional sex lets me explore and discover emotions that translate into an intimacy between the main characters. And I've found, from talking to readers, that when they read my books, they tend to want to escape reality, to go into a world that's different than their own, both intellectually and emotionally. Fictional sex, if only as a backstory in my head, helps me give my readers what they want. If people want real sex, there are a number of ways to get it, including with a different kind of book or with an actual person."

"You make *real* sex sound so easy."

She arched a brow at him. "You're not honestly going to tell me it's that hard for you to find a partner? 'Cause that's not what I've heard."

He opened his mouth then shut it. Smart man. "Okay, so then what's the problem with these two characters?" he said instead.

"I can't seem to put my finger on what it is that will tip them over the edge from where they are to what they can be, together."

"Meaning?"

"There's a moment in every romantic relationship that gives the people involved a choice. To jump in or not? I'm not saying there is only ever one moment, because I don't believe that, but there is always at least one moment when the parties have to make that decision."

"And," he said, leaning forward.

"And I can't quite seem to construct that moment for these two characters. I can't quite figure out what they need to be thinking or feeling, or what needs to be happening for that moment to even present itself."

"A plot issue?"

She lifted a shoulder. "Maybe, but I think it's more of a feeling issue. The characters are both strong, but she's been lied to and betrayed by so many people she's not really sure she can trust herself anymore. The lies and betrayals are work related, not from former boyfriends or anything like that. But what has happened is she's been put in a position where she's starting to question her own judgment."

"Including what she might feel for the guy or might think she feels," Dash said.

Matty nodded. "So, when she questions her own judgment,

what needs to happen to make her take that leap without making her seem like a helpless princess?"

Dash laughed a bit. "I've read your books, you don't write helpless princesses."

She smiled at that.

"You want to know what I think?" he asked.

She nodded.

"I think he needs to overwhelm her with *his* certainty." As Dash spoke he leaned across the table and traced a finger up the back of her hand. Such a small touch.

"Reassure her?" she managed to say as her eyes fixed on his finger making its way back down her hand.

"No, not reassure her. If she's been betrayed, only time and consistency will reassure her. But if he wants the chance to *have* that time and the opportunity to be consistent, he needs to push her over that ledge once and then let her see that he's with her the whole time."

Matty swallowed and looked at Dash. His eyes were almost black. "You sound like you're speaking from experience?"

He shook his head. "In real life it isn't so thought out, is it?"

Her eyes held his for a long moment. "No, it isn't." It didn't escape her notice that what Dash was suggesting was almost the exact opposite of what he himself had been doing for the past few days.

But as his fingers moved up and circled her wrist bone, she wondered if that was about to change. "How did you hear about the family tradition?" he asked, changing the subject but keeping his voice low and intimate.

"People talk."

"More than they should, apparently. It bothers you, doesn't it?"

"That people talk? No, I live in DC, gossip spreads faster in my city than it does in a fifth-grade classroom."

"Don't be obtuse, Matty."

She let out a breath but held his gaze. "Honestly, Dash, I'm not sure what to make of your family situation. I think it's crazy, I really do. And so, in some sense, I don't think it's worth thinking about. But then again, it's not my family that's had this experience, is it?"

"And what if it isn't crazy?"

"Then I can understand why you flipped hot and cold on me faster than a politician in an election year, because if I thought it was remotely real, it would freak me out, too."

A small smile touched his lips. "So, if you don't think it's real, does it bother you?" he pressed.

She looked at him and, for the first time, *really* wondered if it mattered whether the tradition was a real thing or not. She had said it didn't, but that had been more of a knee-jerk reaction. But now? Now that she really thought about it, she was more convinced than ever that no, it didn't matter to her if it was real or not. It didn't matter because she wanted Dash, and she knew he wanted her too. And it didn't matter because no one was going to *force* either one of them to get married if they didn't want to. She didn't foresee wanting to, but knew herself well enough to know that when she decided to take that step, *if* she decided to take that step, it was something she would only do after giving it a lot of thought—not on the notion of a family tradition.

She turned the hand he'd been holding and curled her fingers around his. "I'm not much of a fatalist, Dash, but the truth of it is, if it *is* real, then there's nothing we can do about it, right? And if it's not, then there's no reason we can't enjoy each other's company in the time I'm here."

She saw Dash suck in a quick breath and his grip tightened on hers. Good lord, she wanted this man.

"So, you're saying it doesn't matter to you?" he clarified.

At the moment, very little mattered to her other than leaving this public place. She shook her head.

"Even knowing what it might mean?" he pressed.

She still didn't really believe in it, but if things worked out that way, she knew she'd make the right decision based on what they felt for each other, not because of the tradition. "Even knowing," she said.

"Then let's get out of here," he said, pulling her up. The best words she'd heard all night.

She let go of his hand just long enough for him to throw some money on the table, then he was reaching for her and they were out the door. He unlocked his truck as they approached and opened the passenger door for her. Rather than climb in, she turned, slipped her hand behind his neck, and pulled him down into a kiss. He braced one hand against the truck's door and the other, the one holding her hand, he wrapped around her back, arching her up into him as he deepened the connection.

The heat of the night had nothing on what they were generating with this relatively simple touch. A little sound of need escaped her as she untangled her fingers from his, brought her hand from behind her back, and began pulling his shirt out of the waistband of his jeans, needing to feel more of him. When the tips of her fingers brushed his bare skin she felt it go taut under her touch. And when she slid her hand around his hip and across the small of his back, pulling him closer, he took his hand off the door and speared his fingers through her hair, taking the kiss from hot to scorching.

"The truck, Matty. Get in the truck," he said when she drew her mouth away from his and trailed her lips down his neck.

"Hmm," she said, bringing her hands up to unbutton his shirt. He tilted her head up and covered her mouth again with his. Even as she finished with the buttons and smoothed her hands over his cotton undershirt, feeling his chest and muscles under her touch, she wanted more.

Dash dipped his head and began moving his lips over her shoulder, pushing the strap of her sundress down. She tilted her head away to give him better access and ran her fingers along the waist of his jeans and up his sides.

"Dash, I don't want to wait," she said, moving her hands back down to his jeans and unbuttoning the top button.

"We're in a parking lot, Matty. Get in the truck. We can be at your house in less than five minutes."

But he wasn't making it easy. One of his hands had dropped to her thigh and was making its way back up, pulling her dress along with it. The other was splayed across her lower back, making her aware of his size and strength.

He must have sensed she was close to not caring because, in an instant, she found herself in the passenger seat. But before he closed the door on her, she grabbed his shirt and pulled him into another kiss, this time wrapping her legs around his body. She didn't want to let him go, not even to walk around the truck to get in on the other side so he could take them home.

"Jesus, Matty," Dash said, forcibly pulling himself away. "I knew it would be like this," he added, before bringing his lips back to hers. More than anything else, there was something about that phrase, about the assurance in his voice about her, about them, that sent her hurling over the edge.

"We need to leave, Dash," she said, reining in every bit of what she was feeling and experiencing in an effort to keep it from exploding.

He drew back and his eyes searched hers. She knew what he saw there because it felt like everything she was feeling, everything she wanted, was written not just on her face but on her body.

He nodded and stepped back. She swung her legs back inside and jerkily closed the door as Dash rounded the truck. He paused for a moment and looked at her through the windshield, his hair tousled, shirt open. Their gazes met and held for a heated moment and then he was beside her in the driver's seat.

And she didn't want to wait anymore.

• • •

Matty's leg came across his lap and the next thing Dash knew, she was straddling him in his truck, pulling his undershirt up to touch his skin as she dipped her head to kiss him.

"Parking lot," he reminded her, even as he moved his seat back to give her more room.

"Do you want to wait?" she asked with her hands unbuttoning his jeans. She paused for a moment, met his eyes, then slid her hands inside.

"Oh, hell, no," he said, searching for the zipper on her dress. She lifted her arm a touch and he found it. Tugging it down, the top of her dress fell, revealing her bare chest.

He swore again as she arched back, presenting herself to him as she worked his jeans down and freed him from his boxers.

"God, Dash," she said, her hands on him as he made it his mission to taste every inch of her he could reach.

He moved a hand between them and could feel her, hot and ready. When he brushed a finger across her barely-there underwear and heard her moan, he let out a throaty chuckle. She drew back to look at him and nearly took his breath away. Her dark hair was draped over her bare shoulders, the tips curling around her breasts. Her mouth was swollen from their kisses, and her eyes, thankfully, looked as needy as his.

"Something funny?" she asked, still stroking him.

"Condoms are going to magically appear, is all," he said with a smile. She looked confused and stopped moving her hand, which was probably a good thing.

With his right hand, he reached forward and, after a few botched attempts, managed to get the glove compartment open and pull out a box of condoms. He held them up and her expression turned to one of amused curiosity.

"I bought them the first day I met you. Unopened, see," he said, showing her the sealed sides of the box.

"Let me guess," she smiled and leaned forward, nuzzling his ear and neck and giving him the space he needed. "You were a boy scout?"

"Are you complaining?" he asked as he opened a condom packet and began rolling one on.

Matty raised herself up and met his gaze. "Not in the least," she replied as she sank down on him.

Air flew out of his lungs as her heat surrounded him. Tangling one hand in her hair and gripping the other firmly around her waist, he let her pick the pace but held her at just the right angle. She moved up and down, taking him deep inside her as she sank against him. The slow rhythm let Dash feel every centimeter of her as she covered him, feeling every part of him inside her.

Given how quickly things had heated up physically between them, this deliberate, sensual tempo gave his mind time to catch up and appreciate what was happening. He knew how it would end for both of them, and so, as she moved over him, he let his mind absorb the fact that he was with Matty. That she was as greedy for him as he was for her. That, despite his earlier misgivings and doubts, she wanted this as much as he did. It was a heady sensation and made the physical aspects, the act, of what they were doing that much more powerful.

She quickened her pace just a touch and let her head fall back as she spoke his name and other small, pleading words; he gave her neck a little nip then leaned back and savored her urgency. And then there was that heart-stopping moment when her body locked around him and she cried out, driving herself down on him. He curled his body up to meet her, feel every bit of her. And only when he was sure she had finished, he lowered his hips a few inches, gripped her waist with both hands, and drove himself up into his own release.

Spent, Dash let his hips sink back down and Matty fell forward against his chest. As her head rested on his shoulder and his hands lay limp against her hips, they gasped for air in the truck's warm cab. And Dash knew exactly why sex was nicknamed "the little death."

After a few minutes, when they were both breathing if not normally, then regularly, he reached up and brushed some hair away from her face. She pulled back just enough to see him, then offered a small smile.

He didn't have any words and neither, it seemed, did she. So he pulled her back to him and gave her a soft, sweet kiss before resting his forehead against hers. They stayed like that for another few moments until the sound of Anderson's back door slamming shut brought them both back to a sudden reality.

Matty shrank against him, as if to hide herself in case anyone looked toward the truck.

"It's dark where we're parked and there are lights by the door. Whoever it is isn't going to be able to see into the truck unless they walk right up to it," he said.

"Maybe," she said. "But have you noticed the windows?"

He glanced around, then chuckled. They'd gone and fogged up all the windows. "And teenagers think they have all the fun," he said.

She smiled and then let out a little sigh of relief when whoever it was who'd come out went back inside. She pulled away from Dash and looked around.

"Here are some perfect examples of the differences between real sex and fictional sex. Now that we're done, you're going to have to figure out how to clean up without a bathroom nearby. And I'm going to be sore tomorrow from the door handle digging into my leg and the steering wheel at my back. Not that I'm complaining," she added, leaning back in for a deep kiss, pressing her body against his.

When they ended the kiss she pushed off of him, managing to get herself untangled and into the passenger seat without too much trouble.

"Just to be clear," he said, reaching for the paper towels he always kept in his truck. "We aren't done." As efficiently as he could in his car and with Matty watching, he cleaned himself up then turned to her. She hadn't taken her eyes off him.

"Your place or mine?" he asked.

She smiled. "Mine. It's closer."

CHAPTER 9

MATTY ROLLED OVER TO FIND Dash sitting on the bed, dressed and tying his shoes. "That time already?" she asked, squinting in the morning sun.

"Hmm," he said, turning toward her. Picking up her still-bandaged arm, he examined it then placed a kiss on her inner elbow. "How does this feel?"

"It's fine," she said with a lazy morning smile.

"You're taking care of it, though?"

She gave him a look then rolled over and buried her face in the pillow.

"Matty?"

"Yes," she grumbled, her voice muffled. "I'm taking care of it."

"Good."

His hand spread across her bare back and she felt his lips press against the skin between her shoulder blades. Then they were at her ear.

"I'll talk to you later?"

She smiled into the pillow and moved ever so slightly against him. "Count on it."

Dash was still chuckling when he left the room. From her position in the bed, Matty heard him feed the dogs and let them out. Good man. A few minutes later, he called Bob back in and she heard Isis join them in the kitchen. A few more minutes passed and her little slice of Hudson Valley was silent, the sound of Dash's truck having faded away.

Fortunately, the memories of the night before had not faded

away and she stretched and luxuriated in the satiated feeling. She thought about getting up and showering but realized Dash had inspired her—in more ways than one. She slipped into a robe, popped downstairs, and grabbed her laptop. She paused for a moment when she spotted Brad's computer on one of the shelves. She frowned, thinking it had been one shelf higher the last time she'd noticed it. But then, not being certain and not wanting to lose her focus, she turned and headed back to bed.

And there she stayed, for several hours, writing the scene that would never be in her book. But at the end, when she hit save, she knew her characters would be the better for it. Their connection was solid in her mind now and she knew the rest of their story would come to her much easier.

With a smile, she closed her laptop and looked at the clock. She hadn't showered or even brushed her teeth, let alone bothered with breakfast or coffee. And it was close to two o'clock. With a shake of her head, she jumped into the shower and cleaned herself up then headed downstairs to eat and take care of the neglected animals.

Thankfully, it wasn't too hot and the rabbits had plenty of water. She let the chickens out, collected some eggs, and made a mental note to ask Dash about the pancake breakfast, since she now had over two-dozen eggs and had only been in town for a week. After spending some time futzing in the garden, pulling weeds and watering, she collected some lettuce and herbs, along with some tomatoes and peas, and made her way back inside.

Realizing she hadn't called her mom in a few days, she picked up the phone and dialed.

"Mama," Matty said when her mom answered.

"Matty, Mija, how are you?"

"I'm fine, Mama. I just wanted to call and say hello."

"And check in, in case Charlotte calls me. This is so I can tell her you called."

Matty laughed. "And maybe that, too. How are you?"

"I am fine. It is hot down here, as it always is this time of year. But everything is well. Everyone is well. How is that place?"

She could tell that her mother was trying hard to be fair to Brad. He had no more created the situation they'd all found themselves in than Matty did. But even so, she tempered her answer and told her mother only that it was fine. She didn't say anything about the cool, clean breezes or the beautiful sight of a storm making its way across the valley. Or the fresh vegetables from the garden. Or Dash.

She didn't like keeping things from her mother, but for right or for wrong, she felt as if she would be betraying her mom if she revealed just how much, even in such a short time, she had grown to like the Hudson Valley. That's not to say that she was going to pick up and move here, but she could understand why Brad had chosen this area. It was different than the society world he'd grown up in—still beautifully northeastern and historic like Greenwich, but quieter and more peaceful.

And so she kept these parts of her experience to herself, not wanting to hurt her mother in any way. Instead, she talked about her book and the progress she was making, they talked about the opening of a new modern art museum that her mother was helping with, and they caught up on their DC friends and neighbors.

When she hung up, Matty took a glass of iced tea out to the patio, called Bob down from his bed upstairs, and sent him out to do his business under her watchful eye. He had several more days to go in the bandage and cone, and while he bumped into things and occasionally looked confused as to why he wasn't fitting into places the way he normally did, in typical Lab fashion, he seemed to take everything in stride.

She was smiling, watching his attempts to sniff around when his nose wouldn't touch the ground when something caught her eye. Glancing toward the small table on the patio, she frowned. Something was lying in the middle of the table that she was certain was not there when she'd cleaned the patio area the afternoon after Bob's incident.

Taking a few steps closer, she cocked her head to get a better look. And her stomach lurched. Instinct kicked in and her eyes scoured the hill behind the house and the driveway for signs of anything, or anyone, out of place. Finding nothing, but still feeling entirely creeped out, she pulled her phone out of her pocket and dialed Dash.

"And how was your day?" he asked when he picked up the phone.

His voice sounded very male and she had no doubt he was remembering the night before, but her mind was now elsewhere. "Uh, good." She paused, not sure how to proceed.

"Matty, is everything okay?" he asked. The satisfaction she'd heard in his voice had been replaced by concern.

"I don't know. Did you notice anything on the patio table last night when we came in?"

He gave a short bark of laughter. "You're kidding, right?"

She had to give him that, it's not like she'd noticed anything, other than him, either. "Okay, well, I just found something on the table and, um, I'm not sure what to make of it or when it might have come to be here."

"What is it?" he asked.

She paused again and took one more look at it. A wave of nausea washed over her. "I'm not completely sure, but I think it's Bob's toe."

● ● ●

Dash's mind went blank for a moment, then jumped into gear as his heart crawled into his throat. It wouldn't have been unusual to find Bob's toe out in the field he'd been in when it was separated from his foot, but to find it on the table on the patio couldn't be a good thing.

"Can you bring it to me?" he asked.

"Uh, sure," she answered.

"Take a plastic bag, turn it inside out and pick it up using the bag. Then flip it closed and seal it."

"Like evidence or something?"

"Like something," he muttered.

"What?"

"Nothing. I'm almost done for the day, can you bring it down here?" he asked.

"Sure. I'm done doing what I need to do. I can be there in a few minutes."

They hung up and Dash sat for a moment, staring blankly at the paperwork in front of him. He didn't know what Matty's find meant, but it was just too weird to ignore. So he picked up the phone and called Ian.

"I don't know that it's anything," Dash said after telling Ian what Matty had found.

"Yeah, I don't either. But it is strange, I'll grant you that. Are you planning to take a look at it?" Ian asked.

"I was, unless you don't want me to."

"No, go ahead," Ian said. "I'd be interested in your thoughts and I know you'll handle it carefully. I'm just about to leave Riverside and head home. Why don't I stop by on my way and we can take it from there."

Dash agreed to Ian's plan and, after ending the conversation, forced his mind to focus on the paperwork in front of him so that when Matty arrived he'd be done for the day. Except for dealing with the toe.

He finished reviewing the last of the monthly accounting sheets just as the bell on the clinic door rang. He'd locked up after closing so went to open the door for her. He couldn't help the smile that crept onto his face when he saw her standing there, hair down, in a sundress and flip-flops.

"Now that's a way to say hi," she said, stepping inside. Without a thought, his arms came around her and pulled her against him for a long kiss.

"And that's even better," she said when he drew back to look down at her. "Not to spoil the mood or anything, but I have this for you," she said, holding up a paper bag. "It's in a Ziploc bag inside this but I didn't like looking at it so I put it in the second bag."

He could hardly fault her for that. Taking her to have a seat in his office, he proceeded down to one of the exam rooms that had a microscope. Using a small pair of forceps, Dash retrieved the toe and placed it in a thin, glass container. Before looking at it under the scope, he held it up to examine with his naked eyes.

He couldn't say for certain that it was Bob's, but he'd bet the farm it was—same color fur, same size, and with the same kind of incision along the skin and bone. Not liking what he was seeing, he placed it under the microscope.

And he liked what he saw there even less. Based on what he could tell from the toe and what he remembered of Bob's paw, the cut looked like it was made with a thin, knife-like blade, not glass. He wouldn't wish an injury on any animal, but he had hoped to find something on the toe to indicate that it had been an accidental slice caused by glass left over from some long-ago house. He sat back and sighed. He was glad Ian was coming by. Like Matty, Dash didn't know what it meant, but even the possibility of someone out there mutilating animals wasn't one he liked to contemplate.

"Dash?" Matty walked into the room. "Is everything okay?"

He rolled his chair away from the desk. "It's what I thought it would be."

She eyed him for a minute then came forward and placed her arms around his neck. "That's an answer that doesn't really answer the question, isn't it? Is it Bob's toe? And if it is, how did it get back to my patio? Could one of the other dogs have brought it? Or one of the cats?"

He looked up at her and nodded but said nothing. He didn't want to give her any more reason to be concerned, but any answers he might have would do just that. She eyed him again as he brushed a strand of hair from her face, then she lowered herself onto his lap, dropping her purse at his side.

"Did you have a good day?" she asked, feathering kisses along his neck.

He slipped one hand onto her thigh and held her waist with the other. "It's definitely getting better," he responded, grateful she'd changed the subject but knowing she'd likely done so because she knew she wouldn't like the answers if she continued to press him.

He felt her smile against his skin and pulled her closer. Tilting his head back, he maneuvered his mouth to hers and, just like the night before, his body went from zero to sixty in about two seconds. Wrapping his arms around her, he stood, lifting her with him, and walked the two steps to the exam table. She jumped when her bare legs touched the cool tabletop, but the protest was short lived when he pulled her to the edge and pressed himself against her.

• • •

Matty let her head fall back as he trailed his lips along her collar bone, nudging the top of her dress down as he went. He tugged the straps down her shoulders far enough to trap her arms and expose her breasts to him. Gently, he pushed her back onto the table. She arched her back against the cold metal but he kept one hand on her belly, holding her in place, as he began unbuttoning his pants with the other. She would like to think she hadn't planned for this to happen, but taking a lesson from Dash, she had grabbed a couple of condoms to carry in her purse before she'd left the house. If their first time had been in his car in a public parking lot, clearly inhibition wasn't going to be a problem.

The hand on her belly drifted down and Dash's fingers found the edge of her underwear. Slowly, he slid them off and touched her softly as he took himself in his other hand.

"Close your eyes, Matty," he ordered, and after a moment she complied, focusing her senses on his touch and the sounds they were making.

He pulled her hips to the edge of the table and draped her thighs over the side. She sucked in a breath and arched into him as he slid a finger inside her then slowly drew it out.

"Condoms, Dash. In my purse," she managed to say, keeping her eyes closed, as she'd been told.

She heard him let out a quiet chuckle as he withdrew his finger from her and moved his hand back to her belly. Immediately she felt the loss of his intimacy but her anticipation ratcheted up when she heard the sound of him searching inside her purse, then the muted ripping noise of a little foil packet being torn open. Moments later, she felt the tip of him replace his finger and she was more than ready.

"Keep your eyes closed, Matty," he said as he ever so slowly eased himself in. She didn't need the gentleness; he was doing it to torture her.

Other than his hands on her hips, the only parts of their bodies making contact were the most intimate ones. And while the slow torture was building to a sensuousness she'd never experienced before, she wanted more. And she wasn't shy about letting him know.

Dash didn't say a word when she pleaded with him; he just gave her everything she asked for. And when she wanted more, when she wanted him faster, he gave her that, too. And then, finally, between the friction, the connection, and everything else, she arched off the table and locked herself around him. He pressed into her impossibly deep and she felt him pulse against her insides as he let out a very primal sound.

Once all the tremors died down, she lazily opened her eyes. His hands were resting on the table beside her thighs, his head was bent down, and he was breathing hard. She lifted a hand and traced a finger along his forearm. His eyes came up and he smiled.

"My day definitely just got better," he said, making her laugh.

"Maybe we could just stay here for a while. The chair in your office is pretty comfortable," she suggested, only partly tongue in cheek.

"Nice thought—"

Dash cut off whatever else he was going to say when, as if on cue, they heard a knock on the front door. She sat up and they disentangled themselves.

"Ian," he said in explanation.

"You called Ian?" she asked as she pulled on her underwear and pulled up her dress straps, making sure everything was in place.

Dash nodded. "I didn't like the idea of Bob's toe just showing up, so I called to get his opinion." He was doing his best to clean up and make himself presentable but it was little more complicated for him than for her.

She walked by him and placed a kiss on his cheek. "I'll go let him in. Come out when you're ready."

Ian's upper body was visible through the door's window as Matty approached. He raised his eyebrows at her as he entered.

"Did I interrupt anything?" he asked, knowing full well he had.

"Nope," she countered. "Perfect timing," she grinned, making Ian laugh.

"Perfect timing for what?" Dash asked, entering the room.

"For not interrupting anything," Ian responded.

Dash's eyes went from Matty's to Ian's. "I was just looking at the toe under the microscope."

Matty laughed and Ian chuckled as he crossed his arms over his chest. "So that's what they're calling it these days?"

"That's not what *I'm* calling it," she said. "But if it makes Dash feel better," she added with a shrug. Ian shook his head and tried to stop grinning.

"The toe," Dash said holding out the paper bag.

In a flash, Ian was all business. "And?"

Dash glanced at Matty and she gave him a look that let him know that he shouldn't even think about hiding anything from her.

He let out a deep breath. "It looks like it was sliced off with a very sharp blade."

"Intentionally?" Ian asked.

Dash wagged his head. "It's possible Bob walked into an old bear trap or something like that."

"But that's not what it looks like to you, is it?" Ian asked.

With obvious reluctance, Dash shook his head.

Ian let out a grunt of disgust. "Great, just what we need, someone mutilating animals."

"On top of the body that dropped into Brad's truck," Matty added. Ian shot her a look and she shrugged. "Sorry, just stating the facts."

"Such as they are," Ian said. "Well, I guess I'll take that," he reached for the bag Dash held. "And we'll get a team up to have a look around Brad's property, if you don't mind, Matty?" he added.

"Of course not," she responded.

"We'll need you to show us where Bob was when this happened and where you found the toe today," Ian continued. When she nodded, he seemed about to say more, then thought better of it and changed topics. "Vivienne and I are going to The Tavern for dinner tonight. Do you guys want to join us?" he asked.

"The Tavern? Where's that?" Matty asked.

"Just south of town about a half a mile," Dash answered.

She looked at Dash and raised her shoulders. "I've only ever been to Frank's or Anderson's, I wouldn't mind trying someplace new. And it would be nice to see Vivi again."

Dash and Ian shared a look. "You went to Frank's?" Dash asked, his lips twitching.

"Frank and I are like this," she said holding up her crossed fingers. "We have a little understanding now. He makes me the iced mochas I want and I don't actually order them out loud, so the rest of his customers won't find out. It's our little secret."

Dash and Ian laughed.

"Of course it is," Dash said. "Come on, Matty, I want to go home and change. I imagine Ian does too. Meet you there in an hour?" he asked and Ian nodded. Dash locked the front door after the sheriff left then turned toward her.

"Ready?"

"It just dawned on me that I've never seen your house," she said as they headed toward the back door. "It makes sense and all, but still." And it actually did seem strange, and that it was strange at all was even stranger. Because it felt like she should know more about him than she did, it felt like she *did* know more about him—even though they'd only spent one night together.

"It's nothing too special, but I like it. Let's drop your car at your place, we can check on the animals, and then we'll take my truck back to my house. You can poke around and be as nosy as you want while I shower and change."

And they did just that. She'd thought about showering too, but curiosity had gotten the better of her and she'd spent the time exploring Dash's house and the surrounding land instead. His place wasn't as big as Brad's, but it had a great screened-in porch with a swinging bench seat that overlooked a field and a swimming pond. It was the same Greek Revival style as most of the older homes in the area and had three bedrooms with two baths upstairs and a kitchen, dining room, living room, and powder room on the bottom floor. The grounds were mostly grass, which made sense—with the amount of time Dash spent away from home, it would be hard for him to tend any kind of elaborate garden. But the whole piece of property was tucked up on a quiet dirt road and it felt peaceful and, with its warm colors and inviting furniture, cozy.

By the time Dash came trotting back down the stairs, Matty had decided that his home, whether intentional or not, was a perfect reflection of him: strong enough to withstand the years, yet welcoming, unfussy, and comfortable.

Right on time, they walked into The Tavern, a building that also looked to double as an inn. The restaurant and bar were to the left of the door and, as they entered, Matty caught sight of Vivi talking to the bartender and Ian leaning against the bar listening. When he saw them, Ian signaled Matty and Dash to meet him at a table in the back.

"Vivienne is just finishing some wedding plans with Rob, the owner," Ian said as they sat.

"Are you having the reception here?" Matty asked.

Ian shook his head. "No, Rob is providing the bar services. The wedding will be at the church downtown and the reception will be at a bed and breakfast near our house." When he spoke a small smile touched his lips.

"You like saying that, don't you? 'Our house,'" Dash said.

Ian cocked a brow and his smile spread. "It ain't bad," he said.

"What isn't bad?" Vivi asked, joining them.

"Marriage, being together," Matty answered.

Vivi cast an affectionate look at Ian. "No, it's not. Although the *getting* married part isn't quite as fun."

They paused in their conversation when Rob, whom Vivi introduced to Matty, stopped by to take drink orders and drop off menus.

"Big wedding?" Dash asked, returning to the topic when Rob had departed.

Ian shrugged. "Vivienne has a huge family."

"And every one of them wants to be involved in every part of this," Vivi added.

"Only because they love you," Ian pointed out.

Vivi let out a little laugh. "I know. Believe me, I know. And it will be fun. But it's going to be crazy, I can promise you that. My father was one of four and my mother, one of six," she said, looking at Matty. "I think Windsor may be in for a shock when my Italian brood descends on the town. Then again, they're a fun, easy-going bunch and they tip well, so I'm sure everyone will have a good time."

Matty murmured her agreement. She couldn't imagine what it would be like to have such a big family. When she got married, if she ever got married, she'd have lots of friends to invite, but for family it would really just be her mom and Charlotte, plus Charlotte's mom, Nanette. Her dad wasn't in the picture and with her grandmother gone, it was a pretty small group.

"Oh, Matty, I meant to touch base with you on those numbers," Vivi said, bringing Matty back to the conversation. "We've had a couple of busy days at the lab so I haven't had a chance to look at them. But things should calm down in the next day or two, so I'll dig into them then."

Matty wasn't ready to talk about what she'd found quite yet, so when Rob returned with their drinks, she hoped he'd also serve as a distraction.

No such luck. "Numbers?" both Dash and Ian said at the same time as soon as Rob stepped away.

Matty cast a quick look at Dash. For some reason she felt a little niggling of guilt for not having told him about the numbers. "Uh, it's okay, I figured it out. Have you been able to ID the man who fell into the truck, yet?" she asked, trying to change the subject.

"No, she hasn't. The fingerprints were degraded, the facial recognition didn't give us any hits, and the guy wore dentures, so no dentals. It may take a bit longer than we thought. But just what is it that you've figured out?" Ian pressed, his voice somewhat stern.

"Yes, I'm curious, too." Dash's tone was laced with more than just curiosity.

Vivi must have sensed something; her eyes went from Matty to Dash and then back again with a look of question and apology.

Matty sighed. "I found an old racing form at Brad's and there were some bumps on it. Vivi's cousins told us it was braille and that it was a string of numbers. Vivi and I were trying to figure out what the numbers meant."

Ian sat back and crossed his arms. "Let me get this straight. Brad left you what amounts to a secret message?"

"More like a string of them, right Matty?" Dash added. And he was not happy.

"Meaning?" Ian pushed.

"You found the form in the liquor cabinet, didn't you?" Dash asked.

Matty nodded. Dash then filled in the blanks for Ian, telling him of the set of directions Brad had left that included the reference to the cabinet, where she found the racing form, which led to something else.

"So what are the numbers?" Vivi asked. Her voice was soft,

no doubt trying to balance out the tension coming from the male side of the table.

"It was an ISBN number. To one of my books, actually. One that has a very significant character who is blind."

"And?" Dash pressed with a piercing look.

Matty looked away for a moment then shrugged one shoulder. "And Brad had a copy in his library and inside it were some pictures. Nothing incriminating, just strange," she said, cutting off both Dash and Ian's inevitable questions about the content of the images.

"Strange in what way?" Ian asked.

Matty wagged her head. "There were a couple of pictures from New Orleans after Katrina. A few from what I think is Haiti after the earthquake and a couple others I didn't recognize. They aren't nice pictures but they aren't anything you wouldn't have seen in the media."

"And that was it?" Dash said.

Matty nodded, then paused a moment before adding, "There were two pictures that had names written on the back, but I don't know who they are and haven't had a chance to look them up. The names are written on the back much like my mom used to write the names of other kids in pictures with me, so she wouldn't forget who they were. It kind of reminded me of that."

The table was silent for a moment while Rob brought their meals.

But when Rob was gone, Ian leaned forward. "I don't want to make you worry or anything, Matty, but have you talked to Brad since he left?"

Stalling for time, Matty ate a spoonful of onion soup before answering. She wanted to respond to Ian's question but didn't really want to get into the dynamics of her family.

"Brad and I aren't close, but the answer to your question is no, I haven't heard from him. I've called and left a few messages, but he hasn't gotten back to me."

To her surprise, Dash laid a reassuring hand on her leg under the table. She gave him a grateful look. She didn't feel under attack, or even all that worried, but it was nice that he recognized her unease in discussing family.

"I'll call him tonight and leave a message myself," Dash said. "Maybe if he thinks I'm calling about one of his animals he'll call back."

Ian looked like he was about to say something but Vivi cut him off. "So, how's the book coming along, Matty?"

Matty smiled at Vivi's show of support, even though Ian had a little frown lingering on his lips. "It's going really well; between talking with Chen Zheng, a friend of Brad's and an expert on Chinese politics, and just having some time away, I'm almost back on track—nearly done, actually. But enough about me," she added. "Tell me about the wedding plans?"

And they spent the rest of the dinner talking about the invitations, the food, the drinks, and how over the top Vivi's family was being about the whole thing. The two women even got Ian and Dash to smile and laugh a few times. All in all, the second half of the meal was much more enjoyable than the first—as far as Matty was concerned. But that didn't mean she was oblivious to what Ian had been suggesting earlier.

Pulling Vivi to the side as they walked toward their respective cars after the meal, Matty spoke. "I'm not naïve, Vivi. I know that the things Brad left for me to find, along with not answering his calls, could mean something not very good. It's possible he got himself mixed up in something and needed to get away, but the truth is, I don't know. And I don't know enough about him to know whether he's the kind of person who'd get mixed up in something bad or the kind of person who'd just take off camping in the wilds for two weeks."

Vivi gave her a sympathetic look. "So, what do you want to do?"

Matty shook her head. "I don't know. I don't know what I *can* do other than what I'm already doing—calling, leaving messages.

Maybe if he doesn't come back when he said he would, then I could do something then?"

Placing a hand on her arm, Vivi made a suggestion. "Why don't you let me look into a couple of things over the next few days? I'll see if I can get a trace on his cell, maybe check his credit cards, that sort of thing. It might not tell us anything, but it may give us some indication if he's traveling."

Matty let out a small sigh. "Can you do that legally? I don't want you to get in trouble."

Vivi smiled. "I'll come by tomorrow and you can fill out an official report that expresses your concern about him being a potential missing person. It should be enough to justify my actions if anyone ever questions them."

"And what about them?" Matty asked, gesturing to the two men engaged in conversation a short distance away.

"We'll keep it between us, for now."

"Thanks, Vivi, I really appreciate it."

"Appreciate what?" Dash asked, walking toward them.

"Nothing," Matty said. Judging by the look on both men's faces, neither was buying it.

"Time for us to go," Vivi interjected, preventing any questions. "I have an eleven o'clock dress fitting in Boston tomorrow. Lucky me."

"Oh, I think you're pretty lucky," Matty said with a smile and a pointed look at Ian.

Vivi laughed and wrapped her arms around her fiancé, who draped his arm over her shoulder and kissed the top of her head. "No doubt about it," Vivi agreed.

CHAPTER 10

FROM HER POSITION LYING PRONE on the bed at Brad's house, Matty watched Dash step out of the shower. It was quite a nice morning show.

"I'll be late for work if you keep looking at me like that," he said, shooting her a smile.

"Do you ever have a day off?" she asked, genuinely curious. She hadn't given it much thought, but he seemed to have been working every day she'd seen him or spoken to him since she'd arrived.

He pulled on his boxers and a pair of jeans. "It's not usually so busy, but the part-time vet I have to help out at the clinic is on vacation. She gets back in a few days. I do have a half day today, though, so I'm off this afternoon. Maybe we can do something." He pulled on his undershirt before sitting on the side of the bed to put his socks on.

"Like what?" she teased, inching her bare leg from under the covers and nudging him with her big toe. He caught her calf and ran his hand up her thigh.

"I'm sure we can think of something," he said, placing a kiss on the inside of her knee.

"I imagine we can."

"Imagine away. All day," he said, leaning over her and brushing his lips first against her cheek, then settling them on her mouth. Pulling away he grinned, showing his dimple. "I'll call you this afternoon."

And for the second morning in a row, Matty listened to the sounds of Dash taking care of the animals and then his truck fading down the driveway. Only this morning she wasn't going to write. She felt that the book was in a good enough place that it could wait a few hours, so instead she rose, showered, checked on the outdoor animals, and tended the garden again. She didn't have to think too hard about how the day would end, but she thought it might be fun to actually make a nice dinner using things from the garden. She'd pick up some local meat later in the day and a good bottle of wine.

She was looking forward to the leisurely afternoon and evening ahead when she a heard a car coming up the drive and the dogs, predictably, going crazy. Coming around the house, basket of lettuce and other veggies in hand, she watched as a beige luxury sedan pulled to a stop.

Matty didn't recognize the older man opening the driver's door so she stood her ground beside the house, still a bit of a distance away. She knew he was probably harmless, but the cautious city girl in her wasn't going to be dismissed.

The man didn't seem bothered by the dogs quickly advancing on him in a mass of squirming bodies and tails. He patted them and looked around until he caught sight of her.

"Hello, I'm Alexander Traynor. I'm here to meet with Brad Brooks," he called out.

Matty took a few steps forward. "In regards, to?" she asked.

He inclined his head. "I'm from First Federal, Brad's employer, he and I had an appointment today."

She frowned. "When did he schedule the meeting?"

"He didn't, I did. We spoke about ten days ago. He suggested I come by. Is he here?"

"I'm sorry, he's not here."

The man pursed his lips. "I see."

"Is there a problem?"

"Do you know when he'll be back?"

Matty shook her head.

"I see," he said again.

Matty took another few steps forward. Maybe this man would

have some insight into what was going on. "I'm Matty, a friend of Brad's," she said, offering her hand. "He asked me to house-sit for him while he's away. I'm sorry you've had to drive here all the way from—?"

"New York City," he supplied.

"Would you like to come in for a glass of iced tea or lemonade?"

He looked about to decline, but something must have changed his mind. "Yes, thank you. That would be nice."

Matty ushered him inside and offered him a seat at the kitchen table while she poured two glasses of tea. "It has some fresh mint from the garden, I hope you don't mind?" she said, setting the glasses down.

"No, thank you. This is great. Brad has some extensive gardens," Mr. Traynor commented, his eyes turned toward a window with a view of the chicken coop and several of the more elaborate flower beds.

Matty inclined her head. "I'm a city girl myself so I'm not used to it, but I've definitely found myself taking advantage of all the work Brad must have put in earlier in the season," she said, gesturing toward the basket full of goodies. "Do you garden?"

He shook his head. "My wife used to, but she passed away two years ago. Since then, I moved into the city and just have a small terrace. It's not as homey as where we lived, but it's just me and I didn't need all the space. Or upkeep."

"There is sense in that. Have you ever been up here?"

He shook his head. "No, Brad just started working for us about a year ago. I'm sure you know he manages investment portfolios."

She hadn't known that, but she nodded, encouraging him to go on.

"He's very good at what he does. Our clients love him."

She heard a "but" in there, but didn't press. "It's always good to have good customer service. Especially in today's economy," she said. A small frown touched his lips and Matty sensed she had touched a nerve.

"I'm not sure what the nature of your meeting was today, but maybe he left something for you? Would he have done that? I can always look for you, if you like," she offered, hoping Mr. Traynor might give her some more information.

He seemed to debate the propriety of this before inclining his head. "We were going to talk about a specific account he's managing. Maybe he left a file for me? Or perhaps it's on his computer?"

"Let's go have a look," she said, standing and leading him into the office. She opened a file cabinet and asked, "Is there a name I should look for?" Having already gone through the cabinet when she was on one of her cleaning missions, she knew there would be nothing in it; it held only Brad's personal tax files, bills, and other sorts of documents relevant to his life, but Mr. Traynor didn't know that.

"He wouldn't have filed anything under the client's name, for security purposes. But the ID he would have used was 5639."

Matty made a show of thumbing through everything. "Would it be a big file or a smaller one?"

"If he did what I asked him to do, it should be a big file with the complete records of the accounts of the client."

That was interesting.

"I don't see anything in here," she said. "Is there something else I can or should look at?"

"Is that his computer?" Mr. Traynor asked, pointing to the laptop on the shelf.

"It's *a* computer," Matty answered, taking it in hand. "But I think it's probably his personal computer since it doesn't have any asset tags or anything that would mark it as the bank's."

She handed the device to him and he looked it over. "Would you mind if I kept this?" he asked. That he was interested in looking at Brad's personal belongings didn't come as too much of a surprise; it was obvious he wasn't happy with either Brad or something he thought Brad had done. But that he'd asked to keep the device *was* surprising.

"Actually, I'm sorry, but I do. If it were the bank's computer, I wouldn't mind at all, but since I don't even know if it's Brad's and, even if it is, it's clearly a personal computer, I'm sure you can understand," she said, holding out her hand to take it back from him. After a slight pause, Mr. Traynor handed the computer over.

"I don't mean to pry, and you probably can't say anyway, but has Brad done something wrong?" Matty laced her voice with so much innocent concern that even she had a hard time not laughing at herself.

"You're right, I can't really say. If you talk to him, or the next time you see him, will you have him give me a call? It's very important." He took a card from his wallet and handed it to her as he spoke.

The visit was clearly over so Matty slid the card into her pocket, nodded, and walked him to the door. "I'm sorry you had to come up here for nothing, Mr. Traynor, and I'll be sure to tell Brad to call you."

The man nodded in response and left. She stood on the patio, holding the computer, watching the driveway for several moments after his car had disappeared. She let the meeting and Alexander Traynor's words, expressions, and actions settle into her mind. And the picture they were forming wasn't good.

She had just put the computer back in the office when the dogs went ballistic once again, heralding the arrival of someone else. Walking back out onto the patio, she recognized Chen's car driving toward her. While she wasn't annoyed at seeing him, she certainly wasn't excited. What she wanted to do was boot up the laptop, figure out if it was Brad's in the first place, then see if she could find anything in the files. She didn't hold out much hope, but it was better than doing nothing.

Only it wasn't Chen who slid from the driver's seat. "Matty, I was out and about—I hope you don't mind me stopping by?" Mai, Chen's sister, said as she walked across the gravel toward Matty.

"Of course not, Mai. It's nice to see you. How was the concert the other night?" she asked. She'd liked Mai when they'd met at dinner. It had turned out that Brad was friends with many members of the Zheng family, not just Chen. Mai was incredibly intelligent but also quick to laugh, and Matty liked how she tended to poke fun—affectionately—at Chen.

"Tanglewood is always a pleasure. Listen, I hate to bother you, but I was hoping to get in touch with Brad. He doesn't seem to be answering his cell phone. Do you happen to know where he might have gone?" Mai asked.

"No, I don't." Matty shook her head and ushered Mai inside, out of the heat. "I wish I did though. There're a few things I'd like to discuss with him. Iced tea? Lemonade?" she asked as they entered the kitchen.

"Iced tea, please, thank you. You don't sound very happy with him." Mai observed.

Matty shrugged, not wanting to get into it with Mai. She still didn't know what to think about Mr. Traynor's visit, but she wasn't going to discuss it with anyone. As much as she disliked her half brother, she still believed a person was innocent until proven guilty and didn't want to be the one responsible for starting rumors.

"Brad didn't exactly let me know what I was getting into when I agreed to come up here, but he did introduce me to your brother and I have access to a bountiful garden and incredibly productive chickens, so I can't complain too much," Matty said, handing Mai a glass of iced tea.

"But you really have no idea where he might have gone? Maybe visiting family? Or friends?"

Again Matty shrugged. "Your guess is as good as mine. Probably better."

"Why do you say that? Because you two aren't close?" Mai asked as she leaned against the counter and took a sip of her tea.

"Something like that," Matty answered. "Can I get you anything else? Maybe some eggs, some tomatoes?" she asked, deliberately changing the subject.

"How about lunch one of these days? I know a great local farm-to-table place about twenty minutes from here. A good girls' getaway," she added with a smile.

Matty was debating accepting—she liked Mai, but didn't

want to get too embroiled in Chen's family. He seemed interested in her in a way that wasn't reciprocated and until she felt that the air was clear between the two of them, spending time with his family didn't seem to be a good idea. She was trying to think of a polite way to decline when her phone rang. Excusing herself, she answered Dash's call.

"I got an emergency call this afternoon. I'm not going to be able to get off work until it's over," he said.

Glancing at Mai, Matty wondered if she could fit a couple of hours of writing in after her guest left. Or a couple of hours trying to break into the laptop.

"That's fine. Any idea how long it will take?" she asked.

"Several hours probably. If everything goes okay, I should be done between four and five, but of course, I can't promise anything."

"Of course, not. Is everything okay?"

"Hard to say until I get there. There's a colicky horse at Blue Meadows farm. It's a thoroughbred farm that usually calls in a specialist vet from Saratoga, but he's on vacation this week."

"I bet you're just as good," she said with a smile.

He chuckled. "At this, yes. Colic is colic in horses. If it were an injury, that would be a different story. I just don't have the equipment or experience with racehorses that the specialists do. But as for tonight, why don't I call you when I'm done and maybe we can head to this little sushi place over the border in Massachusetts."

"Hmm, sounds good. And then maybe an early night here?"

"I think you read my mind."

"Not hard, Dr. Kent. You know, great minds and all," she said with a laugh. They said their good-byes and hung up. She had walked into the office when she'd taken the call and now she stood looking at the computer that had been the center of most of her thoughts for the past hour or so.

"Matty," Mai called as the dogs erupted. "I think you have another visitor," she said, laughing at the obvious statement.

"I very rarely have any visitors and this will make three today already," Matty said, moving toward the door.

"Someone else was here?" Mai asked.

But before Matty had a chance to answer, Vivi climbed out of her car.

"Vivi, what a surprise, I thought you were in Boston," Matty said, coming out of the house.

Vivi bent down and gave each dog a little rub. "Just a fitting for me. It's been busy at the lab this week so I wanted to be back today to put in a full day tomorrow. Oh, hello," she said, as Mai stepped outside behind Matty.

Matty introduced Mai to Vivi and it turned out they knew *of* each other, Vivi being a part-time professor at the same university as Mai's brother.

"I didn't realize you lived up here, Dr. DeMarco," Mai said.

"Please, call me Vivi, and it was only recently that I moved. I'm getting married in October and my fiancé lives here."

"My congratulations to you, then." Mai turned to Matty. "I'll leave you two be and perhaps we can set up that lunch? I promise you, you'll love it."

Matty simply nodded, then glanced at Vivi who was watching her with an expression of curiosity.

"Her brother is a very handsome man, if I recall," Vivi said as Mai's car turned out of the driveway. "I hadn't put two and two together when you mentioned his name the other day. Is that who you were having dinner with the other night?"

"Yes," Matty said. "He's providing me some information and research material for my next book."

"I bet he'd like to provide a bit more than that," Vivi suggested with a grin.

"Probably," Matty admitted, walking into the kitchen with Vivi following. "But that's not going to happen. It wasn't going to happen before Dash and it's certainly not going to happen now."

"One man kind of woman, are you?"

"Honestly, what woman in her right mind would want more

than one man at a time?" Matty said, making Vivi laugh. "But even if I weren't a serial monogamist, Chen isn't my type. He's very handsome and cultured and all that, but given my background, I prefer men who don't mind a little grit."

"Amen to that, sister," Vivi said with a smile.

"I've been drinking iced tea all day so I'm going to pour myself some lemonade, but I can get you either."

"Lemonade would be great," Vivi said, pulling up a stool at the island. When Matty joined her with the two glasses, they spent some time chitchatting about the wedding. Matty was intrigued by Vivi's huge family, and though she learned that Vivi had lost both her parents and her brother just over a year ago, Matty couldn't help but feel a twinge of jealousy. If she ever had a wedding, it would be hard for her to fill a single pew, while Vivi, on the other hand, was going to have to pack people in just to fit her immediate family. But still, Matty couldn't help but be happy for Vivi, and even if she didn't really consider herself a girlie-girl, she *loved* hearing all about the dress.

And it took her mind off of Mr. Traynor's visit and the unsettled feeling she'd had since he'd left.

"Sometimes I feel like I shouldn't feel so happy," Vivi said, her voice suddenly tinged with sadness. "Not just considering what happened with my parents and brother last year but also what happened just a few months ago," she added.

Vivi's look told Matty that her friend was fishing to see how much she knew. Matty inclined her head. "I don't know much about the specifics of what happened, but a friend did mention that a killer had been caught up here, and Marcus and Carly said he'd planned to come after you before you caught him," she responded. She didn't want to pry, but if Vivi wanted to talk about it, Matty wanted to leave that door open.

Vivi let out a long breath. "We did catch a killer. A man who we think killed at least twenty-one women. But he was also a family friend, almost like a cousin to me. I'd known him my whole life. And he did it all because he was obsessed with me."

By the way Vivi's eyes darted away and her lips drew into a thin line, Matty knew the woman was still struggling with these facts. Reaching across the table, she laid a hand on Vivi's, "I'm sorry you had to go through that and I'm very sorry for all those women. But considering what you have been through, I'm pretty sure your family is more than relieved to see that you are happy now, starting a new life with someone you love and who loves you. A lot of people would go running in the other direction or break under the weight of all that pain. You're not doing either of those things, and I think you deserve everything you have right now."

A small smile touched Vivi's mouth. "Thank you for saying that, and I know, intellectually, you're right. My parents and brother would have loved Ian, the way the rest of my family does, and they would have hated for me to let that slip away."

"They sound like they were wonderful people."

At that, Vivi did smile, even as she blinked back a few tears. "They were. They were great." She took a deep breath and reached into her bag. "But," she said, pulling out a piece of paper and sliding it to Matty, "I'm not here about my family. I'm here about yours. Here is the missing persons report; you can fill it out for Brad. I'll file it and then do some looking around up at the lab the next chance I get."

Matty took the sheet of paper and quickly reviewed the questions. She felt a fleeting sense of loss when she realized how few of them she could actually answer. She knew his hair and eye color, but other than that, she knew almost nothing—not his height or his car make and model, assuming he had one other than his truck, or when he was last seen. The sheet was practically empty when she slid it back across the counter to Vivi with an apology.

Vivi shook her head. "Don't apologize, Matty. Families come in all shapes and sizes. Some are close, others aren't. It's just a fact of life. And besides, I have enough here to get started." Vivi folded the paper, slid it back into her bag, then drummed her fingers on the counter.

"Yes?" Matty prompted.

Vivi bit her lip for a moment then asked, "You mentioned some pictures the other night, would you mind showing them to me?"

The mention of the pictures brought Matty up short; she'd all but forgotten them in the events of the day. Which seemed ridiculous—since Brad had obviously gone to the effort of hiding them away for her, they must play a part in whatever was going on. She nodded and the two made their way upstairs to the guest room where she pulled down the journal, slid the pictures out, and handed the stack to Vivi.

Vivi flipped through them then turned them over one at a time, making note of the names written on the backs of two of the pictures. "These are definitely of Haiti," she said, holding up several of the pictures. "You were right about that. I was there. I was also in New Orleans and again, you're right about these being taken after Hurricane Katrina. But these?" She held up the two pictures, the locations of which Matty had also been unable to identify. "I have no idea where these were taken. Definitely not a disaster site, judging by the people in the background."

"I was thinking it might be some kind of sporting event, given the structures around the main subjects. But where or what event, I haven't a clue. Maybe a racetrack, considering that Brad left a racing form for me, but..." Her voice trailed off.

Vivi held the pictures up again and examined them more closely. After a few minutes, she sighed, restacked them all, and handed them back to Matty. "I think you may be right, but without more detail, it's hard to know where they are. The other two are disaster sites, so you would think the last group would be of the same, but there haven't been any major incidents at a sporting event in years—certainly nothing on the scale of Haiti or Katrina."

Matty was musing over this point as she put the pictures away. Both women jumped when the dogs suddenly went berserk again.

"Another visitor?" Vivi asked, heading to the window. "But one I think you'll like, this time," she added with a smile.

Matty joined her at the window and saw Dash's truck pulling

up. "Yeah, I kind of like this one, though I liked your visit, too. It was just the first two that threw me."

"First two?" Vivi asked.

Matty hadn't meant to let it slip that someone else had been by before Mai, she had intended to keep Mr. Traynor's visit quiet until she figured out what was going on with him and Brad. *If* she could figure out what was going on.

"Just an old friend of Brad's that stopped by earlier," she said as she turned and headed out of the room, ignoring the look of curiosity on Vivi's face. Thankfully, her friend followed, and soon both women were greeting Dash on the patio.

If Dash was surprised to see Vivi, he didn't show it. In fact, he acted like it was completely normal for Matty to have visitors, even though she'd only been in town a little over a week. But within minutes, Vivi was in her car, driving away, and Dash was getting a proper hello.

"I thought you were on a call," Matty said, pulling away from the kiss.

"I was. It's an older horse, a brood mare that isn't expecting this year. I did all I could for her and now we'll just have to wait and see how she does through the night."

"As in, she could die?" she asked, leading Dash inside.

"Yes, unfortunately. Given the structure of the horse's digestive system, they are more delicate than they look. She could pull through, though. But her case is severe enough that she might not ever make a full recovery."

"So that means no dinner tonight?" Matty asked, not altogether displeased. The day had been a strange one and the thought of spending a few hours exorcising the demons in bed with Dash didn't sound like a half-bad idea, even though she hadn't had a chance to eat since breakfast with all the visitors coming by.

"Actually, I should have a little bit of time. I think we could still hit that sushi place in Massachusetts I was telling you about. It's a bit of a drive, but the food is good and they can be quick once we get there."

She hadn't thought to find a sushi place this far away from a city, not to mention the water, but as soon as he mentioned it, her stomach growled, making him laugh.

"I guess that's a yes, then," he said, wrapping his arms around her.

"I guess it is." She rose up on her toes to place one more kiss on his lips. "Just give me five minutes to change."

True to her word, ten minutes later they were heading toward the state border for dinner. On the way they passed the spot where the body had fallen into her truck, which reminded her of Vivi and the missing persons report she'd filled out earlier. Thinking of Brad, Matty's mind wandered to Alexander Traynor and the pictures. She'd had every intention of trying to go through the computer but just hadn't had the chance. She also wanted to look through Brad's files again and maybe even have a look through some of the other rooms in the house she never went into, including the basement.

"Matty?" Dash's voice cut into her thoughts.

"Hmm?" she responded, turning from the road to look at him.

"Are you okay?"

She frowned. She was fine. She just wasn't sure Brad was, and not knowing was starting to worry her. But she didn't want to share this with Dash. She told herself she didn't want to say anything because she didn't want him to worry, and it was probably just her overactive imagination anyway. But even as she shook her head "no" and told him she was fine, a little niggling of something crept into her mind. The reason she was keeping everything close to the vest wasn't really to protect Dash from worry, it was just what she'd always done—handled everything on her own because it was easier that way.

Dash didn't look like he believed her when she said she was fine, but whatever he might have been about to say was cut off by the sound of his phone ringing.

"Do you need to get that?" Matty asked after Dash glanced at the number then didn't answer. "Maybe it's about that horse?"

He shook his head. "It's not about the horse. It was my mom. It *is* my mom," he added with a sigh when the phone rang again.

"Maybe it's important," she pointed out. Dash gave her a look that clearly expressed his doubts about that but hit the answer button anyway.

"Hi, Mom," he said.

"Hi, honey. How are you?" a woman's voice responded on the truck's speakerphone.

"I'm fine. And you?"

"We're fine," she answered. "Your dad and I are just fine. Just leaving Stockbridge, as a matter of fact, and thought maybe you'd want to meet for dinner. We haven't seen you in a while," she added.

"Thanks for the invite, Mom, but I'm headed to dinner at the sushi place in Great Barrington with a friend," he answered, casting a glance at Matty that she felt more than saw. Even though the conversation was happening over the speakerphone and filled the truck's cab, Matty was trying to give Dash the impression of privacy by keeping her eyes turned out her side window.

"Oh, that sounds great. Why don't we join you?"

Matty knew she should be more subtle, but her eyes shot to Dash. He gave her a sardonic look.

"Nice of you to offer, but we're going to be quick. I may have to take a call, so I can't actually promise we'll even be there when you get there."

"Nonsense. We're ten minutes away. We'll head there and grab a table. If you can come, come. If you get called away, just give us a call."

Dash cast Matty a look telling her he'd lay down the law if she wanted him to. And part of her wanted him to. Not because she didn't want to meet his parents, but because she'd been looking forward to a relatively quiet dinner. But another part of her really didn't mind if his parents joined them. She wasn't all that caught up in what it may or may not mean to meet them, so dinner with Mr. and Mrs. Kent felt more like it would be dinner with new acquaintances than potential family members. And so she looked at Dash and shrugged.

He raised an eyebrow.

"It's fine, really," she mouthed.

His eyes searched hers for just a moment before he refocused his attention on the road and answered his mother. "Fine, Mom. That's sounds fine. We should be there in twenty minutes."

"Excellent. Drive safe and we'll see you soon."

Matty watched Dash press the "end call" button and then couldn't help but laugh. "I really don't mind either way, Dash," she said. "You look a little green around the gills. If you didn't want them to come, it was fine with me too."

He cleared his throat. "It's just that, well, I'm pretty sure they know who you are," he said.

"Know who I am?" she repeated. And then she got it. She felt her eyes widen and her mouth form a little "o" before the word itself escaped her lips. "Oh, I see," she added. "And how might they know this?"

She saw Dash's Adam's apple bob. "That first day I met you, I kind of panicked and called my sister. I have no doubt, judging by the tone of my mother's voice, that my sister mentioned something to her."

Matty mulled this over before letting out another little laugh. "I think it's kind of cute you called your sister. It's sweet."

Dash scowled at her. "It's not sweet."

"Okay," she faux conceded.

"And so you know what this means, right?"

"Spell it out for me," she responded. Dash shot her a look that made it clear he was not as amused as she was. "Seriously, Dash, I'm fine with this," she added.

He let out a breath. "Even when you know that when you meet her she'll be looking at you as her future daughter-in-law?"

Matty lifted a shoulder. "That is a bit weird, but we've had this conversation before, Dash. Whatever we do or don't do is going to be decided by us, based on what we do or don't *want* to do.

And given that we've known each other such a short time, I'm not really focused on what your parents might think of me. As far as I'm concerned, what's more important is what you and I think of each other, and that is something that can only develop over time."

Dash's eyes flicked up from the road to meet hers and in just that split second she knew he saw only her honesty and sincerity. With a sharp nod, he turned his attention back to the road.

"Now, do you want to tell me what was on your mind earlier, since we are no longer going to have a quiet dinner to ourselves?" he asked.

Matty stilled. She thought she'd swept everything under the rug when he'd first asked her. Apparently, it wasn't going to be that easy. And feeling a little caught out in her efforts to avoid the topic, she did what a lot of writers do very well, she made something up.

"It was just a busy day. I thought I would have plenty of time in the afternoon to write, so I took the morning off to work in the garden. But then Mai came by, and then Vivi, and then she and I got to talking, and next thing I knew, the afternoon was gone. It's not a big deal, but I'll have some catching up to do. I suppose I was just mentally rearranging my work schedule."

Matty didn't examine why she'd held back from telling Dash the truth about everything; she didn't have the time or space to do so at the moment. But more to the point, she didn't have the inclination and suspected she wouldn't like what she discovered if she went down that path.

She saw Dash frown. "Do you have time for dinner tonight?"

And that tiny kernel of guilt she'd felt got just a little bigger. "Of course I do. With the odd exception here and there, I don't write much in the evenings. In general, I find that after five or so, my mind just doesn't work the way I need it to. So yes, I have time and it's actually perfect because this way I won't be sitting around the house ruminating on the fact that I didn't get anything done today."

"Ruminating?" Dash repeated with a grin.

"Yes, it's a big word we writers like to use. The word 'think' isn't grand enough and the word 'ponder' sounds too whimsical. And ruminate has more syllables," she shot back making him laugh.

"So, you're sure?" he asked again, pulling into a parking lot.

"Yes, I'm sure," she answered.

"Good, because we're here."

Even without ever having met Dash's parents, Matty spotted them right away. Dash's facial features were identical to his father's, as was his build, which she noted when the tall man—who was still lean, even in his late sixties—stood to greet them. Unlike Dash, his mom was rather short, but she had her son's dark brown hair, which was stylishly streaked with gray, and the same dark eyes.

"Matty," Dash said, "these are my parents, Mary and Will Kent. Mom, Dad, this is Matty Brooks."

Matty shook hands with them both and didn't miss the curiosity lurking in their eyes. But their expressions were open and friendly and as they all sat, Mrs. Kent kicked off the conversation.

"So, Matty, how are you liking the area?"

"It's beautiful, really. I hadn't ever been here before and though my half brother Brad used a bit of false pretense to get me up here, I'm glad I came," Matty answered. "How long have you lived in the area, Mrs. Kent?"

"Please call me Mary," Dash's mom responded as the waiter brought water to the table. "We've been here since before the kids were born. William's family is from this area. I'm from Boston, but we met in college and wanted to settle here since we thought it was a great place to raise a family."

Matty hid a smile at the look Dash gave his not-so-subtle mother. "I know Dash has at least one sister, are there others?"

"Oh yes, Dash is the second of four, two boys, two girls. Jane, the eldest, lives in New York City, and Sam and Nora, our twins who are several years younger than Dash, are in Chicago at the moment, both starting their last year of medical school."

"You must be very proud."

"Of all of them," Will interjected. "We're lucky to have such great kids."

"I imagine luck may have had something to do with it, but certainly not everything," Matty countered. Then something dawned on her. "Wait a second... Jane Marple, Dashiell Hammet, Nora Charles, and Sam Spade? Tell me that wasn't an accident." Matty asked about the possibility that all the kids were named after famous literary detectives, or in Dash's case, a writer.

Mary laughed. "She's good, Dash," she said to her son. Then, turning back to Matty, she answered, "I'm a little bit of a mystery fan."

"Just a little," Will emphasized.

"So yes, it was all planned," Mary finished.

"But you have three characters and one writer, how did that work?" Matty asked.

"I picked Jane, Sam, and Nora," Mary started.

"And I had no say in those, but since we were obviously stuck with the mystery theme, I argued that we should have at least one writer in the mix. So I picked Dashiell, one of my favorites," Will added.

Matty laughed, it was hard not to like a family that named their kids after classic characters and again, in Dash's case, one of the most iconic writers of the genre.

"Matty is a writer," Dash said.

"Oh really? What do you write?" Will asked. She got this question a lot and for some reason it always amused her. Because writers, in general, weren't as publicly visible as their books and, for the most part, people never knew what their favorite author even looked like. So when people asked her that question, their faces inevitably held both hope that she *would* be someone they had read and doubt that she *could* be someone they had read.

"I write political thrillers," Matty answered then added, "under the name Hilde Brooks." Judging by the looks on Dash's parents' faces, both had heard of her, read her, and, even better, liked her.

When the waiter came by to take their orders ten minutes later, Matty, Mary, and Will were still talking about her novels. She always loved talking to her readers, and having the chance to spend time with two who were so well read was such a pleasure that she all but forgot that they were Dash's parents—and everything that might entail.

Until Dash's phone rang, catching everyone's attention.

Pulling his phone from his pocket, he rose and excused himself. When he returned to the table a few moments later, Matty could tell it wasn't good news.

"We have to go, don't we?" she asked.

He nodded. "Yes, the mare has taken a turn for the worse and they've asked me to come talk over the options."

Matty didn't like the sound of that and she could see from the look on Dash's face that this was his least favorite part of the job. She rose from her seat, not wanting to delay him.

"Stay, Matty," Mary said. Then, turning to her son, she said, "We can take her home, if you all don't mind. That way at least she'll have eaten."

Dash turned to Matty, a question in his eyes. Did she want to be left with his parents? Her eyes darted over to Mary and Will, and though she could see they were eager for her to stay, it was also clear they weren't going to press her. If she left with Dash, he would drop her at home where she'd be alone and eating leftovers. If she stayed, she'd not only eat good food but she'd also have a chance to get to know two people she was beginning to like. Pushing aside the loaded issues of just who she was or might be in Dash's life and just what his parents might be thinking, she made her decision.

"I'll stay, if you don't mind?"

For a moment, Dash's eyes searched hers. Then he answered, "Of course I don't mind. At least this way, like my mom said, you'll get to eat."

"Do you want me to bring anything back for you?" she asked.

He shook his head. "No, I'll grab something while I'm out, but I'll swing by later?"

She liked the sound of that, even if the look on Dash's face made it clear that he wasn't done pressing her about what had been bothering her earlier. She had great faith in her ability to distract him, so she nodded. He bent down and kissed Matty's cheek before saying good-bye to his mom and dad. She watched him leave and when the door closed she turned back to his parents. His very eager parents.

"Now," Mary said, leaning forward, "where were we?"

Where they were and where they went was a long conversation over a leisurely dinner. Matty found Dash's parents to be a lot like him in many ways—laid back, smart, interested in life, and interesting. They were easy to talk to, even if they dropped more than a hint or two about her role in their son's life.

By the time they brought her to Brad's, Matty was actually feeling a bit tired, though anxious to see Dash. Thankfully, he called to say he was on his way less than ten minutes after she walked in the door.

When she heard his truck, she went to the patio and stood with the screen door ajar. Watching him climb out of the vehicle, Matty could tell the night did not end as they had hoped for the sick mare and Dash's movements looked tired and a bit heavy.

But that didn't stop the small smile that touched his lips as he approached her. "You're wearing my shirt," he noted

"Yes, I am." He'd left one of his button-down shirts in her room that morning and she'd decided to put it to good use. She held out a hand to him and he walked straight to her, wrapping his arms around her waist.

"I like the look," he added.

Smiling up at him, she took his right hand in hers, dropped it to her thigh, then slid it up.

"You're not wearing anything else," he commented as his eyes got *that* look.

Her smile widened. "No, I'm not."

CHAPTER 11

MATTY KNEW SHE WAS DREAMING but, even so, she was stuck; she couldn't end it. She was driving in her convertible, the top down, the wind blowing through her hair, Dash beside her. They were laughing, but there was something about the colors or the tone or the persistent weight on her body that hinted at something darker to come.

Her eyes skirted to her side mirror and then back at Dash, only it wasn't Dash anymore, it was her mother.

"Don't let them see your fear, Matty," Carmen said.

"What fear, Mama? I'm not afraid."

"They'll use it against you, Mija," her mother said, using her Spanish term of endearment.

"What are you talking about, Mama?" Matty asked. She was confused but she was also beginning to feel unsettled, her heart rate picking up in an erratic rhythm.

"You know what I'm talking about, Mija. You know. I know you haven't forgotten."

Matty glanced in her rearview mirror as if she might find the harbinger of the threat her mother was so worried about behind them. But when her gaze returned to the passenger seat, her mother was gone.

And then the body hit her car again. That same sickening feeling of having something slam into her car as she sped along assaulted her body and her senses. Her heart raced and she could feel her hands shaking against the steering wheel as her stomach churned. "Don't let them see your fear," her mother had said. But how could she not?

In the dream, she pulled her car to a stop and tried to heed her mother's warning. She took a few deep breaths and flexed her fingers, loosening them from the steering wheel. Once she felt a little more composed, a little more in control, she settled her hands in her lap and focused on preparing for what she might see when she turned around.

She forced herself to remember the body in the truck. If she could remember the details, maybe when she saw him again, she wouldn't be so shocked. And if she wasn't so shocked, maybe she could hide her fear. Like her mother told her to. When she felt a little more confident in her own control, she turned around, slowly.

Feet were the first thing she saw. Only neither of these feet were bare and rotted. They were clad in well-kempt shoes and were at the ends of legs dressed in pressed khakis. Matty twisted her body around and let her eyes travel up the form to a striped polo shirt. She could see a man's forearm, well muscled and covered with fair hair. Confused because this was not the body she'd seen before, she took a moment to debate with herself what she should do—turn to look at the whole figure or do something to force herself awake?

She paused, tempted to try to rouse herself. But a small part of her, the part that kept reminding her it was just a dream, was urging her to turn around and look. Her heart beat a heavy rhythm in her chest and she knew she didn't have much time to make her decision before her body made it for her. So, with a deep breath, she pulled herself all the way around.

And her eyes landed on the face of her half brother.

• • •

Matty bolted upright in bed, her heart hammering in her chest. Dawn light was seeping through her windows and Dash was breathing softly beside her. Bob, who lay at the end of the bed, glanced up to see if she was okay, while Isis came over to her bedside and nudged her leg with a cold, wet nose.

Absently, Matty reached out and stroked Isis's head, the motion and the feel of the dog beneath her hand slowly lowering her heart rate and steadying her breath. Within a few minutes, she was feeling less shaken up, but still unsettled by the dream—by the things her mother had said and by the look she'd seen on Brad's face, a combination of confusion and disappointment.

Rising quietly from the bed, she pulled on her robe and padded downstairs. Bob and Isis followed, but the other dogs remained in their beds when she gave them the signal to stay, not wanting to wake Dash with the clamor the dogs made when they all descended the stairs at the same time. After putting some coffee on, she entered the office and pulled out the computer she assumed was Brad's. She was pretty sure it would be password protected, but she wasn't going to let that stop her.

Matty booted it up and even though she'd been expecting it, she was disappointed when the password request window popped up. She sat back for a moment debating about what to do. Based on what little she knew of Brad, she would guess he would have a password that contained the name of one of his animals. But in what format and which pet, she couldn't begin to fathom.

She knew coffee wouldn't really help her solve this problem, but she felt the need to hold a cup in her hands, feel the comforting heat, and smell the familiar scent. Once her mug was full, she came back to the office and looked around, hoping to find some hint of what his password might be. He'd left her clues before—if he'd wanted her on his computer, maybe he'd left more.

She spent a few minutes letting her eyes wander around the room; they eventually landed on the file cabinet. She had been through it before, and then again when Alex Traynor was standing in the room, but she hadn't really gone through each folder, she'd just read the file names. Still, something nagged at her memory.

Walking to the files, she pulled open the same drawer she'd opened the day before then stood back and looked at all the labeled tabs. Most were basic files with straightforward names like "Taxes" and "Bills." But two-thirds of the way back there was a file called "Betty."

Frowning, she set her mug down and pulled the file out. Inside was a picture of a horse, two pictures actually, one where the horse was emaciated and looking extremely neglected and the other where she was well rounded with a shiny coat and proud stance. Matty turned them both over to see that each picture was marked with a date—dates that were approximately nine months apart. Sliding them back into the file and the file back into the cabinet, she closed the drawer.

Opening the second drawer, she found more generic files about the appliances, house plans, gardens, and all sorts of things one would expect to find in a file cabinet. But the folder labeled "Rescues" was what caught her attention; it was much thicker than the "Betty" file. She pulled it out and sat down.

The folder contained pictures and documents of dogs, cats, horses, and all sorts of other animals. Based on what she could tell, Brad was involved in several rescue societies for animals of all kinds. It didn't appear that he actually sponsored all of the animals, but it did look as though he helped the organizations find them homes, and then he kept track of them and their welfare.

It shouldn't have surprised her, knowing what she knew now about how well he treated his own animals, but for some reason it did. It was one thing to see her half brother, the legitimate son of a man who had all but left her and her mother to languish in the hells of the projects, taking care of his own pets. It was another to see a man so obviously committed to the care and welfare of all animals.

This insight into Brad unsettled her almost as much as the dream and she was just about to close the file when the last record caught her eye. At the bottom of the pile was more information about Betty, the horse. It was clearly the same horse and, judging by the date on the paper she was looking at now, which lined up with the dates on the photos, she might have been Brad's first rescue project.

Knowing she had to at least *try* to gain access to his computer, she set the file down and typed in the date Brad had received Betty as the password. It was rejected.

Unwilling to give up, she tried Betty's name and then the date, but this was also rejected. She gave a fleeting thought to how many tries she might have left before the computer locked her out altogether and changed her tactic. She typed in Betty's name and a second date Brad had written on the paper—the date a healthy, rehabilitated Betty had been given to a little girl.

And the laptop's desktop came to life.

The sun was well up when Dash walked into the office and startled her. Lost in the minutiae of what she was reading, time had gone by unnoticed. Instinctively, she stood and turned her back on the screen in an effort to keep him from seeing what she was doing. She knew she shouldn't feel guilty for going through Brad's things; after all, he'd all but asked her to when he'd left her his cookie-crumb trail. But still, hacking into his computer felt different than looking through his liquor cabinet.

"You're dressed." She frowned as she noticed Dash's clothes. He was supposed to have the day off, but judging by his expression, that was no longer the plan. Which, in all honesty, left her feeling a little relieved. And even guiltier because she felt relieved.

His eyes traveled behind her, then back to her face. "There's a problem out at one of the farms. I need to go check it out. It might be a while. Is everything okay?"

"Everything is fine," she answered quickly. "Do you know what's going on or how long you'll be?"

He shrugged, still looking at her curiously. "Hard to say, I won't know until I get out there."

"Your job is almost like being a cop, isn't it? You have to go when called?" Reaching behind her, she closed the laptop and headed toward the kitchen.

Dash followed her. "A bit, although it's not usually so bad. My part-timer will be back soon and then my schedule will be more predictable."

Matty opened a cupboard and pulled out a travel mug. "Here, I don't have any breakfast made, but I can at least get you some coffee to go." She cringed at the eagerness in her voice. She didn't want him gone just to have him gone and she wasn't kicking him out. She just had some things she wanted to do that she needed to do on her own.

"Matty? Something was bothering you yesterday and clearly something is going on right now. I don't think it really has anything to do with your writing; any interest in telling me about it?"

She didn't like the sardonic tone in his voice, mostly because he was justified. "I told you last night, I just have a lot on my mind, that's all. I'll spend the day writing, catching up, and maybe even getting ahead. By tonight, I'll be back on track. One of the pitfalls of being with a writer, I suppose, is that our minds are often somewhere other than where we are physically," she said, handing him the coffee.

"Is that why you were looking at Brad's computer?"

For a split second, she froze. And then the words her mother had spoken in her dream came floating back, "*I know you haven't forgotten.*" And, for good or for bad, she hadn't. She hadn't forgotten how to bury everything she thought and felt so deep down that she was almost able to lie to herself. She hadn't forgotten how to hide her shame and guilt and use apathy as a weapon of self-defense. She hadn't forgotten how to lie about who she was.

She shrugged. "I'm nosy. I was putting off my own work," was all she said. She knew it didn't cast her in a positive light. But right now, with the dream lingering in her memory and the pleas of her mother ringing in her ears, she simply wanted to be left alone—if only to figure out how to handle the unwanted intrusion of her past into her present. And maybe her future.

Dash's eyes narrowed and she could see the tension in his jaw, but just then Lucy, the crazy terrier with, as far as Matty was concerned, perfect timing, came bounding into the room. In the commotion, Dash's eyes went to the clock on the wall behind Matty.

"I need to go," he said.

She nodded.

"I'll call and let you know when I'm done."

Again, she nodded. And as he walked out the door, she ignored the little pang she felt in her heart when neither one of them made any plans or promises for the future.

• • •

Ruthlessly shoving down the almost vertigo-like feeling that had overcome her when, with the memories her dream evoked, her past had crashed into her present, Matty didn't bother waiting for the sound of Dash's truck to fade into the day before heading back into the office and opening the computer again. Over the next hour or so, she found almost nothing, but every now and then there were obscure references to people or places that stood out, primarily because they didn't fit in. But even those held nothing that pointed one way or another to her half brother's involvement in any wrongdoing.

Leaning back in her chair, she stared off at the valley sloping away from her and wondered why she hadn't just told Dash about Alexander Traynor's visit, or for that matter, told Vivi. She wasn't a child; she wasn't living in that world anymore. Keeping things to herself—handling them herself—might not be the best solution. But still, old habits died hard and she she needed more information before she decided if she could, or should, say anything to anyone. So in her mind she went through the facts, again, and everything Brad had left her—from the welcome letter, to the newspaper with the braille, to the pictures.

The pictures.

Rising from her seat and jogging up the stairs, Matty chastised herself for not thinking of them sooner. Returning to her seat in the office, pictures in hand, she flipped them over revealing the names Brad had written on the back. Taking a deep breath, she typed the first one into the search engine and waited to see what, if anything, came up.

Five hours later, she was more confused than ever. Well, about Brad anyway. She'd run a search on each of the names and what she'd found wasn't good. The names listed on the pictures from Haiti were people who were charged and convicted of fraud, having provided sub-standard water filters to the United Nations and various other relief agencies in the wake of the massive quake.

The people noted on the back of the photos from New Orleans were also charged and convicted of fraud. Acting as intermediaries between people needing FEMA trailers and FEMA itself, they'd stolen money, provided false invoices to the government, and offered hollow promises to the people in need. None of the names were well known since all the cases, from what she could tell, were kept as quiet as possible—she assumed for political reasons.

That people could take advantage of such horrible situations didn't come as a surprise to Matty, but still it made her stomach churn to be reminded of just how awful and unethical people could be. Even so, even knowing now what those people were involved in and what they had been convicted of, that wasn't the worst of it.

When she'd first begun to see the pattern in what her research was revealing, she'd felt a sense of relief. Brad was a banking guy, how could he be involved in FEMA trailers and water filters? But as she dug deeper and deeper into the results that popped up on her screen, her heart had sunk.

In all her research, there'd been a consistent piece of information she hadn't liked one bit. Each of the people named in the photos had also been accused of stealing money and secreting it away in foreign bank accounts. The reports she found, which consisted of short newspaper articles and a few scattered court documents, noted the missing and unaccounted-for amounts, presumably the convicted felons' ill-gotten gains, but each defendant steadfastly denied having any knowledge of the missing funds.

Making funds go missing *was* something a banking guy could do. Had Brad been their accomplice?

She ran a hand over her face and through her hair. What she needed to do was find out what bank the convicted offenders might have used and then figure out where Brad had been working at the time of the crimes. From there, maybe she'd see a connection between Brad and the people in the photos, if there was one.

But she knew she wouldn't be able to do that. The information was too obscure for the general public and there were too many possibilities. It was possible that, if she had the entire case file, she could come up with some ideas, but not with just what she'd found online; though it was a lot, it wasn't enough. She was beginning to realize that there were really only two options to the scenario. Either Brad was involved in the illegal behaviors or he wasn't. If he was, he was probably either dead or on the run. And neither of *those* options sounded all that great.

But if he wasn't involved, where was he?

She didn't have an answer to that. Nor did she know just what to do with the information she'd discovered. If Brad was involved in something illegal, what she'd found might help with an investigation into him. In which case, she should hand it over to Vivi and Ian.

But if he wasn't, what then? She knew all too well how dangerous information, especially incomplete information, could be if placed in the wrong hands. And despite not having a relationship with her half brother, she didn't want to see him caught up in something that could very quickly spiral out of control given the political sensitivities of the crimes. At least not if he didn't deserve it.

She needed to know what, if anything, Vivi might have found in her investigation of Brad's financial transactions before she made any decisions. She picked up her phone and dialed Vivi's number.

It barely rang once before Vivi picked up. "Matty, how are you?"

"I'm doing well, thanks. And you?" Matty asked.

"Fine, inundated with evidence at the moment from a couple of car accidents and murders from various places around the state, but other than that, I'm okay. What can I do for you?"

"I was calling to see if you'd had a chance to look into Brad's movements, but it sounds like that's a bit on the back burner at the moment?" She knew she shouldn't be too disappointed, Vivi was doing her a favor; but still, knowing what Vivi's answer would likely be, a wave of frustration swept through her.

"I'm so sorry, Matty. I haven't had a chance to look into it. I could give it to an intern, but I figured it would be better if I did it myself."

Matty's shoulders slumped, but she put on a brave face. "No, no need to be sorry, Vivi. You're doing me a favor so whenever you have a chance. I just thought I would check in."

"Thanks, Matty. I know you must be anxious and I think I should be able to get to it tomorrow. I'll give you a call and let you know as soon as I know anything. Or," she added, "if I'm going to be delayed."

Matty thanked her and hung up. Not knowing what else to do, she closed Brad's computer and slid it onto a shelf. Walking into the kitchen, she made herself a late lunch and tried to bring some calm to her frazzled thoughts. But eating alone and in the silence of the house wasn't very comforting, so as soon as she finished, she decided to keep herself busy by searching the house.

She wasn't sure what she was looking for or if she would find anything, but it gave her an excuse to keep moving and not make a decision about what she should, or would, tell the authorities. She scoured the books on all the shelves, opened cupboards and drawers, and even explored the heretofore never-entered basement. She had assumed it would be a standard, dank basement, but when she descended the stairs she found a lovely extra guest room and full bathroom, as well as a large, tidy storage area. The windows were small, but there was a charming, large arched doorway that led out, she assumed, onto the lawn on the side of the house facing the cows. Because the vegetable and flower gardens lay on either side of the house and she'd had no reason to make her way to where the door came out onto the yard, she hadn't seen it before.

But as charmed as she was by the basement room, she focused her attention on the storage room, and after another hour, she'd found nothing more on the people or places she'd investigated that morning.

She had found pictures, though. And a lot of them. Most were of family and she had to admit, if only to herself, how odd it was to be sitting in her half brother's basement looking through family pictures where her father, a man she'd met even fewer times than her half brother, looked back at her, smiling and comfortable. As if his actions thirty-some-odd years ago hadn't shredded the fabric of a young woman's life—Matty's mother—or set the course for her own.

Looking at a photo of her father and his wife Sandra, Brad's mother, Matty didn't wish she'd been a part of that family. No, she was happy with who she was—and who she was, was a result of having lived through what she had. But still, she wished it had been easier on her mother.

As a child, she'd lived with the belief that her mother was bigger than life and would always protect her. But Carmen Viega had been a twenty-one-year-old immigrant from Puerto Rico when she'd moved to the Bronx and given birth to her only child. Now, as an adult, Matty comprehended how scary it must have been for her. Given where they'd lived, there were never any promises of life or death, and more often than not, there was little a parent could do to keep her child safe. But Carmen had always tried. And they were both the stronger for it.

With a sigh, she put Brad's family pictures aside and started to go through another set. These were more like the photos Brad had left her. There were pictures of Japan after the tsunami, Rwanda, the Sudan, Afghanistan, and even some of tornado-ravaged towns in the US. The pictures were labeled with places and dates, but no names. Matty was just beginning to wonder if Brad had a little bit of a savior complex and was involved in rescuing more than just animals when the dogs started their collective barking, signaling the arrival of a visitor.

She checked the time on her phone, it was much later than she'd thought, closer to dinner than lunch, and though Dash hadn't called, she assumed it was him making his way back. She smiled at the thought of having Dash nearby—her day had been filled with enough turmoil and his calming presence would do her good. But even as the awareness flowed through her, a hint of discomfort made itself known. She didn't want to talk about what she'd been thinking or feeling or discovering the past day or two and she just hoped that maybe Dash would see that and let it slide, let her just escape it all for a short time. Again.

• • •

Dash pulled his truck up into Brad's drive, put it in park, and killed the engine. He wasn't sure what to expect when he walked in the door, so he took a few seconds to prepare. He'd been thinking of little else all day—wondering just what Matty was up to and why she didn't seem to want to talk to him about it. Though he didn't like it, he could grudgingly admit that maybe it was because they were both in new territory when it came to dealing with one another. Maybe that explained her hesitancy. But maybe not.

Because he was at such a loss as to what was going on in *her* mind, he'd spent quite a bit of time thinking about what he wanted—from Matty *and* from and for himself. He knew with dead certainty that he wasn't going to let her push him out completely and he was pretty sure that wasn't what she really wanted either. But he also knew he needed more from her than just easy companionship and sex. He didn't expect her to treat him like she'd known him her whole life, but he needed some indication from her that she was interested in building a real relationship—one with real give and take and compromise and work.

Sliding from his seat, he approached the screen door. She was standing in the kitchen, watching him with the same wary expression he probably held on his face.

"Matty," he said as he walked toward her.

She said nothing but held out her arms to him. He came to her and she wrapped them around his waist and leaned against his chest. It felt good. Like she wanted his familiarity, his comfort.

"Matty, what's bothering you? What's going on?" he asked after a long moment. Although he felt her stiffen in his arms, what he felt the strongest was her pulling away—not physically, but mentally, emotionally. He took in a deep breath, let it go, and dropped his arms back to his sides.

"Nothing," she said. "I'm fine," she added, stepping away.

He frowned. "I never said you weren't fine, but something is on your mind and talking about it might help."

She eyed him for a moment. "I'd rather not talk about it, Dash. If you don't mind."

He did mind, and he decided to tell her so. "Look, don't tell me it's your writing, because I know it's not. Some weird shit has been happening around you. Stuff that may or may not involve Brad, and even knowing you the short time I have, I'm pretty sure you're not letting sleeping dogs lie. If you talk to me, if you tell me what you're thinking, maybe I can help." He tried to keep his words reasonable, but even he could hear the frustration he was trying to hide. Frustration with her, with Brad for putting her in this weird spot, for the situation in general.

She took a few more steps away from him and turned toward the big picture window. For a moment, she just stared out across the pasture below them, a picturesque scene of cows and wildflowers. Then she spoke.

"Look Dash, I appreciate the offer, but Brad left a trail for me to follow. I know it might sound crazy to you, but I need to do this. I need to follow it. And I need to do it before I can share it with anyone any more than I already have."

It sounded reasonable. Only it wasn't. "Did it ever occur to you that *I* might be part of that trail?" he asked.

Her head came around and her eyes shot to his. He could see the question she wouldn't ask, because to ask it would bring her into the conversation he wanted to have. So he did her a favor and answered anyway.

"Brad called me the day before you came into town, the day, I believe, you finally agreed to come up here. He was very insistent that I come at that specific time to vaccinate the cows."

Matty crossed her arms over her chest. "Maybe because he wanted it taken care of before he left and it was the day that worked best for him."

Dash inclined his head. "It's possible, but I don't think so. The cows weren't due for their shots for another month. Beth, my scheduler, thought it was a little unusual, since Brad has always been meticulous with his records, but he was insistent."

She eyed him, clearly weighing this new information. Dash would have preferred that she talked to him because she *wanted* to, not because he might serve a purpose. But at this point, he opted to give her a reason that was more in line with the logic she seemed to be feeding him than what she may or may not want.

"It's possible, Dash." She let out a deep sigh. "But I'm just not sure, and until I'm sure, I want to do this on my own. I really need to do this on my own."

"Why?" It was a simple question, but at the heart of the issue, and they both knew it.

She turned back to the window and waited several beats before answering. "Because for some reason he trusted me to do it. He didn't ask you or Vivi or Ian. He left the trail for me."

"And that means you have to do it alone?" he pressed.

Matty nodded. "It's how I work. How I've always worked. I know this isn't one of my books with fictional characters. This is a real person. I'm not sure what he wanted me to find and because I don't know what he intended, I need to respect what I do know—that he left information *for me*, not for anyone else."

Dash pressed his lips together. He couldn't say he was surprised to hear this from her, but he was still disappointed. Intellectually, he understood what she was saying, but he also heard something deeper in her tone. Maybe it was pride or maybe it was a declaration of independence from him, but he was all but certain that there was something keeping her from talking to him other than the unknown wishes of a half brother she'd only talked to three times in her life—a man Dash probably knew better than she did.

So he had a choice to make: stay and hope he could get her to talk or go and give her what she wanted, time alone to work it out. Neither option gave him a good feeling, but he knew, for his own sense of self, which one he had to choose.

"Okay," he said. She turned to face him as he came closer. "Do what you need to do and I'll leave you to it." Raising his hand to her face, he traced his thumb along her cheek before dipping his head and brushing a soft kiss there. "Let me know if you need me—call anytime," he added before stepping away.

Judging by her furrowed brow and frown, his response wasn't what she'd expected. "You're leaving? You don't have to leave," she said, confirming his impression.

"Yeah, Matty, I kind of do."

She drew back and her eyes narrowed. "So, you're saying if you don't get your way then you're just going to leave?"

Dash's stomach twisted at her words but he forced himself to stay focused. Reaching up again, he cupped her face in both his hands so she couldn't look away. "I am *not* leaving you. You told me you needed to do whatever it is you're doing on your own; I'm trying to respect that the best way I know how while still respecting myself."

"And by staying with me you'll lose respect for yourself?"

He hoped it was anger driving her derisive tone, but at this point he wasn't sure. "As appealing as it can be at times to be used for sex, or as a distraction, now isn't one of those times."

She tried to turn away from him, but he held her still and continued. "You want to do this on your own, but you want me to stay and make you feel better. It sounds like something couples should do for each other, right? Only you don't really want me to help you feel better, you don't want me to help you deal with whatever it is you're discovering, you don't want me to comfort you because that would mean I would have to understand. And in order for me to understand, you'd have to talk to me, if only just a little bit. No, what you want is for me to distract you. To take you away from what you're finding, what you're thinking, what you're feeling. But you don't want me to be any part of it. I'm not willing to play that role, not right now, at this point in our relationship. I want to be your partner, Matty, not your doormat."

He took another deep breath and intentionally softened his tone. "And just to be *very* clear again—I'm *not* leaving you. This is what I assume will be the first of many bumps in our relationship. We'll hit them, like everyone else, get jostled around a bit, and then find our footing again."

He rested his forehead against hers and looked into her eyes. "Now, go do what you think you need to do. I'll call you to check in, and when you want to talk, call me. Anytime." He didn't want to let go and walk away, but he knew he had to if he wanted his relationship with Matty to stay on solid ground. So he brushed one kiss across her lips, then another across her cheek, turned, and walked out.

CHAPTER 12

It was late the next morning, maybe even early afternoon, when Matty watched the sun crawl through the window and spread into the bedroom. She hadn't slept at all during the night so, after tossing and turning for ages, she'd gotten up to give the dogs an early breakfast and then gone back to bed and tried again. Judging by the light now, she'd at least been able to grab a little bit of sleep, even if it hadn't been restful.

The conversation with Dash the evening before kept ringing in her ears, and like cycles of grief, she'd gone through what felt like every emotion possible—from anger and righteousness to loneliness and fear.

Her cell rang, bringing her out of what was promising to be another first-rate spiral into either self-pity or rationalization. Grabbing the phone, she hit the answer button before looking at the number—at this point, she wasn't too picky about distractions.

"Hello?"

"Were you asleep?" Charlotte asked from the other end of the line.

Matty sat up and rubbed a hand over her eyes. "You're back from Greece?" Charlotte was an independent financial consultant who worked mostly with the IMF and the World Bank. Lately, she'd been spending a lot of time in Europe.

"Yes, just now. What were you doing asleep? You never sleep this late unless you're sick or, well, I don't know what else."

For a second, Matty thought about telling her best friend that she was fine. But the truth was that she wasn't—for more reasons than one—and if anyone would understand, Charlotte would. And so she spilled the beans, about everything. It took longer than it should have; Charlotte interrupted more than once to point out that she'd thought the trip to Windsor was a bad idea from the get-go. And she threw in a few choice curse words for good measure, especially when Matty told her about the body in the truck and Bob's toe. But by the end of the saga, when she relayed her last conversation with Dash, much to her dismay, Charlotte was laughing.

"It's not funny," Matty pointed out.

Charlotte cleared her throat but couldn't quite stop chuckling altogether. "You're right, it's not funny that your estranged brother brought you into some weird-ass shit, and it's really not funny that some poor guy got killed and landed in your truck. And maybe the worst part is knowing someone mutilated one of the poor dogs. But I take it back, maybe going to Windsor was the best thing you've done recently. After all, this Dash guy sounds like an interesting catch."

"He's not a fish, Char."

"No, he definitely has more backbone than a fish. I just would have loved to have been a fly on the wall last night."

"So you could bug me even more than my last conversation with Dash has?"

Charlotte laughed again. "No, so I could actually see what it's like when you're confused by someone."

"I have no idea what you mean," Matty retorted, even though she kind of did. And leave it to Charlotte to point that out.

"You know exactly what I mean. Believe me, honey, no one knows better than I do what our childhoods did to us. We learned early and well what it might cost to be involved with the wrong person. And so we spent a great deal of our time not getting involved at all. And now you've met someone who makes your instinct to protect yourself war with some other, more primitive, instinct."

"You make me sounds like a character in *Clan of the Cave Bear*," Matty said.

Suddenly, all the teasing left Charlotte's voice. "You're not a character in anything, Matty. This isn't fiction, and all joking aside, you need to figure out this thing with Dash; but also, don't be a jerk about the Brad thing. I'm with Dash on that one. Whatever trail Brad left you—who gives a rat's ass if he left it for you? You don't owe him anything and you certainly don't owe him anything that might put you in danger. Tell Dash, tell Vivi, tell Ian. At this point, I think the more people who know about it, the safer you'll be.

"And I also agree with Dash that it's possible Brad orchestrated the two of you meeting for a reason. Seriously, I don't know where this misplaced sense of pride has come from, because you've got to be crazy to think you can sort all this out on your own. And even if you could, to what end?"

Matty pursed her lips, wanting to deny the reality of what Charlotte was saying; there was nothing like a best friend to ruin your day. When she heard Charlotte parrot the situation back to her, it did sound ridiculous that she was keeping it to herself. Charlotte was right that she didn't owe Brad anything. Maybe it was a misplaced twinge of familial duty that was driving her to find the answers, but that didn't mean she had to do it on her own.

She sighed. "You're right. I don't—" she paused. "I don't really know what's gotten into me. When I hear you say it, it makes perfect sense why you think I'm crazy—why Dash must think I'm crazy."

"I can tell you what's gotten into you. Dash. And in more ways than one, from the sound of it. But you're trying to protect yourself by keeping him out of everything, except your bed, whether it's rational or not."

"Thanks, Dr. Freud," Matty replied, not bothering to hide the sarcasm in her voice.

"Do you want me to come up there?" Charlotte asked. Matty didn't miss the hopeful sound in her friend's voice.

"No way. Not right now," she answered without missing a beat. She knew exactly why Charlotte wanted to come up and it had nothing to do with Brad and everything to do with Dash.

"Then don't be an asshole and go talk to Ian and Vivi, now."

"Yes, Mom."

"And sort this thing out with Dash," Charlotte added.

"Easier said than done."

"Don't I know it, but then again, you've done a thing or two that's harder."

Matty couldn't argue with that, so she murmured her assent and they hung up. She sat for a good long while before wiry little Lucy jumped on the bed, spun around a few times, sat down, and stared at her.

"Need to go out, girl?" she asked. Lucy dropped into her pounce stance and wagged her non-existent tail. "I take that as a yes," Matty said to herself, flinging the sheets back. Lucy bounded off the bed and they made their way downstairs side by side. Absentmindedly, Matty noticed the clock on the kitchen wall telling her it was close to one o'clock.

She let all the dogs out then went back into the kitchen to make a cup of coffee. She stared at the fridge knowing she should eat but having no real appetite. A scratch at the door let her know that at least one of the dogs wanted back in; when she opened the door, Bob stood there. He entered the room, sat down and stared at her with his big, brown eyes—heedless of the cone encompassing his head.

Looking at him sitting there made her smile, and when she glanced at the calendar hanging by the phone, she realized today was the day she could take the cone off. He thumped his tail a bit as Matty walked over to him but sat quietly as she dropped to her knees, wrestled the seam apart, and freed him. She'd expected an exuberant display of Lab joy, but all he did was shake his head then return to staring at her.

She let out a deep breath. "I need to call him, don't I, Bob?"

Bob wagged his tail.

"I don't think I was very fair to him."

Bob stood and nudged her hand.

"Yeah, yeah, I get the picture." So she picked up her cell and dialed the now familiar number.

"Matty," Dash said when he answered.

"Hi, Dash, how are you?" she asked, knowing how lame it sounded.

"I've been better, but I'm working. How about you?"

She took a deep breath. "Do you have some time today, to talk?" She could feel her heart thudding in her chest. The seconds dragged by and it felt like forever before he answered.

"My last client is at three o'clock today. Would three-thirty work?"

Matty nodded then remembered to speak. "Yes, that would be fine. I'll come down to the clinic and then maybe we can go for a walk or a drink or something?" She thought if they were moving or in public, it might be easier to talk, even though she still had no idea exactly what she was going to say to him.

"That sounds nice," he answered.

"Good, then I'll see you in a little bit?"

"See you in a little bit," he repeated before they ended the call. She placed her phone back on the kitchen counter and told herself she was doing the right thing. But it was a tough sell when she had no idea what she was actually doing.

When she walked into Dash's office a few hours later, she still didn't know what she was going to say or do. Beth, his receptionist, had let Matty in on her way out, so now it was just the two of them in the building. She knocked on his office door before poking her head in. He looked up from the paperwork scattered across his desk.

"Is now still okay?" she asked.

He nodded. "I just need to fill out this last form and then I'll be done."

She sat opposite him, remembering that just a few days ago she'd been in the same exact spot, but in a very different frame of mind. She had teased and flirted with him then, playing a game she knew well. But sitting here now, in this situation, she knew she was out of her depth and going to have to fly blind in some ways. The thought didn't sit well on her shoulders, or any other part of her body, and with every second that went by, Dash's calm focus on his paperwork seemed inversely proportional to the tension building inside her.

And so, when he finally tucked the form into a file, closed it, and looked up, she blurted out the first thing that came to her mind.

"Trust doesn't come easily for me, Dash. For a lot of reasons, the biggest one being how and where I was raised. We might feel some connection to each other, but trust takes time to build, and even more time to believe in."

For a long, long moment, he just stared at her. Try as she might, she couldn't read anything in his expression. And then, finally, he spoke.

"Sorry, Matty, that's bullshit and you know it. I'm not saying that, under normal circumstances, trust doesn't take time, but I *am* saying that trust isn't the issue between us."

Okay, not exactly what she wanted to hear. "How can you say that when we've known each other less than two weeks?"

He placed his forearms on his desk and leaned forward. Very deliberately, he held her gaze, not letting her eyes escape his as he spoke. "Look at me. Do you honestly think trust is the issue? Do you think I'm out to hurt you? Or that I'm going to betray you or lie to you? Look me in the eyes and tell me you think that's a possibility."

She searched his dark, dark eyes and knew he was right. She knew, in her heart, that he wouldn't betray her, not even after so short a time together. He wouldn't hurt her, not intentionally, and lying wasn't in his nature with anyone. It was possible that he'd hurt her unintentionally, but that was part of being human and she couldn't fault him for that. Especially not when she knew, beyond a doubt, that if that ever happened, and it was bound to happen at some point, he would make it right, they would make it right, in whatever way they could.

She felt like she wanted to throw up.

"Dash," she said, her voice soft. But what she was going to

say next was interrupted by his phone. He glanced at the number and she didn't miss the small frown that touched his lips, but he didn't answer.

"You should answer that," she said when it rang again.

"I think this conversation is pretty important. The call can wait."

Only she knew it couldn't when, after a brief respite, it rang again. "Answer the call, Dash. We'll have this conversation, but if someone needs your help, you need to help." Her voice was sure, and for the first time, she was beginning to feel the same way. Sure about him, about them. It wasn't going to be a walk in the park, but she knew they *would* have the conversation.

He seemed to sense her change, her new commitment to the next step, and to understand that her request for him to answer wasn't an evasive tactic on her part. He nodded and answered the phone.

"Dr. Kent," he said. "Hmm… I see… how long?" His eyes flicked to hers as if to ask a question but he said nothing, keeping himself focused on the phone call. "I see… yes, I can be right there." And he hung up.

He took a moment to collect himself and his thoughts—probably struggling to bring his mind back to his work—then his eyes met hers again.

"Have you ever seen a foal being born?" he asked.

She shook her head.

"Any interest in seeing a foal being born?"

"A baby horse?" she asked, making him smile.

"Yes, a baby horse. Trudy White has a mare that's foaling right now but seems to be in some kind of distress." He stood as he spoke and Matty followed suit. "I'm not sure what's going on, but she's asked me to come out and take a look."

"I'd like to come, but not if I'm going to be in the way."

He rounded the desk, slipped a hand behind her neck, and kissed her. Pulling back, he kept his hand in her hair. "You're not going to be in the way. But I also can't promise you that it will be a happy event. I'm hoping it's something we can work through, but like all births, there's a risk—and it may not be pretty."

She gave him a small smile. "Life isn't always pretty, Dr. Kent, but we do the best we can, don't we?" She wasn't just talking about the horse and he knew it. Taking her hand in his, he raised it to his lips and brushed a kiss across her skin before releasing her. With a nod, he headed into the back office to collect supplies.

The ride out to the farm was a relatively quiet one. Dash explained that Trudy was really a barn manager for a local, well-respected thoroughbred farm. But part of the deal she'd made with the owners when she'd come to run the place included board for a couple of her own horses, jumpers she bred and trained herself. The mare in question was one of her own, the thoroughbreds giving birth mostly in January and February.

When they arrived, a short woman with a long brown ponytail shoved through the back of a baseball hat greeted them in the parking lot. She wore jeans, work boots, a t-shirt, and a no-nonsense expression.

"She's back here," was all she said once Dash had gathered a bucketful of supplies from the back of his truck.

"Trudy, this is Matty. Matty, Trudy," Dash said as they made their way through the barn. A couple of curious equine heads popped out of stall doors, but most of the huge animals seemed completely disinterested in their arrival.

"It's nice to meet you, Trudy," Matty said.

"It's nice to meet you too, Matty," Trudy responded over her shoulder. "Normally, I'd offer you a tour and all that, but I'm worried about my mare right now. She was my jumper five years ago and I've promised Mara, that's my daughter," she clarified, "that the baby can be hers. I meant it to be something good, something for her to look forward to. The last year has been a little rough for her. And now I'm just hoping that I haven't made it worse."

"Let's not get ahead of ourselves," Dash said. "We're going to do everything we can to make sure Mara gets her foal."

Matty said nothing more. She could see the tension on the

woman's face and wondered just what had happened to her and her daughter in the last year. She glanced at Dash and guessed that he didn't know either, but she also knew that, at this moment, he didn't care. All he cared about was doing what he could to help the horse and, yes, its owner and her little girl. He and Trudy discussed horse things Matty didn't understand as they made their way to the end of the row of stalls. Trudy unlatched the door and both she and Dash walked in. Matty stayed at the entrance and took in the scene, her heart breaking just a little with every strained breath the mare took.

She didn't have to know anything about horses to know this poor girl was in pain. The mare was sweating profusely, despite a couple of fans blowing in the stall, and Matty could see the whites of her eyes as she struggled to get up at their arrival. Trudy quickly went to the horse's head as both she and Dash spoke soothingly to her.

Matty watched as Dash ran his hands over the mare's big, brown body, well rounded with the foal. He stopped to check for a pulse, listened to her heart with his stethoscope, then put his hand on her belly. Whether he was counting breaths or feeling for the baby, Matty didn't know.

"I'm going to need to do an examination. Will she be okay?" he asked.

Trudy looked up from where she sat cradling the mare's head in her lap and nodded. "She's in a lot of pain, so she may not even feel it. But even so, she's well behaved."

Dash nodded and pulled a few things out of his equipment bucket. He rolled up his sleeves, donned a pair of long latex gloves, and proceeded to examine the horse. After a few minutes, he looked up at Trudy.

"The foal is backward, but its position is the best we can hope for in this situation. I'm going to try to maneuver it a bit to make it easier for her."

Matty didn't know what that meant, but Trudy nodded and went back to soothing her horse. After he pushed, pulled, and pressed various parts of the mare's abdomen, Dash looked up. Sweat was dripping from his face, but he didn't seem to notice.

"I think we're going to be fine, Trudy. Do you want to go get Mara? I think she'd like to see it."

Matty could see the conflict in the woman's eyes. "I don't want her to see it, Dash, if the foal isn't going to make it," Trudy said.

"I can feel the foal just fine, and trust me, Trudy, I think Mara will want to see this."

The woman's hesitation filled the stall, but then Trudy nodded and looked at her. "Will you come sit with her?"

Something akin to panic set in on Matty's body. "I've never been around horses before," she managed to say.

"Then come in here and meet Never. She's a good girl and all you have to do is stroke her, pet her, and tell her she's pretty and she's going to be okay."

Matty cast a look at Dash, who was clearly going to leave the decision to her, but was just as clearly hoping that she'd make it soon. She looked at Trudy and saw a woman trying to do the best she could for her horse and her daughter. If Matty could help, she needed to step up.

She took a hesitant step into the stall and then another as Trudy beckoned her over. And within minutes, much to her surprise, Matty was seated on the straw with the massive head of a horse lying in her lap. After that, instinct took over and she cooed and stroked the mare, telling her what a beautiful girl she was and how Dash was going to help her with her baby. She didn't really know what she was saying, but it felt right and it felt good to have the trust of such a large animal.

Within minutes, Trudy returned with a young girl of about four in tow. She had the same straight, brown hair as her mother, but her coloring was darker and her eyes a bright green.

"Mom says Never is going to be okay?" she said.

Dash looked up and smiled. "She's going to be fine, Mara. I thought you might want to see your first jumper being born. I heard that was the plan for this little baby. To be your first big jumper?"

Mara nodded and Matty watched as Dash charmed and reassured the young girl. His eyes were kind, his voice soothing, and though he used words that were appropriate for a child, his tone wasn't the least bit condescending. Listening to him, Matty realized that he spoke to Mara much the same way he would if he were explaining the situation to her, an adult.

A few minutes later, Mara was on Dash's lap waiting to catch the baby horse. Trudy was standing by with towels and Matty, still stroking the mare's head, was glad that Dash was talking his way through the birth, so she could know what was going on even if she couldn't see it. When the legs of the little animal made their appearance, Dash gave Matty a quick look, telling her without speaking that on the next contraction, the one that would push the foal out, Never would need all the support she could give. Matty nodded, tuned the others out, and focused on the mare.

Never's head came up, her eyes rolled back and she let out a long grunt. Matty wrapped her arms around the horse's head and did her best to keep her calm. As the mare's nostrils flared, Matty could feel the sweat from the horse's neck on her arms as it soaked through her long-sleeved linen blouse. After what seemed like an hour but was probably no more than three minutes, Never's head dropped like a dead weight back into her lap, hot air from the horse's nostrils pounding into her thigh. In a panic, Matty looked up to find the other three people in the stall smiling.

Dash was backing up with Mara still on his lap and they were pulling on two little legs, Mara's hands wrapped around Dash's. Matty's eyes went back to Never, and as she felt the horse's breathing become more regular, she let out a deep breath of relief.

"Dash?" she asked.

He glanced up with a huge smile. "She's going to be okay. Both of them. We're just going to help Never out with this last bit by pulling on the foal as she has her next contraction. Everything is looking great though, and we should have mom and baby safe and together in just a few more minutes."

Matty looked down at Never, who looked exhausted, and then back to Dash, who was holding a smiling, laughing Mara.

"It's a little girl, isn't it, Dr. Kent? A filly," Mara said.

"It is. Nice job, Mara. I bet she's going to be as pretty as her mom," Dash answered. Though the words didn't sink in, Matty continued to watch Dash as he and Mara talked and smiled and, eventually, helped Never finish the birth of her first, healthy baby. Matty was aware of the weight in her lap but she couldn't take her eyes off of Dash as he helped Mara clean off the foal and do something he referred to as imprinting.

"He's pretty amazing, isn't he?" Trudy said. She'd made her way back to Matty's side and was now stroking her mare.

"I think you're all pretty amazing," Matty responded, making Trudy laugh. "Is she really going to be all right?" she asked, running her hand down Never's nose.

"Dash will check her as soon as the foal is up, but she's already breathing better, so I think she's going to be fine."

Just then, the foal gave a little shake, startling Mara, who fell back into Dash's lap. "Now is the really fun part," Dash said with a glint in his eye as he met Matty's gaze.

She turned her attention to the impossibly tiny horse and watched as it first stretched out its legs then rocked its body. Slowly, inch-by-inch, the little foal brought her legs underneath her and then, with a final, mini-Herculean effort, rose up on all fours. Matty stared, transfixed. With legs shaky but strong, the little foal stood for the first time then, seeming to know she had an audience, took her first step while giving a little toss of her head as if to say, "What were you all so worried about?"

Dash laughed as he rose to his feet. Never was already making moves to stand, so Dash came over, reached his hand down for Matty, and helped her up. A few seconds later, Never was up on her feet, too, and nuzzling her new baby. Matty leaned into Dash as she watched the sweet scene before her.

"I'm a mess," he said quietly to her.

"I don't care," she responded. A second later, his arm, sans glove, wrapped itself around her waist. Together, they watched the new mom and baby get to know one another as Trudy and her own daughter talked affectionately to both animals.

Still in a state of wonder over an hour later, Matty gazed out at the horses in the fields as they drove away from the thoroughbred farm. Dash had wanted to stay and keep an eye on Never for a while and Matty hadn't objected to hanging around to watch the new baby on its first day in this world. Eventually, they'd washed and cleaned up as best they could, Dash had given some final instructions to Trudy and Mara, and they'd climbed into his truck and pulled away.

"That was amazing, Dash. Thanks for inviting me," she said.

"You're welcome. I'm glad the outcome was a good one."

"You and me, both," she murmured. They rode in quiet for several minutes as she let the emotions of the day sink in. It had been a roller coaster but now, having seen what she'd just seen and watched Dash do what he'd just done, she felt stronger than she had even just a few hours earlier.

"You're right, Dash, it's not an issue of trust," she said. From the corner of her eye, she saw his head swivel to look at her but she kept her eyes focused out her window. What she was going to tell him wasn't pretty and she couldn't bring herself to look at him as she spoke.

"You know I grew up in the Bronx, in the projects, but you don't know all of it. It's not something I talk about often, and never before with someone who wasn't also there, because it's hard to describe what it was like."

He reached over and covered her hand with his, but said nothing.

"I was four when I was caught in my first armed robbery. My mom and I had stopped to get some milk on our way home from the park one day. Someone came in, shot and killed the shopkeeper and a customer. There were four other people in the store, we all huddled in the corner, praying not to be noticed."

She remembered that day vividly, even though she'd been so young. But that wasn't the worst of it. "I was six when I saw my first drive-by shooting. It killed a little boy I was playing with. And

167

then, at school, it just seemed best not to have any real friends—or feel anything for anyone, for that matter."

She took a deep breath and tried her best to describe what it was really like for her, something she'd never done, not even in the privacy of her own mind. "You see, where I grew up, it wasn't just emotions like fear that people exploited, but emotions of *any* kind. They were used as weapons against you. God forbid you were happy about something, because if you showed it, it was inevitable that someone would come and smack the smile off your face. And if you and your friends were having too much fun, someone would come along and pick a fight, pull a gun or a knife, do whatever it took to stop the joy.

"Everyone was so beaten down—by society, by their families, by themselves—that any kind of emotion at all almost served as a reminder of the humanity we'd all lost. I still remember my mom telling me, when we were huddling in that convenience store, not to show any fear, not to give them any reason to notice me."

Matty paused to run a hand through her hair and noticed she was shaking. It seemed that, even after all these years, that place still had a hold on her.

"And so we learned not to show any emotion in order to survive, in order to protect ourselves and our families and the few friends we allowed ourselves to have. But after a while, at least I think for me, not being able to show any emotions got easier, because I just stopped having them. I loved my mother and in our home it was different—and it was different when I was with Charlotte and her mom, too—but everywhere else? Everywhere else in the real world, well, that was another story."

The gentle hills and delicate summer flowers she saw through her window as they traveled the country roads were at such odds with what she was telling Dash. But still, she continued. "I remember, when I was eleven, just before my grandmother found us, a family moved in above us. I never saw them but knew they had a little girl. You know how I knew?" she asked but then answered before Dash could say anything. "Through the vent in my room, I heard her brother rape her almost every night before he went out to sell his drugs. She was the same age as I was," she said with a choked cry.

For the first time in many, many years, Matty felt a tear fall down her cheek. She closed her eyes and waited for Dash's judgment; he did nothing but hold her hand. She took several deep breaths, opened her eyes, and then continued. She wasn't done yet.

"Because of my experiences growing up, I'm not much of a sharer, especially when I've felt uncertain about things. It was always safer that way—not exposing my vulnerabilities, keeping things to myself. I've been using my past to justify not telling you anything, and then, when you pushed, I used it as an excuse for my actions.

"But the truth of the matter is that I think I'm backing away from you not because I don't trust you, but because I'm not sure I'll be able to give you what you want, what you deserve. I don't know if I know how to really love someone or how to really *feel* much of anything beyond a surface emotion. That ability should be fostered in kids; it should be tended to and grown. But we didn't have that luxury if we wanted to survive. And now I don't know if I'll be able to do it, or if I can even learn how. You make me want to ask the question, Dash, but I'm terrified of the answer. What if I can't?"

They were pulling up in front of Brad's house. Dash shut the engine off and didn't say anything. When he let go of her hand and got out of his truck, she wanted to crawl away and curl up in a tiny, dirty pit. But then he came around to her side of the truck, opened the door, and held out his hand. She took it, sliding from her seat. In silence, he used her key to unlock the kitchen door and then he led her upstairs to the bathroom.

Not letting go of her hand, Dash turned the shower on, then faced her. Without a word, he undressed her first, then stripped himself down before leading her under the cool spray. He ran his fingers through her hair, tilted her head up and forced her to look into his eyes.

"You may not know the answer to the question, Matty, but I do." And with that, he bent his head down and kissed her.

CHAPTER 13

DASH LAY STARING AT THE ceiling, his arm wrapped around Matty. It had been an intense several hours, between the birth of the foal and her revelation about her childhood and the effects, or one of the effects, it had on her. When he'd pushed her the day before, he hadn't actually been sure of what was holding her back. He thought it might have been pride or maybe just a fear of getting too close to someone too fast. He should have known it was something deeper than that. For all her fears about her ability to learn and grow, she wasn't one to just sit back and let things happen to her. She would have told him to back off if that was what she'd really wanted.

But she was right about one thing, her childhood and the things she had experienced weren't anything he would ever be able to completely understand. He could empathize and he could support her, but those experiences she'd shared with him—and he suspected they were only a few of what she'd lived through—were so far out of the realm of his childhood reality. Intellectually, he knew things like that happened, but he had never met anyone who had lived through them, or at least talked about living through them.

"Tell me about your grandmother," he asked now, rubbing his hand down her bare arm. It had gotten dark and neither seemed inclined to rise from the bed to eat, so they stayed there in a contented quiet. He could feel her smile against his chest.

"She was an amazing woman. You know about the letter my mom wrote and how Gran found it. But I still remember her riding into the Bronx in her chauffeured car with "assistants" to help us move out of our apartment and into her home with her. And then, of course, you know she also took in Charlotte and Nanette, Charlotte's mom, too."

"It sounds great, but I can't imagine it was easy," he said.

She shook her head against him. "It wasn't, it was really hard. For me, at least. My grandmother was very, very wealthy, and the house she moved us into, her home, was as big as the entire apartment building we'd left. We had a garden and a pool, but of course, I didn't know how to swim. We had people to clean and garden and cook. All the things my mom had been hired to do for other people were now being done for her. It felt unreal for a long time and it took ages for me to believe it wasn't all going to disappear one day—taken away from me as quickly as it had come.

"Luckily, though, I think my grandmother knew that, and the first year we all stuck pretty close to home so that I could begin to grow some roots. She hired the best medical care for my mom. And she wanted us to go to good schools, but that would mean being in class with kids who had grown up so differently than we had. So she hired tutors and social workers for Charlotte and me to be sure we were ready, academically and emotionally, before we went. By the time we did enter school, both of us were much better adjusted than we would have been if we'd just been thrown in and we both did quite well, especially Charlotte, who has a scary way with numbers *and* people."

"And you grew close to her, didn't you, your grandmother?" Dash asked.

"Yes," Matty said on a sigh and he could tell from her voice just how much respect and affection she held for her grandmother. "It took a little while, but, over time, we grew very close. Completely different beginnings, but we were more alike than not. We had many of the same mannerisms and ways of talking or thinking about things. As I got older, we also enjoyed the same kinds of theater and books and movies. My mom, once she was healthy, delved into the world of art and has spent years volunteering with various museums and sitting on boards and all that. But Grandma and I, while we liked art, also enjoyed a good slapstick comedy or blockbuster action flick."

"And what of her son, your father?"

Matty rolled up onto an elbow and met his gaze as she answered. "It was sad, really. She didn't talk about it much, but I always got the sense she was disappointed in him. Not just because of what he did to my mom and me, but more like that was the straw that broke the camel's back. It was clear she loved him, but it was also clear that she didn't really understand him. And he made no effort to understand her. I suspect it had a lot to do with his wife, Sandra, but I'm not sure."

"And Brad?"

"Brad was an enigma to me. I knew I had a half brother, but he wasn't a part of my life. Again, I think Sandra refused to allow him near me, so as a result, he never really got to spend time with his grandmother, which was also sad. And then there was the disposition of my grandmother's estate, and I think, after that, there was no way Sandra was going to let Brad or my father have anything to do with me."

"Meaning?"

"Meaning she left most of what she had to me. There was a substantial trust for both my father and Brad and a few family heirlooms that went to one or the other of them, but the bulk of her estate, including the house in DC, went to me."

He raised an eyebrow at her. "So, does that mean you're a wealthy woman?"

A sly smile touched her lips. "Yes, very."

"How very?"

"*Very* very."

"So if this family tradition of mine works out, I could be a kept man?"

She laughed and he reveled in the sound of it, in the feel of it against his bare chest. "Yes, you could, as could any children we have, and, if we're smart about it, our grandchildren and great-grandchildren, too."

He grinned, "I knew there was a reason I liked you." The information that Matty was as wealthy as she was came as a complete surprise. If he allowed himself to think about it, it might be a bit intimidating and so, for now, he opted not to think about it at all, deciding to focus on her and what was happening between them instead.

"I can think of a few better reasons you might like me," she said, sliding up over him with another smile and dropping kisses down his neck.

He wrapped his arms around her, flipped her over, and pinned her underneath him. "I can think of more than a few," he said and then proceeded to show her at least three or four.

• • •

The early morning light was seeping through the windows in the bedroom as Dash stood at the foot of the bed and watched her sleep. He needed to get home, shower, and change before going to work. He wanted to stay with her, but that wasn't an option; he had clients that were expecting him. At least his last client was at one o'clock today, so, pending any emergencies, he and Matty could spend the afternoon together—maybe go his place, take a dip in the pond, and just have a lazy summer day. The thought of them just *being* at his house brought a smile to his lips.

"You're leaving and you're smiling, I'm not sure how to take that," Matty's voice, heavy with sleep, drifted up from the bed.

Dash chuckled and walked to her side. Sitting on the edge of the bed, he brushed some hair from her face. "I was just thinking about this afternoon," he answered and then told her of his suggested plan.

She stretched then rolled toward him, closing her eyes. "Sounds like a plan. My car is still at your clinic so at some point I'll need to get it. But in the meantime, I'm going to go back to sleep. You kept me up last night."

"You weren't complaining," he pointed out.

The corners of her mouth tilted up, her eyes still closed. "No, I wasn't."

He smiled and bent down to give her a kiss good-bye. "Rest well, I'll call you around one." He stood to leave but she caught his hand.

"Dash?" she said, still not opening her eyes.

"Hmm?"

"Thank you."

He looked down at her and knew she wasn't thanking him for the physical parts of the night before but for letting her have her space, for letting her regain her footing after sharing some of herself with him, for not pushing her further into that place.

"You're welcome. Now sleep."

She brought his hand to her lips, kissed his palm, then released him. He stood still for a moment, listening to her even breathing, then turned away.

• • •

Matty rounded the house with a basket of eggs in hand and reminded herself, one more time, to ask Dash about that pancake breakfast. She had a way with eggs, but even so, she had way more than she knew what to do with.

She put the basket down on the little patio table so she could open the door, but two of the dogs caught her attention before her hand reached the door handle. Lucy, in her very Lucy way, was bounding down the hill behind the house—half leaping, occasionally spinning, and constantly barking. Her ears flew up like little wings each time she took a gigantic leap and, for a moment, Matty wondered if her little body was going to be able to stop the momentum when she reached the bottom of the hill. Behind her, at a casual lope, was Rufus, his huge stride covering about ten of Lucy's.

It was such a comical site that she watched as they made their way all the way down the hill to the driveway. Expecting them to stop at the door and wait to be let in, she was surprised when Lucy came to a halt in front of her and promptly dropped onto her belly, her paws in front of her and her eyes looking up at her temporary master. Matty frowned; she'd seen all sorts of crazy behavior from Lucy, but this was new. This didn't look like the playful, goofy Lucy she was used to; the wiry mutt actually looked like she was trying to tell her something.

For a moment, Matty studied the dog but couldn't for the life of her figure out what she might be trying to say, so she opened the door, picked up the eggs, and made her way into the kitchen. Then Lucy whined. Actually whined. And inched forward a few steps on her belly.

She looked at the dog again, and Lucy looked back at her. "Just a minute, Lucy," she said. "I'll be right back," she added. It didn't escape her attention that she was talking to a dog as if she might understand. But she had to wonder, given the way Lucy brought her head up but didn't move her body while she watched Matty put the eggs in the house, as if she were waiting for her to keep her word and come back, if maybe Lucy did understand.

"Okay, Lucy, what's going on?" Matty said when she'd stepped back onto the patio. Lucy whined again. Matty glanced at Rufus who was sitting quietly in the shade watching them both.

"Lucy, go," Matty said pointing to the hill. She wasn't sure what she expected to happen, but Lucy seemed to take it as a command, or maybe permission, and she leapt to her feet and bolted toward the hill. She'd made it about five feet up when she stopped, turned, and looked back at Matty, as if to say "Well? Are you coming?"

Matty looked at Rufus, who didn't seem to have anything to say on the matter, shrugged, and followed the little dog. As soon as she set foot on the hill, Lucy seemed to undergo a transformation that, in all honesty, Matty found a bit disconcerting. The normally happy-go-lucky dog was all business. Her nose was down and she didn't bound or spin once, though every few strides or so she turned to make sure Matty was still behind her.

Not knowing what to make of the situation, she followed Lucy for about ten minutes. They walked up to the top of the hill, which leveled out onto a gently rolling field. In the distance, Matty could see other farms and fields and smell the fresh cut grass. She paused and took in the scene. For a moment, she felt like she should be riding horseback with a pack of hounds through the countryside, maybe sidesaddle with a duke or an earl at her side. If it weren't for the distant sound of a plane, she could be in nineteenth-century England.

Then Lucy yipped, not her usual high-pitched little-dog yip, but something deeper, and strange as it felt to Matty, something that sounded more businesslike. Focusing her attention back on the dog who had gotten ahead of her, she marched forward, wondering if this property was even Brad's. But she didn't have too much time to think about it as she followed Lucy around a small copse of trees and a barn came into view.

Matty paused as Lucy ran to the barn and dropped onto her belly again, just as she'd done on the patio. Not for the first time was Matty getting a creepy feeling from the dog's behavior. She glanced behind her but saw no one and nothing but fields in the immediate vicinity. She felt for the phone in her pocket; luckily, she'd grabbed it out of habit when she'd walked out of the house earlier that morning. Of course that didn't mean she had any service.

Lucy yipped again, but Matty still didn't move forward. Instead, she took her phone out and made sure she had coverage. One bar was blinking on and off. Not the best, but better than nothing.

She jumped about a foot when she heard something coming up behind her, panic bursting through her body. And though it was followed by a flood of relief when Rufus's nose touched her hand, she did wonder just what it was that was telling her to be worried.

She glanced at her phone and wondered if she should call Dash, or maybe even Vivi or Ian. But what would she say? My dog is acting weird and I have the heebie-jeebies? She wasn't a woman who embarrassed easily, but even that would be too much for her.

"Okay, Rufus," she said, looking down at where he sat and placing a hand on the huge dog's head. "Shall we go see what has Lucy up in arms?"

His steady brown eyes looked back at her.

"Okay, then, let's go." With Rufus, she approached the barn. When they neared, Lucy stood but didn't bark or make any other noise. Instead, she walked to the sliding door of the barn, nosed the closed door, then dropped onto her belly again. Matty glanced around. She didn't know whose barn this was. It could be Brad's, but it could just as easily belong to someone else.

Lucy let out a small whine. Matty glanced down again.

"You want me to open that door?" she said to the dog.

Lucy gave a single yip.

"There's not going to be a serial killer or ax murderer behind there, is there?"

Lucy cocked her head to the side.

"Okay, I'm crazy. But you're acting weird, so what am I supposed to think?" she asked as she made her way to the door. Gripping the handle, Matty expected Lucy to bolt inside the second the opening was big enough for her. But much to her surprise, and rising anxiety, Lucy did no such thing. Using her body weight, Matty slid the door open, pulling hard. When it was open far enough for her to get through, she stopped and eyed the dog. Lucy was on her belly again—nose down, whimpering.

Matty fingered her phone as her heart rate kicked up again. But knowing she'd have to sooner rather than later, she stepped toward the opening and looked into the barn.

CHAPTER 14

IT WAS DARK, TOO DARK to see anything until her eyes adjusted. But she didn't need her eyes to know that something very bad had happened in the barn. The smell of decay hung in the humid, stagnant air and the sound of flies, thousands of them, echoed in the wooden structure.

The urge to know what had died in the barn battled with the knowledge that if it wasn't an animal the barn might be a crime scene. And so for a moment, she stood frozen in indecision.

Then Lucy whined again, a sad, knowing whine.

If only for the dog's sake, Matty needed to know more. Stepping inside and staying to the inner perimeter of the barn, she edged her way along the wall, careful not to touch anything. The smell clawed at her nose and while she tried to block it with her hand, it did little good. She thought about taking off the button-down shirt she wore over her tank top and using it to dampen the stench, but the flies, and the idea of them landing on her any more than they already were, stopped her.

And then everything coalesced—the buzzing of the flies got louder, her eyes adjusted to the dim light, and she was close enough to see what it was that Lucy had been trying to tell her.

Sprawled in a chair was a human form.

Covered with so many flies, it was almost unrecognizable. But Matty had seen enough in her life to know beyond a doubt that the form was human and, judging by the size, a man. She blinked back tears as her vision began to swim and she tried to control the pounding of blood through her veins because she knew, in her heart, that she was looking at her half brother.

Rufus let out a low growl, bringing her back from the dark place she'd been teetering into. Lucy followed up with a bark of her own. Matty did her best to shut her eyes, if only mentally, to the image of the figure and slowly made her way back out of the barn, trying to use the same path she'd taken on the way in.

When she emerged from the structure, she took several steps away and inhaled deeply, trying as hard as she could to purge the smell from inside her nose and tamp down the nausea. When she felt she was capable of having a cogent conversation, she pulled her phone out and, with shaking hands and fingers, dialed.

"Vivi," she said when the other woman answered. "This is Matty Brooks and I don't think you need to run that search on my half brother anymore."

• • •

Dash squeezed Matty's fingers that were intertwined in his. She turned her gaze from the barn to look at him.

"It might not be him," Dash said.

The look on her face told him that, while she appreciated his efforts, they both knew different. He tugged her back against him and she came willingly, resting her head on his shoulder. They were seated on the lowered tailgate of his truck, watching Ian, Vivi, and various other law enforcement officers do their jobs in the old hay barn. The field, which looked like it should be a quiet and peaceful place, held several vehicles including the medical examiner's van and a special truck from the state crime lab.

It was all a far cry from the tranquility they'd been basking in that morning.

"We should go," he said.

Matty nodded but didn't move. "I don't have much empathy for my father or Sandra, but I would never have wished this on them. I can't imagine anything worse than losing your child, even if that child is a grown adult."

Dash couldn't agree more, but even so, he was wondering what kind of effect it was going to have on Matty. True, she and Brad hadn't been close, but based on the fact that he had asked her to come up to Windsor and she'd accepted, maybe they had both reached a point in life where they were finally open to getting to know each other. And knowing what he knew about Matty, she wouldn't have reached that point easily. But now it was never going to happen. He pulled her closer and rubbed her arm, saying nothing.

They sat for a long while, watching people go in and out of the barn until, finally, a stretcher with a body bag on it was wheeled out and into the medical examiner's van. Vivi had followed the body out and stood by as it was loaded. Once the van was making its way down the hill, she turned and started toward them. Within a few seconds, she was joined by Ian.

"I'm sorry you had to see this," Ian said.

"For the second time," Matty said, referring to the first body that had fallen into her car. "For a small town, Windsor seems to see a lot of violence."

It wasn't a mean comment; instead, it was laced with a sadness that Dash thought he understood better after hearing her revelations the evening before. In the Bronx, she had expected things like this, things like death and violence. But out in the country, out in a place that seemed so quiet and calm, people should be able to find peace. And the fact that they couldn't, the fact that violence was everywhere, was a cause for sorrow for all mankind.

"Is it Brad?" Matty asked Vivi.

"We don't know for sure," Ian interjected.

Dash watched Vivi's eyes dart to her fiancé and then soften as they landed back on Matty. "Ian is right, we don't know for certain. But given what I know, I would say that yes, it's Brad."

It was a small thing, but as Matty leaned her body against his,

Dash felt her sag just a bit. He knew it was all she'd allow herself. He held her hand tight in his.

"If you're up for it, Matty, I'd like to ask you a few questions?" Ian asked.

Dash felt her stir against him before she answered. "Of course. I'm not sure how much I'll know, but you can ask."

"Maybe we could go to the house, sit somewhere more comfortable, and then I can have a look around once we're done?" Ian suggested.

If anyone else noticed Matty's moment of hesitation, they didn't show it.

Soon, all four of them were seated in the kitchen drinking iced tea. The dogs, having sensed something was off, huddled around them in a steady, if somewhat bothersome, show of support.

"Will they be up there long?" Matty asked, referring to the crime scene officers with a gesture of her head toward the hill.

Ian inclined his head. "They'll be there for a bit longer and then Carly and Marcus will come down here to help me look through some of Brad's things. Do you mind?"

She shook her head and made a vague all-encompassing motion with her hands. "Please, whatever you need."

"Thanks, we appreciate that. But for now, I just want to ask you about your last conversation with Brad and anything you can tell us that might shed some light on what happened in that barn."

For a long moment, Matty just stared at Ian, her mind sluggishly processing what he was saying. Then, with a little shake of her head, she started speaking. "I last spoke to Brad the day before I arrived here. It wasn't a very long conversation. He just asked me to come up and house-sit for him."

"But the request wasn't a usual request, was it?" Vivi asked.

"No, you both know it wasn't. I hadn't spoken to Brad in years, and to be honest, the only reason I took his call was because I was looking for a distraction from my writing. But we talked for about ten minutes. At first I thought he was crazy and then I made some offhanded comment about needing an expert in modern Chinese politics and he said he could hook me up with one if I came up. I figured, what the hell, and so I did."

"And who is the expert?" Ian asked.

"Chen Zheng," Vivi supplied, earning her a look from Ian. "I met his sister the other day when I dropped by to see Matty. He's a professor at the university," she provided.

"So, you know how to reach him?" Ian asked.

"Matty probably knows better than me. I can get his contact information from the school, but she probably has it," Vivi answered with a look at Matty, who nodded.

"It's here," she said, rising from her chair. She plucked a business card from a drawer, returned to the table, and handed it to Ian. "He and his sister, Mai, may know more about Brad than I do, they seem to be good friends with him."

Ian thanked her and tucked the card into his shirt pocket. "Now, is there anything you think we should know about Brad? How did he sound when you spoke to him? Did he sound depressed or worried about anything? Distracted?"

She gave a half-hearted shrug. "No, but you have to understand, even if he was any of those things, I didn't know him well enough to necessarily pick up on it. He was insistent that I come up. That alone was strange, given our history. But he'd called a couple of times over the past year and I thought that maybe he was just trying to extend the olive branch or something. How did he die?" she asked abruptly.

Ian looked at Vivi, who gave a small nod then answered. "It was a gunshot wound to the head. It wasn't an accident and he was holding a shotgun, but as of right now, we can't tell if it was self-inflicted or not."

"So, murder or suicide, then," Dash said.

Vivi nodded. "We'll know more tonight or tomorrow. Now, Matty, I think it's time to mention why I was here the other day," she added gently.

Dash turned toward Matty and knew that whatever Vivi was talking about was part of what had been holding her back from him a few days earlier. As if to confirm it, her eyes flickered to his before she looked back to Ian and spoke.

"I've been trying to get ahold of Brad since the first day I arrived and found out that I didn't have just the dogs to take care of but all the other animals, too. I've called maybe a dozen times since I arrived? After the conversation we had at The Tavern the other night, I asked Vivi if she wouldn't mind looking into it, looking into whether or not Brad could be found."

"Did you think something might have happened to him?" Dash asked.

Her eyes met his briefly and he saw a hint of an apology in there. "Like I told Vivi that night, I don't—didn't," she corrected herself after a pause. "I didn't know him well, so I didn't know if he was the kind of guy to hike off into the woods for two weeks with no cell phone or if there might really be something wrong. But given that I couldn't reach him and I found those weird pictures, I thought it might be worth looking into." She finished her sentence a little uncomfortably and Dash wondered if there was something more. But before he could ask, Vivi interjected.

"And because I could understand her confusion, I agreed to look into it myself. I came by a few days ago and collected a missing persons report that I took up to the lab. I was just getting around to looking into it when Matty called me this morning."

Dash watched Vivi communicate this information to Ian, who couldn't have been happy about Vivi doing this on her own. But Ian's expression, though fixed on his fiancée, remained utterly unreadable. At least to Dash. Vivi on the other hand, arched an eyebrow at Ian in what looked like a subtle challenge.

"We'll discuss protocol later, Vivienne," Ian finally said before turning back to Matty. "Is there anything else you think we should know? Any phone calls or mail or other messages? Any letters he left or that have come for him?"

She looked around the room, as if it might tell her something, then lifted a shoulder. "Nothing really. There were a couple of bills that were stamped and addressed that I dropped at the post office the first or second day I was here. But I don't know if he has a PO Box, because I haven't seen any mail in the mailbox at the end of the road. As for the rest, the house was tidy when I got here and the only note for me was the one about the animals."

"And the suggestion to look in his liquor cabinet," Dash interjected.

"And that. And there haven't been any calls, either," she added.

"There was the incident with Bob's toe," Dash added. At the sound of his name, the yellow Lab stood, ambled over, and nosed Matty's hand. Absentmindedly, she stroked his head.

"Yes, there was that, but you're looking into that already," Matty added with a look at Ian who nodded.

"Yes, we are looking into it, but I think we should bump it up on the priority list given the circumstances," he said. Vivi nodded as the sound of a car in the driveway caused the dogs to bark and stir toward the door.

"That's probably Marcus and Carly. Do you mind if we have a look around?" Ian asked, rising from his seat. For a brief moment, Dash wondered what condition Matty had left the bedroom in. Her clothes had been scattered on the floor, the sheets twisted, and the blankets tossed aside when he'd left that morning. He didn't really care but didn't want Matty to feel uncomfortable about anything.

But she didn't seem to notice or care; she just nodded her head and let the three officers get to work as she sat with him and Vivi in the kitchen, listening to the rummaging going on throughout the house. On occasion, Ian, Marcus, or Carly would pop in and ask if something was either Brad's or hers. More often than not, it was Brad's, with the exception of her laptop that, once identified, was brought to the table, presumably to keep it from getting mixed in with the other items the team was either rifling through or collecting.

"Will you stay with Dash tonight?" Vivi asked softly from her position on the other side of the table.

"Yes," he answered for her.

But Matty shook her head. "There are too many animals here,

Dash. I can't stay away for the night and leave the cats and rabbits and dogs and chickens. There is too much to take care of here."

Vivi must have heard the same hint of desolation he heard in Matty's voice because she cast him a look warning him to tread carefully. He didn't know Vivienne DeMarco well, but he did know that, in addition to being a doctor, she was also a psychologist. He thought her specialty was forensic psychology, but even so, she'd know much more about what was probably going on in Matty's mind than he would.

"Of course you don't have to come to my house if it's easier to stay here. Maybe we can just swing by my place after Ian and the team leave. I'll pick up some clothes, then we can grab some food and we'll just have a quiet night here," he said, brushing her hair from her neck. For the first time in several hours, she looked at him, really looked at him. He couldn't tell what she was thinking, but she offered him a small smile and a simple thank you.

A couple of minutes later, Ian came down with a comb in what Dash assumed was an evidence bag. "Is this Brad's?" he asked.

Matty looked at the item and nodded. "Yes, but why are you taking his, oh," she paused, the reality of the situation sinking in. They wanted his comb for DNA. She cleared her throat. "He was meticulously clean. Well, his house is anyway. You may not find what you need with that," she said with a nod toward the comb. "My toothbrush is the electric one. His is the green one in the cabinet. Or at least I assume that was his since it was here when I got here," she said.

Ian gave a nod and muttered a quick thank you before exiting again.

Matty turned to Vivi. "You can take a sample from me if it would help to have someone you know would be a half-familial match," she offered.

Vivi inclined her head. "Thanks. I may ask Ian to do that, just in case."

"Will you tell his parents?" Matty asked.

Vivi shook her head. "Not until we're sure it's him and then, yes, Ian will make that call. Unless you want to?" she added, her tone suggesting she was testing the waters.

Matty gave a little laugh. "No, if it turns out to be Brad, I don't want to be the one to tell his parents. I know we share a father, but it's only biologically. I haven't seen my father since my grandmother's funeral and, before that, only pictures of him. Besides, my feelings for him aside, if it is Brad, this is going to be devastating to him and his wife and I don't need to complicate things further."

Vivi looked about to press her more, but Ian entered the kitchen, followed by the two other officers. All of them were carrying either a box or several large envelopes.

"We're done here," Ian announced. Vivi rose from her seat and asked Ian to take a DNA sample from Matty. Ian didn't hesitate to do as his fiancée asked, and within two minutes, he was done. Matty stood as Ian capped and sealed the sample he'd taken from her mouth.

"Thank you, Matty." Ian said. "Marcus and Carly will take these items to the lab with Vivienne and we'll let you know what we find out as soon as we know anything. In the meantime, take care of yourself—and be careful," he added with a look at Dash.

"Thank you," she responded and they all moved toward the door.

Matty leaned into Dash as they stood on the patio watching the four leave.

"How are you doing?" he asked, rubbing his hand up and down her arm. The afternoon had gone by and dusk was beginning to fall. The crickets were singing in the fields and a few birds of prey were circling in the sky.

"I'm not really sure," she answered. "I mean, it was horrible to find what I did today and it's horrible to think a man's body may have been up there this whole time—time that Ian and Vivi could have been doing their jobs if we'd just found him sooner."

"But what about the fact that it might be Brad," he pressed, ushering her inside.

"That's the part I'm feeling a little, well, nothing about. If it's him I will be sad, but I'm not sure I will be any sadder than if it is anyone else. I know I should feel more because he's my half brother, but, well…" Her voice trailed off and she let out a deep breath. "Then again, considering what I told you yesterday, maybe this is just another one of those instances where I should be feeling something but don't because I'm lame and can't."

Dash's gut clenched. He knew what she was or wasn't feeling for Brad had *nothing* to do with her childhood, but on the heels of their recent and raw conversation about the subject, he could understand how she might take her ambivalence as further proof of her lack of ability to feel.

"There's no *should* about any of this," he reassured her. "You feel the way you feel, even if that feeling isn't overwhelming sadness for a man who was little more than your biological half sibling."

She offered him another small smile. "I know, but it feels coldhearted not to be potentially devastated by it. I can't even say I'm sad about lost opportunities because I'm not sure that those opportunities would have ever come up, even if he was alive. Listen to me," she stopped speaking as she poured herself a glass of water. "I'm talking about Brad like we already know it was him up there in that barn. There is always a chance it wasn't him, right?"

Dash was pretty sure she didn't think that was the case so he said nothing. He watched her take a few sips of water before she raised her eyes back to his.

"I know," she said. "I do think it is him. But it will be good to have Vivi confirm it whenever she can. And I know it could have something to do with the note he left me and maybe even what happened to Bob." Her eyes darted away from his for a just a moment and he wondered if she was avoiding his gaze because of emotion or something else. The thought brought him up short, reminding him of the one argument they'd had. It seemed like ages ago but had really just been a few days past. She'd been looking into something that had to do with Brad and hadn't wanted to tell him what. The situation had sparked what had become a much deeper conversation, but while wading through those depths with her, he'd forgotten what had originally piqued his interest.

He opened his mouth to ask her about what she had been looking for on Brad's computer, but she cut him off.

"There are more questions than answers right now, Dash. But do you mind if we just not try to answer them, or think about them, too much tonight?"

Given what she had gone through, it wasn't a request he could deny. So he nodded and held out his hand to her. She came to him and he pulled her close.

"Let's go for a drive. We'll stop at my house, eventually pick up some food and maybe a movie, and then come back here. Sound good?" he offered.

She made a little hum against his chest. "That sounds like just what the doctor ordered."

CHAPTER 15

Matty knew Dash suspected that she wasn't telling him everything about Brad. She could tell by the hint of a question that crept into his eyes whenever she brushed off talking about her half brother. When Dash had first raised the subject in his truck that night as they drove to dinner with his parents, she had brushed him off because of habit, because of her underlying fears about where she stood, or could stand, in their relationship. But now it was something different. Now, though she wasn't overwhelmed by sadness, she did feel a bit of a protective streak for her half brother creeping into her psyche and she wanted to know more about the body before she said anything about what she suspected Brad might have gotten tangled up in.

First and foremost, she wanted to know if, in fact, the body was really Brad's. And if so, how he'd died. It shouldn't matter, but it did. Had whoever the man was that she'd found in the barn committed suicide or had he been killed?

If he'd been killed, then the hints that Brad had been involved in some sort of financial misdeeds would be important. But if he'd killed himself? What would anyone have to gain by knowing of his potential transgressions?

The banks might be able to close the books, but they'd do that anyway once they found out Brad was dead. As it was, the only thing she could see coming out of disclosing such information, if in fact it was Brad and he had committed suicide, was the additional emotional devastation Brad's parents would feel. And again, while she didn't feel any affection for either of them, no parent should have to go through what may lay ahead of them.

So, instead of talking about what she had or hadn't found in her search of Brad's computer and house, Matty and Dash spent the evening curled up on the couch watching old movies. Without her asking him to, Dash took the next day off and they spent it together, quietly running errands about town. They dropped off several cartons of eggs at Dash's parents' house and were invited to stay for lunch. In the afternoon, they went down to Main Street, where Matty did a little shopping in the quilt store, Spin-A-Yarn, picking out a beautiful quilt of fall colors for her mom. After that, they wandered around in the wine shop and then she bought a new pair of fall boots at the only shoe store in town. They avoided Frank's because they figured that, by now, many people in town would know about the body and they worried that if they sat down it might look like an invitation for people to come and talk. And neither she nor Dash was interested in talking about what she had found.

She paused outside a closed ice cream store and Dash told her that the young woman who owned it had been attacked several months earlier. She was doing well and a full recovery was expected, but she hadn't been able to reopen her shop yet. The town, it seemed, had pitched in and paid her rent and utilities for six months so she wouldn't lose her business while she healed. Matty thought that sentiment probably wasn't particular to small towns, but she liked the idea of the community coming together to help one of their own. She made a mental note to make a donation herself.

After picking up her car from the clinic, they made their way back to Brad's farm. Evening was settling over the valley and Matty and Dash were out on the patio sipping wine when they saw head-lights turn onto the driveway. Predictably, the dogs were up and barking within seconds, but recognizing the vehicle as Ian's, she and Dash stayed seated until the engine cut out.

Ian was out of uniform and Matty could tell by the look on his face that the news wasn't good. Dash moved to her side as, hand in hand, Ian and Vivi approached them.

"Do his parents know?" Matty asked quietly.

Vivi nodded.

"They're out on Prince Edward Island in Canada right now. They'll arrive in Windsor tomorrow," Ian said.

"And was it suicide?" Matty actually brought herself to ask.

Vivi leaned against the patio railing and lifted a shoulder. "We're still going over the evidence. I'm the ME on the case, but I work with Sam Buckley who runs the lab. Neither of us are prepared to make a call on cause of death yet."

Matty gave that statement a moment of thought. It was strange to think a man could die and that the cause of his death would not be easily known. Oh, she knew it happened on television and in movies, but real life wasn't usually as gruesome, or at least as consistently gruesome, as fiction. In real life, people died in ways that weren't a mystery.

"When? Do you know when it happened?" Matty asked, not really knowing if she wanted to know the answer, if she wanted to know just how long her half brother's body had been left out and exposed.

"Twelve days ago," Vivi answered, her voice quiet. "The same day the man who fell into your truck died," she added.

Matty frowned. "The same day I arrived," she said. "Do you think they are related? Do you know who he is yet?"

Vivi lifted a shoulder. "At this point, we still don't have an ID. But as to whether or not the two incidents are related, we don't have any evidence indicating that they are, but the investigation into Brad's death is still in its early stages. Honestly, I'd be surprised to find out they weren't. Though, how they might be related, we'll have to figure out."

Dash and the others gave Matty the space and time to let the information sink in. For a moment, she stood in the silence. Then she gave a small shrug and a shake of her head. "I guess, well, I'm not really sure what to think. I suppose over the next few days we'll have to sort out what to do with Brad's animals and all that, and I'm really not exactly sure what, if anything, I should be doing, but…" Her voice trailed off.

"When my grandmother died," Matty started speaking again, "we all knew it was going to happen, and by that point, I'd been living with her for over fifteen years. We knew who her friends were, who we needed to tell. She was very clear about what kind of service she wanted and all that. But with Brad, I have no idea and I'm not even sure I'm the one who should have anything to do with it."

Dash reached over and took her hand in his.

Ian wrapped an arm around Vivi who leaned into her fiancé. "You don't have to do anything tonight," Ian said. "Vivienne is still doing her thing and I would imagine, knowing what little I know of Brad from what we took into evidence, that somewhere in the house he left a will, or some kind of document, that will explain what his wishes were."

Matty frowned and dropped her gaze. She'd been through a lot of Brad's files and paperwork and hadn't seen a will, but she hadn't really been looking for one either. "I guess I can see what I can find. He has files in his office, but he also has a room full of documents and other things down in the basement."

"Why don't you start that tomorrow," Dash suggested. "There's nothing to be done about it tonight," he added, looking out for her more than anything. She looked up from her wineglass and met Dash's gaze. For a moment, her breath caught at the emotion, at the caring she saw in his eyes. With a small smile, she squeezed his hand.

"I think that's a good idea. Vivi, Ian," she said, turning back to the pair. "Dash's mom sent us home with a huge lasagna this afternoon, and I have some greens from the garden. Would you like to join us for dinner?"

Vivi and Ian accepted her invitation and the four of them spent the evening like old friends, eating, talking, drinking, and even laughing. That she'd only known them all less than two weeks did not escape Matty's notice, but for the first time she could remember, she let herself go with it. In her life, real friends were forged over years of loyalty and consistency. But on this night, in this quiet place, she let herself believe that time need not always be the arbiter of what is good or real.

• • •

By ten o'clock the next morning it was clear that news had gotten out about Brad's death. Elise, his neighbor, had stopped by and Chen had called, as had a few of Brad's other friends. Matty had called her mother and Charlotte to let them both know what had happened. To say that they weren't happy with her staying in Windsor was a huge understatement.

While Charlotte was concerned about the possibility of Brad having been murdered not half a mile from where Matty was staying, her mother was more concerned about the arrival of Sandra and Douglas Brooks. Matty assured both of them that she would be fine and that, while she was living in the house, mostly because of the animals, she wasn't alone. And as for her father and his wife, well, Matty knew she could handle herself with them. She actually hadn't given their arrival much thought—not real thought—until her mother brought it up.

"Everything okay?" Dash asked when she'd hung up the phone with her mom. He'd taken another day off from his clinic but was still on call for emergencies.

Matty frowned. "My mom is worried about what might happen when Brad's parents show up."

Dash came to her side and propped his hip against the kitchen counter next to where she sat. "Do you think it will be a problem?"

She mulled it over before answering. "I'm not really sure. I know I can treat them civilly, for sure. But this situation is going to be so much more emotionally charged than the last time I saw them. I mean, my god, they just lost a son. Their only child. I really can't imagine what they must be going through, what they must be feeling right now. And then to find me here, well," she paused. "Well, I'm an easy scapegoat given who I am and what happened after my grandmother died, with me inheriting most of the estate and all."

"Do you want to leave?" he asked. "You can always stay with me," he added.

Again, she thought before answering. "I don't think I should leave quite yet. There are the animals that Brad entrusted to me and then, depending on what Vivi finds, the police may need to be here again. I just think that someone should be here to handle things for Brad and I'm not sure his parents would be able, or should even be asked, to do that."

Dash reached over and brushed a lock of her hair back from her face. "That's very fair of you."

She gave a small laugh. "I know." The irony that she was the one who would have to maintain the peace after everything her father had, or had not, done was not lost her. "But again, taking me out of the picture, Sandra and Douglas are two people who just lost their son. They'll need someone to handle the details."

Dash opened his mouth to say something but his ringing phone cut him off. Pulling it from his pocket, he glanced at the number, frowned and hit the answer button.

"Kristen? Is everything okay?"

Matty watched his expression as he listened.

"Whoa, slow down. How long?" he asked. "Left hind?" He waited for an answer. "It's okay, Kristen, I'm glad you called. I'll be right over. Just try to keep him calm until I get there, okay?"

Dash must have received the reassurance he was looking for because he hung up and looked at her with a far-off expression, like he was trying to figure something out.

"Everything okay?" she asked, repeating the same question he'd asked the caller.

He gave a shake of his head and held out a hand. "I need to make a vet call, will you come?" he asked. She nodded and he filled her in as they locked up the house and climbed into his truck.

"That was Kristen, my neighbor to the east. She's a kid, fourteen. Her dad leaves her alone a lot so she has my number in case of emergencies. About a year ago, her dad bought her a horse as a guilt gift and now the horse, Bogey, is tangled up in the fence."

"That sounds bad."

"It can be, depending on how much they thrash around," he answered.

"But something else is bothering you?" Matty pressed. Dash had looked like he was pondering more than just a common problem when he'd hung up the phone.

After a moment, he spoke. "Yeah, it's weird that he's only tangled up on his left hind leg. It's possible he rolled near the fence and rolled into it with that leg, but usually when I see a horse tangled in a fence, it's a front leg or both back legs. It may be nothing, but I'll know more when we get there."

Ten minutes later, they were walking down a hill toward a distraught young girl who was alternately trying to soothe a clearly frightened horse and wave them toward her. As they approached, Dash introduced Matty to Kristen, a waify-looking girl with the biggest, deepest pair of blue eyes Matty had ever seen, offset by Mediterranean coloring and dark blonde hair. Kristen very politely murmured her greeting but promptly turned her attention to Dash who was running his hand down the side of the enormous brown animal as he made his way to the entangled leg.

Matty watched Dash as he made a quick visual examination of the mess, then turned her own eyes to the situation. And cringed. It wasn't just a single wire from a fence wrapped around the poor horse's leg; it was five or six. Even to her, it looked strange, like five or six strands of wire had come unwound from each other and had all wrapped separately around the horse's back leg in various places.

Matty's eyes went to the fence. It was made of heavy gauge wire and constructed much like a rope, which would explain all the different strands. It sure as hell didn't look like it would come apart easily. In fact it seemed like the kind of wire that would require either years of wear and tear to come apart, or opposable thumbs.

"Dash?" she said, calling his attention to her. His eyes looked up, even as his hand stayed on the shaking horse. She made a small gesture to the fence with her eyes, not sure if the situation was as weird as she thought it was and not wanting to call Kristen's attention to it if she was wrong.

But the look Dash gave her told her he was thinking along the same lines.

"What can I do?" Matty asked.

"I brought a tranquilizer in with my stuff," he said, nodding to the box and bucket of supplies he'd unpacked from his truck. "But I'm going to need some wire cutters to get this off."

She turned to head back to his truck but was surprised when Dash stopped her. "Actually, Kristen, can you run up to my truck and get the cutters? They are in the back, on right hand side, fourth drawer down. Matty can stay here with Bogey. She's good with animals and probably doesn't know her way around a vet truck as well as you do."

Not sure what Dash was thinking, she stilled while Kristen, who looked about to protest, finally turned her eyes to Matty.

"Come over here," Kristen said, motioning Matty to her place at Bogey's head. "Talk to him. He's a cuddler and will like resting his nose on your chest."

Matty did as she was asked and as soon as Kristen looked convinced that Bogey was going to be okay, she turned and started to run up the hill, being careful not to startle her horse.

"Dash?" Matty made a silent inquiry.

"I don't want to freak Kristen out, but this looks intentional. I want to get some pictures to give to Ian and Vivi. If they agree, I think someone needs to have a talk with Kristen's dad."

"Once you've taken them, I think you should send them straight over," she suggested. "If Ian agrees and thinks it looks suspicious, he'll want to come over and have a look around."

Dash inclined his head even as he took several pictures with his phone. "That's a good point. When Kristen gets back, why don't you take my phone up to the truck, e-mail them to Ian, and then give him a call. That way we'll know what he thinks before we're done here," he added as he made his way to the other side of Bogey and took a few more photos.

"Do you think this could be related to what happened to Bob?" she asked.

Dash's head came around, and judging by the look on his face, he hadn't considered that.

"Shit."

"It was just a thought," Matty said. "I don't know much about what kind of crime happens up here, but it would just seem weird that there would be two animal-related incidents in such a short period of time, that is, *if* something was done to Bogey."

Dash swore again. "Kristen's coming back. I'll tranquilize Bogey and once he's down, I'll cut him free. Take this," he said, handing her his phone. "Once she's here, go on up and get the photos to Ian."

Matty nodded and slipped the phone into her pocket. A few minutes later she was walking up the hill to the truck, phone in hand, e-mailing the pictures. When she was done, she dialed Ian's number and told him what was going on. After taking a look at the images, Ian wasn't any happier with the situation than they were and was on his way over to have a look for himself.

As Dash made his way back up the hill, Matty was pondering a grumpy-looking sheep in one of Kristen's pastures. Bogey was up and moving slowly behind his owner as they made their way to the small barn. The horse's back leg was bandaged, but at least he was walking with only a minimal limp.

When Dash reached her side, she nodded toward the sheep. "He always look like that?"

The poor thing, covered in wooly dreadlocks sticking out at all angles, looked like it hadn't been sheared in ages. But what was most noticeable was his expression. Matty hadn't known sheep could have expressions, but this one sure looked to be telling them to fuck off.

Dash chuckled. "Yeah. That's Bad-Hair-Sheep. He's too mean

to shear so Kristen just lets him be. What did Ian say?" he asked, turning serious.

She paused then gestured toward the road where they could see Ian's truck making its way toward them. "He didn't like what he saw any more than you did. He says he doesn't know much about horses, but having grown up with cattle, that kind of tangle would have caught his attention, too. Not to mention it happening on the heels of what happened to Bob."

As Ian drove the rest of the way over to them, Matty went silent and contemplated the past two weeks. Despite the events earlier in the summer, Windsor didn't strike her as an area prone to violence—but there had been two deaths and two animal mutilations in her short time there. As a city girl, and one from DC at that, it didn't necessarily scare her, but it did make her wonder just what was going on. Were they all related? Were they all a coincidence? It all just seemed too, well, *odd* was the only word she could come up with, to be unrelated. But then she knew how much Brad loved animals, so how or why he could be tied to someone who could do what was done to Bob and Bogey, didn't make sense.

As if reading her mind, Dash wrapped an arm around her waist, pulled her to his side, and dropped a kiss on her temple. "Ian will figure it out. You have other things to think about right now. Let's just get through this day, through Brad's parents' arrival."

For a moment she'd forgotten—not about Brad, but about the situation. It was much easier to try to solve the puzzle of just what was happening in Windsor than think about the emotional quagmire that awaited her when Sandra and Douglas showed up. Matty nodded.

"How is Bogey?" she asked as they watched Ian climb from his truck.

"Thankfully, not as bad as it could have been. He didn't need stitches, but we cleaned him up good. Kristen will have to keep an eye on him for the next couple of weeks."

That was good news, she thought. At least he hadn't lost any pieces of his anatomy, like Bob, or been permanently injured.

"Dash, Matty," Ian called as he walked toward them.

"Ian," Dash responded and, with a gesture of his head, he began to lead Ian down the hill.

"Hey, Dash," she said, stopping the two men. "I'm going to go be with Kristen. She'll probably wonder why the sheriff is here and I don't want her to worry too much."

"Thanks, that would be great," Ian said, then he and Dash continued down.

Walking into the barn, she spied the young girl leaning against a stall door, arms resting on the top of the lower half, her chin on her hands, staring into the box.

"Kristen?" Matty said, coming closer. The girl turned her head but didn't raise it. "I hear he's going to be okay," she continued as she approached the stall. Bogey was standing but looked a little groggy. His head hung low and he wasn't moving much.

"Yeah, that's what Dr. Kent said, I just don't know how it happened in the first place," she answered. "I mean I'm super careful about that kind of stuff. I turn him out at night because it's cooler and there are less flies, but I'm always checking the fence 'cause I don't want anything to happen to him." Kristen paused for a moment, then a look of guilt crossed over her face. "I guess I just didn't check good enough yesterday and now look at him," she added with a gesture to Bogey, who made a half-hearted attempt to perk his ears at his owner.

Matty sighed internally. On one hand, telling Kristen what was going on in her pasture, that Dash and Ian thought what had happened to Bogey was intentional, would erase her guilt. On the other, it might terrify her.

"Is your dad around?" she asked.

Kristen shook her head. "No, but he gets back today. Flying back from Singapore or someplace like that."

"What time is he supposed to get home?"

Kristen shrugged like it didn't matter. Based on what Dash had told her, it probably didn't, since he would most likely turn around and be off somewhere else in the next day or so.

"I don't know, two or something like that."

"Do you have anyone else who comes to stay with you?"

Kristen wagged her head. "I did, but not after I turned fourteen. Now he says I'm old enough to be on my own. I catch the bus to school and he has someone who comes in and helps with shopping and cleaning and things like that, but mostly I'm on my own."

Matty couldn't tell from Kristen's tone whether she thought this was a good thing or not. In fact, it sounded a bit to her like the girl just didn't care because caring about it, one way or the other, wasn't going to change anything. Matty knew a thing or two about what that felt like.

"Look, Kristen, you should know that whatever happened to Bogey isn't your fault."

That got the girl's attention and Kristen straightened and looked at her. Matty continued. "Ian MacAllister, the sheriff, is here right now, down in your field with Dash. Dash didn't like the way it looked when he arrived, how the wire was wrapped around Bogey's leg, so he took a few pictures and we sent them to Ian. Ian agreed that it didn't look right, so they're down in the field right now, looking into it."

Kristen stared at her for a long moment, her huge eyes blinking as the information sank in. "You mean you think someone was *here* in the field and did this to Bogey on purpose?"

Matty pursed her lips and gave a tight nod.

Kristen's eyes widened and went back to her horse. "But who would do that? Who would hurt an animal like that?"

"We don't know, Kristen, and that's why Dash wanted to call Ian out. Look," she paused, looking for the right words to say to a fourteen-year-old who was, for all intents and purposes, living as an adult. "I don't think you should stay here alone. Not until Dash and Ian sort this out. I know you're not going to want to leave Bogey, but I don't like the idea of you being here alone."

It was clear from the look on Kristen's face that, until that point, she'd been more concerned about Bogey than herself; that it hadn't occurred to her just how creepy it was to have someone coming onto her property.

"But I don't want to leave Bogey," she said.

"I understand that," Matty said. "Maybe we can find a compromise," she added, not wanting to make things worse for the girl.

"We have a compromise," came Dash's voice at the barn door as he and Ian walked in. "Kristen, none of us like the idea of you being alone. I hope you don't mind, but I called my parents and they're going to come hang out with you until your dad gets home. That way you can keep an eye on Bogey but aren't alone. How is that?"

Matty thought Kristen would have done just about anything Dash said, not because she had a crush on him, but because he'd saved her horse. The young girl nodded.

"I'll call your dad this afternoon and fill him in," Ian added.

Matty held her tongue, opting to wait until she was alone with Dash to ask him about what he and Ian had found. She figured they would have already said everything they were comfortable saying in front of Kristen and anything else could wait.

On the way back to Brad's house, the quiet of the truck had an eerie, creepy feel to it, given what had just happened. But even so, Matty's mind wasn't so much on the deed but on trying to sort out why. And so she asked Dash his opinion on the matter.

He shrugged. "I'm not sure why someone would do that. Same way it's not really in my realm of comprehension as to why someone would have cut off Bob's toe. The easy answer, as disgusting as it is, is someone just gets a kick out of hurting animals."

"I know that's the most obvious, but it just seems strange to me. Two animals, in the same small town. Has anything like this ever happened here before?" she asked.

He shook his head. "Not to my knowledge."

She was silent for the remainder of the trip but gave the dogs a little extra love when they arrived at the house. Deciding that she needed to cook a big lunch, just to give herself something to do, she left Dash in the kitchen and went into the office to look up some egg-based recipes online. She'd dropped off dozens of eggs to Dash's mom the day before but had many more just from that morning. Scanning the office for her computer, she frowned. She was pretty sure she'd left it on the desk but it was nowhere to be seen. Acknowledging that she could have brought it upstairs, she turned to head to the bedroom but was stopped by an eruption of barking.

When she and Dash got to the door, they discovered an older man standing beside a white van in the driveway petting the dogs. He was tall and robust but the hunch of his shoulders and the slowness of his movement spoke of his age.

Straightening, he came toward them. "I'm Casper Collins, I heard about Brad this morning and I wanted to come give my condolences. You must be Matty?" he said, coming toward her, hand outstretched.

She took it in hers, nodded, and introduced him to Dash; she wasn't sure what to make of a friend of Brad's knowing about her.

"He told me about you—just a little, mind you," Casper said, returning to the rear of his truck. "He was proud of what you've done with your life, the writing and all," he continued, his voice muffled as he reached into the rear of his van. Coming out with a big box, he ambled back to stand in front of her.

"He said he didn't think he would have survived what you had, let alone succeeded at the level you have. Anyway," Casper said with a vague gesture of his shoulders. "He was a good man and I wanted to bring you some of this," he added, lifting the box just a little.

"What is that?" she asked.

"Wine. My wine, or wine from the family winery," Casper answered. Dash must have realized how much weight the man was bearing at the same time she did and he stepped forward to relieve Casper of the box.

"Wine?" Matty asked.

"Hmm," Casper nodded. "It was a favorite of Brad's, it's actually how we met him all those years ago."

Matty thought about the situation for all of two seconds before making a decision. "Come in for a drink, Mr. Collins. It's a bit early for wine, but I do have some iced tea and, well, to be honest, I didn't know Brad all that well and wouldn't mind hearing a little bit more about his life from one of his friends. That is if you have the time?"

Casper nodded his head in agreement and the three of them made their way into the cool of the house. Dash set the wine down on the table and they headed to the kitchen island. Casper and Dash pulled up stools as she poured the tea.

"I know you and he weren't close," Casper said as she handed him a glass. "Brad regretted it. Understood your hesitance, but regretted it."

"So, tell me about him," she prompted, not wanting to wade into the mess of her familial relationships. "Tell me how you met."

Casper's expression changed and a faraway look, a look tinged with sadness, stole across his face before he spoke. "He came into the winery one day, said he'd had some of our wine at one of the local farm-to-table restaurants. Hard to say why, but he struck up a conversation with my son—it's my son who really runs the place—and next thing I know, Brad is back the next week, and then the next, just helping out with odd chores, things like that. I don't think he wanted to be in the business, but I think he liked the physical work he did for us; it was a lot different than the banking he did to make his money. It also came at a good time. My son's wife had just died and left us with a hole that couldn't be filled. My grandson, Robby, was twelve at the time and he and Brad spent a lot of time just walking around talking about the winery. I think it did Robby good to be able to teach an adult something. Maybe Brad knew that, maybe he didn't, but after that first summer and the next fall, he was kind of a regular fixture at the winery, and often at our dinner table, too."

Matty stroked her fingers along the condensation of her glass. She hadn't known any of this about Brad, and while that didn't surprise her, the sadness creeping into her mind, the sadness she hadn't felt since finding the body, did.

"How old is your grandson now?" she asked.

Casper smiled. "He's twenty, just getting ready to enter his junior year at the University of California in Davis. Brad helped with that, too."

"That's a long way away," Dash commented.

Casper inclined his head. "It is that, but given the school's location next to wine country and the viticulture program they have, Robby didn't want to go anywhere else. He loves the business and didn't want to go to college at all, but when he figured out that wasn't an option, he picked Davis."

"And Brad?"

"Brad helped him get a scholarship. My son, Steve, was called up from the reserves and deployed to Afghanistan last year. He's proud to serve his country, we're all proud of him, but his absence meant hiring yet another person to help out at the winery. With both Robby and my son gone, we've had to bring on more than two extra people, since no one works like family does. Anyway, we were able to afford the out-of-state tuition at first, but then with Steve gone, it was going to be tough to find the money for housing, books, a stipend, travel—all those extra things that college costs."

"It doesn't sound like Robby was averse to working, though?" Matty said.

Casper gave a strong shake of his head. "Not at all. In fact he convinced his department to create a job for him and that was enough to cover his housing costs. He wanted to get a weekend job but we decided he should focus on his studies. He reluctantly agreed with us, though I wouldn't put it past him to be out there working with one of the other wineries on the weekends."

Matty smiled at the tone of bemused pride in Casper's voice. He was proud of Robby, and from what she heard, he had every right to be.

"But the scholarship?" she asked.

"Brad knew someone from his college days who runs a huge

winery, one of the ones that's ten times the size we are. The family is loaded—not from the winery, but from other investments. Turns out they have a foundation to support people in the study of viticulture. I don't think it's really one of those things that a lot of kids go into so a lot of their "scholars" are probably people entering a second career; but Brad talked to them about Robby and, next thing we knew, his tuition was covered. Of course, Brad wouldn't let us thank him or anything, but that was just Brad. He just did things for people."

"And, with housing and tuition covered..." Matty said.

"Picking up the rest of the costs, including the costs for us to go visit him, was something we could manage."

Matty looked down and drew her finger through a bead of water on the counter. The story Casper had just told her about Brad had touched her in a way she hadn't expected. The way her half brother had reached out to help, in his own quiet way, was, well, it was sweet. It was what those in a community should do for one another when they have the chance. Not that everyone in a community could do what Brad had done for Robby, but it just seemed like he'd done what he'd done for the right reasons—not because he wanted his name on a brick or a building. Not the way his mother would have done it.

It also reminded her of the story Dash had told her about the young girl, Meghan, who owned the ice cream shop in town. After listening to Casper, she'd wager that Brad had made a hefty contribution to the fund to help Meghan. She was planning on doing the same but hadn't gotten around to asking Dash about it yet. She was definitely going to do so now, in Brad's name.

"How is your son?" she asked Casper.

He smiled. "Better now that he's coming back. He's in Germany right now, left Afghanistan two weeks ago. He has some leadership things he has to turn over and finish up, but he should be back in time for the harvest."

She smiled at the good news then jumped when the dogs, once again, went into a frenzy of barking madness. She looked at

Dash, who rose from his seat and opened the kitchen door. With a look back at her, he shrugged. "I don't know who it is," he said.

He stayed standing at the door until two women bearing baskets came into view. They were older, Matty would place them in their early seventies, and stylishly dressed. Both had white-gray shoulder-length hair, but one was several inches taller than the other.

"I'm Candy Rose and this is my sister, Autumn," the taller of the two women said. "We heard about Brad this morning. He was a good friend to us so we wanted to drop by."

Matty slid from her stool and beckoned the women inside as she introduced herself and Dash. "Please do come in. This is Casper Collins, also a friend of Brad's. He brought by some of Brad's favorite wine that maybe we can use for the memorial reception, if you think that would be appropriate?" she added, turning to Casper to ask for his consent.

"I think Brad would like that," he answered. Matty didn't miss the catch in his voice.

"He was also telling us how he met Brad," she continued, turning back to Autumn and Candy. "I'm not sure if you know, but Brad and I weren't close. In fact, I barely knew more about him than his name, I'm embarrassed to say."

"Yes, we know all about that," Candy said, handing her basket to Matty while Autumn handed hers to Dash. They shook hands with Casper and then, without asking, pulled out two chairs from the table. Matty smiled as she and Dash set the baskets down on the counter. She wasn't sure what was in them but she could smell cinnamon and chocolate.

"Brad always regretted what happened to you and your mom," Autumn said.

That brought Matty up. "He told you about that?" Dash came to her side.

Candy nodded. "Of course he did. Brad wasn't one to dust things under the rug, so to speak. We were visiting him the day after he got back from your grandmother's funeral."

"And the reading of the will," Autumn interjected.

"And the reading of the will," Candy repeated. "He was on the phone to his mom, who wasn't happy. Anyway, it all came out then."

"I don't think he was very happy about it either," Matty said.

Candy shrugged. "Actually, he didn't seem to care one way or the other. He was sad for his dad because it was so obvious from the will what his mother, your grandmother, thought of him. But Brad's mother's self-righteousness bothered him."

"A lot," Autumn added and Candy nodded. "But, it was Brooks family money and money from your grandmother's family, so as far as Brad was concerned, his grandmother could do whatever she wanted with it."

"That was very generous of him," Matty said, not quite believing what they were saying. Her memories of the months after her grandmother's death weren't so blasé. But then again, in the fleeting moment she thought about it, she hadn't heard much from Brad, just from Sandra and the attorney Sandra and Douglas had hired.

"Bah," Autumn waved a hand in the air dismissing her. "It wasn't generous, it was just the way he was."

"And I think he felt a little guilty for what his mom and dad had done to you and your mom," Candy added.

"Yeah, there was that," Dash muttered beside her.

"Maybe we should open one of these bottles of wine now?" Matty suggested, turning to Casper, who immediately pulled a wine opener from his pocket and made for the box of bottles. "I'm glad I'm meeting all of you, but I won't say it's not strange to meet people who know so much about me when I know nothing of you or even much about the person who connects us, Brad."

Dash and Casper filled wineglasses and when everyone had one in hand, Matty raised hers. "To Brad. While I didn't know him well in life, I'm glad to at least begin to know him now, through his friends—whom I'm happy to have here with me today."

And it didn't end there. Matty learned that Brad had met Autumn and Candy while doing volunteer work with the Catholic church in town. And then Pamela stopped by, a friend of Brad's from the animal shelter he'd donated time and money to. After Pamela, Matty met a woman who finally enlightened her as to why Brad had decided to keep rabbits. She should have guessed; they were rescues from an illegal fur farm. When Elise noticed the cars making their way up the shared road, she decided to come back over with some pictures she had of her and Brad. The photos were taken over a period of several months during which she and Brad had worked together to get his beautiful garden in place. And then Tommy stopped by, the local lead for one of the big international disaster relief agencies—one that Brad had worked through several times, including on his trips to Haiti and New Orleans.

While Matty made a mental note of Tommy's information, now was not the time to bring up her questions for him, questions about Brad's activities in those regions. No, even as more people arrived—and Candy and Autumn's baked goods were spread over the kitchen island and more of Casper's wine was popped open— now was the time to listen and learn and celebrate the person Brad had been. A person she was just now realizing she would have really liked and, even more, respected.

CHAPTER 16

"GET OUT! ALL OF YOU! All of you—just get out!" a voice screeched at the door.

Matty, who had been laughing at a story Elise was telling, turned at the sudden invasion into what was turning out to be an impromptu wake. With so many people, over twenty now, the dogs had ceased barking at every new arrival, so she'd been unaware of the entrance of Sandra and Douglas Brooks until she heard the shrill voice and laid eyes on them standing just inside the kitchen doorway.

Sandra looked livid; her white hair in its harsh bob and her fair skin flushed red added to her sharp look. For a second, Matty could see her point; it did look like they were having a party in the aftermath of Brad's death. On the other hand, if she'd taken even ten seconds to look around, Sandra would have known what they were doing. Pictures of Brad were laid across the table and kitchen island; people were standing around, holding photos up and talking, laughing, and, yes, some were crying. It was so obviously a celebration of his life that any sympathy Matty might have felt toward the woman vanished.

And her father, well, he did what he usually did when it came to Sandra. Nothing. Tall and well dressed with sun-streaked, brown hair that was remarkably free of gray, he stood behind his wife saying nothing. But as Matty watched his eyes, eyes the same blue as Brad's, take in the room and register what was going on, she also noted the redness there and the dark circles underneath.

His gaze landed on her and she took a deep breath. These

people had just lost their son, she reminded herself; there was probably very little in life worse than that.

"Sandra, Douglas," she said, stepping forward. She felt Dash come up beside her in a silent show of support. "This is Casper Collins, a friend of Brad's." As she introduced Casper, he came forward but didn't hold out a hand. "And this is Tommy and Candy and Autumn..." Matty continued until she'd introduced Brad's parents to everyone in the room. "They were kind enough to come and share their condolences, as well as their stories of Brad," she explained.

Sandra's eyes glistened in fury—an anger Matty knew was born of sadness, but there was so much history between the two of them that it was hard to grant her that sentiment. It didn't help when Sandra straightened her shoulders and took a moment to glance at each person in the room, stopping only when her gaze focused on Matty.

"In that case, I just want you out."

Matty had thought that Sandra could no longer shock her, but she had. And judging by the uncomfortable shuffling in the room, she wasn't the only one shaken by Sandra's words.

"Sandra," Douglas said, putting a hand on his wife's shoulder. A small conciliatory gesture that was too little too late by Matty's standards.

"Stop it, Douglas," Sandra shot back, shaking off his hand. "I want her out. If she thinks she can just move into Brad's house, use Brad's things, and, and..." Sandra's voice faltered but Matty knew what was coming next, an accusation that she would be gunning to inherit even more of the Brooks family fortune.

"Excuse me," Albert Redmond, an attorney in town who was also a friend of Brad's, stepped forward. Albert and Brad had been playing chess together for nearly ten years. When talking to the man earlier, Matty had been drawn to his gentle voice and calming manner. With everything that Brad had done in his life, in his community, she suspected he'd probably liked the same things about the lawyer.

"No, I won't excuse you," Sandra spat back with a sharp look at the man. "I want you out," she said, her eyes back on Matty.

For a moment, she wasn't sure what to do. She didn't want to make her guests, Brad's friends, uncomfortable. But she also didn't want to miss the opportunity that had landed on her doorstep, a chance to know her half brother. What she really wanted to do was shake Sandra, get in her face, and remind her that she wasn't the only person who'd lost Brad. But thankfully, Albert stepped in before she'd contemplated that course of action any further.

"I was Brad's friend, but I was also his attorney. It's really not the time or the place to discuss such things, but in this circumstance, I think it might behoove us all to go over the basics."

That brought Matty up short. Ian had said Brad would probably have a will, but she hadn't had a chance to look for it yet, and Albert hadn't mentioned anything so far. Why he would bring it up now, she couldn't fathom. Unless… Her stomach sank. She knew what Albert was going to say and if the color draining from Sandra's face was any indication, she knew, too.

"No," Sandra said, shaking her head.

"Is there a private space we can talk?" Albert asked.

For the first time in her life, Matty looked to her father for direction about what she should do. She didn't want to have the conversation any more than Sandra did, but here they were. Her father gave her a small, sad nod.

"The formal sitting room," she said, gesturing to her left. It was on the other side of the house and could be closed off.

"Then, shall we?" Albert said, taking the lead.

• • •

Dash watched Matty, her father, and Sandra Brooks follow Albert out of the kitchen. He hadn't offered to go with her; whatever was going to go on behind those closed doors was a family affair. But he had given her a small hug of support just before she'd left. He hoped it was enough for her to know he was here for her.

"Well, that explains a lot," Candy said, plopping herself down on a stool and taking a sip of wine.

Dash raised an eyebrow in question at her even as many of the others seemed to murmur their agreement. "What explains what?" he asked.

"Brad," she said. "He never really talked about his parents much."

"Oh, he was never disrespectful," Casper interjected.

Autumn nodded, "He just didn't talk about them often."

"Or when he did," Tony added, "He always seemed a little confused, a little sad."

"Like he wasn't sure what to do with them," Pamela chimed in. "I remember once, we were cleaning out one of the animal pens at the shelter and I made some offhand comment about how proud our mothers would be at our cleaning abilities. I was a complete slob as a kid," she said as an aside. "Brad laughed a little—not the funny kind of laugh—and said his mother would be horrified to see him on his hands and knees scrubbing a floor. I asked him what he meant and he just shook his head and said the only kind of cleaning his mother ever did was making sure the fork and knife lay properly across the plate when she was done with dinner."

As soon as Pamela finished her story a few others jumped in, rehashing pieces of conversations they'd had with Brad about his parents. Dash only half-listened as he kept his eyes on the hallway, waiting for Matty to return.

After about fifteen minutes, he heard the door to the sitting room open and shortly thereafter, Albert walked back into the kitchen. Dash excused himself and made his way toward the sitting room. He found her standing at the front door, the one that was never used but would have allowed Douglas and Sandra to leave without having to walk back through the kitchen. Her father stood in the doorway.

"I had no idea he was going to do that, Douglas," Matty was saying.

"I know, Matty. I know," he replied.

"I don't—" Dash heard her voice catch as he came beside her and took her hand. "You just lost your son, Douglas. I don't want to do anything that will make this harder. I know what Brad's wishes were, but if there is anything, anything, you want or need or, well, just anything at all, please feel free."

"Thank you."

Douglas looked about to say something else, but Matty spoke again. "I can go stay with Dash. I'll need some time to pack up the animals and everything, and I'll have to come back every now and then to check on the cows until we figure out what to do with them, but I'll leave and you can come back and just be here. If you want," she added.

Douglas blinked and lifted a hand as if to pat her on the shoulder then let it drop back to his side. "Thank you, Matty. I think," his voice cracked and he cleared his throat. "I think for now, it's better for us to stay in town, but maybe, maybe after a little while," his voice drifted off and she nodded at what was left unsaid—that after a while, when the shock had dulled, he would take her up on her offer.

"You know where to find me," she said.

He nodded.

"And Douglas," she said as the man turned to leave. "I'm sorry, I'm so sorry for your loss."

Douglas's eyes filled and he bit his lips as if to keep himself from howling in pain. Nodding, he turned and left.

"You okay?" Dash asked, wrapping an arm around her shoulders and pulling her close after they watched the Brooks leave.

She nodded against him and, after a moment of silence, she spoke. "Brad left everything to me, Dash. Well, almost everything. I don't know why. Honestly, I have no clue. He even made it clear that he left me the animals."

"Maybe he knew you'd take care of them," Dash offered.

"Hmm, maybe. I don't know, it just doesn't make sense to me."

"I think a lot of what has happened in the past few weeks probably doesn't make a lot of sense. Starting with him asking you to come up here in the first place. Not that I'm taking any issues with that," he added, dropping a kiss on her forehead.

"Yeah, no kidding," she said then gave a little shake of her head. "Whatever," she added, conceding, for the moment, to the confusion. "Maybe it's just not something to think about right now. Maybe we should just go back into the kitchen and join his friends."

"Matty?" A new voice came from the hall and they both looked up.

"Chen," she said, stepping away. "Mai."

Dash watched as Chen, and the woman he assumed was Chen's sister, Mai, gave Matty quick hugs and handed her a box of something Dash guessed must be food as the scent of honey and cinnamon drifted toward him.

"These were some of Brad's favorites from a small bakery in Chinatown," Chen said solemnly. "We were in New York visiting family when a mutual friend from the university called to tell me."

"Thank you, both," Matty said, taking the box. "Will you stay for a bit? Some of Brad's other friends are here and we're reminiscing about him. Well, I'm learning about him. A little late, I know," she added, her voice drifting off. Dash stepped forward and put an arm around her waist. "Chen, you remember Dash Kent," she said. Then she introduced Dash to Mai.

As Dash shook the man's hand, a bag hanging from Chen's shoulder bobbed forward. "Can I take that for you?" Dash asked as the bag bumped back into place.

Chen gave him a blank look then followed Dash's eye. With a shake of his head, he spoke. "Sorry, I forgot I even had this. I was doing some consulting work while visiting family and I've been carrying it non-stop for two days."

"And he wouldn't be caught dead without it," Mai added with a smile at her brother. "We would love to stay for a bit if it's no problem? Brad has been a friend of the family for years and we'll miss him greatly," she added, blinking away a tear.

"Of course," Matty said with a gesture toward the kitchen.

"But perhaps I can put this down somewhere out of the way?" Chen asked, lifting the bag.

"I'll put it in the office, Matty. You three go on in," Dash said. There was something about Chen Dash just didn't really care for. But as he placed the well-heeled leather bag in the office, a bag that probably cost more than his first car, Dash acknowledged that it was entirely possible that his distaste was rooted in Chen's obvious sophistication. And though Matty didn't seem to care about that sort of thing, Dash couldn't help but think someone like Chen—a professor, a traveler, a wealthy, urban man—would probably fit more into Matty's life—her life in DC—than he ever would.

"Dash?" He looked up to find Matty at the door to the office. "Are you coming?" she asked, holding out her hand.

Dash gave a small smile and reached for her. When her fingers curled around his, he tugged her toward him. She came willingly and he wrapped his arms around her. "You're really doing okay?" he asked, drawing his head back to look at her.

She seemed to think about it for a moment before she nodded. "I am. I think it's good to have everyone here. I'm glad you're here, too," she added.

For a moment, he just looked down at her. He could worry about how they were going to work things out—families, jobs, houses, lifestyles. He could worry about being a small-town guy with a city girl. He could worry about her trust issues and their different backgrounds. There was a lot he *could* worry about. But right then, he was only interested in being there, with her, in that moment.

"I'm glad I'm here, too."

CHAPTER 17

AFTER THE EMOTIONAL DAY OF the impromptu wake, Matty and Dash had tried to spend a quiet evening together, but that hadn't quite worked out. First, her mother had called and insisted on coming up, which, after an hour or so, Matty had been able to talk her out of. Then Charlotte had called and insisted on the same thing. Matty had tried to talk her out of coming up too, but she was less certain of her success with her friend than with her mother. And then even Nanette, Charlotte's mom, had called and offered to make the trip. After that, Dash's parents had stopped by, and though in the grand scheme of things it wasn't a flurry of activity, it was a constant stream of interruptions well into the night.

At around eleven, after seeing his parents to the door, Dash handed Matty a shot of whisky and sent her off to bed. She tossed and turned for a while, until Dash joined her, curling his body around hers, and then she fell into a fitful sleep. A sleep filled with frenetic dreams of Brad, Dash, the earthquake in Haiti, and all sorts of random images. There hadn't been a story to her dreams, as there usually was, just images. And so when she finally woke the next morning, just as the sun was creeping over the hills and shining its light through the window, she still felt exhausted.

Leaving Dash in bed, she slipped into a robe and headed downstairs. After making a pot of coffee, she headed into the office to print up the daily crossword, a habit she'd had at home in DC but had fallen out of since her arrival in Windsor. She glanced around the office and a small frown touched her lips. It looked different, if only subtly so. Her laptop was off to the side and it looked like the cord connecting it to Brad's printer had been pulled loose. The chair was positioned to the right side of the desk, which was odd because all the desk accessories were placed to the left, since that's where she usually sat. Not to mention that she could have sworn she hadn't even seen her laptop in the office the last time she'd looked for it.

She paused in the middle of the room and turned around, surveying the rest of the space. The edge of a piece of paper was sticking out from the closed top drawer of the file cabinet and two of the three pictures on one of the bookshelves had been moved. Taking a closer look at the bookshelves, she thought it was also possible that one of the many binders that lined the bottom shelf was missing. She'd looked through them all during her search of the house but didn't remember how many there were.

"Everything okay?"

At the sound of Dash's voice, Matty whirled around, a little yelp escaping from her mouth as a hand came up to her chest.

"You startled me," she said, letting out a breath.

Dash eyed her then stepped into the room. "Obviously. Sorry, I certainly didn't mean to, but you looked like something was on your mind." He reached out and brushed his palm over her cheek.

She bit her lip and hesitated for just a moment before speaking. But then she remembered this was Dash; if she told him what she thought she was seeing, he would be a voice of reason, a voice of calm.

"It looks different. Just a little off," she said, turning back to the room.

"What looks different?" he asked, coming to her side.

Matty glanced around again before answering. "The room, the things in it." Then she pointed out all the small things she'd just noticed. She watched Dash's eyes sweep the space before landing on her computer. They lingered there for a moment, before returning to hers.

"Remember, Ian, Carly, and Marcus were in here conducting a

search the day you found Brad. Neither of us has really spent much time in here since then," he offered.

She tilted her head in thought. "I suppose things could have gotten moved around when they were in here searching. Or when all Brad's friend were here. I didn't see anyone come into this room, but there were a lot of people and it *is* right off the kitchen."

"That would be my guess, but if you're concerned, given everything that's been going on, we can ask Ian," he offered.

For a moment, Matty considered it. She wasn't one to go running to the police every time someone said "boo," but she also wasn't one to play the dumb victim, like all those horror movie kids who blithely tramp off into the woods when they know an ax murderer is on the loose. But then she thought about all the other things both Ian and Vivi were probably doing to find out what had happened to Brad, all the important things. She shook her head.

"No, it's fine. I'm sure you're right—it's just been a few days since I've been in here so I'm seeing it with new eyes." She stepped over to her laptop and reconnected the printer cord tightly. "I was just about to print up a New York Times crossword, care to join me?" she asked, popping open her computer and keying in the URL.

"As much as I would love to, I have a few clients I need to take care of at the clinic this morning."

She could tell by the tone of his voice that he didn't like leaving her. "I'll be fine," she said.

"I'm done around eleven-thirty and then I have to make a few calls out to some farms this afternoon. I wish I didn't, Matty. I could try and cancel them."

"Don't. I'll be fine," she insisted, giving him a smile. "Elise, my neighbor, was talking about showing me her collection of antique photos of New Orleans this morning. Then maybe I'll go with you this afternoon, if you don't mind the company?"

He gave her a long look and she could see the struggle in his eyes. Finally, he crossed over to her and slid a hand behind her neck. "I don't mind the company and it would be nice to have you along." He looked about to say something else but then seemed to change his mind, dropping a kiss on her lips instead. "Lock the door behind me. I'll grab some lunch and bring it back. We can eat here and then head out. Sound good?"

She smiled up at him. "Sounds perfect."

The dogs made a beeline for the fields and yard as soon as Dash opened the door. Matty followed them all out, stepping out onto the patio behind Dash. Not yet touched by the morning sun, the flagstone felt cool beneath her bare feet. Even so, she could tell it was going to be another hot day as the humid air swirled around her bare legs.

As his truck pulled down her driveway, she waved to Dash and then, in the silence that followed, took a deep breath. She could smell fresh-cut hay and hear bees already buzzing in the garden. Her eyes lifted to the hill and for a moment she stood there, caught between the peace the country seemed to bring her and the knowledge of the violence that had so recently touched it.

She knew she needed to find out what had happened to Brad, what he'd been doing in Haiti and New Orleans and what, if anything, his employer thought he'd been involved in. But somehow, standing there on the patio with the clean, quiet air sliding over her skin and into her lungs, she couldn't bring herself to think about it much. For the first time in a long time, Matty simply wanted to *be*. And so, in quiet, she went back into the house, poured herself a cup of coffee, walked back out to Brad's garden—to the little swinging bench he must have put up at some point—and just sat.

But life wasn't so accommodating and within the space of two hours Lucy had been stung by a bee, one of the cats had deposited a dead mouse on the doorstep, and she'd gotten caught in the wild raspberries trying to toss the thing out. She was propped on the kitchen counter with her leg hanging over the sink, cleaning out the scratches, when she heard a car pull up. Dash's reminder to lock the front door floated through her mind. Quickly scanning the counter, she spied a knife nearby. If worst came to worst, at least she had a weapon.

Then a cooler head prevailed when she realized Rufus and the other dogs weren't barking their heads off. If they were relatively quiet, that meant that whoever had driven up was known to them. And sure enough, within a few seconds she heard Vivi and Ian talking to each other as they came toward the house.

"Come in," Matty called when they knocked at the door.

Vivi stuck her head around the door then stepped into the room. Ian followed.

"Everything okay?" Ian asked, eying Matty.

"Wild raspberries," she responded as she pulled out what she hoped was the last thorn. "Just give me a second, I'm almost done. Help yourselves to some coffee while I finish," she gestured to the pot sitting beside the stove as she rinsed her leg.

"What were you doing in the raspberries?" Vivi asked. Matty told her about her hectic morning as Vivi poured a cup of coffee, handed it to Ian, and then poured another for herself.

"Well, unfortunately, I don't think we're going to make it any better," Ian said, leaning against the counter.

"You have news?" Matty asked, drying her calf. She looked up when neither answered. Vivi wore a small frown and Ian stared at Matty with his characteristic straightforward gaze. "By the looks of it, I'm not going to like what I'm about to hear, am I?"

"It's, well," Vivi paused, her lips pursed this time. "We don't know what it means, but what we found is odd."

"And that is?" Matty swung herself off the counter and looked at the couple.

Vivi glanced at Ian, who answered. "The bullet that killed the guy who fell from the tree and the bullet that killed Brad were fired from the same gun."

Matty blinked. "The same gun that was found with Brad?" she asked, confused.

Vivi nodded. "Yes, but like I said, we don't know what it means."

Now it was Matty's turn to frown. "I don't understand. It seems like that would mean that Brad killed the man in the tree and then killed himself." It was a logical leap to make and, even though it didn't make any sense to her why Brad would kill someone, it also didn't make sense that Vivi was hesitating to see the logic.

Vivi lifted a shoulder. "Normally, that is what we would think, too. But there were some inconsistencies that make that conclusion less certain."

"Inconsistencies?" Matty pressed, taking a sip of her own coffee.

"We found a shoe imprint in the barn from someone other than Brad," Ian said.

"And we didn't find the levels of gunshot residue on Brad that we would normally see on someone who'd recently fired a shotgun," Vivi added.

Matty looked at her visitors, trying to read their expressions, trying to figure out what they were saying. "So, maybe he didn't kill the other man? Or himself?" she asked.

Again, Vivi lifted a shoulder. "We think that either Brad killed him and then killed himself or that there was a third person involved."

"Someone who killed both of them," Ian interjected.

"And framed Brad." Matty mulled the idea over a bit before positing a scenario. "So, maybe the man in the tree saw someone kill Brad and then was killed because he was a witness?"

Ian dipped his chin. "We think that's a possible scenario."

"And then the killer went back and placed the gun in Brad's hand to make it look like Brad had killed himself after killing that man," Matty voiced her thoughts out loud. Yes, she wrote thriller stories, but they were fiction. It was surreal to be having this conversation about real people, real events. Or possible real events, anyway.

"I guess it's a possibility," she conceded. She hated that she didn't know Brad well enough to know if he was capable of murder or suicide. But of the two options Vivi and Ian were considering, she preferred the option where Brad was killed—it sounded harsh, even in her own mind, but she'd rather not find out her half brother was a killer. There were already too many unknowns about him. And despite her own lack of relationship with her father and his wife, it was clear Douglas and Sandra cared deeply about their son and she still wouldn't wish that kind of pain on either of them.

"Did you ever find out who the man in the tree was?" Matty asked.

Vivi nodded. "We actually ID'd him shortly after we last talked about him. The couple who own the property where the barn is located are weekenders and were away on a cycling holiday in New Zealand, unreachable by cell. They called as soon as they got our message and were able to give us a name," she paused to take a breath. "His name was Randy Smeltzer. He is, or rather *was*, a banker from New York but had taken some time off work. He was up here staying at his friends' house while they were away. No one had any cause to think anything had happened to him because he was not due back in New York until after Labor Day," Vivi answered.

Matty frowned thinking how sad that must be, that he'd been dead for several days while his family and friends assumed he was simply enjoying some time off. Not unlike Brad.

"Do you mind if we go through Brad's things one more time?" Ian asked, interrupting her thoughts.

"We'd like to see if we can find any information that would point us one way or another," Vivi added.

For a fleeting second, Matty thought about the pictures and what she'd learned about the people in them. But Vivi had already seen those and Matty had no doubt that if Vivi wanted to recall the names of the people, whether they took a second look at the pictures or not, she would be able to.

Matty nodded. "Of course."

Ian gave a small nod of thanks. "I'll let Marcus and Carly know and they'll probably be out here later this afternoon. I'll come assist, but as sheriff, it's better to have the police in on the search even if it is technically my jurisdiction."

"I may be out with Dash. We talked about running some of

THESE SORROWS WE SEE

his rounds together this afternoon. I think I have an extra key, can I just give that to you?" she asked.

"That would be great," Vivi answered. "I'll probably come along too, in my capacity as a consultant to the crime lab."

Matty set her coffee down and proceeded to test the extra keys hanging by the door until she found one that worked on the kitchen door. She handed it to Ian who thanked her, looked at Vivi, then said his good-byes before walking back to his truck.

Vivi lingered for a moment, placing a hand on Matty's arm. "How are you doing?"

Matty was touched by the concern in the woman's voice. "Hangin' in there," she answered with a ghost of a smile. "It's all a bit surreal, that's for sure."

"I'm sure it is. I've worked with death and violence every day for years, but when it was happening to me earlier this year, right here in Windsor, it didn't feel real. It kept feeling like someone was going to jump out and yell 'You're on *Candid Camera*!' or 'You've been punk'd!' or something like that."

Matty gave a soft laugh. "Yeah, it kind of does feel like that. Especially considering how little I knew Brad and how our lives never touched. Now, I'm living in his house, going through his things, and trying to figure out if he was a murderer or a victim."

Vivi gave her arm another quick squeeze and then let go. "It's tough. If you ever need anything, you know where you can find me. Normally, we'd tell people to let us do our jobs and not do any investigating on their own, but if you think of anything, maybe something you learned living here, don't hesitate to call me or Ian."

Matty let out a little breath. She wasn't sure what she was going to do in the long run about what she'd found out about the people in the pictures, or the visit from bank executive, but for now she held it back. Even as she did, she didn't feel very good about the decision, but she just wasn't ready to cast an even darker shadow over her half brother now that it was possible he was a murderer. It's not that she didn't trust Ian and Vivi, but her long-held prejudice against law enforcement in general was definitely rearing its head. If she had evidence that tended to point toward Brad, she feared it would become the only path they would look at. That was something she definitely didn't want.

"Thanks, Vivi. I know you guys are working hard on this and I know it's got to be hard on the community, considering what happened here with you just a few months ago. If I think of anything, I'll let you know."

Matty thought she saw a fleeting look of disappointment cross Vivi's features, but if it was there at all, it was gone so quickly, she couldn't be sure. They said good-bye and she walked Vivi to the door. She was still standing on the patio a few minutes after seeing Ian's truck disappear down the drive when Dash's truck pulled up.

As if he sensed her need to avoid talking about Brad, he let her know he'd run into Ian and Vivi on his way up and heard the latest. After that, he said nothing more. They made a light lunch together, played with the dogs a bit, and then packed up to make the afternoon's large-animal rounds.

After visiting the third farm, Dash waited until she'd closed her door then turned to her and asked, "Okay, Matty, what's on your mind?"

She blinked at him. "Nothing?" She sounded about as convincing as she felt.

"Bull. I know you well enough by now to know something is going on in that complex mind of yours. I know what Ian and Vivi told me, and I intentionally gave you some space to think about what they said, but there is something else bothering you and it's been bothering you for a while now."

She met his gaze, his dark eyes unwavering on hers, but filled with concern and kindness rather than frustration. And it occurred to her that he was worried about her. He wasn't mad about the fact that she wasn't talking; he wasn't hurt. He was worried. And sitting there in his truck, something shifted inside her. Dash wasn't the kind of man who was governed by his own needs or wants, but by what was right and what was necessary. And right now, he believed she needed to talk, not because he needed to hear what she had to say, but because something was eating her.

She motioned for him to start the drive to the next and last farm. It would be easier to talk while he was driving. After a moment's hesitation, he complied, starting the truck, and pulling out of the farm's drive onto one of the county roads. As soon as they hit the pavement, she told him everything. Some he already knew, but she started from the beginning, with the weird phone call from Brad when she was still in DC, the strange letter he'd left her, the newspaper in the cupboard, the pictures, the visit from Alex Traynor, and the research she'd done on the people in the photos. And the one photo with no identification on it all.

By the time she was done, they'd pulled into the next farm. Dash killed the engine and they sat in silence. Matty watched as the owner of the property emerged from the shadows of a big red barn and started toward them.

"Matty," Dash said. It sounded like he was at a loss for words, and she kind of understood that. She didn't know what to think about it all either.

"I know, Dash. It's a lot. And to be honest, I know I should probably have told Ian and Vivi by now," she paused and then told him of her fear—her probably irrational fear—that the information might sway them to an easy answer, even if it wasn't the right one.

"I've known Ian a long time. He was a Ranger for over a decade before he came back here. I have no idea where he's been or the things he's done—I doubt anyone, other than maybe Vivi, does—but I do know that you don't have the kind of career he had by taking the easy way. And as for Vivi, she started college at sixteen, was a homicide detective with the Boston Police and a county medical examiner before coming here. She's also an FBI consultant and a professor in addition to the work she does for the state crime lab. 'Easy' isn't really her MO either. I think you need to tell them."

Matty looked at Dash for a long moment. In her peripheral

vision, she saw the owner of the farm, an older man in a button-down shirt and jeans, standing by the fence waiting for them, looking unsure about what was delaying them.

Slowly she nodded. "I know. It just feels," she hesitated, searching for the right word. "It just feels *big*, I guess. But I know I need to tell them. I even knew it earlier today when I chose not to say anything."

Dash reached over, picked up her hand to kiss it, then gave it another reassuring squeeze. "We have this call to finish, then we can go home and clean up. You have some time. Sit with it for a while, get used to the idea. We can call them over after dinner."

She squeezed his hand back and gave him a small smile. "You're a good man, Dashiell Kent."

His lips tilted into a grin. "Yeah, well, on occasion, I like to think I can do the right thing."

Matty laughed at his self-deprecation and leaned over to brush a kiss across his lips. "Now, let's go take care of that man's cows before his feet start growing roots."

CHAPTER 18

AFTER THE FARM VISITS, DASH and Matty had gone back to her place to clean up and have dinner, then Matty had bitten the bullet—so to speak—and invited Ian and Vivi over. Now Dash sat beside her, absentmindedly running his fingers over the stem of his wineglass, as he watched his friends take in everything she was telling them.

"This is the only picture with no name on it," Matty explained as she handed a photo to Vivi, who sat across the table from her. Ian, sitting next to Vivi, leaned over to take a look.

Carly, Marcus, and the others hadn't been able to make it to the house that afternoon to search for evidence because of a multicar accident that had required their attention. Dash thought maybe that was a good thing, since, judging by Ian and Vivi's interest, they would've probably wanted to come back anyway, once they'd heard the new details Matty was sharing now.

And he was very glad, though not entirely surprised, to see no censure in either of his friends' behavior when they found out that Matty did, in fact, have additional information that she hadn't shared earlier. Both of them seemed to take everything in stride and focus on the main task at hand, collecting the information Matty had and understanding it in the best way they could.

So far, she'd gone over everything with them, including the visit from Brad's former employer, Alexander Traynor, and her suspicion that there was some kind of issue with one of the accounts or funds that Brad had handled. Then she'd brought the pictures down and walked them through what she'd found out about the subjects. Dash had no doubt Vivi and Ian would be able to dig up more information on them, but what Matty had found was pretty amazing considering she'd only used public search engines.

Right now, they were all examining the picture of the young woman, the only photo with no name written on the back.

"And you have no idea who she is?" Ian asked.

Matty shook her head. "I don't and I haven't seen any other pictures of her around the house, so I'm thinking she wasn't someone Brad knew personally."

"Or someone he knew well," Vivi interjected. "It's possible he might have met her recently."

"Matty, do you mind if we take these?" Ian asked. Dash knew Ian didn't really need to ask. He had a search warrant for the house that just hadn't been executed yet, but it was nice of him to go through the motions.

She lifted a shoulder. "No, go ahead—but if you don't mind, I would like to make copies of them?"

Ian motioned for her to go ahead and both women rose, gathered the pictures, and headed into the office where Brad kept a printer with a scanner.

"Did you know about this?" Ian asked as soon as the women were out of the room.

Dash shook his head. "Not until today. She told me this afternoon." He saw the question in his friend's eyes, but he didn't want to betray Matty and what she'd shared with him about her past. But still, he felt the need to defend her. "Matty had a different kind of childhood. One where law enforcement wasn't very, well, wasn't very good, or effective, or even really around much in a good way. She trusts you and Vivi, but old prejudices—especially those ingrained at such a young age and in such brutal ways—die hard. She just needed some time," he said.

Ian eyed him for a moment then nodded. "She has an edge to her, doesn't she? And I mean that in a good way. Vivienne is tough, but Matty strikes me as a different kind of tough. She's a survivor.

I don't know what her childhood was like, but I can imagine. She's done remarkable things with her life."

Dash couldn't agree more but didn't want to push the conversation any further; he simply nodded. Ian must have sensed his sentiment, so the two men sat in a comfortable silence, sipping their wine until the women returned.

Matty and Vivi came out of the office laughing about something, which Dash took as a good sign. But before she was halfway across the room, Matty's phone rang and he saw her frown as she read the number on the screen. She hesitated for a moment, met his gaze, then motioned with her free hand that she was going to take the call. He nodded as Vivi sat back down at the table.

"Hello, Douglas," Matty said. That got Dash's attention. He felt the tension rise in his body, even as Matty leaned casually against the counter. He was pretty sure it was a ruse; he was pretty sure this conversation wasn't one she wanted to be having.

"Her dad," Dash said as an aside to Vivi and Ian. They probably already knew, but they seemed to sense something was going on, so he reminded them, with just those two words and his tone, how complicated the relationship was between father and daughter.

"How are you?" Matty asked then paused as, presumably, Douglas answered. "Yes, I can only imagine how you must be feeling… No, I hope I don't ever have to go through it, too," she said, her eyes rising from the counter to meet Dash's. "I can't imagine what it would be like to lose a child," she added.

She waited a few more moments in silence and Dash could hear an occasional muffled voice filter through the phone. He had no idea what Douglas was saying to his daughter and Matty's face was worryingly blank.

"How's Sandra?" Matty finally asked, then waited again as she listened to Douglas's answer.

"You have an appointment to talk to the police tomorrow?" Her eyes moved to Ian, who gave a short nod. "Good, I'm glad to hear that," she said. "Marcus Brown, the deputy chief, is a good guy and Carly Drummond has also been involved in this situation since the beginning." She paused again as Douglas must have asked a question. "Yes," she answered. "The sheriff has been involved and he's good at his job, too. And if it makes you feel any better, his fiancée is a former Boston Police homicide detective and a medical examiner. She also works for the FBI and the state crime lab. Windsor might be small, Douglas, but there are good, smart people here," she finished.

Dash caught hints of smiles from both Vivi and Ian. He often dealt with people's perceptions of a small-town vet—which weren't usually complimentary—and imagined it was probably even worse for small-town cops. He also figured that whether or not a cop—or vet—was good or bad had more to do with the person than with where they lived.

"I'm not sure, Douglas," Dash heard Matty's voice, bringing his attention back to her. "Marcus and Carly are going to be here at the house tomorrow going through a few things and I may be out... Yes, I understand, of course you can come by. I'm just not sure I'll be here, but please, feel free."

Dash watched Matty cut off a sigh before speaking again. "Yes, you can call me. As to the rest, well, let's just take it one day at a time." That seemed to mollify Douglas a bit, and after another moment, she ended the call and rejoined them at the table. She didn't say anything when she sat down next to him but did take a large sip of her wine.

Dash took her hand in his. "Everything okay?"

She bobbed her head. "I guess. He wants to spend some time with me. I know I'll probably sound selfish saying this, considering he just lost his son and all, but I'm just not sure I'm ready for that. As his daughter, I know I'm not ready, but as a human being, it seems cruel to deny him some comfort."

"You don't have to do anything you don't want to," Vivi said. "At least when it comes to your relationship with your dad," she added, ever practical.

"He doesn't know any of what you've told me today, about the second victim, does he?" she asked Ian.

Ian shook his head. "No, we were waiting to see if we found anything today, but since we didn't get to look through Brad's things this afternoon, we held off. Mr. and Mrs. Brooks know we're investigating and they know we haven't ruled the death anything other than suspicious at this point, but they don't know any more than that. Marcus will walk them through everything tomorrow," he added.

Matty sat in silence for a long moment, absentmindedly twirling her wineglass between her fingers. Bob wandered into the room, took a look at everyone, then turned and wandered out. A few seconds later, Dash heard the Lab climbing the stairs. Since Matty had moved in, all the dogs had taken to sleeping in the master bedroom rather than the kitchen where Brad had relegated them. Dash was about to let a small smile touch his lips as he thought of the changes in the house in just the short time since Matty's arrival, but the sudden tightening of her hand in his brought him back.

"Matty?" he said, concerned.

Matty's eyes met Dash's then traveled to Vivi before landing on Ian. "She is going to blame me," she said.

Ian frowned. "Who is going to blame you?"

"Sandra. If there's any possibility that Brad was murdered, she is going to try to blame me," she explained.

"That's ridiculous," Dash said instantly.

Her eyes swung around to his. "Is it?" And he remembered her telling him about what had happened with her grandmother's estate, and then there was Sandra's spiteful behavior at the house the other day.

"And why would she think that?" Vivi asked, leaning forward and resting her elbows on the table.

Matty cast Dash a look, silently asking him to intercede, so he did. "For a few reasons. First, Sandra hates Matty because she is a living reminder of her husband's infidelity. And then there is the fact that, when Douglas's mother died, she left the bulk of her estate to Matty rather than to Douglas or Brad. And last but not least, Brad left his entire estate to her, too."

"I had no idea he was going to do that," Matty jumped in.

"Of course you didn't," Dash reassured her as he shot Ian and Vivi a look communicating just how ridiculous it would be to suggest otherwise.

"I…" Matty paused, shook her head, then took a deep breath. "Honestly, it was probably more of a surprise to me than anyone else. I didn't know Brad *at all*. We never talked, never met. At least not more than once or twice. I still can't fathom why he left everything to me."

"How much are we talking about?" Ian asked. Dash frowned at his friend. He knew Ian had to ask, had to understand what kind of motive Sandra might say Matty had; but he didn't like traveling down that road.

Matty lifted a shoulder. "I don't know what he has left of the trust my grandmother left him because she did leave him something, just not what she left me. I also don't know what his personal financial situation was. But I can tell you that when he received the trust, there was somewhere around twenty-seven million in it."

Dash almost choked. She hadn't been kidding when she'd said she was set for life, as were probably many generations after her. If Brad's portion of his grandmother's estate was only a fraction of what Matty had received, he couldn't begin to guess what she was worth.

Ian's eyes shifted to Dash. "I take it you didn't know you were courting an heiress?" His sardonic tone poked fun at Dash's obvious surprise.

Dash shook his head and Ian let out a little chuckle.

"Don't be mean to him," Vivi said, bumping her shoulder against her fiancé. "It's not every day a man finds out the woman he's dating could buy the town he lives in," she added.

"I don't mean to be crass," Matty said, "and I appreciate you all making light of the situation rather than taking it as potential motive, but I just want to be clear about a few things, Ian."

Ian, ever the sheriff, leaned forward—all business now. "Twenty-seven million is a ton of money," Matty said. "And I know Sandra will use that against me. But you need to know a few more things. Not things that would give me more motive, but things that will counter her arguments—arguments I know she will make."

She paused to take another sip of wine, then a deep breath, and spoke. "As for the money, I have a lot of my own. Twenty-seven million isn't anything to laugh at, but I think my entire net worth is somewhere close to one hundred thirty million, between the properties and other assets. Another twenty-seven million isn't going to change my life all that much. Brad also asked that I donate half of his estate to charities."

Dash blinked. The fact that twenty-seven million probably wouldn't change her life was an astonishing statement.

"Did he specify which charities?" Vivi asked. Her eyes darted to Dash for a moment before returning to Matty.

"No, and I can't believe he didn't. He was involved in a lot of things, from animal rescue to disaster relief. But he left it up to me. It's actually not even a requirement, but he made the request in his will that I consider it. Of course I will—I'll probably give his entire estate away—and I already have a good idea of some of the causes he would have liked me to consider, but it still surprises me that he trusted me that much, that with everything that went on between our families, he placed that responsibility in my hands without really having any idea what I'd do with it."

"Maybe he knew you better than you think?" Ian suggested.

Again, Matty shrugged. "I'm not sure how he could, but regardless, that's the story with the money."

"What else?" Vivi pressed.

"I arrived in town on the day you said both Brad and the other man were killed. I'm not sure what their actual times of death were, but if you need to track my whereabouts, I was driving up here from DC. I made several calls on the drive—on my Bluetooth," she clarified when Ian's eyebrows went up. That small diversion brought smiles to everyone for just a moment.

"I called my agent at nine in the morning from somewhere

north of DC and then my mom about an hour after that. And then, just as I was coming into Windsor, I was on the phone with my friend Charlotte. You should be able to track those calls if you need to. I'll give you whatever permission you need to look at my phone records."

"And what time did you get here?" Vivi asked.

Matty frowned. "I think it was around two o'clock in the afternoon. Actually," she said, drawing her head back as she seemed to remember something. "When I pulled off the Taconic, I passed the gas station and I saw the two of you talking," she smiled, pointing to Dash and Ian. "I remember because you both looked so unlike the dressed-up suits I see all the time in DC."

Vivi laughed, "They do, don't they."

Ian shot her a look.

"Hey, I happen to like the rugged small-town cop look," Vivi added with a grin as she leaned over and curled her arm through her fiancé's. Ian looked at her for a moment and Dash recognized the look in his eyes. He was pretty sure it was the same one he got when he looked at Matty. He squeezed her hand.

"I remember that day," Ian said. "Yeah, two sounds about right. I had Rooster, my dog," he said to Matty. "And we were talking about the upcoming pancake breakfast and who was going to be back in town for the event."

Dash chimed in as his memories were jogged. "It was definitely around two—when I left you, Ian, I came straight up here because Brad had scheduled a two-thirty appointment."

Ian nodded. "That's good to know—thanks, Matty for providing the information. I don't think we'll need to look into it, but if Sandra pursues you as a potential suspect, we'll be ahead of the game."

Matty glanced back and forth between Ian and Vivi. "I," she hesitated. "I know I should have said something sooner about all this," she continued with a sweeping gesture to the pictures, "and thank you for not berating me for that. But I just didn't want to make things worse for Brad. I didn't know him, but it seems like he was a good guy. I think we both paid for the sins of our parents, so to speak, when it came to any relationship he and I might have had, and I guess maybe I was just trying to make amends to him for not taking the olive branch I think he tried to extend when he was alive. He called a couple of times, but I just never..." Her voice trailed off. "Did you ever find his phone?" she asked suddenly.

By her tone, Dash knew she was remembering the many frustrated calls she had made to Brad in the past few weeks. None of which were efforts to extend a truce between them and the regret rang clear in her voice.

Ian glanced at Vivi, who reached across the table and laid her hand on Matty's free one. "We did. It was on him when he died. And as to the rest, you told us now, so now we can put what we've learned in the context of what we already knew and we can also use it to inform where we look from here. It would have been good to know all of this right away, but despite everything, he was family and sometimes we do funny things when it comes to family."

Ian raised his hand and rubbed it up and down Vivi's back, as if to give her reassurance, and Dash knew why. The serial killer that had killed so many women, the man they'd caught earlier in the year, had been like a cousin to Vivi, someone she'd known her entire life.

Dash gave Matty's hand a reassuring squeeze. "I second what Vivi said. Now that they have this information, they can use it however they need to. So," he said, releasing Matty's hand and rising, "I don't mean to be a killjoy, but I have an early morning tomorrow and Matty is planning to come with me, so we should probably think about bringing this night to a close."

Taking Dash's cue, everyone else rose as well. It was true, he and Matty did have an early morning, but more importantly, he thought she needed some downtime. She wasn't a woman used to sharing and she'd had to lay a lot out on the table today. Not just what she'd found out about Brad, but also her relationship with her father and the reality of just how tense her interactions with Sandra could be.

She was also dealing with the very real possibility that Sandra would try to point a finger at her for Brad's death. There wasn't a shadow of a doubt in Dash's mind that Matty was not involved, and it looked like Vivi and Ian agreed, but still, knowing that her father's wife might make the accusation, and that her father would be caught in the middle, couldn't be easy for Matty.

A few minutes later, after saying good-bye to Vivi and Ian, Dash followed Matty up the stairs. By unspoken agreement they said nothing and crawled into bed, finding a quiet kind of comfort in each other.

• • •

A powerful wind blew Matty's hair across her face as she stood on her patio watching Dash drive away. They'd spent most of the morning together, driving from farm to farm, meeting Dash's clients and handling all sorts of matters—from shots for cows and sheep to emergency stitches on one of the local performance horses. They'd also stopped for lunch at Frank's Café in town and had even done a little bit of comfort shopping—well, at least she had. She'd picked up another beautiful quilt at the store on Main Street, this time for Nanette. Now Dash was off to handle his afternoon appointments at the clinic and she was going to spend her time alone cleaning the house and writing.

Carly and Marcus had been searching the house while she was out. Judging by the car in the driveway, at least one of the officers was still present, so it wasn't a surprise when the kitchen door popped open behind her.

"Oh, hi, Matty," Carly said.

"Hey," Matty answered with a smile. She might have met Carly under bizarre criminal circumstances, but she liked the woman. Quick to assess both of the situations and just as quick to start dealing with them in an efficient and business-like way without being too uptight or tense, her easy-going and attentive manner conveyed a confidence that put Matty at ease.

"Are you close to being finished in there?" Matty asked.

Carly nodded. "I just put away the last of the files."

A gust of wind came up and blew Matty's hair into her face again. Carly's shorter hair stayed in place and Matty took a moment to envy the woman's blonde curls. It wasn't that she disliked having long hair, but it could get a bit unruly, especially in the wind and in any weather that wasn't seventy degrees and sunny with no humidity.

"Want to join me for a glass of iced tea or something before you leave?" Matty offered, moving toward the door and out of the wind. "I don't know what is up with this weather, but this wind is going to make me crazy."

Carly laughed. "Thanks, but I need to get back to the station and keep an eye on things. There's supposed to be a storm system moving in. I doubt there's much flooding up here since you're on a hill, but you may want to make sure you have batteries and flashlights and things like that."

"Is it going to be that bad?" Matty asked, her hand on the door. She'd noticed the change in the weather, of course, but being a city girl, and one who lived in DC where most of the power lines were below ground, losing power had never really been something she'd worried about.

Carly shrugged. "It's hard to tell right now. Summer storms can grow or collapse pretty fast, so it's always good to be ready just in case."

Matty thought that was good advice and made a mental note to do as Carly suggested. They said good-bye and she retreated into her house just as her phone rang. Glancing at the number she smiled, it had been a few days since she talked to her mom, it would be good to hear her voice, if not fend off questions about Dash. Actually, as she thought about it, between Brad's death and the appearance of Dash in her life, Matty was kind of surprised her mother hadn't just shown up. Like a lot of mothers, there was nothing her mom wanted more, other than the happiness of her daughter, than grandchildren.

"Mama," she said as she entered the kitchen. She wasn't sure what she had expected after walking into a house that had just been subject to a thorough search, but it was in the exact same condition in which she'd left it, which was kind of nice.

"Matty, how are you?" her mother responded.

"I'm good. It's been an interesting trip, that's for sure," she answered and then filled her mother in on what had happened in the past few days, including the possibility that Brad had been murdered. She sat down at the desk in the office as she talked and watched the wind whip the trees back and forth outside. Her mother made occasional, appropriate sounds and when Matty was done talking, Carmen did exactly what her daughter had been expecting.

"Mija," she said, her voice serious and her accent touching every word. "I think I should come up there. Charlotte, well, she too is worried."

Matty sighed. "I'm fine Mama, really. I'll call Charlotte next and touch base with her, too."

"Someone was killed not one hundred feet from where you are living, in the middle of nowhere. I don't like that you are alone."

"It was more like a quarter mile from where I am and I'm not alone all that much." She caught herself too late; she'd walked right in to her mother's trap.

"You are not alone much? Then you are spending time with that boy, Dash. If you are spending that much time with him, I think I must come up and meet him."

"He's a man, Mama, not a boy," she responded.

"Mathilde."

Matty sighed again. "Now just isn't a good time." She did not want her mother showing up when Douglas was in town or Sandra likely on the warpath to declaring Matty a suspect. She hadn't heard anything from Ian, and Carly hadn't mentioned anything either, but she would be more surprised if Sandra *hadn't* accused her than if she had. And Carmen Viega was a very different woman now than she had been when Sandra Brooks ran her out of the house all those years ago.

"But this boy, he is special, no? Different?" her mother pressed.

For a beat, Matty thought about lying to her mother—saying no, Dash wasn't special. But as much as she didn't want to talk about it, she also didn't want to belittle her relationship with Dash. Not only did she not want to demean her relationship, there was also the fact that Dash *was* different and her mom, who loved her and had given her so much in life, deserved to know.

"He's a *man*, Mama, not a *boy*," Matty repeated, more to tease her mom than anything else.

"Mathilde."

Matty bit back a laugh at her mother's predictable response. She could almost see Carmen sitting at the kitchen table, coffee in hand, rolling her eyes at her daughter.

"Yes, Mama, he is special. And yes, prepare yourself, because I *would* like you to meet him. But now really isn't a good time. Both Douglas and Sandra are in town, and to be honest, I don't want to deal with having all of you in the same town at the same time." Matty decided not to mention that little issue of a possible murder accusation.

Her mother made a small sound on the other end of the line that gave Matty next to no indication of what she was thinking. "It's very quick, no?" she said.

Matty was relieved that Carmen hadn't picked up the conversation thread about Douglas and Sandra, but the concern in her voice as she asked about Dash gave Matty pause. It didn't sound disapproving, but she didn't really sound excited either. And then it came to her and Matty felt like she'd been smacked in the face with the true sentiment behind her mother's concern. Carmen herself had been swept up by Douglas Brooks all those years ago. And though Matty knew her mother didn't regret having had her, she was not oblivious to the destruction and pain her parents' brief relationship had caused in the lives of many people. That it had turned out okay in the long run for most of them was good, but there were years her mother had suffered for what had happened in that whirlwind moment.

"Mama, I'm not getting swept up in this relationship," Matty said in all seriousness. She wanted her mom to know she wasn't throwing caution to the wind. "Dash and I aren't doing anything dumb and we're taking things as they come. Yes, it's moving faster than any of my past relationships, and yes, Dash *is* different than the others, but I'm not going to lose my head over this. You don't need to worry about that."

Her mother was silent for a moment, then Matty heard her let out a little laugh. "No, Mija, you mistake my hesitance. You are not the girl I was when I met Douglas," she said, reading her daughter's mind. "You are thirty-two, educated, successful. You have a career of your own, money of your own, friends, and a very different kind of life. I was twenty-one when I met your father and a new emigrant. I spoke little English, was poor, and had no support other than a distant cousin in Connecticut. No friends, no family, no money," she repeated. "You are a very different woman, Mathilde. I do not worry about you getting 'swept up,' as you say. Truly, what I worry about is that you *won't* let yourself get caught up in something, or someone."

Okay, that *wasn't* what Matty had expected. "Mama?"

Her mother sighed. "Our life in your early years wasn't easy, Mathilde. It was the best I could do—"

"And you did a great job," Matty interjected.

She could hear the smile in her mom's voice. "Thank you, Mija. But it was not easy and you did not learn to trust because there were so few to trust. And you did not learn to see the joy because there was so little of it where we lived. We couldn't care about people, because if we did, it was used against us. We had to be cautious in everything. We had to doubt and we had to protect ourselves—physically and emotionally—to survive. *That* is what you learned when you were little."

"Mama?"

"You are a remarkable young woman and I know I don't have

to tell you how much I love you, but things that are sometimes easy for other people do not come easy for you because of how you grew up. I lived there with you in the Bronx, but my childhood, when I was a girl, I was very happy. I grew up with a loving family, a big family. There was much laughter, and while there was not much money, there was much love. When I left for the states, they cried and did not want me to leave. And then when I got pregnant, I could not afford to go back. But I tell you this, because even though I lived in the same world as you when we were in New York, my memories of my childhood, of how people could and should be with each other, were still strong. I *knew* there was a different way of life because I had lived it. I couldn't provide that for you, Mathilde, and I know it has impacted you—in ways that I see and, I'm sure, in ways that I don't."

For a moment, Matty was speechless. Her mother very rarely spoke of her family in Puerto Rico. By the time they'd had money to go back and visit, her mother's parents had both died and each of her siblings had moved away—her brother to Los Angeles and her sister to South America. Matty had met them each once, but just as her mother's poverty had kept her from her family in the early days, her subsequent wealth had had almost the same effect later on. Her brother and sister had both seemed uncomfortable during their individual visits to the DC mansion and neither had expressed any interest in building a relationship with Matty afterward. She knew her mom kept in touch with each of them, regularly, but it was only over the phone or e-mail, never in person.

But now, aside from her mother's insight into her family, Matty was struck by how accurately her mother had, to put it bluntly, hit the nail on the head. Carmen had just hit upon the very issues Matty had been struggling with ever since she'd met Dash, issues she'd even discussed with him. All along, Matty had assumed that her mother was like her—that she struggled with the same questions. But she'd been wrong. The way they'd lived in the Bronx was all Matty had known at the time, but for her mother it was just a role she'd had to play to survive; it hadn't become a part of her the way it had become a part of Matty.

Quietly, Matty responded. "You're right, Mama. It did impact me in ways that I am just beginning to realize—just beginning to deal with and confront."

"And this boy—this *man*," her mother corrected herself with a small laugh, "he is helping you, no?"

Matty thought about Dash. About his quiet way. About his insistence that she not back down from her own fears and his confidence that she could overcome them. She thought about the way he pushed her just enough to challenge her but then backed off to let her think things through. And she thought about the way he quietly listened to her stories, especially those about her childhood, and didn't judge or overreact. He didn't want to *fix* her, but he wasn't going to let her hide from, or behind, her past either.

"Yes, Mama, he is helping," she said softly.

Her mother let out a long breath. "Then I am glad and I will be happy to meet him. Perhaps after Brad's funeral?" she suggested.

Matty nodded to herself. "Yes, Mama, I think that would be a good time to come up."

Feeling drained and exhausted when she ended the call, Matty stared absently at the floor for a long moment. It hadn't been too long of a talk, but it had packed a lot of emotional punch and left her with a lot to think about. She had never given much thought to her mother's life before she'd come to the US because the move itself, in both good and bad ways, defined so much of Carmen. Her mother's comments had not only opened Matty's eyes to the fact that Carmen's childhood experience was different than her own, they had echoed so much of what she was already feeling, or becoming aware of, through her relationship with Dash. She had internalized so much of what she had experienced in her youth in a way that, until recently, she hadn't even acknowledged. And it wasn't that she thought her life would take a one-eighty if she really tried to understand her childhood, but maybe understanding it could help her live the kind of life that seemed so easy for Dash—the kind of life she was beginning to think she might want.

She put on a kettle of water, mulling over the scary reality of what it would mean to talk about her childhood and acknowledge the ways it had affected her in adulthood when she was startled by the jumping and barking of the dogs. They'd been lying peacefully about the kitchen just moments before, and with the wind, she hadn't heard the car that was now obviously pulling into her drive.

Glancing at her watch, she frowned. She knew it wasn't Dash because his afternoon appointments didn't end until five. But thinking it might be Carly coming back to pick something up, she walked to the door and peered out.

To her dismay, Douglas was climbing out of his luxury sedan, his shoulders slumped and his movements sluggish. His face still carried the look of shock she'd noticed a few days before, but now it was tinged with a deep, unfathomable sorrow.

He closed the car door and made his way to where Matty stood in the kitchen doorway. She hesitated when he stepped up onto the patio, then moved aside and opened the door, silently inviting him in.

"Thank you," he said quietly as he came inside. Perhaps sensing the grief that enveloped her father, the dogs stayed quiet and nearly still. The kettle whistled and Matty returned to the stove to shut the burner off. Pulling out a mug for herself, she gestured to Douglas, asking if he would like to join her. He shook his head then cast a look around the kitchen as if he wasn't sure what to do next.

"Have a seat," she said. He sat down at the kitchen island and watched as she made her cup of tea.

She sat on a stool across from him. "How are you?" she asked gently.

Douglas tilted his head, his eyes still downcast, but didn't give her more of an answer than that.

"Did you meet with the police this morning?"

His eyes came up and another look of sorrow crossed through

them. "Yes, we did. Sandra went home, back to Connecticut, after we talked to them. Since they aren't," his voice cracked and he paused for a moment to clear it. "Since they aren't releasing Brad's body until they are done with the investigation, she wanted to be home, near her friends."

"And you?"

Douglas's eyes drifted away. "Our social circle is hers. It should come as no surprise to you, Matty, that I don't have many friends of my own. Besides, I wasn't quite ready to leave yet. It doesn't, it just doesn't feel right," he added.

Matty had nothing to say to that, so she simply sat and sipped her tea in silence. Douglas sat across from her, tracing patterns on the countertop, his eyes fixed there.

After several minutes, Douglas cleared his throat. "I don't," he paused again then looked up. "I know it's too late, Matty. I know I can't change the past and probably not even the future. I'm not a very good person. I'm weak and I've led a passive life, letting everyone—letting Sandra—make all the decisions, define who I am and what I am. It's been so long since I made a decision for myself, I'm not even sure I know how anymore. And even if I did, I suspect no one would take me seriously since I've never done it before."

Matty set her mug down and watched Douglas as he looked away, hiding the glimpse of shame she'd caught in his eyes.

Keeping his eyes averted, he continued. "At this point in my life, there's only one good thing that's left." Douglas turned his eyes back to hers, "You. And I know I have no right to even claim that," he added.

He didn't, but Matty was never one to kick a man when he was down. Besides, despite who he was, despite everything that she and her mother had gone through because of his cowardice and weakness, she wasn't unmoved by the despair she heard in his voice. It was as if he believed he'd had no will or ability to change anything; that everything in his life, all his past sins, even those of omission, were so overwhelming that he didn't deserve anything other than what life threw at him. It didn't escape Matty's notice that this attitude, too, was a sign of weakness, but given that he'd just lost his son, she didn't feel the need to point it out.

She took another sip of tea and listened to the wind gust against the house. "Where are you staying?" she asked.

Douglas looked about to say something else, then answered her question, "The Tavern. It's downtown."

Matty nodded. "And how long do you think you'll stay?"

He managed a small shrug, "I don't know. As long as they are still investigating? Until I feel like I can leave," he added.

She had nothing to say to that so they lapsed back into silence. After several more minutes passed, Douglas put his hands on the table and pushed himself up. Matty, following his lead, rose as well.

"I guess I should be going," he said.

"Is there anything here you'd like to take with you? Really, Douglas, I'll take good care of everything, I don't want you to think otherwise, but if there is something you want, I'd like for you to have it."

For a long moment he just looked at her with his sad, blue eyes. "Maybe a picture, if he has any?" he finally said.

She thought for a moment and then remembered an album she'd seen downstairs. Excusing herself, she jogged downstairs and quickly located what she was looking for. It was the one she'd found several days ago that was filled with images of Brad, Douglas, and Sandra over a period that looked to cover Brad's high school and maybe early college years. Returning to the kitchen, she handed the album over to Douglas.

"I found this the other day. I think you'll like it," she said. He took the album and flipped it open to the first page. She watched as his eyes filled. Blinking back the moisture, he closed it and, with a cracking voice, thanked her. She nodded and walked him to the door.

He was about halfway to his car when she called out. "Douglas?" He paused and turned. "There's a storm coming," she shouted over the wind. "Be safe."

Again, he looked at her for a long moment, before nodding.

"You, too, Mathilde. You, too," he replied. Then, through the gusts, he made his way to his car and drove off.

Feeling inexplicably sad after the visit, Matty reentered the kitchen and knelt down to give Bob a good rub, hoping that seeing his happy face would make her feel better. And for a moment, it did. But still, the rest of the afternoon was somber as she alternately worked on her book, picked up a bit, and mulled over what to make for dinner. The house was silent except for her movements, the occasional sounds of the dogs moving about, and the frequent gusts of wind. She found herself gratefully sinking into the peace, using it to soothe and calm the emotions that had been drummed up by her conversations with her mother and with Douglas.

As evening fell, Matty found herself at the desk in the office, staring out the big, picture window, thinking of nothing in particular—especially not her latest book, which sat almost complete on the laptop in front of her. She was watching one of the cows make its way toward the barn when she noticed the unusual color of the sky.

She frowned. It looked green.

Glancing at the clock, she noted that it was close to five—Dash would be coming back soon, but it was too early to be quite so dark. Her frown deepened as she continued to stare at the sky, not quite sure what to make of it. She was fascinated by the color, a hue she'd never seen before that looked slightly sinister.

Lost in thought, Matty jumped when, simultaneously, the dogs started barking and a radio came on. Shaken by the sudden onslaught of noise, she was momentarily confused. Why was the radio on? And *where* was it?

Hoping that it was Dash the dogs were barking at, she rose hesitantly from her seat, a little freaked out by the radio going on by itself. She followed the sound and realized it was coming from the kitchen. Pausing at the kitchen door, she tentatively looked around the room, wondering if whoever had come after Brad—*if* someone had come after Brad—might be back.

The kitchen appeared empty and she was about to step in when the radio, what it was actually reporting, registered in her brain. At the same time, the patio door slammed open and Dash came charging in. His eyes scanned the room until they landed on her, still standing in the office doorway trying to grasp the situation.

"Matty! We need to get down to the basement. There's a tornado alert in the county and one has already touched down just north of Riverside," he exclaimed, coming toward her. She felt like she was in an alternate world, the reality of what was going on just skirting the edges of her comprehension. She'd read about tornados, donated quite a bit to the recovery after they'd hit Joplin, Missouri, but she'd never been anywhere where they actually occurred.

"Matty, come on," Dash said, grabbing her arm and dragging her to the stairs. That brought her out of her fog.

"The dogs, Dash?" she asked, suddenly frantic.

"Are they all in the house?"

She nodded.

"Then call them and they'll come with us." He was pulling her closer to the stairs.

"But the cats?"

"Trust me, the cats will take care of themselves, so will the cows. They'll go where they feel the safest."

"What about the chickens and the rabbits? We can't just leave them out there, Dash," she pleaded, knowing in her heart that it was ridiculous to care about them so much when the situation could turn deadly at any given moment. But still, she couldn't bring herself to be so callous as to disregard them; there'd been enough bystanders in her life, enough people who'd sat by and watched terrible things happen, that it was hard for her to consider leaving behind animals she had promised Brad she'd take care of.

"Matty," Dash said, his tone of voice trying to reason with her.

And then something unexpected happened. Maybe it was the stress of the past few days or the emotional conversations with her mom and Douglas, but her eyes welled up. Dash froze.

She bit her lower lip. "I'm sorry, Dash. Just ignore me—it's been a long day. Let's get down to the basement room. We'll be safe there and there's even a bed and a bathroom if we need to stay the night." She took a step toward the stairs and Dash stopped her.

"Find some cardboard or tape and cover the windows. I've only seen them from the field, but if I remember correctly, they aren't very big so it should be a quick job. Then find a place to put the rabbits. There are too many chickens for me to carry, but I can bring the rabbits back for you."

A single tear fell. "I swear this isn't normal for me, Dash, and I don't want you to risk your life for the rabbits—"

He cut her off with a quick kiss then turned and started jogging away. "If there is a bathroom downstairs, the tub or if there is an enclosed shower, would make a good spot for the rabbits," he called back. And then he was gone.

Matty stood for a moment before a gust of wind hit the house, rousing her into action. She hurried down the stairs and tackled first things first. She found some duct tape, emptied a few of the boxes that held Brad's files and used the cardboard to tape over the windows. It wouldn't totally protect them from flying glass, but it would help. She was just tearing up some paper she'd grabbed from the storage area and dumping it in the tub when she heard Dash coming down the stairs followed by a clattering of doggy toenails.

Within seconds, he appeared in the doorway. It must have started raining because he was soaking wet. His shirt was plastered to his body, his hair flat against his head, and his jeans, darkened with water, clung to his thighs. And in his arms were two wet bunnies.

She motioned him over and he gently placed the rabbits in the bathtub. They scrambled around, their feet trying to catch purchase on the ceramic tub, then finally settled down.

"Thank you," she said, wrapping her arms around him, heedless of the cold soaking through from his wet clothes. His arms came around hers and he rested his cheek on the top of her head.

"I'm glad I got them in here before things turn too bad," he said. "Rabbits are more delicate than people think. They should be fine, but they are wet and I can't vouch for how they are going to handle the sudden change in location."

"That's okay," she said, still leaning against him. "I know it's totally irrational, but I just couldn't stand the thought of leaving them out there. Not when they are dependent on me," she added. She felt Dash take in a deep breath and let it out before he spoke again.

"Want to tell me what happened today?" he asked gently, resting his cheek on her head.

It didn't surprise her that he hadn't missed, or forgotten, the reference she'd made earlier about the long day she'd had since he'd dropped her off. And whether it was the events of the day, or the current situation, or even the possibility that she was actually "growing up," the thought of really just laying everything on the table didn't seem too scary.

She pulled away and inclined her head. "Yes, I will, but I want to make sure we're set for what's coming first. I fed the dogs already so they should be set for the night. I don't have anything for the rabbits to eat or drink, will they be okay?"

Dash nodded. "They'll be fine for the night. This storm system shouldn't last more than six or seven hours so, if we're still awake when it's over, we can either take them back outside or bring them food if we feel they need it."

Matty glanced at the rabbits, who seemed to have settled down. She was glad they were there, glad they were safe, and though she still didn't get the point of pet rabbits, knowing they were rescues and guessing at what kind of life they'd had before Brad had taken them in did soften her toward them.

"I don't have any food for us," she commented as they moved toward the main room of the basement.

"I'll be fine for a while," Dash said. "Like I said, this system shouldn't last too long. Don't get me wrong, it could do a lot of damage in a short amount of time, but provided we don't get caught in the direct path of a tornado, within a few hours we should be able to venture upstairs for food."

She considered this, considered the fact that he had way more experience in this type of situation, and simply nodded. "Why don't you take off your wet clothes so they can dry?" she suggested, gesturing with her hand toward the heating vent. She figured as long as they had power they could turn the heat on and dry his clothes. And even if they didn't have heat, she had no doubt that the two of them could stay warm, if needed, tucked up under the quilts lying on the big bed.

Following her gaze to the bed, Dash began pulling off his wet clothes. Matty took them as they came off, turned on the heat, and laid them over the vent. Down to his boxers and white undershirt, he climbed into the bed with Matty and they curled up against each other, listening to the wind, with the dogs scattered around them on the floor.

"Your parents?" she asked, suddenly remembering that the universe consisted of more than just her and Dash.

"I spoke to them just before I arrived," he answered. "They were already set up in their cellar and ready to wait it out like the rest of us."

She let out a little sigh of relief.

"Now do you want to tell me about your day?" Dash prompted as the lights flickered. "Wait, do you have flashlights?" he asked first.

Matty nodded against his chest, where she lay with her cheek against him. "In the side tables," she answered as the lights flickered again and then went out. It wasn't all that dark for a basement, or at least on a normal day it wouldn't have been. But between the clouds and the small, covered windows, the room fell into a sort of a dusky stillness. "Do I need to be worried about pilot lights or anything?" she asked before answering Dash's first question. She could feel him shaking his head.

"No, we'll check everything once the power comes back on; but for now, it's just you and me and no technology." *So talk to me* was the unspoken end of that sentence. So she did.

The siren at the volunteer fire department had gone off not

long after the power had died and a few phone calls had come in on their cell phones from concerned family. But still, despite these interruptions, despite the storm raging outside, they talked. They talked for several long hours in the dark—about her, about him, about life in general. She told him about her conversation with her mother, about their different childhoods and how those childhoods influenced how each of them had internalized their experiences in the projects. And that led to more conversation about just what her life in the projects had been like—what it had been like, on a day-to-day basis, to live and survive in the part of the Bronx she'd come from.

Then she told Dash about the visit from Douglas and how she'd realized she no longer felt any anger toward him. Oh, she didn't particularly *like* him, but when she thought about Douglas, her overall feeling was one of sadness.

Dash told her about what usually happened when tornados hit, which they didn't do often—only a few times in his life. He talked about the destruction and then the cleanup that would be needed in the next several days. Thankfully, no one had ever been killed in a tornado locally, and they both hoped that record would stand.

Hours into their time tucked away in the basement, the storm seemed to ease. It was nighttime by then, so hard to tell if the skies had cleared through the blocked windows, but Dash got up from the bed and cautiously pulled back one of the cardboard window coverings.

"I can see the stars," he said.

Matty let out a small sigh of relief and they made their way back upstairs, followed by the dogs. Though it was late in the night, neither had eaten dinner, so Matty began putting a light meal together while Dash called family and friends, checking in on everyone.

As she gathered the ingredients for omelets, she gave a moment of thought to the time they'd just spent downstairs. She *could* feel vulnerable if she thought about, if she thought about everything she'd told Dash. But the truth was, she felt strong, she felt settled, and she felt sure—not necessarily sure of the future, but sure that she had done the right thing. It was the right time and Dash was the right man.

"Everyone all right?" she asked when he hung up from his last call.

He wagged his head. "More or less. As far as we know no one has been killed, but at least one tornado touched down not far from the thoroughbred farm where Trudy works, where we went the other day when I delivered that foal," he reminded her. She nodded, remembering the birth.

"And we know another one touched down just north of town," he added.

"What about your parents and Kristen? Was her dad in town? Is she okay?" she asked.

Dash smiled. "My parents are fine. They actually went and got Kristen after I talked to them. They weren't sure if her dad was around, and apparently he's not, so she spent the last few hours with them."

Matty shook her head. "What is his deal? I don't know the man, I hardly know Kristen, but it seems extreme to continually leave your fourteen-year-old daughter on her own."

Dash agreed with her as they sat down to eat. "I barely know him myself. He pays his bills on time and I've only seen him maybe a handful of times. I know his wife, Kristen's mom, died when Kristen was five and he's an executive with an oil company, but other than that." A shrug completed his sentence.

Matty thought the situation seemed awfully sad, maybe because she could identify with an absent father. But then again, she didn't know what was worse, a father completely out of the picture or a father that flitted in and out of the picture at will.

"So, cleanup will start tomorrow?" she asked.

Dash nodded. "Yes, but we should try to get as much sleep as possible now. If any animals were hurt, I'll have some calls coming in tonight."

Matty hadn't really thought of a vet being on call like other doctors, but of course it made sense, especially in an emergency situation. They finished their meal in companionable quiet and then, even though the storm was over, opted to be safe and head back downstairs to the most protected part of the house. After curling up in bed, they didn't talk much more; the first call came not long after they'd finally fallen asleep.

Dash was already up and moving toward his now-dry clothes, even as he answered his phone. Half asleep, Matty listened to his side of the conversation. She woke more each second as it became clear through Dash's questions that something had happened up at Trudy's farm. Knowing how close a tornado had come to them and the number of horses they had, she couldn't even begin to fathom how spooked the animals must have been and what they might have done. At least she hoped it was something like that, rather than any injuries resulting from a direct hit of the storm.

Thinking of Trudy and her daughter Mara, Matty pulled back the covers and made to rise just as Dash finished the call.

"You don't need to come," he said, buttoning his shirt.

"What happened? It wasn't Mara's little foal, was it?"

Dash had disappeared into the bathroom to splash cold water over his face but popped back out to answer her question as he dried himself off with a small hand towel. "No, both Trudy and Mara are fine, as are the barn help they have and Mara's foal. Two of the broodmares are in distress and Trudy's afraid they are going to miscarry."

Matty frowned, she'd never heard of a horse miscarrying before. Then again, everything she knew about horses she'd learned in the last few weeks.

"What does that mean?" she asked, her feet hanging off the bed.

Dash came back into the room and sat at the end of the bed to pull his shoes on. "Well, for the owner it could mean a huge financial loss. The mares are top producers for him and the babies come from stallions that the owner paid well into the six figures to breed to the mares. But more importantly, if the mares lose the babies, they may also lose their own lives, which is what we really want to prevent. Hopefully, if we can get them stabilized, we can save both; but if things go bad, we'll be focusing on saving the mares."

"I'll come with you. Trudy may need help with Mara or something," she said, rising.

Dash walked over to her with a smile curving his lips. "I appreciate it, I really do. But I suspect this will be the first of many, many calls tonight. I'll probably even call in some favors from some out-of-area vets that don't usually serve this region but will at a time like this. You should stay here and sleep," he added.

She frowned. "And be useless? I'm not very good at 'useless,' Dash."

That made him chuckle. "I hadn't noticed," was his sardonic reply. "But seriously, if you want to help, and I know you do, there will be tons of cleanup tomorrow. And neighbors will be checking on neighbors—people may need help getting to doctor appointments, that kind of thing."

"Things where I can actually be useful," she said, still not loving the idea of sending Dash out into the night, but seeing his point.

He nodded. "Yes, things you'd be very good at. I have no doubt my mom will be in the thick of it. Why don't you get some rest? When you wake up, text me and I'll call my mom, or you can call her directly."

Matty thought this over for about a second then nodded. It just made more sense to go where she would be the most useful; and keeping Dash company, as appealing as it was, probably wasn't the best use of her energies.

Dash bent down and kissed her. "Thanks, now get some rest. Or actually—before you get some rest—do you happen to know if Brad had a chain saw?"

She blinked at Dash. "A chain saw?"

Dash nodded. "I keep a small handsaw in my truck, but if there are trees down on the roads, I'll need something more powerful."

Matty thought for a moment. "I'm not sure if there is a chain saw, but he does have a lot of tools in the garage."

Dash motioned for her to stay in bed, saying he'd check the garage on his own, then gave her one more kiss before heading up the stairs. She heard his boot-clad feet on the floor above her and the kitchen door opening then closing. When she heard the key turn in the lock, she lay back down, pulled the covers up, and thought about just how much her life had changed since she'd answered her half brother's call.

A few minutes later, she heard a chain saw rev, run a minute or so, and then go off. Figuring Dash must have been testing it to make sure it worked, she smiled, imagining him wielding the tool. Then it really hit her what he might encounter out there—not just downed trees, but possibly downed power lines and flooding, as well. And if the rest of the area had lost power, too, there would be no streetlights in town, no working traffic lights. Quickly, she grabbed her phone and, not wanting to distract Dash but not wanting to keep silent, she texted him a short message telling him to be safe.

His reply, "Always. Go to sleep," made her smile. After a few moments, she cuddled down into the blankets and let the warmth lull her back to sleep.

CHAPTER 19

MATTY WOKE UP JUST BEFORE dawn. Even though her body was still sleepy, she roused herself—she knew the day would be long and, depending on the destruction from the storm, emotionally difficult. The dogs jumped up as soon as she threw the covers off and she remembered that they hadn't been out since the evening before. They were probably both hungry and in need of a bathroom break. Lucy, who'd jumped onto the bed sometime after Dash had left, cocked her head and started to bounce from side to side.

Although Lucy put on a good show, Matty went to check on the rabbits first. They seemed content to be hanging out in the tub, but she knew they too would need food and water soon. She pulled on her clothes from the day before figuring she could shower and change into something clean once she'd taken care of the animals and done a check of the property. At some point in the night the power had come back on and when she walked into the kitchen the clocks were all blinking at her.

Not wanting to let the dogs out without first checking things outside, she pushed past them and locked them inside as she stepped out into what looked like just another beautiful summer day. If branches hadn't littered the fields behind the house or mud caked the gravel driveway, there would have been no indication of what had happened less than twelve hours before.

As she headed for the chickens, she pulled out her phone to text Dash, then called his mom to arrange for a time to meet. Her plans were set by the time she reached the chicken coop and the chickens, in all their chicken glory, looked completely oblivious to everything that had happened. They sat on their perches in their coop and looked at her as if to ask what she was doing up so early. Their vacant little stares made her laugh as she opened the coop to let them out into their garden area. One by one, they rose, made a few clucking noises, and ambled down the ramp.

Matty collected the eggs to add to her ever-replenished stock, then swung by the rabbit hutches to make sure the cages were in good condition before she brought the animals back out. The gardens looked beaten down, but nothing seemed to have been pulled from its roots and the cows were already back to grazing in the field—assuming they'd ever stopped. With everything looking a little worse for wear but safe and in decent repair, she headed back to the house and let the dogs out.

All five went tearing in different directions. She watched them for a moment before stepping back inside and filling their food bowls. At the sound of kibble hitting metal, all the dogs were back inside within seconds and in such an ecstatic rush that they nearly knocked her over, even as she laughed at their behavior.

Once all the animals were taken care of and back in their rightful places, including the cats who had each made an appearance at feeding time, Matty grabbed her own quick breakfast, showered, and changed into jeans, sturdy shoes, and a long-sleeved shirt, then climbed into her car and made her way into town to meet Mary Kent.

The roads weren't too bad. A couple of large, downed branches had turned two-lane roads into one-lane roads in some places, but the few drivers she encountered between her house and downtown Windsor were cautious and conscientious—no one wanted to cause any more problems than the community was already faced with.

As she pulled into town, she grabbed a parking spot in front of Spin-A-Yarn and walked the rest of the way to the central meeting place of the cleanup volunteers. Mary had given her directions and told Matty she would meet her there. She wasn't sure what to expect, had never been involved in anything like cleaning up after a tornado, but Mary had assured her she would be much needed.

When she reached the meeting spot, a parking lot on the north end of Main Street a few doors south of the police station, she was momentarily taken aback by all the activity.

A large tent had been erected, giving shade and shelter to the volunteers and coordinators. A generator was running and she saw both Rob, from The Tavern, and the infamous Frank, handing out coffee and bagels to anyone who asked. A few firemen were partaking of the donations at tables scattered throughout the space.

Matty knew that the firemen had probably been on the job for hours, and though she could see fatigue showing through in a few of them, most of them looked more interested in wolfing down their breakfasts and getting back to work than taking a break.

"Matty."

She turned to her right and saw Dash's mom coming toward her. To Matty's surprise, Mary enveloped her in a hug then stepped back.

"I'm glad you're okay and made it through the night," the older woman said.

"And you too," Matty responded. "Now, tell me what I can do," she said with a sweeping gesture of her hand encompassing the tent. There were a number of people on phones, some bent over what looked like maps, and several going through boxes.

"We're pretty covered here, but I was hoping you might be able to head out and check on some of our seniors that live alone? All the churches in town have given us lists of the seniors they provide services to and we've all added anyone else we might know that probably should be checked up on. You'll have to be in the car most of the day, but it would be really helpful."

"And I can help, too, Mrs. Kent, if you like."

Matty spun at the voice and saw Kit Forrester, the author Vivi had introduced her to, walking toward them. Matty smiled. "Kit, it's good to see you."

"You too, Matty," Kit answered as she, too, stepped forward and gave Matty a hug. "I'm glad you all are okay."

"Kit, dear," Mary said, also greeting her with a hug, "it would be lovely if the two of you could go together. It's always better to travel in pairs. Now, come with me," she said, directing them to a table.

After reviewing the list with Mary, Kit and Matty spent some time looking at the map of the county and selecting a route. Once they felt fairly confident in how they should proceed, Matty followed Kit to her Land Rover and they plugged the first address into the GPS.

Thankfully, the weather that day was cooperative. The heat of the previous few weeks hadn't returned, and though the storm had cooled things off, it wasn't too cold either. Which was good because most of the people they visited still didn't have power. Several of the folks were just fine and happy for the visit, but not in need of anything. Some were in need of food and a few needed their prescriptions filled. To the best of their ability, Kit and Matty worked with Mary over the phone to get everything done that needed to get done. They also made notes on property conditions so that later, when all the vital recovery work was finished—fallen trees removed from roads and power restored—volunteers would be able to go back and help clean up yards and gardens and make minor repairs.

They'd reached everyone on the list by about one o'clock, so Matty and Kit returned to the volunteer tent to help Frank and Rob serve food and coffee. Vivi and Ian stopped by in the late afternoon to check in and Matty and Kit shared a cup of coffee with Carly just as the sun was starting to set. It was a long day, but people were buoyed by the fact that there were no fatalities. Everything else they could deal with.

She and Dash had touched base several times. One of the two pregnant mares at Trudy's farm had miscarried but he'd managed to save the mother. The other mare had settled down and looked to be holding on to her foal. As for other calls, there were several animals that had gotten caught in fences when they'd panicked, a few dogs and cats with cuts and scrapes, and the worst was a partial barn collapse at one of the local dairy farms. The farmer had lost several cattle, but Dash had joined in with the farm hands to clear the rubble and had been able to save most of those left trapped.

As she headed back home, looking forward to a hot shower and long night's sleep, she dialed Dash's number on her Bluetooth.

"Matty." She could hear the fatigue in his voice.

"Hey, how are you?" she asked.

It took him a second to answer. "Tired, really tired. A lot of good people have been through a lot today."

"I know. Is there anything I can do?" She turned left and crossed over the railroad bridge.

"Thanks, but no. I think I'm good. I have one more call I need to get to, then I want to check in with my folks."

"Want me to have dinner ready?"

He sighed. "I wish I could come over tonight, I really do. Believe me, very little sounds better than that right now. But I need to restock the truck with supplies. Most of the things are at the clinic, but I also have some stuff at home. I'm tempted to let it be, but if I don't get to it this evening and I get another call tonight and I'm not ready…" His voice trailed off.

"You do what you need to do, Dash," Matty said. She'd miss him tonight, but she understood that he needed to be stocked up on supplies. He sounded so tired that she would rather he just stay home once he got there and get a few more minutes of sleep. "Just let me know if I can do anything to help."

"Thanks, Matty, I appreciate it, I really do. I wish—"

"I know what you wish, but go take care of yourself," she said, cutting him off. He didn't need to feel guilty for not spending one night at her house. "I'll see you tomorrow. I'll probably be back at the volunteer center, so just give me a call when you wake up."

He paused then let out a long breath again. "Okay, will do."

She smiled to herself. "And be safe," she added.

She heard the answering smile in his voice. "Always, and you too. Sleep tight."

They ended the call just as she pulled onto the road that led to her house. As she drove past her neighbor's house she was relieved to see the lights on and Elise moving around inside. The yard looked picked up already, and though Matty knew it would be neighborly to stop by and check, she decided that Elise looked safe and well enough that tomorrow would do.

She drove on and pulled to a stop in front of her house. Her house. It was weird to think of it like that now. It really was *hers*. Not just a place she was staying.

With that thought bringing back memories of her half brother, she climbed out of the car and let the dogs out. As they foraged and gallivanted, she called Douglas. She knew from Rob that her father had weathered the night just fine, but Douglas had called earlier in the day to check on her. She hadn't answered the phone, but rather texted him that she was fine.

She kept the conversation short then called the dogs in. Phoning both her mom and Charlotte as she took care of the evening feeding for all the animals, she was done with everything she needed to do in a short amount of time. Showering and crawling into bed, she thought about her day; she thought about what it was like to help the community recover, about the senior citizens she'd met, about her conversations with Kit and Carly. It had been the long, exhausting day she'd known it would be, but when she finally closed her eyes, a feeling of contentment rested easily on her shoulders.

• • •

Dash was beyond exhausted when he walked into Frank's Café. He'd stopped by the volunteer tent, and though it was still buzzing with activity, his mom had gone home and Frank had moved operations back to his regular location after the power had been restored. Dash called and checked in with his folks as he walked the short distance to the café. He was pretty sure Frank was suspending the no-cell-phone rule, but Dash didn't want to take the risk since he desperately needed a cup of coffee, so he hung up before opening the door to the empty café.

"Dash," Frank said, looking up from cleaning the espresso machine.

"Frank, I'm glad you're still open," Dash said as he approached the counter.

"I'll be open for a while," Frank said with a shrug. Dash eyed the man. Despite his surliness, Frank was committed to his community.

"Have any coffee left?" Dash asked.

"For here or to go?"

"For here, if you don't mind. I'd like to sit down for a while before I go by the clinic to restock."

Frank poured a big cup as they talked about the injuries to the animals Dash had seen throughout the day, but by the time Dash sat down at one of the tables for two, Frank had disappeared into the back, leaving him to sit alone in the quiet café.

He was almost done with his coffee when a man he didn't recognize walked in. It wasn't as though Dash knew *everyone* in town, but this man, with his pressed khakis, button-down shirt opened just so, and sports jacket, just didn't look like he fit in. Not today, especially. Dash frowned and wondered if he was a reporter. He knew a few had been in town throughout the day, but while the tornados were big news to people who lived in Windsor, with no fatalities, most of the media had wandered off by early afternoon.

"Excuse me," the man called, stepping up to the counter. Frank came out from the back of the café, wiping his hands on a dishcloth.

"Can I help you?" Frank asked.

"I hope," the other man said, pulling out a piece of paper. "I'm looking for this road," he said. Dash had almost tuned the man out, but when he mentioned the name of the road, the same road Matty lived on, his ears perked up. He turned his eyes back toward the counter.

Dash saw Frank's eyes glance briefly at him. "Can I ask why?" Frank said.

"I've been trying to reach my fiancée all day and I'm getting

THESE SORROWS WE SEE

worried, she isn't answering her cell. I live down in DC and she's up here attending to some family business. I finally decided to drive up and check on her."

Dash frowned.

"Did you try using a GPS?" Frank asked.

The man gave an annoyed sigh. "Of course I did, and my staff did, too, but we can't seem to find this exact road."

Dash knew it was because the road was technically private and not on most maps, but anyone who'd been in town for any length of time knew the road. There were a number of them like that in the area, along with several roads that had legal names, names required for 9-1-1 access, but that everyone referred to by a different, historic name. It was all part of the charm of living in a rural part of the country with a long memory.

Frank cast another glance at Dash. There were only two people who lived on that road, Elise, who was in her eighties, and, now, Matty. Chances were slim that Elise was engaged to this man, who couldn't be more than forty, from DC.

"Doesn't sound like much of a staff," Frank replied gruffly, in true Frank style.

Dash saw the man's eyes narrow. "Look, I just need to find this street. I'm a congressman and I don't have much time to waste, I actually have work I need to do. But I'd like to find my fiancée first. So, can you help?"

Dash watched Frank eye the congressman and imagined a few choice words the café owner was probably biting back—Frank was not the kind of man to be impressed or swayed by a person's position—especially not that of a federal official.

Frank picked up the dishcloth he'd laid on the counter and began wiping his hands again as he turned away. "Nope, good luck," Frank said and walked away without looking back.

The man stood there for a moment, gawping as if he'd never had someone turn his back on him before. Since he was a congressman, Dash doubted that was actually the case.

Finally the stranger turned to Dash. "Do you know the road?" he asked.

Dash stared at him for a long time before shaking his head. Finally, he allowed the crush of emotion he'd been repressing since the man had first mentioned his fiancée to surface. His stomach fell and his heart thudded heavily in his chest. He managed to keep his emotions in check as the man left, then he let his head fall into his hands, too shocked to actually do or say anything. Or even think coherently.

"He might be lying," Frank said, back at the counter.

Dash looked up.

"He's a politician, every time he opens his mouth he's probably lying," Frank added.

Dash appreciated the support, but he didn't know what to think. He rose from his seat, murmured a thank you as he placed his coffee cup on the counter, and walked out in to the clear, dark night.

On autopilot, he made it to the clinic, restocked his truck with the supplies that he needed, then headed home. After adding what he needed from the supplies he kept in his barn, he made his way into his dark house. Not bothering with the lights, he took a shower in the blackness, the moon providing enough light to see what he was doing, then crawled into bed. And lay awake for a very long time.

CHAPTER 20

MATTY AWOKE TO ANOTHER CLEAR morning. She'd slept in enough that the sun was shining brightly in her room, causing her to squint when she finally opened her eyes and saw five sets of doggy eyes staring back at her. Her own eyes traveled to the clock and she sighed. Once again, it was long after their usual breakfast time.

A few minutes later, she padded downstairs, let the dogs out, and went through the morning routine of feeding all the animals, collecting eggs, and doing the myriad of chores that had become second nature to her over such a short time.

She texted Dash when she came back from the coop, letting him know she was up and asking him to call her when he had a chance. Then she called his mom to check in and see what needed to be done for the day. The cleanup was being handled and was under control, but Mary asked Matty if she would mind helping some of the locals get ready for the pancake breakfast that was scheduled for the following day. Power had been restored to most of the county, and given how hard the firefighters had been working over the past two days, everyone involved felt strongly that the event, which was a fundraiser for them, should go ahead as planned.

Matty readily agreed and even offered to bring more eggs, which Mary accepted. After getting the specifics of when and where she should show up to help, she hung up and, after eying her property, launched into some of her own cleanup.

The sun was hanging high in the sky several hours later when she stood on her patio, frowning to herself as she looked at the field behind the house. The gardens, those that were planned and planted by Brad, were mostly cleaned up now, but the field still looked somewhat sloppy and she wasn't sure how to approach picking up the small branches and twigs strewn across the large area.

Lucy caught her eye as she came trotting down the left side of the hill, her tiny, almost non-existent tail wagging. Matty smiled at the sight then blinked as something reflected off the hill, casting a sharp light into her eye.

Surprised by the sudden flash of light, Matty stepped back. Glancing around the field where the light seemed to have come from, she scoured the area, looking for the source. When she saw nothing, and nothing flashed back at her, she took a step forward, back to her original position. Moving her head around, she caught the flash again.

Curious, she called Lucy to her side then headed in the direction of the object. The storm had turned up some soil and wind-blown branches had gouged small trenches in places. She carefully made her way to where she thought the light had come from, looking down, searching the whole way. And when she found it, when she found what she was looking for, a wave of unease swept over her.

Not one to jump to conclusions, even though her gut was telling her something definitely wasn't right, she knelt down to take a closer look. And when her eyes confirmed what she'd suspected, her stomach roiled.

Lying in the dirt, the textured handle caked in mud, was a switchblade. It lay open, the blade remarkably clean considering it had obviously been buried or, more likely, carried in the wind and rain and dumped near the house. Matty didn't dare touch it, not because she was afraid of knives or unfamiliar with switchblades. But because in the hinge, right at the base of the blade, she could see fur. It was darkened with dirt, but there was no doubt in her mind that it was Bob's fur she was seeing.

She looked up and glanced around her, as if she might see who had deposited the knife there a few weeks ago. Seeing nothing, she weighed what to do next. After a moment's thought, she simply pulled out her cell and called Ian.

Ian was in the middle of dealing with an accident out on one of the busier state routes, but promised he would call Carly and Marcus and have them come over. So she found a stick, which wasn't hard, and stuck it straight up in the ground near the knife to make it easier to find it again when the officers arrived.

It wasn't too long before a car drove up, only it was just Marcus inside, without Carly.

"Everything okay?" Matty asked when he stepped out.

He inclined his head. "Carly's out directing the cleanup of an old oak that fell across a road early this morning. Thankfully, no one was hurt. People were cautious yesterday, but now we're going to see the weekenders coming up to check on their houses. Not that they're bad drivers, it just puts more people on roads that aren't completely functional yet," he said. "So, what did you say you found?" he added.

She crossed her arms and a flicker of doubt crossed her mind. What were the odds she would find the knife that was used to hurt Bob? But if she had? Maybe it was related to Brad and maybe it might help give Vivi and her team at the lab something to go on.

"I think I found the knife used to cut off Bob's toe," she said.

Marcus gave her a flat look; one that was meant to hide his thoughts, but didn't.

"I know, it seems weird to me too," she said and then proceeded to tell him what she'd found and how she'd found it. He asked her to show him and, rather than walking back up, she pointed him to the stick, clearly visible from where they stood.

She watched Marcus make his way toward the marker. When he arrived at the spot, his hands went to his hips and his gaze dropped down to look at the switchblade. After a few minutes, he looked around at the ground and Matty suspected he was looking to see if there were any footprints or any other indication of how the knife ended up where it had. But with the storm, she knew he would find nothing and, after a moment, he fished something out of his pocket and dropped down closer to the ground.

About three minutes passed before he started walking back toward her, carrying the knife in a sealed evidence bag.

"I can't say for certain that you're right, but it would surprise me if you weren't," Marcus said when he stopped in front of her.

"I can't decide whether I want to be right or not," she answered.

One side of his mouth tilted up into a smile and it occurred to Matty that Marcus Brown was a good-looking guy. She'd put him at about her age, with dark brown hair, cut very short, that was offset by a pair of light brown eyes. She wasn't attracted to him at all, but the fact that she hadn't even really noticed until now that he looked like he could have just stepped out of a J.Crew catalog—if he were wearing something other than his uniform—was a bit befuddling and made her think about Dash.

"Have you seen Dash today?" she asked Marcus suddenly. She'd texted him twice but hadn't heard back.

A shadow crossed the officer's face.

"Marcus?" she pressed, her heart starting to race. Surely, if something had happened to Dash, Mary would have told her when they'd spoken earlier.

"It's not that, Matty, he's fine," Marcus said, sensing her rising panic. "But," he hesitated. She fixed him with her best Bronx-inspired stare and crossed her arms over her chest. He sighed.

"There was a congressman in town last night claiming to be your fiancé. He came into Frank's, asked for directions to your house. Dash was there."

Matty let the information sink in, and as it did, she gained new insight into the word "deflated." "I see."

"Most of us don't believe the guy, but when a man hears another man say he's engaged to the woman he loves, well, we men aren't always as secure as we'd like to be."

Matty's eyes held Marcus's and then she looked away. "How many people know?" she asked.

Marcus shrugged. "I only know because Dash stopped by the

station this morning and mentioned it to Ian while I was there. Of course, Ian thought the guy was full of it," he said, then added "and I do, too."

Matty allowed herself a small smile at the loyalty of Marcus and Ian. "Thanks, Marcus. Thanks for telling me. And just so you know, I am not, nor have I ever been, engaged to Congressman Steven White."

She saw Marcus lift a shoulder. "I didn't doubt it for a second."

But Dash had. And maybe still was—doubting it and doubting her.

"So, are you going to give that to Vivi?" she pointed to the bag Marcus held, needing to change the subject.

He opened his mouth, then shut it and nodded.

"How long do you think it will be before the lab will know anything?" she asked.

Again, Marcus shrugged. "Depends on their backlog, but given that it might be related to Brad's death and the death of the man in the tree, I'm thinking it will get as much priority as they can give it. After Kristen's horse was attacked, we had every intention of coming up here to see if we could find anything related to your dog's toe, but then with everything already going on…" His voice trailed off.

"And the department being relatively small, I know—priorities and resources don't always let us do everything we want," Matty finished.

Marcus gave her a half smile, acknowledging the truth of her words. "Well, this is one good thing that's come from the storm, I guess," he said, holding up the bag with the switchblade. "Maybe this will give us something. Thanks for being so quick about recognizing it."

She nodded. "Of course, and thank you, Marcus." She meant for more than just coming over, and by the look he gave her, he knew it.

He started back to his car but before he climbed in, he paused.

"I know Dash is being a jerk about this right now, but don't be too hard on him. It's not always easy being a guy in love."

She didn't want to touch that comment so she laughed. "You speaking from experience?"

He mock shuddered, "No way, no how," he said. Then, with a smile and a jaunty salute, he slid into the driver's seat and drove away. Leaving her to ponder just how betrayal felt.

Hours later, Matty was still contemplating the emotion. She'd spent most of the afternoon helping Mary and some of the other locals prepare for the pancake breakfast, but the entire time she'd felt like little more than a hollow robot. Now, as she sat alone at her kitchen island absently swirling a gin and tonic, she let her mind wander not just to the past afternoon but to the last several years of her life. Her lack of trust in humanity in general wasn't something she held up as a badge of honor, as some people did. In fact, it was such an ingrained part of her that it wasn't something she'd really even noticed about herself.

Until she'd met Dash. In those dark hours in the basement she had talked about things she'd never spoken about out loud—things she'd barely acknowledged in her own mind. She had trusted him enough, and trusted herself enough with him, to venture into new territory—new emotional territory.

And he had repaid her by doubting her. By doubting her fidelity and honesty. By betraying that trust.

A sad smile touched her lips as the sound of a voice floated through the screen door. Matty looked up and watched as Elise's figure appeared in the frame.

Not bothering to ask for an invite, the older woman stepped in, swept off her sunglasses, glanced around, then let her eyes land on Matty and the drink she held in her hand.

"I'd say something witty, but really I think I should just make a drink and join you," Elise said, already moving into the kitchen.

Matty motioned to the drink ingredients she'd pulled from the liquor cabinet and placed on the counter.

"What did Dash do this time?" Elise asked as she started measuring and pouring.

"This time?" Matty repeated.

"I've seen him come and go, young lady. I can tell by the way he drives up or down our road if he's content or agitated. And there have been a few times it's been clear he hasn't gotten his way. Not that that's a bad thing, necessarily," she added as she slid onto a stool next to Matty and looked at her expectantly.

Matty dropped her eyes to study the mint leaf she had added to her drink, noting that it was almost the exact same shade of green as the slice of lime.

"Well?" Elise prompted.

"It's a long story," Matty answered, taking a sip.

"It always is. Or we always think it is, even if it's not." Elise countered.

Matty contemplated this for a moment before realizing Elise was right. It wasn't really a long story, it just felt that way.

"How much do you know about my relationship with Brad and the Brooks family?" Matty asked.

Elise lifted a shoulder then took a long sip from her drink. "I know the basics. You and Brad share a father. You and your mom lived in the Bronx while Brad grew up in Greenwich. When you were twelve, your grandmother, Brad's grandmother, moved you to DC. From there you flourished into the woman you are now."

Matty managed to smile at that. "You make it sound so easy."

Elise let out a bark of a laugh that suggested she'd been a smoker back in the day. "It's never easy. Life is never easy. It's complicated and messy and chaotic. For some more so than others." She finished off her drink with a long draw then stood to make another. "Of course, life is all those things, but that doesn't mean we don't often make it more complicated than it needs to be. So, let me make us both a fresh drink and you can tell me all about what Dr. Hubba Hubba did to make life messy."

Matty smiled at Elise's assumption it was all Dash's fault and handed the woman her now empty glass. In silence, Elise mixed the two drinks, using more gin than tonic, then handed one over as she returned to her seat.

"Now that you've got a little liquid courage in your system, tell me all about it," Elise said.

Matty took a deep breath and let it out. "The night of the storm we camped out in the basement," she started then paused. For a moment she debated whether to repeat some of the things she'd told Dash, things she never even talked about with her mother. But then, in a rush of awareness, she realized that the stories themselves weren't what had brought her closer to Dash. No, what had brought her closer to Dash, what was the true sign of the trust she had placed in him, was *him* being the first person with whom she'd shared that part of her. The first person with whom she'd walked an unknown path, with whom she'd held open her own vulnerability.

She recognized that the stories themselves no longer held any power over her now that she'd shared them and survived. Not that they didn't affect her—they did and probably always would—but they'd been brought out into the light, losing the power to haunt her from the shadows.

"We talked. A lot," Matty continued. "I told him things about my childhood that I've never told anyone else. Never actually even talked about before. Horrible things, of course. Stories about drive-by shootings, rapes, murders, drug dealing. Everything you've ever read about the projects pales in comparison to what it's like to live there."

"I can't imagine what it was like," Elise said, taking a sip of her drink.

Matty inclined her head. "No, you can't. And I don't mean that dismissively. I just mean that, after a while, the press stops reporting things because it becomes old news. 'Another seven-year-old gunned down in the streets,' or 'another fifteen-year-old girl gang-raped and beaten,' begins to lose its novelty after the fourth or fifth in a single year. And if the press doesn't cover it, it's as if it didn't happen." She fell silent for a moment, thinking of all the ruined lives.

"If you were at all like me the night of the storm, you spent a lot of hours in that basement," Elise commented after a bit.

Matty lifted a shoulder. "We did. And they were long hours, too."

"But good?"

Matty tilted her head in thought then answered. "In some ways, yes."

"And last night Steven White came to town and Dash threw all those hours away as if they were meaningless." Elise's comment was so abrupt that Matty's head whipped up in surprise—at the fact that Elise knew about Steven, but mostly at her insight into what was really at the heart of the problem.

Because that *was* what was really the problem. For Dash to have so easily ignored, or not recognized, or not valued, the meaning of everything that had happened between them that night in the basement was what really stung. It wasn't the words that mattered when they'd talked, but everything it meant for her to decide to share them with him.

Matty took a long sip of her drink then swirled the ice around in the empty glass. "It doesn't feel good, that's for sure," she said.

"Of course not," Elise replied, rising and taking Matty's glass with her—this time filling it with water before handing it back.

"I suppose I should just get over it, I mean it's kind of a no-harm-no-foul kind of situation. It felt like a big deal to me, talking to him about my past, but maybe it wasn't, maybe I'm over-reacting. Not that that excuses him, but..." Matty's voice trailed off and she shrugged.

"Don't be ridiculous, dear," Elise shot back. "Putting Dash's behavior aside for the moment, how do you feel right now? And I don't mean how do you feel about Dashiell Kent, I mean how do *you* feel?"

Several beats passed before Matty spoke. "Disappointed, I guess," she said softly. "Sad, too. I feel like I should be angry, but

I'm not. Not really. But none of that, none of those emotions really get me anywhere, do they? They don't change anything."

"Don't they?" Elise countered. Matty looked up from her glass.

"Oh, don't look at me like that," Elise said with a wave of her hand. "Don't look at me like I'm some kind of relationship guru who will tap her magic wand and make everything all right. I'll have you know that my relationship with my late husband was complex and sloppy and definitely not one that inspired sage advice." Elise paused for a moment, looking lost in some sort of memory. That she'd been married at all surprised Matty, though the minute Elise had mentioned it, Matty couldn't picture it any other way.

"But?" Matty prompted.

"But it was also fun and he was the love of my life," Elise said simply. "He died when I was forty-five. It's not that I lacked suitors or male company afterward, but I figured I'd done the marriage thing, I didn't need to do it a second time. Or third, for that matter, at my age. So I've stayed single."

"And avoided dispensing relationship advice," Matty added.

"But I've never shied away from telling someone what I think about them."

"Which means you have something to tell me," Matty responded.

"I do. You think that all the things you're feeling right now, this tangled mass of mixed emotions, won't get you anywhere so you might as well not feel them, right? Wrong," Elise continued, not waiting for Matty to respond. "Whatever it is you're feeling, savor it, wallow in it, absorb it, and understand it. It will change things. It might not change the facts of what happened, it might not change the fact that Dash didn't come straight here to talk to you after he met Steven White, but it will change you. If you let it.

"It can change how you look at yourself, how you think about yourself, and how you deal with disappointments in the future. Because believe me, there will be more disappointments in life. And you should *really* believe me when I say that when you share your life with someone, like I suspect you and Dash might end up doing, you will disappoint each other at some point, probably more than once. It's almost as much a fact of life as death and taxes, but how you deal with it, what you do with that disappointment, is what will really define you, both as individuals and as a couple. It's what will make or break you. And if there is anything I've learned about you, from Brad and my short acquaintance with you, you aren't one to break," she added, fixing Matty with a firm look.

Matty studied her neighbor for a long time, letting the truth and meaning of her words sink in. She had never thought of her emotions as a tool before, as a way to make her stronger, better. Mostly because she'd never let herself really have them, for all the reasons she had talked to Dash about. They would have been used against her in her childhood, but the idea of using them to make her stronger was a novelty. A concept she found both appealing and terrifying at the same time.

"So, if I don't let it break me, how do I let it make me? How do I let it help me deal with Dash?" Matty asked tentatively.

Elise shrugged. "That, my dear, is up to you. But Brad, who followed you and your career from afar, was never shy in talking about how much he admired your strength and resolve. I don't think it will be all that hard for you to figure it out. Of course, it doesn't hurt that Mary and Will Kent didn't raise any idiot children, even though it might not seem that way at the moment."

Matty had to smile at that. She actually had no problem picturing Mary and Will being completely exasperated with their son for his behavior. It didn't change things, it didn't change the disappointment she felt when she thought about how easy it was for Dash to doubt her, but it did make her smile. And it reminded her that Dash had a solid foundation as a person; he *was* a good person, with a good family and good friends. He may not be acting that way right now, but everyone made mistakes. Despite everything, she knew that the core of who he was hadn't changed. And in recognizing that, in allowing herself to look beyond the immediate hurt Dash's reaction had caused, she felt a sense of relief wash through her. The hurt wasn't gone, and she wasn't going to sweep the events of the last twenty-four hours under the rug, but she knew in her heart, and her head, that somehow, they could sort things out.

"If that look on your face is anything to go by, I think I've done my good deed for the day," Elise said, rising from her seat as the dogs started barking. Matty shook her head and shrugged when Elise cast her a questioning glance, asking without words if she knew who was visiting.

Staying in her seat, Matty watched as Elise opened the screen door and poked her head out.

"I think the cavalry is here," Elise said, turning back from the doorway with a huge grin splitting her age-weathered face.

"Excuse me?" Matty asked as she rose from her seat and walked to the patio. Just in time to see Vivi, Kit, Carly, and another woman climb out of Vivi's car. All of whom seemed to be carrying bottles that looked suspiciously like champagne.

Matty let out a groan. It's not that she didn't appreciate the obvious effort to cheer her up, but the thought of champagne following her gin and tonics was already giving her a hangover. And judging by the way Vivi was grinning as she led the group up the drive to the patio, Matty had a sneaking suspicion that what she was imagining she would feel the next morning was nothing compared to what Vivi had in mind.

• • •

Dash was sitting at the bar of Anderson's when Marcus pulled a seat up next to him. It was late, he was tired, and he still hadn't figured out what to do about Matty. In his gut he knew there was more to the story than he knew, than what his imagination was hinting at. But that little part of him, that little part that freaked out at the thought of sharing the rest of his life with someone, wasn't so little right now. If he really thought about it, he might even wager that he was using the congressman's appearance as an excuse to avoid commitment. But that was so lame on so many levels, not the least of which was the fact that spending the rest of his life with Matty wasn't actually scary at all.

But still, something held him back. What if it was true? How well did they really know each other, anyway? Matty was the one who was always pointing that out. What if she'd been trying to tell him something?

He took a sip of his whiskey.

Marcus ordered a beer, saying nothing to Dash. When it arrived, he took a long drink. Placing the glass back on the bar, he spoke. "I saw Matty earlier."

Dash clenched his teeth. He didn't like the younger man's tone, but he said nothing.

"It was interesting, actually. We had an interesting chat. Oh, by the way, she found what we think is the knife that cut off Bob's toe. I handed it off to Vivi to take up to the lab. Kind of freaked Matty out, but she has a good eye for that kind of stuff. Found it out in the field and recognized the fur caught in the hinge of the switchblade."

Dash flinched at the thought of someone with a switchblade anywhere near Matty. "Is she okay?" he asked without thinking.

Marcus took another sip of beer and tipped his head toward his shoulder in a vague gesture. "She'd be better if you weren't being a complete asshole, but other than that, she's fine."

"*I'd* be better if he wasn't being a complete asshole," Ian added, walking up behind the two men and joining them at the bar.

"Vivienne heard what happened," he continued, "and now she's rallied the troops for some girl-power hour or something like that because you're being such an asshole." Ian glared at Dash. "She, Carly, Kit, and Jesse are headed over to Matty's house right now with a couple of bottles of champagne. We have so damn much of the stuff since we got engaged," he grumbled, mostly to himself. "If only our well-wishers would send beer. Or whiskey," he added.

"Jesse?" Dash asked Ian, thinking of their mutual friend. "Matty doesn't even know who she is," he commented. Jesse was another born-and-raised Windsor resident. She ran the hospital down in Riverside, and though she hadn't been in the same class as Dash or Ian, their school had been small enough that most of the kids stayed friends, even into adulthood.

Ian ordered himself a whiskey, too. "Yeah, well, Jesse and Vivienne have become friends, and Jesse's also friends with Kit and Carly, so they included her in the powwow. Now, I'm alone for the evening, without *my* fiancée, so thanks a ton, Kent. Well done."

Marcus chuckled. Dash got the sense that they knew more about what was going on than he did, but he didn't want to talk about it. Mostly because he had a sinking feeling they were right, and now all his doubts were slowly melding into a panic that he'd fucked up big time—so big time that he might not be able to make it right. Especially after the time he and Matty had spent in the basement during the storm when she'd talked to him about everything and everyone. That night, those words, had been a big step for her. And how did he repay her? By doubting everything she felt about him.

"Fuck," he said, taking another sip of whiskey.

"Yep," Ian said, sipping his.

Marcus just laughed.

CHAPTER 21

DASH WOKE UP WITH A mild hangover the next morning. He hadn't had too much the night before at the bar, not enough to impair his ability to get home, but once he was home, when he knew he had a backup vet on call and could actually get a good night's sleep, he'd opened his own bottle of whiskey and partook of another glass or two. Long into the night, he'd thought about Matty. By now, he knew he'd messed things up. He'd let his own insecurity lead him to a bad decision and now he was just hoping it wasn't too late to fix it. He had thought about calling her when he got home, but knowing Vivi and the other women were with her deterred him. Lord knew what they were talking about or saying about him, but he probably deserved every word.

He rolled over, looked at the clock, and groaned. The pancake breakfast started in two hours and if he wanted to catch Matty beforehand, he needed to be up soon. Flopping back onto his back, he rubbed a hand over his face and stared at the ceiling. He was just getting ready to pull himself out of bed when his phone rang.

Hoping it was Matty, he grabbed the phone and answered without looking at the number. And was more than a little disappointed when he heard his mother's voice.

"Good morning, Dash," she said. And somehow his own disappointment in himself paled in comparison to the same sentiment he heard in her voice. Huh, clearly she was on the Matty bandwagon, for which he couldn't actually blame her, even if he didn't feel up to dealing with it this morning.

"I'm on it, Mom," he said, responding to her unspoken accusation.

"I should certainly hope so. I did *not* raise my children to be assholes."

Dash blinked at the curse. His mother never cursed. "I said, I'm on it."

She harrumphed.

"I take it you talked to her?" he ventured to ask.

"Of course I talked to her. Yesterday. Unlike you, I might add."

"I don't need the reminder, Mom."

"Well, you certainly need to be reminded of some things, that's for sure."

He sighed. "How is she?"

His mother's voice softened when she answered. "She didn't say anything specifically about you, which I'm sure doesn't surprise you. But I think she's hurt."

"And angry?"

"You should hope she's angry. Anger is often easier to deal with than hurt," his mother countered. He had never thought of it that way, but now that his mother had vocalized it, he saw the truth in what she said. Especially for a woman like Matty. Anger would come easily for her, but to be hurt, to allow herself to be close enough to someone to be hurt by him, well, that was rare.

"So, what's the story?"

He should have known better than to ask. His mother let out a bark of laughter before answering. "Nice try, Dash, you dug yourself into this. And don't believe it will be the last time you, or she, does something dumb or thoughtless—you've got a lot of years ahead of you, Son. You need to figure your own way out of this one. You both do."

Dash let out another deep breath. He hadn't expected any different, but still, a little part of him hoped his mom would throw him a lifeline.

He sat up in bed and swung his legs over the side. "I'm on my way over to her house right now," he said.

"Good, but you'd better hurry. She's due at the breakfast site in less than an hour."

"And she'll be there all day?"

"Yes, she's planning on it. But I told her she might want to consider leaving early since she helped so much yesterday with the prep work and is going to be there early to help set up."

"Great, thanks, Mom," he said as he headed toward the shower.

His mom paused for moment before answering. "You're welcome. And Dash? For what it's worth, I like her. I really do."

Dash inhaled deeply, amazed at how his mother's approval made him feel. It wasn't that he needed her approval—really, he'd never doubted that his parents would like Matty—but the tone of his mother's voice was so genuine that he knew she liked Matty because of who Matty was, not just because he did. And because she liked Matty, his mother now wanted what was best not just for Dash, but for Matty, too.

"Yeah, I do, too," he said.

"Then you'll go fix it?"

"If you ever stop talking to me long enough for me to get in the shower so I can be presentable, then, yeah, I'll go fix it."

"I can still cause you a world of hurt, Son. You remember that."

Dash laughed at the love he heard in his mom's voice. "I don't doubt it."

She was still laughing when they hung up and quick as he could, Dash tried to make good on his promise to his mom.

When he pulled up Matty's drive thirty minutes later, he saw her walking toward her car wearing shorts and a t-shirt, her favorite kind of outfit. Her black hair was pulled up into a ponytail and she was carrying a variety of cooking utensils in one hand as she pressed her phone to her ear with the other.

She froze when she saw him, just for a millisecond, then continued on to her car. The top of her convertible was pulled back and she easily dumped the utensils into the passenger seat as he climbed out of his truck.

"Yes, I'll be there most of the morning. No, I'm doing okay. If you'd like to come, I'm sure Rob can tell you where it is, but I'll be busy." She stopped talking for a moment then made a conciliatory noise, said good-bye, and ended her call.

She stood facing her car for a moment before she turned to face him.

"I'm sorry," he said as soon as her eyes met his. "I don't know the whole story, but I know you wouldn't have talked to me the way you did the night of the storm unless I really meant something to you, and I also know you well enough to know you aren't the two-timing type. I've been a complete jerk and I just hope that I haven't completely fucked things up."

He'd taken a gamble mentioning that night in the basement. In some ways the fact that that night had happened just before Steven White had come to town, made the situation worse. He knew she was feeling more vulnerable. He knew she had stepped out onto the proverbial emotional limb. But on the other hand, the fact that she had stepped out on that limb, the fact that they had talked about all the things they had talked about, *did* mean something. And he was banking on that *something* to be what they needed as common ground for finding their way back.

She looked at him for a good long while but he didn't flinch or back down. Never even considered it.

"Dash," she started, then paused and glanced away. "I can't do this right now. I just got off the phone with Douglas and, well, I just can't do this right now."

Not what he wanted to hear. Not at all. But what could he do? He'd walked away from her for over twenty-four hours; he didn't really think he had a right to demand that she resolve the issue on his timetable.

"Matty," he said, waiting for her eyes to come back to his. As soon as they did, he continued. "Later then?" He wanted her to see the sincerity he felt.

Her eyes searched his for another long moment before she gave a small nod. "Later. Maybe after the breakfast."

He let out a breath he hadn't realized he was holding and nodded back. She moved to the driver's door of her car and slid into her seat. They didn't say any more, and as he watched her drive away, he held a little bit of hope that later, maybe later, she'd let him try to fix the mess he'd made.

• • •

When Matty arrived at the breakfast site, she spotted Kit and Jesse unloading Kit's Land Rover. She waved as she pulled into the parking space next to them and they waited as she got out of her car. As soon as she'd met her the night before, Matty had liked Jesse—a petite blonde who looked a bit like a modern-day Marilyn Monroe, but with longer hair. And now, seeing Jesse standing next to Kit, with her auburn hair, golden eyes, and five-foot-eleven frame, Matty thought the two looked quite striking.

"You look a little worse for wear, Matty. I take it you didn't get any last night?" Kit teased as they started toward the cooking area.

"I got a lot last night," she shot back. "Of course most of it was shit from you ladies, but hey, you know," she shrugged, making Jesse and Kit laugh.

"So, any word?" Jesse asked as they began placing their supplies on the tables some the volunteers had set up earlier.

"He came by this morning—" Matty started to say just as Mary Kent called her name. All three women turned to see Dash's mother bustling toward them with a younger woman in tow.

"Hi girls," Mary said as she came to a stop in front of them. "Thank you so much for all your help."

All three nodded and mumbled their responses.

"Matty, this is my oldest daughter, Jane. Jane, this is Matty Brooks." Matty looked at Jane as she stepped forward to shake her hand. She looked like Dash—with strong cheekbones and dark hair—but her eyes were more hazel, whereas Dash's were dark brown. And Jane's eyes sparkled with a little something that looked a lot like mischief.

"It's nice to meet you," Matty said.

"And you, too," Jane replied. Then she turned to Kit and Jesse and greeted them, obviously having met both before.

"Why don't Matty and I get the bacon and ham all set up and you three can manage the pancakes and drinks?" Jane suggested to her mom.

Mary nodded then started to hustle Kit and Jesse away. Matty turned to Jane, who was grinning.

"Sorry my brother is being such a jerk," she said, clearly enjoying the hot water her younger brother had gotten himself into.

Matty wasn't quite sure what to say. "Um, he's trying to make up for it."

"Are you going to make him work hard?"

Matty's lips twitched at the apparent glee in Jane's tone. "This is fun for you, isn't it," she said.

Jane laughed. "Immensely."

After studying Jane for a moment, Matty gestured toward the tables with a tilt of her head. "Let's get the bacon and ham started," she said as she moved away.

"And you'll tell me all the details?" Jane pressed, following her.

"Nope."

"Please?"

"I think you already have the details," Matty said, laughing at Jane's approach—an approach that was clearly a holdover from a childhood spent teasing her little brother.

Jane shrugged as she started checking the pilot light on the grill. "I do, but hearing it from Mom isn't quite as fun as hearing it from you or Dash. Although, she did use some colorful language last night recounting what she knew."

"Your mom is great," Matty offered with a smile. She liked Mary Kent—really liked her. And she knew her own mom would like her, too.

"She is. My brother is pretty great, too, even if he is being a jerk right now."

"You don't actually seem all that concerned about the situation," Matty said, handing Jane the lighter to start the grill. Jane was silent for a moment, concentrating on her task, but when the pilot was lit, she straightened and grinned again.

"I'm not. You'll figure it out. I just want some ammunition to use against him later."

"Loving sister that you are," Matty rejoined.

"Oh, he adores me," Jane said, unpacking some of the meat.

"It's because of the family curse right? Your confidence?" Matty asked, knowing Dash had talked to Jane about her.

"It's startling when it happens, but most of us who have come out on the other side like to think of it as a blessing," Jane answered. She paused as a truck pulled to a stop a short distance away. They both watched as Dash's dad climbed out of the front and two boys, who looked to be about eight, poured out of the truck's back doors, arguing loudly about something or other.

"Of course, it depends on the day I'm having," Jane said with a nod to the shouting boys. "My twins, Josh and Derek. There are times, I will admit, that it does seem a bit like a curse," she added with a sigh.

The love in Jane's voice was so clear that Matty knew her words were ones of jest and held not an iota of truth to them.

"Hmm, I can see horns growing from their heads as we speak," she answered, making Jane laugh.

"There's more truth to that than you might think," Jane said, as she turned back to the very serious business of cooking bacon, acquiescing, for the moment, in dropping the subject of Dash.

Matty spent most of the morning between the cooking stations—filling in when people needed a break, running errands for more supplies. She had thought Mary's planning was a bit overzealous, but seeing the number of people who showed up, she vowed never to doubt the woman again.

Several of the local law enforcement officers had made a point to stop by, including Ian and Vivi. When Matty was able to take a break, she visited with them for a short time, then sat and had a cup of coffee with Carly.

Seeing her taking a short break, Jesse brought Matty a plate of food—eating was a little detail she'd forgotten in the morning rush. Then, after a glance to check on her two teenage sons who were staffing the grill, Jesse joined Matty and Carly for a short bit.

Dash had arrived not long after the event started. He'd planned to be there earlier but had texted both Matty and his mother to say he'd been called out to a local farm and would be there as soon as possible. Of course, the moment he arrived, Matty was hyperaware of him.

And it looked like she wasn't the only one feeling the connection between them. Every time she caught a glimpse of Dash, he looked to be watching her. He hadn't tried to talk to her and she was glad for that—this event was neither the time nor the place. But in general, he seemed to be keeping close, helping out when needed.

After finishing her breakfast, Matty chatted with Jesse and Carly for a bit longer, until Carly had to leave for her shift and Jesse decided that leaving her two boys in charge of the grill might not have been the best idea. Rising from her seat to throw her plate into a composting container, she caught a glimpse of Dash playing catch with one of his nephews. She'd met Josh and Derek earlier, but from where she stood, she couldn't tell which of the identical twins was playing with his uncle.

Dash looked at ease tossing the ball around with his young relative. She couldn't hear what they were saying, but the boy was smiling and Dash was laughing. Her mind wandered as she watched the two and she was startled when Marcus approached, calling her name.

She spun, a little embarrassed to be caught out ogling Dash, and Marcus cast her a lopsided, knowing grin.

"Enjoying the scenery?" he asked.

She rolled her eyes. "Shut up," she said. He laughed as she shook her head at him.

"Was there something you wanted?" she asked. Instantly, he sobered.

"Actually, I just wanted to touch base with you on the knife you found yesterday. I don't have much news; between all the cleanup and additional accidents that have happened over the last twenty-four hours, we haven't been able to run it up to the lab yet."

Matty frowned. It wasn't that she blamed them for being short staffed; she just wanted some answers.

"I know," Marcus said in response to her reaction. "But Vivi and Ian were going to swing by the station after this event and take it up. I think Vivi might even be planning to process it today. But I wanted to let you know we did find a print though. We dusted it yesterday and were able to lift a good impression that Vivi will run through the computer databases today."

Well, at least that was something. Matty lifted a shoulder and let her eyes stray across the bucolic setting. Wild flowers dotted the fields and, from where she stood, she could see the rooftops of several barns peeking through the trees. With such scenery, it didn't feel right to be talking about what they were talking about.

Marcus must have sensed the unease that had swept over her and he reached for her arm in a reassuring gesture.

"The fingerprint is a good thing—"

"Uncle Dash!" came frantic cry from behind Matty. Marcus's hand dropped as she spun around to see Dash hunched over, his hand covering his eye.

She saw Dash's nephew run toward his uncle as Jane did the same. And then, before she knew what she was doing, she was beside him, too.

"I'm fine," Dash was saying through his hands—hands that were covering not his right eye, like she had originally thought, but just above it.

"I'm sorry, Uncle Dash." Matty could now see it was Josh who must have thrown the errant ball and was now fervently apologizing.

"I know, Josh, don't worry about it. It was my fault, I looked away."

"Move your hands," Matty directed, leaning over him. He

must have been startled to have her so close because he straightened right away and looked at her using the eye on the uninjured side of his face.

"Let me see," she said, gently pulling his hand away. There was a big red goose egg on his brow and she didn't bother to hide the breath she sucked in.

"Is it bad?" he asked, his face bunched in concern.

"It doesn't look good."

"Luckily, you have a hard head," Jane interrupted.

"Nice, thanks, Jane," he said.

"Stop it, you two. We need to get some ice on it. Jane?" Matty directed.

"On it," Jane replied and then disappeared with her son in tow.

"You going to take care of me?" Dash asked Matty, not bothering to hide a hopeful little smile. She rolled her eyes at him and led him over to a bench. Pushing him down, she pulled his hand from the injury again and gently touched it.

A breath hissed out.

"I guess I don't have to ask how much it hurts," she said, starting to step back. He grabbed her wrist to prevent the movement and she almost tumbled into his lap.

"Ice," Jane said from behind her. In silence, Matty took the towel-wrapped bag of ice, tipped Dash's face up, and gently laid it against the goose egg. She heard Jane retreat again and say something to Mary, who had come to investigate. After a short time, she heard both women walk away, leaving her alone with Dash.

She held the ice pack on Dash's forehead and, for several minutes, they stayed that way—Dash on the bench with her standing over him—without saying anything. Then Dash reached for her free hand and brought it to his lips.

"I'm really sorry, Matty," he said simply.

She sighed.

"And after everything you trusted me with that night in the basement, it was really low of me. A new low, actually," he added.

Matty knew he'd intentionally mentioned that night, the trust she'd placed in him, as a reminder of what he knew he meant to her.

She sighed again then spoke. "Look Dash, honestly, I'm not sure I can blame you for being confused. If someone walked up to me and told me she was your fiancée, I'd be confused too. And probably hurt. But I like to think I would actually *ask* you what the real story was. You know, like your mom asked me, or Ian, or Vivi, or Marcus. To name a few."

She saw him flinch at the list, at the demonstration of just what a jerk he'd been, but he didn't look away. In fact his eyes held steady and sure on hers.

"I'm sorry, Matty. I *know* that man is not your fiancé. Will you tell me who he is?"

For a long moment, she just looked into his dark eyes. She wasn't hesitating to tell, she was, for just a moment, reveling in the honesty and the affection in his expression.

"Steven White and I met several years ago, when my grandmother was still alive," she started. "He came to one of her parties, which, over the years, had become somewhat elite in the political circles. He was a new senator in town and I think he didn't want to miss the opportunity to rub elbows with more senior members of congress.

"Anyway," Matty continued as she glanced around her, not missing the contrast of her life in DC with the very different kind of life she lived here in Windsor. "We started dating. We both agreed to keep it quiet. He didn't want his private life splashed about and I preferred to keep myself out of politics. Don't get me wrong," she added. "I'm a political person and definitely have political views. Some he and I shared and some we didn't, but mostly I wanted to be able to keep my politics to myself. If we had been linked together, given my family and his new status, everything I said would be scrutinized and I wasn't interested in that."

"That couldn't have been easy. Isn't DC the town with no secrets?"

Matty gave a little laugh at that. "In a way, yes. But there is also a bit of a subculture of people turning a blind eye to others' private lives, knowing that if they call attention to someone else's private life, the spotlight can just as easily swing back and shine on them. Of course there are the scandals, but believe it or not, a lot of public people can more or less manage to have a private life," she said.

"So, what happened?"

"We dated on and off for a couple of years, but it was never serious. It was more a relationship of convenience. We liked each other, but we both knew it wasn't anything long term."

"And then?" Dash asked, rubbing a thumb across her palm.

She looked at his big hand wrapped around hers. It was calloused and rough and she loved the feel of it against her own skin.

"And then he started asking me to go to political rallies and events with him."

Dash frowned, not understanding. She couldn't blame him; it had taken her a while to figure it out, too.

"At first I resisted. Like I said, I didn't want to become a public political figure. I don't mind being public for my writing, but politics in that way doesn't interest me. But finally, I relented and his staff scheduled two visits within two weeks of each other. One in Florida and one in New Mexico." She didn't bother to hide the wry cynicism in her voice. To this day, she couldn't believe she'd been so slow to figure it out.

"Florida?" Dash asked.

She met his gaze again. "It was a presidential election year and those two states have huge Hispanic populations. He thought it might be good to get out and stump for his party, which wasn't the same as my preferred party, mind you, and trot out his Hispanic-looking, Spanish-speaking girlfriend. What better way to prove how inclusive they could be than by having a party member actually dating one?" she added with a roll of her eyes.

Dash's eyebrows shot up then he winced at the movement. "Seriously?"

"Hmm," she nodded. "I figured it out when we landed in

Florida, before we even got off the plane. I asked him about it and he said I was being ridiculous, but his staff couldn't meet my eyes. Needless to say, I didn't bother showing up at that event. I got off his private plane, bought myself a ticket back to DC on a commercial flight, and have maybe talked to him a handful of times since then."

Dash frowned. "I don't mean to sound like I'm doubting anything you say, but why would he come up here and claim to be your fiancé now?"

Matty laughed, and it wasn't a funny ha-ha kind of laugh. "It's an election year again next year. He's been calling me lately. I'm not sure why he thinks I won't see through him or why I might have any interest in seeing him. But mostly I've been ignoring him. I have no idea why he claimed to be my fiancé, but my guess is that he probably had some media thing planned."

"As in the good senator running up to check on his beloved fiancée in the aftermath of a huge storm?" Dash said.

Matty cocked her head and made a face. "I wouldn't put it past him. But I never talked to him so I can't say for certain. He called several times the day after the storm, but like I said, I've been ignoring him and that day wasn't any different. I haven't heard from him since so I assume he left town."

Dash looked at her for a long time, then tugged her down onto his lap. "I'm sorry. I'm sorry for being such a jerk and I'm even sorrier *he's* such a jerk and tried to use you."

Matty smiled and settled against him, even as she tried to keep the ice on his injury.

"You two look like you figured things out," came Jane's voice from behind her. Craning around, she found Dash's sister walking toward them, her two boys trailing behind her. "Josh got stung by a bee and Derek didn't sleep well last night. We got in really late." She added, directing the explanation to Matty. "We're looking for Dad so I can take his truck home, since I came with Mom."

"You can take mine," Dash said, reaching for his keys. "I'll get a ride home."

"Or you can take mine," Matty said, digging her own keys out.

"You have that cute convertible, don't you?" Jane asked with a gesture toward Matty's car. Matty nodded. "You don't have to offer twice," Jane grinned and took the keys. "We can drop the car by later today. Or, if you're coming to dinner tonight, you can grab it then."

Matty shrugged, figuring they'd figure it out somehow. As Jane and the twins left, the boys talking excitedly about riding in a convertible, she turned back to Dash, who was grinning a different kind of grin than his sister.

"Want a ride, little girl?" he asked.

"You sound like a dirty old man," she replied with a smile.

"Dirty, maybe. Old, not even close." He surged to his feet, taking her with him. She let out a very girly squeal as he tossed her over his shoulder and started for his truck.

"Dash, put me down," she demanded, still clutching the ice pack.

"Dashiell Kent," Matty heard his mother saying.

"Sorry, Mom, I'm busy. I'll talk to you tonight," he called over his shoulder.

Matty turned beet red as she heard several other people hoot and holler. "I swear to god, Dash, you will pay for this," she said, just loud enough for him to hear.

He opened his truck door and deposited her on the seat. "I'm kind of counting on that," he said, before silencing anything she was about to say with a kiss.

CHAPTER 22

MATTY COULDN'T REALLY COMPLAIN ABOUT the way Dash showed his contrition. They spent most of the afternoon relaxing together—yes, in bed, but also just being. She worked on some final pieces of her book while Dash went out and walked the fence to make sure it hadn't been damaged in the storm. She'd had her eyes on the cows and most hadn't really left the barn area since the storm so she wasn't worried any had escaped, but it had never occurred to her to check the fence and make sure that they *couldn't* escape.

Later, they'd picked up around the house a bit, since it had been neglected with all the outdoor cleanup. When things were back in order, about a half hour before they were planning to head over to his parents' house for dinner, Matty's father called. Dash, without any prompting, had handed her a nice glass of red wine—it hadn't exactly made the conversation easier, but at least it had given her something to appreciate during the awkward few moments she talked with Douglas.

The situation still felt surreal to Matty—having had more conversations with her father in the past three days than in her entire life previously. And though she still didn't think of him as her father in the traditional sense, she didn't have it in her to turn him away.

"Everything okay?" Dash asked after she ended the call with Douglas.

She frowned. "Hard to say. He and Sandra have been told that

Brad's body will be released tomorrow, which is good. They'll be able to hold the funeral service for him now."

"But?" Dash pressed.

"But Brad was pretty clear about wanting to be buried here, in Windsor, which isn't sitting well with Sandra. She wants to take him back to Connecticut; his dad—*my* dad—is trying to stand firm with Brad's wishes. I think he won out, but it was hard to tell."

"Did I hear you talking to him this morning about coming to the pancake breakfast?"

Matty nodded. "Yes, but he decided not to go because he knew several of Brad's friends would be there and he didn't want to make anyone uncomfortable. He said he went to one of the churches in town and volunteered to drive some of the seniors to appointments they might have missed over the past two days."

"That was nice of him."

It was, but she was very carefully trying not to have any feelings about her father. He was going through a rough time at the moment, to put it mildly, and right now she just didn't trust that he had any reason for even trying to reach out to her beyond his own desperation. When the rawness of what he was experiencing dulled a bit, would he go back to Connecticut, to Sandra and the country club, and forget about her again? She really didn't know the answer to that so she was intentionally keeping herself from getting too involved with him.

She and Dash finished their wine in silence then headed to his parents' house, which was anything but silent. Jane, her husband Greg who had arrived from New York City, the twins, and Kristen, whose father was still out of town, were all in residence and having a rowdy game of Twister.

The gathering was unlike any Matty had ever attended. Oh, her grandmother had thrown grand parties, but they'd definitely never included Twister. And while there might have been a game or two of Pictionary at her grandmother's, it was usually just the five of them—Matty, her mom, her grandmother, Charlotte, and

Nanette—and it was never played with crayons, which was, apparently, the Kents' writing utensil of choice.

Matty was still smiling about the events of the night before when she woke up the next morning. The twins had convinced her to write a children's story, Jane had given her the third degree about a character in one of her most recent books, Mary had told her she didn't put enough sex in her books, and Dash and Greg had just sat back and laughed at her indoctrination into the Kent clan.

"Did you have fun last night?' Dash asked, lying beside her.

She rolled over to look at him. "What gave it away, that I woke up laughing or the fact I almost peed my pants last night when Derek drew a woman in a short skirt after he pulled the word 'hoe' from the Pictionary box? I think your sister had what back in the day would have been called an apoplectic fit."

Dash lay on his back and chuckled toward the ceiling. "Yeah, it was fun watching her try to explain where they'd even heard that use of the word to my mom and dad."

Matty rolled onto her back for a moment, then rolled back up to face Dash. "My mom wants to come up," she said.

Dash turned his head, eyebrows raised. "How do you feel about that?"

"How do *you* feel about that?" she countered.

He shrugged, his bare shoulders rubbing against the cotton sheets. "I'm fine with it. You already know the bulk of *my* family. Sam and Nora, my youngest brother and sister haven't been around, but you've met most of the rest of them."

"Yes, but this is a little different," Matty said.

Dash rolled his body to face her. "How so?"

"She knows you're different from other men I've dated."

"Um, my mom knows, well, she knows what she knows about you. And me," he pointed out.

"But your mom is so open and so, I don't know, she just kind of embraced me. My mom will probably be more reserved. She'll probably interrogate you, too."

"My mom embraced you for two reasons. One, you're easy to

like, and two, she knew she didn't really have a choice. Remember she and my dad only knew each other two weeks before they were married. She knows what the family tradition does to people, so she knew when it hit me that she could either embrace you or not, but that it wouldn't have any bearing on what would happen between you and me. She simply chose the path that would keep her family together, the path that would enlarge her family rather than split it. Your mom might not be so quick to get there, but my guess is that she'll make the same choice."

Matty thought about that perspective for a moment, and in the end, had to agree with Dash. Her mother might not be as open and friendly as Mary and Will Kent, but Dash was an easy guy to like and her mother would never do anything to alienate herself from Matty—they'd been through too much together.

She dipped her chin, conceding Dash's point. "You're right, but she'll be more reserved, so please don't be offended if she doesn't welcome you with open arms."

Dash shrugged, "I'd be surprised if she didn't put me through my paces. When is she planning on coming?" he asked, rising from the bed and heading into the bathroom.

She relayed that part of the conversation she'd had with her mom. Carmen didn't have a date yet, but now that Brad's funeral service could be planned and they would know soon when Douglas and Sandra were likely to leave Windsor, they'd be able to set a date for her mom's visit. Dash seemed unfazed about the whole thing and popped out of the bathroom, wearing a pair of jeans, to tell her so.

"So, we'll wait and see," he shrugged. "And, at some point, you are going to have to decide what to do with everything Brad left you—from the house to the money to the cows to even the rabbits. But in the meantime, I was thinking about Trudy and Mara yesterday and want to make a quick run up to the farm to check on the two mares I cared for the other night. Trudy hasn't called, but I didn't see either of them at the pancake breakfast so I just want to make sure everything is okay. Any interest in joining me?" he asked.

Matty thought about it for all of two seconds. Lying around in bed held some appeal, but so did visiting the farm, Mara, and the cute little foal, still only a few days old. "Can I see the baby?" she asked, rising herself.

Dash lifted a shoulder. "I don't see why not."

She went up on her tiptoes and brushed his lips with a kiss. "I'll be ready in ten minutes."

• • •

"Who're they?" Matty asked Mara as they stood at the fence line watching the new foal, unharmed from the storm, frolic in the pasture. Matty was eying two men, one in his early forties, the other several years younger and quite a few inches shorter. They were clearly having a heated argument about something and both men were gesturing emphatically.

"Oh that's John, the owner's son, and Carlo, one of the jockeys that rides for Mr. Green, the owner. One of the horses got hurt and didn't run well yesterday at Saratoga. So now no one is happy," Mara answered simply, as four year-olds often did.

Matty frowned as the taller of the two men stomped off. The jockey, Carlo jammed his hands on his hips and stared at the ground. Matty couldn't help herself, she'd never seen a jockey up close, and she was still staring when his eyes came up and landed on hers. He was too far away to distinguish much detail, but she was almost certain she saw a small feral smile touch his lips before he started their way.

"Hi Mara," he called when he got within earshot.

"Hi Carlo," Mara answered.

"How's Short Stuff?" he asked, gesturing to the foal with his head as he joined them at the fence line.

"She's good. She'll come over for a treat in a little bit, but we just put her out so she's getting her sillies out."

"Who's your friend?" He gestured to Matty with his head.

"This is Matty. She came with Dr. Kent to check on Trouble because she almost died the other night." Matty heard the sadness in the young girl's voice and she knew it was for the baby that Trouble, the mare, *had* lost.

"Yeah," Carlo consoled her. "That was a tough night. I was sorry to hear about Trouble and the baby, but I am glad Dr. Kent could help Lizzie and her foal," he added, referring to the mare and foal Dash and Trudy had been able to save.

Mara nodded, then added. "Matty was also here when Short Stuff was born."

Matty reached around Mara and held out her hand. "Matty Brooks," she said.

"Carlo Ruiz." He took her hand, holding it a bit too long.

"Is that what you named her?" Matty asked Mara. "Short Stuff?" she added with a gesture to the foal, who was making her way toward them.

Mara shrugged. "For now. She'll have some fancy name on her papers when my mom registers her, but she's Short Stuff, or Shorty, to us."

Matty was pretty sure they were being ironic because the foal was only a few days old and already it looked to have grown substantially. She didn't know a thing about horses but she'd bet this one wasn't going to be anywhere near short.

"You ride, Matty?" Carlo asked.

She almost answered "not horses" before catching herself. Not only was Mara there, but she didn't need to be intentionally tossing innuendos around with a man she'd just met. That it had even come to mind at all surprised her. But then again, she had to admit, for a man who was not that tall, he exuded a fair bit of alpha maleness.

"Matty," Dash said, coming up behind her. Glad to have him near, she turned and smiled. There must have been something in her smile, because he slipped a hand around her waist and dropped a kiss on her lips. "Having fun?" he asked with a nod toward the foal, who had decided it was much more fun to tear around the field than have a treat.

"You done good, birthin' that baby," Matty said with a teasing smile.

He let out a little laugh. "I didn't birth anything, but I am glad I was able to help her mom along. Carlo, how are you?" he asked, acknowledging the jockey.

Carlo inclined his head.

"I heard about Tenacity," Dash added. "One of the Green's horses that got injured up at the track yesterday," he filled Matty in on what Mara had already mentioned.

Carlo shook his head and uttered a series of profanities in Spanish. Matty was sorry for the injury, but when Carlo muttered something about a father of a goat, she snorted, causing him to stop.

Carlo turned to her, curiosity in his eyes. "You understand?" he asked in Spanish. She answered in the affirmative and told him her mom was from Puerto Rico. They continued their brief conversation in Spanish, but stopped when Trudy walked up and handed Dash a check, presumably to cover his services. Taking that as their cue to leave, Matty and Dash said their good-byes and made their way back to his truck.

A few minutes later, they were driving back to her place. "What was Carlo saying to you?" Dash asked.

Matty lifted a shoulder. "Not much other than he doesn't often see Spanish-speaking people at the farm who aren't cleaning the stalls."

"It sounded like he said a lot more than that," Dash commented.

Matty felt a smile tug at her lips. "He did offer to let me compare recipes if I ever got tired of the gringo, if you know what I mean."

Dash's head whipped around to see if she was serious, then abruptly returned to the road when he remembered he was driving.

"He didn't."

Matty laughed. "He did."

"Ballsy of him, considering you were there with me."

"He probably weighs no more than 120 pounds and, if what I learned watching the Kentucky Derby is right, he regularly sits atop 1,200 pound, three-year-old thoroughbreds. I don't think cojones, or lack thereof, are an issue for him."

Dash grunted, making her laugh again. She leaned over and kissed his cheek. "If it makes you feel any better, I had the urge to tell him you were my fiancé, just to make it clear I'm off the market—not that you are," she added, in case her announcement made him drive off the road.

To her surprise, he seemed unperturbed by her comment. "You should have," was all he said.

"I think I would have if I thought it would have made a difference, but I don't think he's the kind of guy to actually care one way or the other," she responded. They rode a few miles in silence and she began to wonder why she had even mentioned her errant thought to Dash in the first place. It wasn't a lie, it had crossed her mind, but two things had kept her from saying it to Carlo. One she'd shared with Dash, but the other was that the lie would have rolled easily off her tongue—so easily, in fact, it made her wonder if it was the truth. She and Dash hadn't talked about the whole marriage thing since their first night together, but for the first time in her life, she could actually bring herself to consider the possibility. Not that it was going to happen as fast as his family seemed to think, but she wasn't as freaked out by the idea as she expected. Now, she actually felt open to considering it, open to the possibility that spending the rest of her life with someone could be a decision she would want to make.

"You're awfully quiet over there," Dash said as he pulled onto her road and headed toward her house.

Matty shrugged. "Just thinking about my book," she lied.

He pulled to a stop in front her house and turned toward her. "Liar," he said, but with a smile. "You're thinking about getting married, aren't you?"

"No," the words were out of her mouth faster than a bullet.

Dash laughed. "You are. Admit it."

"I won't." Great, now she was sounding like a petulant child. But still, Dash laughed. Then he pulled her toward him and kissed her properly. When he pulled away, he still held her face close to his.

"I have a few errands to run today and then I need to check in with the clinic this afternoon."

She leaned forward and kissed him again because, well, because she wanted to. When she pulled away, he grazed a thumb down her cheek.

"I have some work I need to do on my book. I'm almost done and I just want to finish up a few things, double check a few things, before I send it to my editor," she said.

"So you're going to stay home?"

She nodded and brushed another kiss over his lips. "Maybe I'll even cook dinner."

Dash smiled and released her. "Don't bother, why don't we go out tonight?"

Matty agreed and opened her door. She was about to slide out of her seat when Dash grabbed her hand. "Call me if you need anything."

"Thanks, but I'll be fine. Hopefully, I'll get the book done today and then I'll be home free for at least a little bit—while my editor tears it to shreds, all in the name of making it better."

After one last kiss, she closed the truck door behind her and though she would normally wait for Dash to leave before entering her house, she knew he'd want to wait until she was inside before he left. And so she waved and entered the house. It was quiet inside, all the dogs having flooded out when she'd opened the door, but inviting. She was looking forward to finishing her book. She wasn't sure what she would do once it was done, but it was so close that she just wanted to tie up the loose ends and launch it into the next step in the publishing process.

But an hour later, she still wasn't feeling it. Something was nagging at her brain and she couldn't quite place it. It wasn't something about her book, although there were a few areas she thought needed cleaning up. And it wasn't about her last conversation with Dash. Sighing, she propped her chin on her hand and stared out the office's big picture window at the cows.

They had finally ventured away from the barn and were out grazing in the field. The scene was peaceful and comforting, like something out of a Monet painting. Which made it that much more amusing when one of the cows suddenly got what Matty assumed was a figurative bug up its behind and launched itself into the air in a frolic-y little dance. She couldn't help but laugh as the less-than-graceful animal arched and bucked and trotted around the field. The fact that the other cows simply stood and watched the show only made it funnier.

She was still chuckling a few minutes later when the cow finally settled down and resumed eating. It was a far cry from the graceful moves of Short Stuff, but still as entertaining, if not more so.

Short Stuff. Thinking of the foal reminded Matty of Carlo. Grabbing hold of the thread that was now taking shape in her brain, she pulled out the copies of the photos Brad had left in the book for her and thumbed through until she found the picture of the young woman, the picture with no name.

Fingering it, an idea came to her. Picking up her phone, she dialed Vivi's number.

"Matty," Vivi answered. "Everything okay?"

"Yes, thanks, but I was thinking. Do you have an ID on the woman in the photo yet?" Matty asked.

Vivi paused and Matty heard her typing away. "Hmm, no, that's interesting."

"What's interesting?" Matty asked.

"We ran her face through the driver's license database using facial recognition and nothing came up."

"Meaning?"

"Meaning she doesn't have a driver's license. Which is unusual for someone her age."

"Is there a database of jockeys?" Matty asked.

"Jockeys?"

"Yes, I just met one today and it struck me, he was built like the woman in the picture—tiny frame, not very tall. I know it's probably a long shot, but it just struck me that maybe she's a jockey and the picture was taken at the track. It would make sense given that Brad also left the racing form."

"Hmm," Vivi said again, typing something else. "There is a database of jockeys since they have to have a license to race. It will take some time to run the recognition program, but it's worth a try."

"I could just be seeing connections where there aren't any," Matty said cautiously.

"But you never know," Vivi countered. "Right now we have nothing else to go on with respects to the picture so we'll take any direction that seems reasonable, and this seems more than reasonable."

They chatted for a few more minutes, catching up on the case. Though the lab had released Brad's body, they were still processing evidence and trying to come up with and track down leads. Vivi was confident they were making progress, but backlogs at the lab were making it hard to move as fast as any of them would like. They ended the call with a promise to get together for dinner in the next few days.

When Matty returned to her laptop, she realized focusing on her book was now much easier. And focus she did. She plugged away for several hours and when she finally sat back there were just three or four points she needed to clarify, and for those she'd need Chen.

Thirty minutes later, Chen pulled up her drive, bringing his sleek car to a stop. Matty had thought to just call him and talk over the phone, but when she had, he'd offered to come over, saying he was out and about anyway. When he arrived, she greeted him on the patio and invited him in. They spent a few minutes discussing the funeral plans for Brad. Douglas had won out and the service was scheduled for the following weekend at the church in Windsor where Brad had only occasionally attended services but had often volunteered. The burial itself would be attended by Brad's parents and immediate family only. Douglas had asked that Matty come, Brad had even mentioned it in his will, but she had yet to decide whether or not she felt comfortable with the idea.

Sandra was intent on not holding a reception in Windsor, so Matty assumed Brad's parents would be leaving immediately after the burial for a reception of Sandra's choosing. Matty, on the other hand, was debating whether or not to host a reception in town for Brad's local friends. She hadn't landed on an answer yet, but figured she'd have a day or two to sort it all out.

After talking about it all and sharing her indecision, Chen offered his place for a reception should she choose to host one in Windsor. She thanked him, but as she was not prepared to make any further decisions, she changed the topic to her book, the original reason she'd called him over.

They were going over the second to last point she wanted his input on when her phone rang. Seeing it was Vivi, she excused herself and answered.

"You were right," Vivi said without preamble. "She was a jockey."

"Was?" Matty asked, her stomach sinking.

"Her name was Courtney Carol, twenty-six years old and a jockey for a number of the local farms. By all accounts, she was good, very good, but not great. And she was killed nine months ago."

Matty swallowed. "How?"

"A single gunshot wound to the head. Up on an exercise track used for the horses about an hour north of Albany."

Matty's eyes sought the quiet view of the cows in the field as her mind processed this information. "Any ties to Brad?"

"We're looking into it. The bullets don't match those we pulled out of the victims in Windsor, so we know she wasn't killed with the same gun. But whether or not it was the same shooter, or if she had anything to do with Brad, or even if she knew him at all, are answers that we will need to find. Now that you have a name, have you seen it anywhere in Brad's things?"

She mentally went through all the paperwork she'd read through, all the files, and shook her head. "No, it doesn't ring a bell. But given what we know about the other people in the pictures, is there a chance she might have been involved in something like that?"

"Fraud or skimming funds?" Vivi responded, more mulling it over than asking a question. "We didn't find anything in her bank statements to indicate that, but you're right, given the company she was keeping, or rather the company her picture was keeping, we'll look into it a bit more. And given she was a jockey, we may want to look into the gambling aspect of it as well, fixing races and things like that."

Matty wasn't sure what to think of the new information and, after a few more minutes, they said their good-byes and ended the call.

"Everything okay?" Chen asked from the door between the kitchen, where she'd left him, and the office, where she now sat.

She frowned. "I'm not really sure. Vivi, who works in the crime lab in Albany," she clarified for Chen. "She just ID'd someone in a photo."

"Someone involved in Brad's death?" Chen asked, straightening away from the door.

Matty shrugged. "Hard to tell. She was a jockey and she was killed nine months ago. Vivi said they don't have any obvious ties between her and Brad, but they are looking into it."

Chen frowned. "I vaguely remember something about this. Was she shot?"

She looked up at Chen in surprise and nodded. "How did you know?"

Chen lifted a shoulder. "My family has horses, we race them around here sometimes. It was a big deal when it happened because there had never been such a seemingly cold-blooded murder in the racing community up here before. By all accounts, she was a good jockey, no rumors floated around about her or anything like that. That was what made it such a memorable event—not only had nothing like that ever happened before, but no one could think of any reason why it had happened to her," he said.

"Did you know her?" she asked.

Chen shook his head. "No. I don't get too involved in that part of the family business. My sister is really the one who is most heavily involved in the stables and with the horses, but I asked her about it after it happened. She knew Courtney but had never used her as a jockey for any of our horses. Though she did ride for a few friends of ours," he added.

"Do you know if she knew Brad?"

Again, Chen lifted a shoulder. "I never saw them together, but Brad knew a lot of people, it's possible he knew some of the owners she rode for and maybe met her through them? My sister might know."

To Matty, anything was possible. But the world of horse racing and jockeys and owners and trainers wasn't anything she knew much about.

"Do you want to go to the track and ask around? I can take you, if you like," Chen offered.

For a moment, she considered his offer. He was an owner and would have access to places she wouldn't if she ever went up to ask around on her own. But what would she find? What would she even ask?

She sighed and shook her head. "Thanks, Chen, I appreciate it, I really do. But I think I'll leave it to the professionals," she answered.

He studied her for a moment, as if expecting her to change her mind. When she didn't, he took a step back and gestured back toward the kitchen with his arm. "In that case, and if you're ready, perhaps we should finish this up and then maybe we can celebrate the completion of your next best seller."

At that, Matty let out a small laugh. She had no thoughts as to whether her book would be another best seller or not. It was true, she had several to her credit, but she preferred not to think about it too much and just produce the best book she could every time. But she could definitely get on board with the rest of Chen's suggestion. So, joining him in the kitchen, she got back to work. But not before putting a bottle of champagne in the refrigerator to chill.

CHAPTER 23

Dᴀꜱʜ ᴛᴏᴏᴋ ᴛʜᴇ ɴᴇxᴛ ᴅᴀʏ off and he and Matty were having a leisurely and late breakfast on her back porch when Matty's phone rang. Dash saw her glance at the number before she looked back at him.

"My father," she said as the phone rang again.

"Are you going to get it?" he asked. He knew she and her father had spoken a few times, but he also knew that she wasn't entirely sure what to make of the situation—not that he could blame her. That she didn't trust Douglas was obvious, but she wasn't unwilling to listen to him either.

Matty quietly debated as the phone rang in her hand then lifted a brow at him, silently asking if he would mind. He shook his head and she rose from the table, answering the call as she walked back into the kitchen and into the office. He watched her retreating figure for a moment then began to clear the table. He was just about to run the hot water in the kitchen sink when the dogs erupted in their usual early-warning style. Matty popped her head into the room, still on the phone, but he gestured to her that he would take care of it. When she disappeared back into the office, he made his way to the door.

Two cars pulled up as he stepped onto the patio. Both looked like rentals, though one was decidedly more sleek and expensive than the other.

A tall man with dark hair, dark eyes, and a dark suit emerged from the first, more utilitarian car; Dash pegged him as a government man. The second car produced an almost equally tall, stunning woman. She looked to be of mixed ethnicity, definitely some African-American heritage, but also some Caucasian, Asian, and maybe even Spanish. Her long, straight, black hair was pulled back by a clip at the nape of her neck and she wore the kind of outfit that looked like it cost more than Dash's entire wardrobe. The tailored skirt hugged her hips and long lean legs, and her blouse seemed made specifically for her, whispering across her body. And then there was the jewelry—a thick gold rope necklace and matching bracelet and diamond studs that could probably blind a man if caught in the light the right way.

The two men eyed her as she walked toward the patio. Aside from her general appearance, which was beyond striking, Dash couldn't help but be impressed by the way she navigated the gravel driveway in heels that should be illegal without appearing to give it a second thought.

Dash cast the man a look, silently asking if they were together. The man shook his head and stepped forward.

"I'm Special Agent Damian Rodriguez with the FBI and also a friend of Ian MacAllister's. I'm here to see Mathilde Brooks."

Dash glanced at the woman who had now joined them on the patio. A look of distaste had flashed across her face at the mention of the FBI, and whoever she was, she did not look like a woman you'd want to displease.

"And just what do you want with Matty?" she asked the agent before Dash could do the same.

Special Agent Rodriguez turned his gaze, one that was only slightly higher than the woman's, toward her. As he watched the two eye each other, Dash realized he now understood the phrase "tension so thick you could cut it with a knife," and for a moment he wondered if these two had known each other before arriving on Matty's doorstep.

But then Agent Rodriguez looked away. "It's FBI business, ma'am," he said. The woman looked at the agent for another long moment before turning to Dash.

"I'm Charlotte," she said. "I hope you've heard of me because I've *certainly* heard a lot about you."

Dash saw the agent's eyebrows go up. There was no mistaking the tone of sisterly conspiracy in Charlotte Lareaux's voice. And that was what Dash knew her to be: Matty's closest and oldest friend—close enough to be her sister.

"Charlotte, it's nice to meet you," Dash said, holding out his hand. She seemed to debate for a moment how to respond to him, then manners apparently got the better of her and she took his hand in hers. "Matty didn't mention you were coming up," he added.

"That's because Matty didn't know," Matty said, stepping out from behind Dash to give her friend a huge hug. "Not that I'm not glad to see you, but what on earth are you doing here?" she asked as she pulled away, still holding onto Charlotte's hand and giving it a quick squeeze before stepping back beside Dash.

Charlotte inclined her head and smiled. "Your mom was fretting about, well, you know," she said with a not very subtle nod of her head toward Dash. "And since she promised not to come until after the funeral, I offered to make the trip myself. Well, actually, it was me or *my* mom and I figured that, even though I'm nowhere near as good a cook as she is, I'm definitely more fun."

Dash watched Matty's face as Charlotte spoke and saw the kind of smile he didn't often see her wear, one of complete joy and comfort. It spoke volumes about just how close the two women were, and despite the surprise, Dash was glad Charlotte had come—was glad to be seeing this part of Matty's life.

He cleared his throat and Matty laughed. "Charlotte, this is Dashiell Kent; Dash this is Charlotte," she made the formal introductions. And then, acknowledging they weren't alone, Matty turned a questioning gaze on Agent Rodriguez.

The agent introduced himself to Matty just as Ian and Vivi pulled up.

"What's this about?" Matty asked when Ian and Vivi joined their group.

"Perhaps we can go inside and have a seat somewhere?" Ian suggested after Matty introduced Charlotte to the couple.

"After you introduce me to Damian," Vivi said. Dash saw Ian blink, as if he couldn't believe the two didn't know each other, then made the introductions. To Dash's surprise, Vivi stepped forward and gave the agent a long hug. Dash, who was standing closest to Agent Rodriguez, heard Vivi say, "I know what you did for Ian when he got back. Thank you."

When she pulled back, Rodriguez gave her a long look before releasing her back to Ian's side. Dash looked at the man, then at Ian, and though they were physically different in size and coloring, he could see some similarities—in their builds, in the way they carried themselves.

"You two served together?" he asked. Both men shared a look then nodded. Dash didn't have a clue what sorts of things they had done as Rangers, but it was clear the bond between them was strong, and based on what he'd heard Vivi say, Rodriguez must have been with Ian when he'd come back to the US. Must have been one of the people who'd helped Ian put his life, and body, back together before he'd come back home to Windsor.

In an obvious effort to lighten the mood, Damian grinned and gestured with his head toward Vivi, "See, MacAllister, I told you she's a dead ringer for a young Sophia Loren. Only she looks a lot happier now than she did in her FBI photo I saw a few months ago."

Dash had never seen Ian look even remotely embarrassed, but he saw a faint rise of color on his friend's cheeks now. Which made Agent Rodriguez laugh.

Taking pity on her fiancé, Vivi wrapped her arms around him and smiled. "That's because she *is* a lot happier now. In every way," she added, making everyone laugh except Ian, who rolled his eyes.

"Now, can we get on with things?" Ian asked, gesturing inside with the arm that wasn't wrapped around Vivi. Rising up on her tiptoes, Vivi kissed his cheek before stepping away and leading them all into the house. Matty and Charlotte followed her, the men came in behind them.

After everyone declined the offer of coffee, they sat at the kitchen table and Matty, holding Dash's hand, looked from Ian to Agent Rodriguez expectantly.

The two seemed to communicate silently with one another, maybe deciding who should go first, when Charlotte broke in. "Well, someone better speak because I have plans for Matty that don't involve sitting around all morning. No offense," she said with a nod to Vivi who lifted a shoulder.

"Ian?" Vivi said, prompting him.

Ian opened his mouth, but Agent Rodriguez cut him off with a look at Charlotte. Ian arched a brow in response and sat back.

"Ms.—?" Agent Rodriguez asked Charlotte, who grudgingly provided her last name.

"Ms. Lareaux, this is a federal matter and while I'm sure you are a good friend of Ms. Brooks, the conversation we need to have is about an ongoing investigation—an investigation everyone else here has been a part of—and isn't one we can have in front of people not involved," he continued.

"Oh, this is going to be interesting," Matty muttered from beside Dash as she, too, sat back.

Dash watched as Charlotte very calmly tilted her head to the side as if considering her response. Then, just as calmly, she sat forward, crossed her arms on the table and tapped her long, pale pink nails on the tabletop. "I'm not leaving Matty," was all she said.

"Ms. Lareaux," Agent Rodriguez warned.

"You can go all 'federal matter' on my ass as much as you like, Special Agent Rodriguez, but if you care to have a look, or call into your mother ship, I promise that you will find my security clearance is significantly higher than yours."

Agent Rodriguez's eyes narrowed. "What do you do that warrants your clearance?"

"I'm a consultant. I consult," she said, daring him to challenge her.

"On what?"

"Like I said, it's above your security clearance, Special Agent," she answered. "But if you'd like a few minutes to call your people, feel free, because now that I'm here, I'm involved and I'm not leaving."

For a moment, Dash wasn't sure what Rodriguez would do, but not ten seconds passed before the agent abruptly pushed away from the table, pulled out his phone, and walked back out onto the patio. When he walked back in, it was clear from his expression that he'd learned something interesting. What it was would remain a mystery, at least to Dash, and he sat back down at the table.

"Ms. Lareaux, welcome to the investigation. You've been authorized to come on board." He paused for a moment then a good-natured smile touched his lips. "Actually I'm glad to have you on the team, I'm not much of a numbers guy."

Charlotte studied Rodriguez for a moment as the rest of them glanced back and forth between the two. Finally, Charlotte gave a nod of acceptance. "Happy to help in any way I can."

Beside him, Matty let out a long breath. "Now that we've cleared that up, what *is* going on, Special Agent Rodriguez?"

"Call me Damian, please. First, you should know that this isn't my usual kind of case. But because it involves Windsor and I know Ian, the agency asked me to lead the operation."

"What involves Windsor? What operation?" Dash asked. From the look on Vivi and Ian's faces he'd wager they already knew. And judging by the frown that touched Matty's lips, she'd noticed too and didn't much care for being one of the last to know.

"I assume this is about Brad?" Matty asked.

Damian nodded. "Do you remember a piece of mail you posted for him—judging by the postmark, it must have been soon after you arrived?"

Matty's brow creased as she thought, then her head drew back as she obviously remembered something. "Yes, I do. There were three and they were right there," she said, pointing to the wooden pocket hanging from the wall by the door. "I noticed the envelopes were stamped and addressed my second day here. I figured he'd forgotten to post them, so I took them with me into town and dropped them in the mailbox near the grocery store," she said, repeating what she'd told Ian and Vivi the day they'd found Brad's body. Dash wrapped his other hand around hers, enveloping hers in his as her voice cracked at the knowledge that Brad hadn't forgotten the letters but hadn't been able to mail them because he'd already been killed.

Damian nodded. "We thought as much."

"How did you know I mailed it?" Matty asked.

"Fingerprints," Damian answered.

"Was there," she paused, hesitant to ask what Dash knew she was going to. She swallowed. "Was there something bad in the letters?"

Damian wagged his head. "Yes, but not in the sense you seem worried about. The letter made it to our office in a few days, but it took a while to move through the channels and be verified."

"What did you need to verify?" Charlotte asked, sitting back now, taking in the conversation. Damian glanced at her before turning back to Matty.

"Brad Brooks provided detailed information to us regarding the activities of a branch of the Irish Mafia that we've been trying to track and bring down for the past ten years. They are based out of Boston, but have significant holdings and dealings in racetracks and horses around the country, including some in this state. Thanks to him and the information he provided, we're collecting and documenting evidence and should be able to execute a raid in the next day or two."

Dash blinked at the information. He didn't know what he'd been expecting the FBI agent to say, but it wasn't that Brad had helped them bring down a branch of the Irish Mafia. Matty looked just as stunned as he was. Charlotte was frowning, looking to be contemplating everything.

"I don't understand," Matty managed to say.

"We don't know how he did it either, and that's why we'll be bringing in a team of people to go through all of Brad's things. They should be here shortly," he added with a glance at his watch before continuing. "We do know that he provided enough information in the letter he sent—including bank accounts, dates of transactions, movements of the members, and those sorts of things—that we might even be able to bring the whole organization down."

"So, he was doing something good?" Matty asked, still sounding somewhat confused, but Dash didn't miss the tiny little spark of hope that interjected itself into her tone.

Damian frowned. "Is there a reason you might think otherwise?"

Dash looked at Ian as Matty looked at Vivi. Vivi gave a small nod of encouragement. Matty took a deep breath and answered.

"I don't know, Damian," she said with a shake of her head. And then she told him everything she'd told Vivi and Ian a few days earlier, about the pictures, what she'd found out about the people in them, the jockey, and the visit from the bank officer. "Don't get me wrong, I don't *want* to find out he did something wrong, but if there were irregularities in the accounts he worked with at work *and* he had ties to all these other people who were convicted of various financial crimes, I just had to wonder. And knowing he had inside information into organized crime, enough to maybe even bring it down, seems to suggest he might have been a part of it, doesn't it?" she asked.

"You didn't tell Damian any of this?" Dash interjected, directing the question to Ian and Vivi.

Ian shook his head. "He called on his way here and we spoke for five minutes. I didn't have much of a chance to say anything other than that we would meet him here."

"It's true," Damian interjected, obviously not wanting to sow any seeds of discontent between friends and neighbors. "I got the assignment a few days ago and we've only been focusing on the information in the letters—trying to verify and confirm it. We didn't know who'd sent the information until Matty's fingerprint turned up on the envelope; we identified her last night and tracked her up here to Windsor through credit card statements. That's when we learned about Brad, his murder, and the other events that have been happening up here. I was on the first flight this morning and called Ian on my way. We may have a head start on the Mafia angle, but we don't know much about Brad Brooks himself, other than it fits that he is the one who provided the details. And as to what you might be thinking, Matty, I wish I had a clearer answer for you, but at the moment, all I can say is we're looking into it all."

"Is there any possibility that the information he gave you in the letter is wrong? Or that maybe he was a part of it, but had a change of heart?" Matty asked. "I guess, I mean," she paused, took a breath, and continued. "I guess I mean to ask, is there any chance, since you don't know much about Brad or his movements or motivations, that what he gave you was misinformation or an attack of a guilty conscience?"

"With respect to the possibility of misinformation, no, absolutely not," came Damian's swift answer. Dash felt some of the tension leave Matty's hand and he rubbed a thumb over her palm as she gave him a soft smile.

"But as for an attack of a guilty conscience," Damian shrugged, "I don't know. Like I said, we'll have to dig into his things to find out. But at this point, we don't have enough either way to say if he was involved in criminal activities or just a Good Samaritan, reporting what he knew."

"Okay," Matty said on a breath. "I know it's ridiculous, but if you discover something bad about him, it will be nice to know he did some good, too. Even if it was just a last ditch effort."

"And we may not discover anything bad about him," Charlotte added, placing a comforting hand on Matty's arm. "We don't know what the bank officer was looking for or what raised the red flag. Maybe it was Brad looking into accounts to gather the information for the FBI. Just because he did something that gave the bank concern doesn't mean he did something wrong."

For a long moment, Matty looked at her friend. Then she sat back and let out a sigh. "Okay, I like the sound of that much better.

I like the thought of him trying to help rather than embezzling, or being part of the Irish Mafia, or something like that. I know you'll find whatever you'll find, but I think I'll do my best to try to think the best of him until you all tell me otherwise," she said with a meaningful look at Charlotte, who gave her an answering nod. "So, this mean you're going to look at the members of this gang, of this Mafia branch, as potential suspects in Brad's death, right?" she asked, turning to Ian and Vivi, who both nodded.

"Yes, we will," Vivi answered. "We'd like to cooperate with the FBI and exchange information. We may not be able to look into specific people until after they conduct their raid, but you can rest assured that if there is a link between Brad's death and the information he sent the FBI—and given what the information is, it's not too hard to believe—we'll do our best to find it."

Matty's eyes swept around the table. Dash knew this wasn't at all what she'd thought her trip up to Windsor would be like. He'd bet that never in a million years did she think she'd be surrounded by law enforcement, her best friend, and her future fiancé—because that is what he was, despite not having said much on the subject the day before—discussing her half brother's death and the Irish Mafia. But she was handling it well. And he wouldn't have expected any different.

"You'll take care of telling Douglas and Sandra what they need to know?" she asked Ian who nodded again. "Okay," she said, turning back to Damian. "What do you need from me?"

Damian smiled and Dash knew they were almost out of the woods.

CHAPTER 24

MATTY GATHERED UP HER THINGS while Dash collected the dogs' supplies. They planned to load up his truck and move her, her car, and the dogs to his house for the time being. Matty didn't mind being usurped from Brad's house while the FBI went through everything. Damian had said she could stay, but she really had no wish to be underfoot all day. With the arrival of the FBI team, there were just too many law enforcement officials around for her to relax anyway.

All that was left to do was bring her bags down, grab her computer, and load the dogs. Coming down the stairs, they were about to take a left into the short hall that led to the office when Damian's voice, sharp with authority, caused Matty to pull Dash to an abrupt halt right outside the door.

"Agent Pearson, I hope you put more thought into how you investigate than how you flirt. Do you have any idea who this is?" Matty heard Damian say to one of the agents who'd arrived not long ago. Matty had briefly met Agent Pearson, a good-looking young man from the Albany FBI office, when he'd arrived. Emphasis on young.

"Her name is Charlotte Lareaux, our financial consultant, sir," came the answer—the last word sounding a bit forced. "And I wasn't flirting," Pearson added, making him sound even younger than he probably was.

Dash raised his brows at Matty as she fought a smile. "For an FBI agent, he's not very good at lying, is he?" Dash whispered. Matty's smile cracked and she shook her head. She'd seen the way

Damian looked at Charlotte and she was curious to hear how this exchange was going to play out. Clearly, he was displeased with the young agent's behavior. It wasn't professional, to be sure, but if Matty wanted to place a bet, she'd bet that Damian just plain didn't like another man flirting with Charlotte.

"You were," Damian countered, his voice brokering no argument. "But more to the point, she's more than just a consultant, Pearson. She also works with the EU, the World Bank, and the IMF. Just last week, she was in Europe meeting with the EU on the debt crisis. In the five days she was there, she met with prime ministers of three of the G7 countries. And her last boyfriend, if you're curious, was Anthony Goulakis, sole heir of one of Europe's wealthiest shipping magnates. She's not likely to be impressed by a twenty-six-year-old FBI agent based in Albany, NY, even if you had—what was it you called it, Ms. Lareaux?" Damian asked.

"A magic cock," Charlotte supplied.

"Yes, even if you had a magic cock. That said, if the badge does give you one, like Ms. Lareaux intimated, maybe we should exchange badges, because I've been wearing mine longer than you and I have to admit, I'm still just a regular guy."

Matty choked back a laugh as Dash did the same. It was just like her friend to feel no compunction with setting down a young agent, even in a graphic way. Charlotte was not a woman who allowed her time to be wasted, and though Matty felt a little sorry for the young agent, she kind of regretted having missed the exchange. Although it wouldn't have been the first time she had heard Charlotte call out an officer for using his badge like it was a magnet for sex. There was nothing Charlotte hated more than someone using publicly granted authority for personal gain.

"Sorry about that," Damian said after Pearson had muttered an apology and shuffled out of the office into the kitchen. "I can't really blame him for trying, but you were right to set him straight when he tried to use his badge, his position, to impress you."

"You do your research, don't you, Agent Rodriguez," Charlotte responded after a pause.

"I try."

"You did forget two things, though," she said. "I also met with two Nobel Laureates, in economics, of course. And I dislike the term 'boyfriend,' as the men I date aren't anywhere near boyish. Of course, Anthony *was* an exception, so I suppose I'll grant you that description this time around."

Damian chuckled and Matty cast Dash another look. She knew she should walk in and pick up her computer, but she didn't want to interrupt this conversation. On the other hand, when Dash suggested with a gesture of his head that they leave the two alone and head into the kitchen, Matty shook her head—she was also loath to stop eavesdropping. Dash dropped his chin and looked at her from under his dark lashes, seriously questioning her behavior. Shrugging and grinning, she dared him to challenge her since she had no doubt he'd done his fair share of eavesdropping on his siblings in his day. Of course, he'd been a child at the time.

"Thank you, Charlotte, for agreeing to help out," Damian continued. He hadn't made another sound and Matty wondered if he'd walked toward Charlotte or kept his distance. "I know we have teams of people that can do this work, but they're in DC. The Albany team will be good for everything else, but they don't have the expertise you or our forensic economists have. You're saving us a lot of time by getting started on all this."

Matty could all but hear Charlotte shrug. "Matty is like a sister to me. She *is* a sister to me in every way but by blood. If I can help her out, I will."

"But it's not what you came up here to do," Damian pointed out, more conversationally than argumentatively.

"No, it isn't," Charlotte agreed. "I came up here because she's all but living with a man she's known less than three weeks. But I know her well enough to know that she won't give *that* any thought at all until this stuff with Brad is sorted out."

Matty frowned. It sounded suspiciously like Charlotte thought she might be with Dash because he was easy, because he was there, because he was a distraction. She looked up to find him watching her and reached out to place a hand on his chest. One of his hands came up and covered hers, the other wrapped around her waist.

"They look pretty in love to me," Damian said. "I'm not sure there's anything to worry about. Dash seems like a good guy. I know Ian likes him."

Startled by the mention of love, Matty's eyes widened. They hadn't ever said those words, and to be honest, she hadn't really given much thought *to* saying them. Not because she did or didn't feel that way, it was just something, yet *another* something, she'd never thought much about—yet another way she was emotionally stunted. As if sensing her thoughts, Dash lifted her hand to his lips and placed a sweet, silent kiss on the sensitive skin at the inside of her wrist, holding her gaze the entire time. It was just a moment, a moment like so many others, yet somehow, standing there in the hallway, it felt like it held so much meaning.

"People like Matty and I don't know much about love, Agent Rodriguez. If she is in love, it will be the first time, and knowing Matty, probably the last. If she does love him, then I want to be sure he feels the same, because if Matty has put herself out there in that way—in the way that kind of relationship would require—and he doesn't feel the same, she won't ever do it again."

"Love is a one-time thing for her?" Damian asked.

"If that," Charlotte answered.

"And you?" he asked.

"Not even going there, Agent Rodriguez."

"Call me Damian, please," he said. "But you know, I think both you and Matty know a lot more about love than you probably think. You have each other."

"No argument there, but I can count on one hand how many people she trusts, really trusts. And I wouldn't even need my thumb," she added.

"And how many do you trust?" Damian asked.

"One less than, Matty. Or so it's looking like," she added.

Matty still held Dash's gaze, even as a tightness spread across her chest. His thumb gently rubbed the hand he still held and his eyes seemed to implore her to breathe, to relax, to trust him. He brushed a strand of hair from her face then slipped his free hand behind her neck. Only he didn't pull her in for a kiss, but rather dipped his head and rested his cheek against her temple, pulling her just close enough to feel—to absorb—his steady, solid presence. After a moment or two, she relaxed against him. She knew she didn't have anything to worry about as far as Dash was concerned. He was there; he wasn't going anywhere. And while he wasn't going to let her go anywhere either, he seemed to have no wish to rush her to any conclusions about the two of them.

She let out a deep breath and heard Damian do the same.

"Well," the special agent said. "Thanks again, and please let me know if you need anything or if I can do anything to help."

Matty heard Charlotte murmur a thank you, then Damian's footsteps heading to the kitchen where he started talking with one of the other four agents that had arrived from Albany. For a moment Matty was frozen in indecision, unable to decide whether to run or stay with Dash in the hall for another long while. As if sensing her indecision, Dash stepped away and, still holding her hand, pulled her into the office.

Charlotte swung around from her spot at the desk. Her eyes dropped to Matty's hand entwined with Dash's before coming back to her face.

"You okay?" Charlotte asked.

She nodded. "I just need my computer and then we'll go."

"This is Brad's though, right?" Charlotte asked, pointing to the computer now sitting on the desk in front of her.

She nodded again, then frowned as a memory floated into her mind.

"Matty?" Charlotte asked.

Matty pursed her lips for a moment, and as the thought took full form her frown deepened. "It could be nothing," she said.

"What could be nothing?" Damian asked, reappearing in the doorway between the kitchen and the office.

"There was a day," she paused and her brow creased in

thought. Because now that she was thinking about it, there were *two* incidents.

"Matty?" Damian prompted.

"A few weeks ago, Bob, the Lab," she added, pointing as the animal himself walked in, looked at them, then walked out. "Well, someone cut his toe off."

"Excuse me?" Charlotte said. Damian's response was a bit more colorful.

Matty looked at Dash who was studying her. She swallowed. "Well, of course I rushed him to the vet, to Dash, with my neighbor's help. But when I got back, I remember thinking that Brad's computer was in a different place than where I'd first seen it."

"Charlotte," Damian said in warning, but Charlotte was already backing away from the device. "Tell me what happened that day and when it was," he ordered.

"There's not much to add," she said after Dash had given the exact date of the event. "It was in the morning. I think I was at the clinic just before noon, maybe?"

Dash nodded in agreement.

"And then back home probably three hours later," Matty added. Damian had already called in two of the other agents to take the computer away and barked an order for them to fingerprint it.

"My prints will be all over it," Matty said quietly, suddenly feeling a little ashamed of her solo, and somewhat sneaky, investigations.

"Say that again?" Damian asked.

Matty pursed her lips. Damian crossed his arms over his chest and leveled a look at her. Dash's arm came around her shoulders.

"I wanted to see if I could find anything on his computer. I, uh, I figured out the password and spent several hours on it. My prints will be everywhere."

Whatever Damian was thinking, it didn't show on his face. Matty cast a glance at Charlotte who was also studying her, her head cocked.

"What?" Matty finally said. "Don't pretend you wouldn't have done the same thing," she said to her friend.

One side of Charlotte's lips tipped into a grin. "Of course *I* would have, but I'm nosy and sneaky. You aren't usually the sneaky one."

"I sneak," Matty retorted, though why she was offended she didn't really know. It must have been some knee-jerk, childish reaction.

"Honey, you're about as good a sneak as a fat man hiding behind a sapling. But I love you anyway," Charlotte retorted.

Matty narrowed her eyes at her friend.

"Anyway," Damian cut in. "That's good to know, we already have your prints on file, Matty. We can eliminate those. Is there anything else we should know about? Anything else you remember?"

"What about the day we went out to take care of Kristen's horse," Dash said, reminding her of the second incident.

"What happened that day, and who is Kristen?" Damian asked.

And so Matty told him. She told him about Bogey getting tangled in the fence. Dash interjected, adding information about the conversation he'd had with Ian after Ian had come out to look at the fence where Kristen's horse had been caught—an event neither man thought was an accident.

"Okay, so you have two suspicious incidents involving animals. What made you think of the horse incident?" Damian pressed.

"Because when we came back, Matty thought things in the office looked different," Dash supplied.

Damian frowned.

"Different how?" Charlotte asked, taking a few steps toward the door to the kitchen, away from the desk.

"I couldn't find my computer when I came in to look for it. But then we had a lot of people stop over that day to pay their condolences when news got out that the body was Brad's. The next day, I went into the office and my computer was there but there were a number of small things that looked out of place, like cords that didn't look like they were in the same position as when I'd last noticed them, paper edges sticking out from the file cabinet. But we've had a lot going on the last two weeks. It's possible I was just imagining it," Matty said.

"Or not," Damian countered, calling in the other two agents. His eyes swept the room and he let out a long sigh. "Sorry, Ms. Lareaux," he said. Charlotte seemed to know what he was referring to because she lifted a shoulder and stepped closer to Matty.

"Pearson, Anderson," Damian directed the two agents. "This room needs to be dusted, too. And as soon as the computer is done, please ensure it gets to Ms. Lareaux." He gestured the rest of them out of the office, leaving just the two agents inside.

"Do you have something you can do for an hour or so?" Damian asked Charlotte.

"I'll go check into a bed and breakfast or something," Charlotte answered, unperturbed by the change in schedule.

Matty, on the other hand, felt ill at the thought that someone might have been in the house while she and Dash were out. If it had happened once, or maybe even twice, how many other times had it happened? Dash squeezed her hand and whispered in her ear, "You're okay."

Bob came up and poked his wet nose against her other hand. She glanced down at the dog and realized that at least she could be fairly certain no one had been in the house *while* she was home or Bob and the other canines would have barked up a holy racket. Which is why, if it was true that someone had been inside, it had only been when they'd known she would be away, likely because they'd orchestrated it that way.

"You can stay with us," Dash was saying to Charlotte as he led Matty through the kitchen toward the patio. Both Charlotte and Damian followed.

"Thanks, but I like my own space and I'm allergic to dogs. It's not bad and a few hours around them isn't anything a Benadryl can't handle, but any more than that and I'll be a mess. And I'd rather not be doped up going through the files later. Any suggestions on where to stay?"

Dash let go of Matty's hand as they stepped out onto the patio. He hung back with Damian as she and Charlotte walked to his truck. Opening the truck cab's rear door, Matty called to the dogs and let them pile in, one by one, as she and Charlotte spoke.

"There are a few places to stay, but the best is probably The Tavern because it has a restaurant and bar downstairs. We've eaten there a few times, and Rob, the owner, is handling the beverage service for Vivi and Ian's wedding in October. Why don't you try that? If he has a room, we can meet there for dinner tonight once you're done here, so you don't have to be around dogs, or dog hair, for the rest of the day."

Charlotte agreed and Matty gave her directions to The Tavern. When she finished, she was struck again at how strange her life had become in the past few weeks. She could almost understand Charlotte's hesitancy when it came to her new situation. Matty was a city girl through and through. Or so she'd always thought. And now, here she was—wearing a sundress and flip flops, her hair pulled back into a low ponytail, giving Charlotte directions to a small-town inn—acting like she'd lived here her whole life.

As if reading her thoughts, Charlotte smiled. "Who would have thought we'd ever find ourselves in this kind of situation? Out here in the middle of nowhere, actually helping law enforcement."

Matty cocked her head then gave a short nod to Dash. "Yeah, the situation is unusual in more ways than one," she said with her own smile.

"It's a long way from the Bronx, isn't it," Charlotte added.

Matty nodded. "Again, in more ways than one."

"He seems like a good guy," Charlotte said, turning her gaze to where Dash and Damian were talking.

"He is. But you're reserving final judgment and I'm okay with that," she responded.

Charlotte's eyes came back to hers and in them Matty saw all their years together. All the tears and the pain, but also the laughter, the love, and the joy they'd shared. "Thank you for coming, Charlotte. And not just because you're helping to sort through the mess I've managed to find myself in. Thanks, well, just thanks for coming. For checking on me. For caring." She cut herself off and cleared her throat.

"Because whatever else happens, we'll always have each other," Charlotte said.

Matty inclined her head. "We always will," she agreed.

Then Charlotte grinned and added, "Even when you're like ten-months pregnant and huge as an elephant and hating your life and Dash for getting you that way. You'll still have me."

Matty laughed, making both Damian and Dash look up. "I will *not* be huge as an elephant, you twig. And even if I am, you better not mention it or I'll have your mom zap you with some gris-gris."

Charlotte laughed too, especially at the reference to her mother's creole past. "Yeah, and if you're carrying the first grandbaby between us, she'd probably do it, too."

CHAPTER 25

"WERE YOU AND CHARLOTTE TALKING about kids?" Dash asked much later that afternoon. They'd been asked not to discuss the case with anyone so had pretty much kept to themselves all day. Currently, they were camped out on his porch swing enjoying the pleasant weather. He'd been reading and Matty had been mostly quiet, lying on the swing with her head in his lap. Her quiet wasn't pensive or worried though; she looked more like she was just enjoying the lack of activity.

Her eyes swiveled to him at his question. "Kind of," she said, her hair spilling across his thighs.

He studied her eyes for a moment then shrugged. "Okay, thought so."

After a minute or two, she spoke again. "Does that freak you out?"

He looked down at her again and though the thought of kids hadn't really been on the forefront of his mind, he found he was far from freaked out by it. He shook his head. "No, it doesn't freak me out. My parents will be happy about more grandkids. Does it freak you out?"

After a moment, Dash realized he'd been holding his breath and he willed himself to breath. Slowly, he let his lungs empty as Matty seemed to mull the question over.

"Not really," she said, sounding more confused by her answer than anything else.

"Good." He glanced at his book again, more in an effort to hide his surprise at the topic of conversation than because he was all that interested in the book. "Ever thought of how many you'd like?" he asked without moving his eyes from the words he held not ten inches from his face—though, if asked, he wouldn't have been able to recall a single one of them.

He felt her shoulders shrug against his thigh. "Not really, but maybe two?"

A heartbeat passed before he let himself answer. "Two's good."

Matty was silent for a long while after that and he wasn't at all sure what she was thinking. Was this idle conversation for her? Was she thinking about having kids with *him*? And if she was, at some point they'd have to figure out their living situation. He had never really lived in a city, not for any length of time, and didn't really want to. But he knew he would for her. She had a big life and a history and her mom in DC. If she wanted to be in DC, he could understand that. He figured he'd have to do more small animal work; it wasn't his favorite but he could deal with that. He was about to mention that to her, to tell her he would move to DC to be with her if that was what she wanted, when she spoke again, rendering him almost speechless.

"You'll have to fence that swimming pond, though," she said, waving toward the pond in question about a hundred feet from the house. "I'd worry too much about the kids if it wasn't fenced in."

"Um, okay," he said. Not a problem. He and his dad could have it safely fenced in a weekend if that was what Matty wanted. She didn't seem interested in saying any more; she just dropped her foot down to the porch and gave the swing a gentle nudge. They rocked slowly for a long moment before Dash spoke again.

"Not to push or anything, but I'm assuming this means you're okay with the whole Kent family tradition of quick marriages."

She made a noncommittal sound that brought his eyebrows up and his book down. He looked down at her; she looked up at him. "I know not everyone needs a piece of paper to be committed to each other," he said, "but call me a traditionalist, because I do. We *will* get married Matty."

She smiled at him. He wasn't sure what to make of that. "Are you laying down the law, Dr. Kent?"

"Yes."

Her smile broadened, though she was saved from responding by her phone ringing. Given everything that was going on, neither of them were ignoring any calls these days. She looked at the number and rose from her reclined position.

"It's Charlotte," she mouthed, before rising from the swing altogether and walking toward the end of the porch. He didn't take offense that she'd moved away, rather he smiled at the fact that she'd quickly realized that the best location for cell reception in his little valley was the east end of the house.

When she ended the call, she came back to his end of the porch looking a little bit like the cat who found the cream.

"Charlotte said she's done for the rest of the afternoon. She's heading back to The Tavern and asked if we wanted to meet her there for dinner and a drink. Of course, I said yes."

"Of course you did," he responded. She held out her hand to him and he let her pull him up. When he stood in front of her, she wrapped her arms around him and started nibbling his neck in the way that always got to him.

"We *are* getting married, Matty," he said. She tilted her head back and grinned then took his hand and started leading him toward his bedroom.

"In a church. We're both Catholic, so that will be easy. With our families," he elaborated as she led him upstairs.

"Now?" she asked as she pulled him to a stop at the foot of his bed and moved her hands to the top button on his jeans.

"What?" he asked, distracted.

"Are we getting married now? Right this minute?" she asked, sliding her hands down along his hips.

"What? No, of course, not." His hands were slowly tugging the straps of her dress down over her shoulders.

"Then can I make a suggestion?" she asked, leaning into him. He looked down at her.

She grinned again then went up on her tiptoes, her lips a hairsbreadth away from his. "I think we should stop talking."

• • •

Matty was still smiling and still not saying much of anything when they walked into The Tavern a few hours later. Charlotte, who'd been sitting at the bar nursing a glass of wine, turned when they walked in, took one look at them, and rolled her eyes even as she laughed.

"Guess I don't have to guess how *some* people spent the afternoon while I was slaving away over computer files," she said as she walked toward them. She was wearing jeans and a sleeveless silk top that fit her figure perfectly. But then again, Charlotte had been wearing nothing but things that fit her perfectly since the day she could afford to. It also helped that she had the kind of body clothes just sat well on. She wasn't skinny per se, but she was nowhere near voluptuous and had none of the curves that Matty had. Charlotte always said she had a body that was neither here nor there—not small enough to be called petite but not quite full enough to have assets to flaunt either. But whatever her body was, clothes definitely liked it.

Matty laughed then glanced at Dash, who was trying not to look too embarrassed. "She's just jealous," she said, giving her friend a kiss on the cheek and then a big hug.

They were about to make their way to a table when Damian Rodriguez trotted down the stairs. Earlier, in his suit, Matty had thought he was a handsome man; now, in jeans, a t-shirt, and even a pair of flip-flops, she thought he looked better yet.

"You're gawking," Dash teased, nudging her as Damian came to a stop in front of them and graced them all with a killer grin.

"I'm just surprised by how different he looks out of his suit," she shot back innocently. Dash rolled his eyes but didn't seem truly concerned.

"Agent Rodriguez," Charlotte said.

"Damian," he reminded her.

"I didn't realize you were staying here, too," Charlotte continued.

"I heard you guys talking about it, then Ian and Vivi recommended it, too. They are actually joining me for dinner. Maybe we should make it a sixsome?" he asked as the couple in question walked in. Vivi must have said something funny because Ian was laughing and shaking his head.

Everyone said their hellos and agreed to eat together. Wanting some time with her friend, Matty sat herself beside Charlotte, who was at the head of the table. Vivi was on Charlotte's other side while Dash sat between Matty and Damian, who took a seat at the head of the other end of the table, and Ian sat beside Vivi.

Drinks and dinner were ordered and lively conversation ensued. As if by tacit agreement, no one mentioned the investigation into Brad's death or the Irish Mafia. Rather, the men slipped into conversation about the area and work while Matty, Charlotte, and Vivi talked a lot about Charlotte's work. Vivi, ever the mental powerhouse, was intrigued by the machinations behind the global economy. Later, when the conversation turned to animals, Dash and the other two men joined in to discuss the use of search-and-rescue dogs at disaster sites.

"Have you used them yourself?" Dash asked Vivi, who shook her head.

"No, they have handlers who live, train, and travel with them. It's highly specialized. Do you have any as clients?" she asked.

Dash inclined his head. "There are a couple of people up here who train them. I went down to help out after 9/11 with a family who had two dogs. I was just starting vet school at the time, but I had some training—enough to help the certified vets who were down there working on the dogs."

Matty frowned; she hadn't known that about him. But it didn't really surprise her. She slipped her hand into his under the table.

"That must have been intense," Damian said.

Dash just gave a nod. Matty would wager that "intense" was a huge understatement.

"You and I were both in the army by then," Ian said to Damian, sitting back, remembering. "Ranger training."

"Training sure as shit got cut short though, didn't it?" Damian added.

"We did okay," Ian countered.

Damian gave a sharp nod in agreement. "Damn straight," he said. "What about you, ladies?" he asked with a nod to Vivi and Charlotte.

"I was working on my doctorate and in medical school, I ended up volunteering in a lab in Boston where they sent some of the remains for identification. They didn't have much need for my medical background," Vivi said, sadness creeping into her voice. "So I did what I could do," she added, then looked at Charlotte.

"I was just starting my PhD in Economics at Johns Hopkins, but I was interning with a professor who was brought in by the government to assess the financial impact of 9/11. Not just the cost of things like lost property, but everything you can imagine, from the cost to the healthcare system, to the interruption in banking systems, to the days of lost productivity that would inevitably follow for years after the attacks as people began to heal. As terrible as it sounds, it was what first got me started looking at financial systems as just that, a system within a much larger system that is our society. I know people like to put finances in a box, but the truth is, money isn't a means to an ends, it's a vital part of how we live and function and if it's not functioning well, the whole system can become sick. So to speak," she added, then looked away somewhat embarrassed by her sentiments.

Vivi cocked her head. "I hadn't really thought of it that way, but I can see what you mean. Have you ever done that kind of assessment after a natural disaster?"

Charlotte nodded. "Several, actually. New Orleans, of course, but also Haiti and the Japanese earthquake and tsunami. Unfortunately, there isn't a short list of work in that area."

"Brad was in Haiti. And New Orleans," Matty said before realizing what was coming out of her mouth. She'd been enjoying the evening, the opportunity to enjoy her friends without thinking about what was really going on. And now she'd just brought it all back.

"He was?" Charlotte asked, sitting back in her chair and taking a sip of wine.

Matty nodded. "I don't really know what he was doing," she said with a look to Vivi and Ian. She was unsure of how much she should say to her friend about what they had found in the photos.

"We don't know what he was doing either, but we did find photos of a few people who were subsequently charged and convicted of various crimes," Ian interjected.

Charlotte frowned. "What kind of crimes?"

"One was fraud. Some sort of defective product, a water filter, I believe, that was purchased by some of the relief agencies," Matty said.

"That was in Haiti," Vivi supplied. "The other people were also convicted of fraud, but also self-dealing and coercion, with respect to the government contracts they were awarded."

Charlotte cocked her head, obviously thinking about something. "I don't remember reading about that," she said.

Ian wagged his head. "It was mostly kept quiet, both of them, because of the implications and fallout."

"Charlotte?" Matty asked.

"Was there a settlement in either case? For the people injured, I mean, not the criminal prosecutions?" Charlotte asked.

Both Vivi and Ian shook their heads. "Not that we know of, or nothing substantial," Vivi added.

For a moment, Matty watched Charlotte mull this new information over, completely in the dark about what was going through her friend's head. And Charlotte didn't seem willing to share.

"Can I get that information from you?" Charlotte asked Vivi and Ian.

"Of course," Ian said. "We can have Carly, one of the police officers here in town who is also working on the case, e-mail it to you tonight, if you'd like?"

Charlotte gave a distracted nod, "That would be great."

Matty was about to ask her friend just what she was thinking when the door to The Tavern opened and her father walked in. Dash must have felt her stiffen because he gave her hand a gentle but reassuring squeeze.

Douglas's eyes caught hers as he removed his hat and a wayward thought floated through her mind that he did not look like a baseball hat kind of guy. He was tall, like both his children, and distinguished looking, even in his grief. But he looked more like he should be having power lunches and wearing suits than eating at a tavern in jeans and a baseball hat.

Tentatively, he took a few steps toward Matty and her friends. When she didn't obviously turn away from him, he walked the rest of the way.

"Matty," he said, rolling the hat between his hands. His eyes swept the table, now cleared of their meals but scattered with a few glasses, then found hers again.

"Douglas," she said.

His eyes moved around the table again, this time taking in the others. When he recognized Vivi and Ian, he nodded a greeting.

"Is there any news?" he asked Ian. "I know this probably isn't the time or place," he hastened apologetically.

"It's fine, Mr. Brooks," Ian said. His voice was soothing, but Matty saw Damian's eyes dart up in recognition of the name—just as Ian intended, no doubt. "We have a few new leads we're working on. A few good ones. It's an ongoing investigation, so we can't say much more than that, but we hope to have some information for you in the next day or so."

For a moment Douglas just stood there staring at Ian. But to Matty, he looked more to be staring into the empty air between them. Then he nodded and turned back to her.

Matty had felt Charlotte straighten as soon as Douglas had

walked in. Giving her loyal friend a reassuring look, she turned back to her father.

"I was out helping the churches with the cleanup," he said, holding up his baseball hat as if it was a sign of labor. "Some of the community centers and schools and senior homes still need a lot of cleanup," he added, sounding more and more lost.

"I'm sure they were happy to have the help," Matty replied.

He looked away, then back again. "Did you get my message? About the service," he added.

She nodded. "Yes, next Saturday. We'll be there," she said.

He seemed to let out a sigh of relief, but it was hard to tell because his shoulders were already so low. "Thank you. Will you sit with the family?"

The request caught Matty so well and truly off guard that her head drew back in surprise. She glanced at Charlotte who was frowning, then to Dash who seemed to be signaling that whatever she decided would be fine with him. She held Dash's gaze for another long moment, before turning back to her father.

"Maybe we can talk about this later in the week?" There was no way she was prepared to sit next to Sandra, but she also didn't know a gentle way to say that to her father. And for some reason, it was important to her to say it right, to not be hasty or inconsiderate in her response.

Douglas opened his mouth, then shut it and nodded. "Yes, that would be fine."

Matty let out her own sigh of relief. This was also *not* a conversation she wanted to be having in front of a table full of people.

"How about I call you tomorrow?" she suggested. Surprising both of them.

Doulas held her gaze for a moment more, then nodded. "That would be nice," he said. Rolling his hat one more time, his eyes flickered around the table again. "Well, I'll leave you to your meal, then," he turned and was gone.

The minute Douglas rounded the corner for the stairs leading up to the rooms, Charlotte turned to Matty and asked if she was okay. She glanced around the table; Charlotte wasn't the only one concerned. Everyone was looking at her with worried expressions except Damian, who knew nothing of the situation.

Matty took a deep breath and smiled. "It's fine, I'm fine. I'll deal with it later." Now everyone cast her a doubtful look except Damian, who was frowning. "It's a long story, Damian. Charlotte can fill you in during your breaks tomorrow," she added.

"Speaking of tomorrow," Damian said, pushing his chair back from the table. Charlotte immediately followed suit. "We have a long day. I'm hoping we can get what we need to move forward," he added, tossing a wad of cash on the table to cover his dinner.

Ian pushed the money back, refusing to let his friend cover the meal. "Don't be ridiculous," he said.

Damian looked to argue for a moment, then grinned. "The government thanks you then, as do I. One less thing to put on my expense report," he said, putting the money back in his wallet.

"Me, too," Charlotte said. Then, turning to Ian, she added, "You'll have those files sent to me tonight?"

Ian nodded as the rest of them rose as well. "I'll text her right now—it might even be in your inbox before you get settled in your room."

Matty hugged Charlotte good-bye and promised a girls' spa day as soon as the investigation closed, which she knew Charlotte would hold her to. Fortunately, one of the top five spas in the country was less than forty-five minutes away so she knew she'd be able to deliver a day they'd both enjoy.

With the rest of the good nights said, Dash and Matty followed Ian and Vivi to the parking lot.

"Why do you think she wants the files on those two cases?" Ian asked.

Vivi lifted her shoulder.

"I have no idea," Matty said with a shake of her head.

"But my guess is if she's asked for them, she thinks they might be related to whatever she's finding in Brad's files," Vivi added.

"Yes, she doesn't strike me as a wild-goose-chase kind of woman," Ian responded, making Matty laugh.

"Yeah, you pretty much have her pegged there. I have no idea what she thinks she might find, but my guess is she'll find something."

They said their good-byes and all the way home Matty wondered just what it was that had piqued her friend's curiosity about Brad's connection to the people in the photographs. She was almost to the point of calling Charlotte when Dash, in his very Dash-like way, reminded her of just how important it could be to take a break every now and then.

CHAPTER 26

EVEN IF MATTY HADN'T CALLED to tell him that something had come up in the investigation into Brad's death, Dash would have known when he pulled up his driveway to find two cars, in addition to Matty's, parked in front of his house.

She came out with the dogs, who weren't let out on their own because of their unfamiliarity with his property, and watched as he got out of his truck and came toward her. Her expression gave away nothing and he had no idea what he would hear when he went inside.

"Charlotte and Damian arrived ten minutes ago and Ian and Vivi shortly after that. We haven't started yet," she said when he stopped in front her.

Then she bit her lip and looked away. He wrapped his arms around her and pulled her close, dropping a kiss on the top of her head. "Are you worried?" he asked.

She pulled back just enough to look at him as she answered. "I don't know. I mean it's not like I knew him well, or was invested in him as a friend, but I just," she paused and took a breath. "I know it's silly but I just don't want him to turn out to be a big jerk. Or a criminal."

Dash could hear the confusion in her tone and rubbed his hands down her shoulders. "I can't tell you anything about what those folks in there are going to tell you," he said, gesturing to the house with his head, "but I can tell you he was a good guy. He wasn't a close friend, but I knew he was good, Matty. He took care of his animals and you heard from all those people that stopped by after word got out about his death about how much he helped people around him. I hope Charlotte and Damian don't have information that will change that, but if they do, remember that he did do some good."

She looked up at him again and he brushed her hair from her face before he dipped his head down and kissed her. "Are you ready?" he asked when he pulled away.

She took another deep breath and nodded. "Lead the way."

It was late afternoon and Matty had clearly already offered everyone drinks. When they entered the kitchen, Vivi and Charlotte were sitting on stools, elbows propped up on the countertop, while Ian and Damian were leaning against the counter on the opposite wall. Vivi and Charlotte each had a glass of wine in hand and Ian and Damian were sipping from bottles of beer.

Damian must have caught the question in Dash's eyes because he raised his bottle and spoke. "Off duty until tomorrow. All of us."

"I'm off duty period," Charlotte added.

"So, the raid happened then? And what exactly were you raiding?" Matty asked, picking up her own wineglass and sliding onto the last of the three stools.

Damian took a sip of his beer but shook his head. "No, it hasn't happened yet, but when it does, it will be on the Mafia's main place of business—a warehouse east of Albany. My team has collected all the evidence it can, so until that happens, we're sitting tight. After the raid, once we have more evidence, I'll be back on duty."

"So you're not leading it then?" Dash asked, grabbing a beer for himself then leaning back against the refrigerator door. His kitchen wasn't nearly as big as Matty's. It was functional, but small; having three decent-sized men standing in it made it seem even smaller.

Damian shook his head. "I don't do that kind of thing anymore. Turns out my hearing's not all that great."

Ian raised a brow in question.

Damian lifted a shoulder. "I know, who'd have guessed. But it turns out all those firefights and IEDs did some damage. It was never checked while I was still a Ranger, but when I started at the FBI they did a full physical and found out that not only is my hearing less than perfect, my peripheral vision's not so hot either. I'm functional, obviously, but probably not the guy people want watching their backs any more."

Dash saw Ian cast a curious look at Damian; obviously this was news to him, too.

"I'm sorry to hear that," Vivi said. "But I'm glad it wasn't worse."

"You and me, both," Damian said. "But enough about me; Matty looks like she's about to down that entire glass in one gulp. Charlotte?" He gestured for her to begin.

Charlotte turned to Matty and laid a hand across her friend's. "You should know that while Brad did do some things he shouldn't have, things that could have gotten him into trouble were he alive, he did them for a good reason."

Dash shifted and frowned, unsure what to make of what Charlotte was saying. Judging by the look on Matty's face, by her furrowed brow, she wasn't sure either.

"Meaning?" Matty prompted.

"Meaning that Brad did embezzle money from people, but he only embezzled it from bad people *and*," Charlotte said, holding up a hand at Matty's pending interruption, "he didn't ever keep any of the money."

For a moment, Matty was silent. Then she shook her head and said exactly what was on Dash's mind. "I don't even know what that means. You make him sound like some modern day Robin Hood, but I can't condone someone acting as both judge and jury."

"I know," Charlotte said. "I don't really condone it either, but I have to admit, once I figured out what Brad was doing, I gained a tiny bit more respect for him."

"So, just what was he doing?" Dash asked, moving to get a better view of Charlotte.

"Well, when we started talking about New Orleans and Haiti last night and you mentioned Brad having been there, it got me thinking about the people in those photos. See, a while ago, I was asked to consult on a case, a consulting gig I didn't take," she added as an aside, "for an executive who was being accused of misappropriating funds. His defense said he couldn't have done it because the funds were nowhere to be found. I didn't take it because I know how easy it is to hide money, but mostly because the guy was a big jerk. But I digress," Charlotte said with a smile.

"Based on the evidence Damian gave me as well as what I was finding on Brad's computer, I had some inklings that Brad *was* embezzling," she continued. "But I couldn't find where it was going or even where it came from. So I started to look into those people in the pictures. I reviewed the files Carly sent over and, sure enough, all of the defendants had similar claims to those of the guy I'd refused to help—they all used the fact that the money they'd supposedly made was nowhere to be found as a defense. In other words, if there was no proof of financial gain, it didn't happen."

"But what about the faulty product?" Matty asked.

Damian lifted a shoulder. "Their argument was that, yes, the product was faulty, but that it was a design flaw, an honest mistake. And because there was no obvious financial benefit to them, at least none that could be found, the defendants had no motive and therefore weren't criminally at fault."

Matty frowned. "Uh, okay."

"Obviously, it didn't work, since they are in jail," Dash pointed out. Damian nodded then gestured for Charlotte to continue.

"So, what I think," Charlotte started again, after taking a sip of wine, "is that Brad knew what those people were doing, knew those people in the pictures were committing various kinds of fraud and ultimately hurting the people they were supposed to be helping, and he took exception." Charlotte paused and glanced at Damian, who straightened away from the counter.

"At Charlotte's request, I looked into how those convictions were brought about." Damian began. "And, in both cases, the evidence that kicked off the investigations came as anonymous tips. We pulled the original files and, sure enough, the evidence in those two cases was presented in a way similar to the information provided for the Irish case. In short, we think Brad was the one who originally discovered *all* the crimes, conducted his own investigations, and then provided us with what we needed to press charges and get convictions."

Matty frowned. "Okay, that sounds good, but what about the embezzling."

Charlotte let out a throaty chuckle; Damian cleared his throat and shot her a look.

"I know, it's totally inappropriate for me to actually respect what Brad did, but I can't help it," she said with a dismissive gesture to the agent.

"And what did he do?" Dash asked.

"All the people he investigated reaped tons of cash from the criminal activities at the expense of others. Brad just took some of that cash back."

"And gave it back to the people it was originally supposed to benefit," Matty cut her friend off, with a look of recognition dawning on her face. Charlotte nodded.

A little laugh escaped Matty, too. Then she looked a little sheepish. "I'm sorry, I know we're not supposed to condone that, but given the background Charlotte and I have, I kind of agree with her. We don't have much faith in the legal system considering the things we've seen, so it's kind of nice to see someone stick it to the big dogs, so to speak."

"I'd like to point out that you *are* a big dog," Dash said, half smiling.

Matty rolled her eyes. "Only by the size of my bank account. So, let me get this straight." She turned back to Charlotte and Damian. "Brad stole money from people who acquired it through illegal means then redistributed that money to the people it was originally supposed to benefit?"

Charlotte nodded.

"It's definitely poetic," Matty said. "But how did he do it?

I don't mean the embezzling part, but how did he redistribute the money?"

"I don't have all the details," Charlotte started, "but from what I can tell, in New Orleans, several of the churches and organizations that were, in fact, providing housing and rebuilding the city—rebuilding to code, not just saying they were—received huge donations around about the time Brad was investigating them. In Haiti, the faulty water filter caused all sorts of problems, so he couldn't just fix that."

"Didn't they have a big outbreak of cholera several months after the earthquake?" Dash asked.

Charlotte nodded. "There are a lot of diseases that can spread quickly and easily in unsanitary conditions. But by the time Brad figured it out, much of the equipment had been replaced, so in that case, he sent the money to medical relief agencies providing support to those who were still suffering from the earthquake and the resulting unsanitary conditions."

"And the Irish Mafia?" Matty asked, rounding out the list of people in the pictures.

"Courtney Carol, the jockey, was a friend of Brad's," Damian said. "Once we knew who she was, we were able to go through her phone records, computer records, that sort of thing. We aren't as certain with her as we are with the others, but what we think is that she provided information to Brad on the activities of the group."

"Which got her killed," Matty guessed, sadness heavy in her voice. Charlotte nodded, and Dash finished her thought.

"And Brad, being as big on justice as we now know him to be, took to investigating the information his friend provided in an effort to bring justice to her killers."

Damian inclined his head. "That is what we think," he confirmed.

"And it's likely that the group he was investigating is the group that killed him?" Matty asked.

Vivi nodded. "It's certainly our best lead at this point."

"Did Brad steal any of their money?" Matty asked, and Dash wasn't the only who heard the curiosity in her tone.

Charlotte let out a small laugh; Damian rolled his eyes, but didn't bother to call her on it.

"Yeah," Charlotte continued, "he did. Courtney didn't have any family to speak of, but she and Brad met through their work with a horse and animal rescue organization. An organization that recently received a substantial—"

"And anonymous," Damian cut in.

"Donation," Charlotte ended.

For a long moment, the six of them sat and digested the information in silence, letting Matty process it all. Finally, she looked up, let out a long breath, then smiled. "Well, again I have to say, it's poetic. So what now?"

"Now," Ian said, placing his empty beer bottle on the counter. "We wait until after the raid, see what Damian's team finds in the aftermath, and use that information to see if we can figure out just who killed your brother."

Matty nodded, then her brow furrowed as if she'd just remembered something, "What about the knife I found after the storm?" she asked. "Wasn't there a print on it?"

Ian nodded. "There was and it matches a print found on a similar weapon used in a knife fight in New York City last year, but whoever's fingerprint it is isn't in the system."

"So kind of like DNA—on its own it's not going to do you any good, but if you have something to compare it to, it could be useful?" Matty asked. Both Vivi and Ian nodded.

"All right then, so I sit around and wait. When is the raid?"

Damian gave the room an inscrutable look.

"Can't say?" Dash asked.

Damian lifted a shoulder, "Soon."

The only response they were going to get.

Matty let out a little huff. "Well, is there anything I can be doing?"

"No," Damian and Ian both said.

Matty arched a brow then looked at Dash. He just shrugged.

"I have something you could do," Vivi said.

"Vivienne," Ian warned.

"Oh stop, Ian," Vivi said, waving off her fiancé's warning. "How are you with flowers?" she asked.

Dash saw Matty cast a confused look at Charlotte who, judging by her own expression, wasn't going to be providing any assistance.

"Uh, I'm pretty good with flowers, actually. Vegetables not so much, but flowers, yes. Charlotte and I both are. We spent a lot of time with our gardener when we moved to DC. We'd never been able to be outside much before that, so it was fascinating to us."

"Great," Vivi said with a beaming smile. "I suck with them, so how do you feel about helping me pick out my wedding flowers?"

• • •

Matty spent a sleepless night that night, and not for good reasons. Earlier that evening, she and Charlotte had spent some time weighing the pros and cons of certain kinds of flowers with Vivi and then made plans to visit the local florist the next day. The activity felt incongruent with everything else going on—the pending raid, the investigation into Brad's death, and the upcoming funeral services—but it was something to do. Something to occupy her time while she sat around and waited. And waited.

She hated not being able to *do* something. While she was able to play god when she was writing—dispensing actions, deductions, resolutions, and justice at will—this was not one of her books. And it did not sit well that there was, in fact, nothing she *could* do.

But that wasn't what kept her awake. In the dark hours of the morning, she finally let herself really think about what Brad had done, think about what he had risked, not just once, but at least three times that they knew about. At any point, the people he was investigating could have turned on him. And yet he continued to do it, seeking justice for those who could not do it on their own.

"Matty," Dash mumbled beside her. She turned to find him watching her.

"What's on your mind?" he asked, brushing a lock of hair from her face.

"Brad, of course," she answered quietly.

"What about Brad?"

She sighed. "I just keep thinking about what he did and why he would keep doing it all these years."

"Because he could?" Dash suggested. "He had skills and access that not everyone has."

"Yeah, but he also has, *had,* a nice life—plenty of money of his own, and no reason to put everything at risk. But he did. Many times," she countered, rolling onto her back.

Dash propped himself on his elbow. "Are you comparing yourself to him?" he asked with a small frown.

She looked up at the ceiling, the shadows darkening the gray light. "I don't know. I mean, well, maybe, in a way," she said. Beside her, Dash said nothing, so she rolled back over to face him. "I'm not comparing myself to him in that I think I should have done what he did, but what he did took courage. A lot of it. I'm not sure I have that much courage."

Dash made a noncommittal sound, but she ignored it and kept talking as she wrapped her hand around one of his. "I mean, I know I lived through a lot when I was younger. Things no young child should have to live through. But that's just the thing, what have I done *since* then? Nothing, really."

"I beg to differ," Dash said. "You went to school, then college, you're a best-selling author, and you manage your grandmother's estate."

"That's not what I mean. What I mean is why did I never go back and actually *face* what happened to me as a kid? I threw myself into my new life, and yes, I've done well. But I've also completely ignored what is a huge part of who I am because it's too painful to think about. Or it's too painful to admit just how much it's affected me as an adult. So I don't think about it, I just move through life."

Dash frowned. "That hasn't been my experience with you," he commented.

Matty offered him a small smile. "That's because you actually got me to think about some of the things that happened to me and made me want to understand just how much they affected me so that I could be a part of something real," she answered. She saw Dash's jaw clench, then he lifted her hand and kissed it.

"But that's just it, Dash, I needed you to give me the nudge. And then there's Charlotte, she's done more or less the same thing as me, only she's thrown herself into work so much that she doesn't even have the time to come to grips with her past. I ignored it, she just doesn't let herself slow down enough to think about it."

"But you and Brad had very different lives," Dash pointed out. "I don't think it's something you can even compare."

She shrugged a shoulder. "I'm not so sure. Yes, he had a very privileged childhood and never had to worry about money, but I can't comment on what kind of emotional support he had. But that's not even what I'm talking about. What I'm talking about is that he saw all the bad things, all the sorrows this world has to offer. He saw death and destruction, he saw communities annihilated, children killed, families torn apart, and what did he do? He went back time and time again to help, to try to make it better, to ease people's suffering; and when he couldn't, he fought for justice in the best way he knew how." Matty stopped talking and took a deep breath. Dash said nothing, waiting for her to continue.

"All my life I either despised Brad or felt little more than antipathy toward him," she said after a few long moments of silence. "But what did I do with all the sorrows, all the injustices I saw? Nothing, Dash. I did nothing. I've *done* nothing. I've just ignored them."

"Living them is different than experiencing them the way Brad did, by choice," Dash pointed out.

"I know it is, and believe me, I'm not belittling everything I experienced as a child. But I just, well, I guess what it comes down to is the man I had very little regard for wasn't some spoiled child. I know it's probably too little too late, but he was a man who deserved not just my respect, but my gratitude. My gratitude for being willing to take on things that many of us aren't willing to take on. I think Brad wasn't just a good man but a strong one, too. In the best sense, he was a man I think we can all learn something from. I know I can," she added.

Absently, she stroked a finger across Dash's hand as she held it, then continued. "Because, these sorrows we see—the sadness and pain and injustice—and yes, the joys, too, it's what we do with them that makes us who we are, Dash. And Brad was a remarkable man."

They lay in silence for several long moments, Matty lost in thought about just how much she had missed by not knowing Brad, but also thankful that even at this late juncture, she had the opportunity to know at least a little part of him, a part of him that she knew would have a lasting impact on her.

"You still have an opportunity to honor him, to respect him," Dash said. She turned her eyes to him in question and he continued. "He asked that you donate part of his estate to charities. Maybe you could take that opportunity and what you know about him and use his money in a way that honors not just the things he cared about but, as you say, who he was as a person, what he did, and what he gave to the world."

Matty mulled this over. She'd originally been inclined to donate the money to just the charities she knew he'd volunteered at, but maybe there was a better way to use the money, or at least part of it.

"I'm not sure what that would be," she started.

"And you don't have to decide now," Dash responded.

She smiled. "But I like that idea. I like that maybe we can figure out a way to honor not just what he did, but the courageous person he was."

Dash picked up her hand. "You have some time to think about it and if I know you, you'll come up with something great."

"*We'll* come up with something great, Dash. It's your idea, too, and since we're kind of in this together, I think we should think it through together."

She saw Dash's eyes sparkle a little and he smiled. "I like the sound of that."

She smiled back. "Me, too. But let's talk about it more in the morning," she said, pulling him toward her.

"I like the sound of that, too."

CHAPTER 27

MATTY CRAWLED FROM BED FEELING a little under the weather for the first time in forever. She supposed it could be the stress of the past few weeks, but she had a sinking sensation it might actually be something like the flu or a summer cold. Her chest felt tight and she had the sudden urge to lie down in the shower and let steaming hot water pound down on her. Stumbling into Dash's bathroom, she reached into the shower, cranked up the hot water, and stepped in. For a long moment, she just stood there, letting the water warm her. When Dash came in to check on her ten minutes later, she wasn't exactly lying down, but she was reclining on the built-in tile bench, blankly watching the drops of water gathering and falling down the sides of the shower.

"Matty? Are you okay?" Dash asked, pushing all five of the dogs that had come into the bathroom to keep her company aside.

She turned her head at the sound of his voice and noted a frown on his lips.

"Not feeling well?" he asked.

She shook her head. "Not so much," she said, then started coughing.

Dash stepped in and shut the water off then wrapped her in a towel. "You're shivering," he said, briskly rubbing her down. She didn't feel the need to agree, since it was obvious.

"Back to bed," he ordered, shoving her toward his big king-size bed. A bed that normally held great appeal to her, but right now looked like a yawning ocean of cold cotton sheets. Her skin broke out in goose bumps again.

"It's too cold," she said, as Dash all but pushed her onto the bed and pulled the covers up. Even though she protested, she grabbed the blankets and pulled them tightly around her.

After a moment of silence, while she lay curled up, still shivering, she peeked out to see Dash. He was standing over her, hands jammed on his hips, nicely clad in jeans. Her eyes strayed to the clock. "You need to go to work," she said, then started coughing again.

"Give me a minute," he said, then he called Bob and Rufus into his room and ordered them up onto the bed. Matty closed her eyes but could feel Dash maneuvering the dogs around her, one in front and one in back. Both dogs seemed born for their roles as body heaters, stretching themselves out alongside her.

"This is just temporary, just give me a minute," Dash repeated and then she heard his footsteps leaving the room. Bob leaned back and nuzzled her; Rufus seemed to scrunch up even closer to her. She smiled. How could she not love a man who trusted dogs to keep his woman warm when he couldn't?

She snuggled down further into her blankets at the thought, enjoying the feel of her two companions beside her, like two sentinels. She was drifting back to sleep when she heard Dash order the dogs back off the bed, and immediately she was wracked with shivers again.

She mumbled a not very polite protest and heard Dash chuckle. Then the bed dipped, the covers were pulled back, and he slid in behind her.

"They were just temporary while I rearranged my day to stay with you," he said.

"You didn't have to do that," she said, or thought she said. Her voice sounded fuzzy to her.

"I know, but I did. Now go back to sleep," he ordered and she did.

• • •

The second time Matty woke up that day, she felt like she'd been hit by a freight train—but in a weirdly good way. In the way a person feels after their body has spent a few hours shivering and tensing its muscles in the fit of a fever then, once the fever has passed, the tired, sore muscles have relaxed. In other words, she felt like her body had run a marathon while she'd been sleeping.

Stretching out under the covers, she noted that her chest still felt a little tight, but she knew her fever was gone. She also knew that Dash was gone. Glancing over at his side of the bed, she frowned. His jeans and white undershirt were gone, but his socks and a button-down work shirt were still draped on the chair beside the bed.

Stretching again, she rolled out of bed and tentatively placed her feet on the floor. Taking heart from the fact that she neither burst into a renewed bout of shakes nor started coughing, she stood, found one of Dash's oversized t-shirts, and slid it on.

Moving slowly, like she would the day after a good workout, she made her way downstairs. Dash was outside, phone to his ear, engaged in what looked like a serious conversation. Matty stood in the doorway and took a moment to acknowledge just how easy on the eyes Dashiell Kent was, especially standing there in his jeans with his bare feet braced apart, emphasizing his lean frame. Of course she'd noticed his looks when they first met, it was impossible not to. But since then, she'd grown to know him and, yes, his aesthetic was still extremely appealing, but now when she looked at him, she saw so much more.

He swung around when he ended his call, as if sensing her presence. His eyes swept over her and she let out a little smile.

"Like what you see?" Matty asked.

He grinned back and walked toward her. "I could say the same to you. You were ogling my butt, weren't you?" He wrapped his arms around her as she looked up to meet his eyes.

"That and other parts," she said.

He ran a hand over her face, his expression going from fun to serious in a heartbeat. "Feeling better?"

"I feel like I just did a two hour workout in my sleep, but my fever is gone and I don't feel quite as tired."

"Your cough? You weren't sounding so good."

"Chest still feels tight, but I think a good night's sleep might cure it. Is everything okay?" she asked, pulling away from Dash and moving toward the kitchen. "You looked awfully serious on that call."

Following Matty, he put a teakettle on the stove for her as he chided, "You couldn't even see my face, how did you know it was serious?"

And that's when she knew it really was something; that the phone call had been important. She could see it in Dash's eyes, in the way his easy-going comment didn't quite reach them.

"It was in the way you stood, the line of your back," she answered, moving toward him. "What was the call, Dash?" she asked, stopping a foot away. His eyes skittered away from her and her heart sank. It didn't seem as if he was trying to hide anything, but he looked like a man gathering strength to say something. Finally, he began.

"The FBI conducted their raid late this morning. That was Ian on the phone."

Her breath caught in the back of her throat. "And?" she managed to say.

"And they are still combing through the evidence. They arrested nine men and the FBI is very happy with what they are finding."

"But what about Ian? And Vivi? Did they find out anything about Brad?" After everything she'd realized last night, she knew that Brad had come to be important to her, even in his death; however, even she was surprised at the desperation in her voice. She wanted justice for her half brother, a man she hadn't had the privilege of knowing in life, but who had given her so much in his death. The changes she'd experienced, the thoughts she'd allowed herself to have, were because of the people she'd met over the past few weeks, and though Brad was dead, she counted him among that group. Perhaps even, with the exception of Dash, the most important.

Dash took a deep breath. "They found surveillance photos of Brad in the office and on one of the computers. They also found a shotgun of the same caliber that killed him, though they haven't had a chance to run ballistics yet. They also found his address written on the back of one of the pictures."

"So it's looking like they might find who did it?" she asked, hope clear in her voice.

Dash nodded. "It's looking that way, but they don't have any concrete evidence yet."

"Like a confession or the matching ballistics?" she asked. He nodded again. "But it's looking good?" she insisted.

He let out another deep breath. "Yeah," he said wrapping his arms around her, "it's looking good."

She rested her head against his chest until the whistle on the teakettle sounded. In silence, she made herself a cup of tea, Dash's presence solid and steady beside her. After steeping the leaves for a minute, she went to the sink and found herself staring out the window at the sweeping view in front of her. It was such a breathtaking place, she couldn't imagine herself anywhere else. The intellectual side of her knew that in the winter it would be brutal. But it would still be beautiful and she was certain that she didn't want to leave. And everything she'd experienced, every person she'd met, every field that took her breath away, was because of Brad. And most of all, there was Dash. She wouldn't have met Dash if it weren't for her half brother.

Standing there in Dash's kitchen, a wave of something that felt like love for Brad washed over her. Blinking away a few tears, she realized she would never be able to thank him. Yes, she and Dash would figure out how to honor him, but she would never be truly able to say thank you.

But maybe she could say her own good-bye.

"Dash," she said, turning toward him. His dark eyes met her gaze. "I want to say good-bye to Brad. And I don't mean at the funeral in a few days. I want to go back to the house, back to the barn, and say good-bye."

His eyes studied her face for a long moment. She thought he might point out that what she was saying was fanciful, but instead he inclined his head. "And you want to say thank you, don't you?" he asked, seeing right into the heart of her.

She unsuccessfully blinked back a few more tears. Dash stayed where he was, letting her feel what she was feeling. She nodded and more tears flowed. Tears she didn't even try to hold back or hide. "I have a lot to thank him for, Dash. Including you."

He stepped forward and took her in his arms. "We both have a lot to thank him for," Dash said, resting his cheek on her hair. "Of course we can go back to the house. Why don't you go upstairs and get dressed, maybe take a few Tylenol in case your fever thinks about coming back, and then we can head over to the house. I can wait there while you go up to the barn."

"You know I love you, right?" Matty asked, tightening her hold on Dash. For a moment he went still, then his arms pulled her closer to him.

"Yeah, I do. And I love you too."

She smiled against his chest then pulled back. "Ten minutes?"

He lowered his head and dropped a kiss on her lips. "Anytime you're ready. I'll be here."

And he would be, she knew. He would be there.

CHAPTER 28

It took Matty quite a while to make it back up to the barn where she'd found Brad all those days ago. Between the tightness in her chest and the reason for her going in the first place, her feet were not moving very quickly.

She paused and turned to take in the view behind her. It was the time of day she liked to call the magic hour. About an hour before dusk, just as the sun was starting to go down behind the hills to the west, the hills to the east were cast in light that varied from gold to pink. Tonight they were most definitely gold, and she took a moment to appreciate their beauty. She didn't know what she would do with her house or life in DC, but she knew she wanted to be here, in Windsor, watching the magic hour as much as possible.

When the light started to change, she turned and continued making her way to her destination. When the barn came into view, she realized that it looked almost exactly as it had that first time. It seemed to her that a lot should be different because so much had happened there, but aside from the tire tracks from the police and crime scene vehicles, it looked just the same.

She slid the door open and stepped inside, blinking at the darkness. Standing there in the doorway, she let her eyes adjust to the dim light then started to take in the scene.

There was no body, no chair, no flies, nothing. It was all but empty with a few bales of hay at the far end. It no longer smelled as it had when she'd found Brad; instead, the scent of the sweet alfalfa mixed with dirt greeted her. It wasn't a clean smell, but it was earthy and appropriate, and Matty thought Brad would be glad to see this place back as it should be.

She walked farther into the barn, toward where the chair had been, and stood, absorbing the silence. She inhaled deeply and let her breath out slowly. She had so much to thank Brad for that for a long moment she just stilled her mind and body and let herself feel. Sorrow for what she and Brad had lost because of their parents, happiness at having been brought to Windsor, and gratitude for what Brad had taught her and was continuing to teach her about engaging in life, about strength, and about character.

A ray of sun shot through one of the west-facing windows and the light danced in front of her, making her smile. She was watching the dust float about when a figure appeared at the door.

Startled, she took a few steps backward.

"Mai?" Matty said. She knew the confusion in her voice probably wasn't that courteous, but she was surprised to see Chen's sister there. Surprised Dash had told Mai where to find her.

"Matty," she said, her voice sounding different than it had in the past, less cultured, less smooth. Less let's-be-great-girlfriends.

"Is everything all right?" Matty asked as Mai came toward her.

"That depends," came the answer.

Matty frowned again as the little warning bells inside her mind started going off. "On?" she said after a slight hesitation.

"On what you can tell me about what Brad was up to before he died," Mai answered, as she pulled a gun from the pocket of her blazer.

CHAPTER 29

MATTY STARED AT THE GUN, the reality of the situation slowly sinking in. Or at least what she knew of it. She was still horribly confused. Though what she did know—that Mai was there, with a gun, thinking that Matty knew more than she did about Brad—didn't make much sense.

"What are you talking about, Mai?" Matty tried to inch her way to the door, taking small steps as she spoke. But Mai, pointing the gun, effectively halted her progress.

"Your brother was looking into things he should have left alone. I know he uncovered some of the activities happening around the horses and tracks, I want to know what else he found," Mai responded.

"How would I know what he was looking into?" she asked, saying the first thing that came to mind because she hadn't quite processed the rest.

Mai sighed. "The raid, Matty. There was a raid this morning on the offices of several known members of the Irish Mafia."

"You're not part of the Irish Mafia," Matty pointed out.

"Of course not," Mai said, disgust echoing in her tone.

Matty eyed the door. "Then just what do you want to know and why do you think I would be able to help you?" She wasn't sure how she was going to get out of this, or even *if* she was, but she wasn't going to go without a fight. That said, looking in Mai's eyes, Matty recognized something she hadn't seen in a long time: the hollow, empty look of a sociopath who neither cared nor valued the life of anyone other than herself.

It was a reminder of everything she had left behind when she'd moved out of the projects. Oh, Mai was dressed better, had more sophisticated mannerisms, but she was no different than those that ruled the neighborhoods, that terrorized the people where Matty had grown up. And Matty knew, without the slightest doubt, the other woman had no intention of letting her live. Even if she didn't know anything about Brad and what he might have found out, Mai would kill her; and if she did know something, Mai would simply wait to hear it and then kill her anyway.

She could fake it to buy herself some time; she knew she could. But only if she knew what kind of information Mai was looking for—what Mai thought she might know. If she could figure that out, or maybe keep Mai talking and occupied, she might, just might, be able to find herself a way out.

"What did he tell you?" Mai asked.

"About?" Matty countered.

"About what he was looking into. About my business arrangements."

"*Your* business arrangements?"

"Matty, don't play dumb, it doesn't become you," Mai said on a sigh.

Matty blinked. Okay, maybe figuring out what information Mai wanted from her wasn't going to work because she had no idea where to start. Maybe she should just focus on the getting-her-to-talk plan.

"You're right, it doesn't. It doesn't generally become anyone. But in this case, I actually don't have any idea what you're talking about. What makes you think Brad was looking into *your* business arrangements and why I would know about it?"

"Your brother talked about you all the time, you know," Mai said, taking a step toward her in designer boots that, for some reason, seemed to stand out to Matty, even as she took one step back and moved little to her left. She was precisely three inches closer to the door now.

"He was always amazed at the life you led, at your success.

Pleased, I might add. He used to say you deserved it after the hell your father, *his* father, put you through. I think he admired you greatly."

"The feeling is mutual," Matty said. At least that was the truth. It might not have been mutual before, but she did feel all those things for him now.

"Be that as it may, I know you two *never* spoke. I know he tried to contact you a handful of times. I know you never responded. I know your estrangement caused him great pain and it was something he thought about often. I also know he felt guilty for what his parents did to you."

Matty wasn't sure what to make of this long statement, or even what seemed to be the hint of jealousy she heard in Mai's tone. She knew the facts were accurate—that Brad had tried to call and contact her, but she had never reciprocated. And as for the rest, she couldn't attest to what Brad had been feeling, so she simply nodded at Mai and began to wonder if Mai and Brad had, at one point, been more than friends.

"So you can imagine my surprise," Mai continued, "when suddenly you agreed to come up and house-sit for him."

"I was surprised myself," Matty interrupted.

"On the same day someone hacked into one of my computers that contained private records," Mai finished.

Matty's brows shot down. She *still* wasn't sure what Mai was trying to say, but she was starting to understand that it was more likely than not that Brad had stumbled onto something other than just information on the Irish. Whether Brad knew it or not was unclear.

"So, you think Brad accessed some of your files—files that contained information he shared with me—and that I came up to Windsor to, what? Help him plan what to do with it? Use it against you?"

Mai tilted her elegant head and studied her for a long moment. "He skimmed money from the accounts."

"And it was the lure of that money that brought me up here?

You think I came because he was able to entice me with *money*?"
Matty asked the question, but it was so absurd she could hardly
wrap her mind around it. She didn't need money. And not that she
could be bribed, but if even if Brad had wanted to try, he wouldn't
have chosen money as the incentive.

"A lot of money went missing, Matty," Mai said.

"I *have* a lot of money, Mai. I don't need any of yours, and
I especially don't need to do anything illegal to get more," Matty
shot back, even as she realized that, based on what Mai had just
said, Brad must have known something if he'd taken the time to
steal her money. If what Charlotte had told them yesterday was
anything to go by, Brad only took money from people who earned
it in illegal and harmful ways. But whether Brad knew it was Mai's
money, or if he thought it was just part of the Mafia's money, wasn't
clear. However, since it was Brad who had put her in touch with
Chen, who had then brought Mai into her life, she was leaning
toward Brad not having had any idea about the Zheng family. And
as her mind raced, Matty gave a fleeting thought to Chen—was he
involved, too? Did he have any idea his sister was here?

"Brad didn't know it was yours," Matty said. "Not that it
would have mattered, because even if he had known you were a
criminal, and I assume you are, given what you're doing and saying
here, he still would have turned you in. Like he did with the Irish."
Of that she was certain.

"He knew in the end," Mai said.

Matty's blood ran cold. She knew a confession when she heard
one. "You killed Brad," she said.

Mai lifted a shoulder. "*I* didn't kill him. But we did what we
needed to do to protect our assets."

"And who does 'we' refer to?" she asked, not sure she wanted
to hear the answer.

Again, a shoulder came up. "The Irish have their little gang
and the businesses they run, my family has a much more enterpris-
ing approach."

Again, Matty found herself blinking at the onslaught of information flowing at her. Of course she knew that there was organized crime in the US. And she even knew that Chinese gangs—families—were a growing concern to not just law enforcement, but other cartels as well. It had just never occurred to her that the family of a respected professor from one of America's top universities might be involved. And it made her feel like a naïve child.

"I see," she said quietly. The more she knew—the more she learned—the more of a liability she became and she already knew far too much. Any hope she had of getting out of this situation alive was rapidly dwindling.

"So, Brad found one of your accounts and syphoned your illegal money?" she asked. Mai nodded. "And just how do you make your money, Mai?"

"Gambling, of course. The betting windows, that sort of thing."

"You control them?"

Again, Mai nodded. "It's a more sophisticated operation than what the Irish control. Although, over the years we've reached a bit of an accord with them. They stick to their enterprises, we stick to ours," she added.

"How very civil of you," Matty all but bit out. But then she paused and took a deep breath. She had hoped to will her heart rate down, but all the breath did was make her cough. She turned her head and out of the corner of her eye, through the window, caught movement. She wasn't sure what it was but just in case it was someone riding to her rescue, she didn't want to give them away, so she turned back to Mai.

"I don't know anything," she said.

"Wrong answer, Matty," Mai said raising her gun.

What did she have to lose now? She shrugged. "I'm sorry, I don't know anything. I don't know what Brad knew, I don't know what he did with the information he had, and I really don't know what he did with your money."

"I do," came Dash's voice from the doorway. Mai spun, gun raised, to find Dash striding toward her with a rifle in his hand.

If possible, Matty became even more still, not liking that Mai's weapon was now pointed directly at Dash.

A few feet in the door, Dash stopped, not dropping his focus on Mai for a second. In fact, Matty was surprised to see just how focused Dash was. Not that she doubted him, it was just that he had always been so laid back with her. He didn't tend to get ruffled about much of anything; he went with the flow, unless the flow was against his grain and then he didn't make a big deal of it, but just quietly stood his ground.

But this Dash, the one in front of her now, was radiating tension from every muscle in his body. He held his rifle as naturally as if it were a part of his body and he wore an expression that said he would fire without a second thought if provoked.

"Matty, I'd like you to leave the barn now," Dash said. Mai said nothing, also keeping her weapon drawn.

"Matty?" Dash said again. Mai swung her weapon around to point it back at Matty. If possible, the tension in Dash's body coiled even tighter and his jaw clenched.

Matty shook her head, not that he could see her with his eyes locked on Mai. "No, Dash, I'm not leaving you," she said as she looked to Dash's waist to see if his phone was in its usual place. Having left hers in his truck with her purse, getting closer to him and using his phone to call for help might be their only chance. She frowned; his phone wasn't there.

She saw the side of his mouth tip into a small grin. "I'm not asking you to leave *me*, but I am asking you to step outside for a moment while Mai and I sort this out."

She looked at the two people in front of her. They both had their eyes locked on each other, though Mai's weapon was still pointed at her. "No," Matty said. "If I leave, she'll only have one target, you. At least this way if she tries to kill me, you can get a shot off."

Mai shifted her position, taking a step away from Matty, making her wonder what the woman was thinking. She couldn't possibly believe that she was going to get away with anything at this point. But then, casting a glance in her direction, she saw the flat look in Mai's eyes, a look that made her suck in a quick breath. Mai knew this wasn't going to end the way she had intended but had no intention of bowing out gracefully.

"No one is going to die today, Matty," Dash said as if reading her mind.

His confident tone irritated her. It shouldn't have, but it did. He was being cavalier about his life. She wasn't feeling quite the same way.

"Then it shouldn't matter if I stay," she shot back. She saw Dash take a breath and will himself under control.

"No one is going to die, Matty," Dash repeated, "but you've seen enough violence in your life that whatever happens in here, you don't need to witness it." Mai made a small, derisive sound.

But Dash's comment had caught Matty by surprise. It wasn't at all what she had been expecting him to say, though she didn't know why. In his own way, every day, he'd shown her how much he cared for her, cared *about* her. And he was still doing it. Even as he pointed a rifle at the head of a woman who'd been involved in the death of her half brother. Dash wasn't being cavalier about himself; he was trying to protect her—not necessarily from a bullet, though there was that too, but from the pain of her past.

"We can get married, Dash," she blurted out. That startled him and, for a moment, his eyes shot to hers before refocusing on Mai. Matty cast another glance at the woman holding the gun, too. Mai had been unusually silent during their exchange and Matty could only guess it was because she was using the time to come up with a new plan and she didn't like the thought of that.

"I'm glad to hear that," Dash said. "My mom's already planning on it so if you want any say in the wedding, you may want to mention it to her, too. In fact, why don't you go do that now?"

While he was talking, Dash had inched closer to her and was now standing between her and Mai, who had taken another step toward to the door. Matty realized that if Mai was able to leave the barn, all she would have to do was wait for them to follow, then she could easily pick them off one at a time as they exited, something they'd have to do at some point, especially if they couldn't call for help.

"Dash," Matty said in warning.

"I got this, Matty. Believe me, I do," he said, his voice pleading with her to leave. A small part of her wanted to give him what he wanted just to make that tone disappear. She didn't like denying Dash what he wanted. But another part of her knew she wasn't going to leave him.

"I know you do, Dash. I know you do," she repeated. "But you're not doing this alone. We're doing it together. I'm not leaving you now, I'm not leaving you ever. I think you need to get used to that."

"Such a sweet sentiment," Mai drawled as she took another step backward toward the door.

Matty saw Dash's jaw clench and she braced herself for what he might say next.

But when she heard a man's voice, it was Ian's, not Dash's.

"Lucky for you two, I think you'll have a long time to get used to the together thing," Ian said as he, Marcus, and Carly entered the barn, weapons drawn. Ian stopped a few feet inside with Marcus and Carly fanning out on either side of him.

Matty watched Mai spin at their entrance. Her eyes danced between the four weapons directed at her. For a moment it looked like she might take a shot just to bring someone down with her. But then, miraculously, she lifted her finger from the trigger, opened her palm, and raised her hands. In an instant, Carly had Mai disarmed and handcuffed.

"Dash," Ian said. "If you wouldn't mind lowering that hunting rifle, we'd all appreciate it."

Ian's voice cut through the fog in Matty's brain and as Dash set the safety and lowered his weapon he turned just in time to grab her as she stepped into his arms. The rifle slid to the floor and he held her so tightly she started to cough. They stood there a long time, not saying anything, until Ian cleared his throat.

Dash pulled back from her, but just enough to see her face. He wound his hands into her hair and tilted her head up to look at him. Their gazes met and held, and in his eyes, she saw everything she felt for him reflected.

"Dash?" Ian said. "We need to take some statements."

Without taking his eyes from hers, Dash answered. "We need a minute, Ian." Then he took her hand and dragged her out of the barn and around to the side, out of sight of everyone else. Pushing her against the barn, his hands raked through her hair again and his mouth crashed down on hers. It was rough, rougher than he'd ever been with her, but she didn't mind. The reality of what had just happened was slowly sinking into her consciousness and she needed him, his vitality, as much he needed her.

His hands were up under her shirt and her arms were wrapped around his neck, pulling him closer to her, when the punishing kiss suddenly lost its power.

"Jesus, Matty," Dash said breathing hard, his forehead resting against hers.

She closed her eyes and gave thanks, once again, for Dash, for the fact that he was okay. "You scared the hell out of me, Dash," she whispered, starting to shake a bit. Or maybe it was Dash.

"If I never have to go through something like that again, it will be too soon," he said, his unsteady hand combing her hair back.

"You and me both." She leaned into him and could hear his heart beating a strong tattoo in his chest. "How did you know?" she asked, finally.

"I guess one of the accounts on the list Brad sent the FBI wasn't linked to any of the Irish accounts. Damian was worried that whoever held the account might have been tipped off because of the raid and just wanted to be sure that everyone involved, meaning you and I, were aware of the situation and safe. So he called Ian, Ian called me," he answered.

"Your rifle?" she asked. "Did you really think I might be in danger?"

Dash shook his head and lifted a shoulder at the same time. "I didn't know, and that's what got my blood going. I always carry a rifle in my truck on the off chance I need to deal with an injured animal quickly and safely. I grabbed it on my way up to get you." And after a moment he added, "Jesus, I'm glad I did."

Matty pressed herself against him again, just to feel his warmth, his body against her, but a coughing fit hit her and she nearly doubled over.

Dash held her through the fit then gently brushed a hand over her forehead. "Your fever is back. I need to get you home."

"What about Ian?" she said. "He needs to know what Mai told me."

Dash looked around them for a moment, then spotted Ian leaning against his car talking into his phone. He hung up when Dash waved him over.

"You guys okay?" Ian asked as he headed their way. His eyes swept over both of them then stayed on Matty. "You don't look so good, Matty," he added.

"She has a fever and maybe bronchitis or something like that. Can you drive us to the doctor and ask your questions on the way? Your car is closer, mine's still at the house and I'd rather not make her walk back down the hill."

She smiled when Ian didn't hesitate for a second. Vivi definitely had herself a good man. But then again, so did she. Within minutes, Marcus was driving them to the hospital. Ian sat beside him in the front seat taking notes, while she sat in the back, tucked in next to Dash, answering questions.

• • •

Much later that night—after getting checked out by the doctor, picking up some antibiotics, enjoying an amazing Italian dinner that Vivi had cooked and that she and Ian had delivered to Dash's and then stayed to share, and drinking more wine than she should have given the state of her health—Matty crawled into bed.

"I shouldn't have let them stay so long," Dash said, lying on his side facing her, his fingers tracing lines across her cheek.

"They know what it means to celebrate life, Dash. To be so thankful for it. I *am* tired, but I'm also glad we let our friends take care of us a little bit tonight."

He was silent for several heartbeats but she could tell from his breathing that there was something he wanted to say. She raised her eyes to his in question.

"Were you serious about getting married, Matty?" he said bluntly.

She studied him before answering. She considered his beautiful face, though he'd hate to hear it described that way, but more than that, she studied his eyes. The way they looked at her—the love, the respect, and even that tiny bit of nervousness that had crept in at his question. She smiled and placed a palm on his cheek, brushing her thumb across his lower lip.

"Well?" he said.

"Yes," she answered. "I was serious, Dash."

He looked at her for such a long time that she actually started to wonder if maybe he'd been hoping she would say no—that all that talk was just that, talk. But then he smiled and a low laugh vibrated in his chest.

"Good, because I was, too. About my mom that is. You may want to let her know. I think she may have already booked the church."

EPILOGUE

THE WEDDING WAS BEAUTIFUL. JUST perfect. Matty looked around her, at all the smiling faces, and couldn't help but smile herself. And take a long sip of some of the excellent champagne Rob had provided for the reception. The flowers she'd picked were exquisite if she did say so herself and as she eyed the expansive buffet her stomach gave a low growl.

Beside her, Dash's chuckle echoed in her ear. "Hungry, Mrs. Kent?"

She turned into her husband's embrace and smiled. "I'm always hungry," she said. "I have no idea how my stomach can be growling right now, I think I just ate half of everything. Vivi wasn't kidding when she said her family was taking care of the food," she added.

They both turned and looked at the bride and groom. Vivi looked stunning in her gown, but even more so for the smile she wore when she looked at her new husband. Beside Vivi, Ian stood, in his charcoal-gray suit, looking just as besotted as his new wife.

"Italians," Dash said with a shrug and a smile.

Dash and Matty's wedding had been very different in form, but not in substance. Matty knew that the expression Vivi had on her face when she looked at Ian was the same one she'd worn the day she and Dash had wed. The same look she probably still got on her face when she looked at Dash. But the wedding itself, which had taken place two weeks after Brad's funeral, had been tiny. They had anticipated only Dash's immediate family, Matty's mother, and Charlotte and Nanette Lareaux. But of course Ian and Vivi had come, along with Elise, Kit, Carly, Marcus, and Jesse, who'd been accompanied by her two boys. Kristen had also asked to come and there was no way either Matty or Dash was going to say no to her—they had kind of adopted her during her father's frequent trips and Matty loved the girl like a little sister.

After the wedding, they'd moved into the house Brad had left her, because as Dash pointed out, once they had kids, they would need a bigger place than his. They weren't quite ready for kids yet, but Matty knew they both hoped to have a family someday and Brad's house—*their* house—was big enough for two or three.

Matty's mom had spent a good two days interrogating Dash, which he'd taken with good humor, and then finally declared him *almost* good enough for her daughter. Since then, Dash had been charming Carmen in every way possible and the two of them were now thick as thieves—Matty suspected her mom was buttering Dash up for grandkids sooner rather than later. She didn't think Dash was fooled, but she also didn't think he probably needed much prodding.

But the biggest surprise of their wedding was when her father had shown up. She was grateful he hadn't asked to take her mom's place and walk her down the aisle; he'd sat in the back of the church, respectful of her wishes for the day. He hadn't accompanied them to the informal dinner reception after the ceremony but had asked Matty if they might meet or talk at a later date. She'd agreed and when they had met, when he'd asked if there was any way to even begin to make amends, she'd surprised herself by telling him about her plans to start a foundation in Brad's name that honored the courage of everyday people. Douglas had readily agreed to help, had even begun to tear up during the conversation. She and her father had spoken a few times since and were beginning to make plans for how the organization might be structured and run.

Her mother was managing the estate in DC and she and Nanette were considering making it available to the public for events. Matty liked that idea, liked the idea of her grandmother's house being used for weddings and other celebrations. And she liked even more that her mom and Nanette had also agreed that they wanted the whole endeavor to be a nonprofit—whatever they took in hosting fancy events would be turned around to cover the cost of hosting events at no charge for local nonprofits.

As for Mai Zheng, she wasn't someone Matty thought about much anymore—at least not intentionally. Although with Chen feeling so deeply horrified by his sister's actions, by the actions of his family, he stopped by more often than she wished simply to continue to apologize.

It had been a surprise that Chen knew nothing of his family's business, but apparently, according to Mai, Chen had been pegged at a young age as too much of a bleeding heart to be brought into the inner circles. Fortunately for Chen, the investigators were able to verify her statements. Unfortunately for everyone else, that was about all Mai said.

She was awaiting trial, but unlike the Irish group Damian's team was able to bring down, they'd only been able to arrest two other people involved in Mai's family, including James Connell, the man she hired to kill Brad and also hurt the animals, causing the diversion Mai had needed to continue her search of Brad's house. After realizing his best chance at escaping the death penalty lay in implicating Mai, Connell had confessed to being a hired gun for the Zheng family and provided as much information as he could to help the authorities prosecute Mai and investigate several others.

Connell had lured Brad to the barn with a tale of an injured dog before he'd had a chance to leave town as planned. Where he was going, they never did find out, but Matty, Vivi, and the others, including the FBI, assumed he was clearing out for a few weeks knowing the turmoil that the information he'd sent to the FBI would cause. And given that they had found photos of Brad and evidence during the raid that indicated the Irish Mafia had been looking into him, it hadn't been a bad plan.

But in all likelihood, one thing Brad hadn't counted on was stumbling across an illegal account held by the Zheng family. The FBI couldn't say for certain if Brad knew he'd found not just one, but two, organized crime families operating in the area, but they were leaning toward the discovery of the Zheng account as being an unintentional find, with the Irish group being Brad's primary investigative interest. Of course, once he'd found it and syphoned money from it, he'd inadvertently tipped the Zheng family off to his activities, as Mai was much more meticulous with her accounts than her Irish counterparts.

When Connell confessed to injuring both Bob and Bogey, he also answered the mystery of just how Randy Smeltzer was involved—or not. It turned out that Smeltzer had simply been in the wrong place at the wrong time. He'd been out for a morning stroll in his robe, slippers, and socks and happened to see Connell leaving the barn moments after he'd killed Brad. According to Connell, he'd had no choice but to kill Smeltzer, who had run and tried to hide from Connell by climbing the tree. Connell had collected the robe and slippers that had fallen off when Smeltzer had run, leaving him in nothing but his red socks.

There had been a lot of surprises and revelations in the past few months, but none more important than Dash.

Matty smiled now as she looked up into her husband's face and wrapped her arms around his waist.

"Have I told you just how good you look in that suit?" she asked.

Dash's eyebrow went up at her intentionally suggestive tone. "I'm pretty sure you'll like me better out of it," he said with his own smile, making her laugh.

"I like you just fine in whatever you are, or are not, wearing." She went up on her tiptoes and kissed him. He followed her lips down, dipping his head, as she returned her heels to the ground.

"That's nice," he said, his voice gruff against her lips. "Because, as much as I love you all the time, I have to say, I'm partial to when you're not wearing anything except me and a smile."

Matty laughed again against his lips. "I'm so glad to hear that, Dr. Kent," she said, lacing her fingers with his and gently pulling him in the direction of the dance floor that was full of couples slow dancing. "Because that aligns perfectly with my plans for the evening."

He let out a low groan as they stepped onto the floor and she slipped into his arms. "You're going to make me wait, aren't you?"

She laughed at his grumpy tone and then slid her fingers into the hair at the nape of his neck, nudging his head down so her mouth was beside his ear. "Since when have I ever made you wait for anything," she whispered. She took his hand and led him back off the dance floor and to the room she had secretly booked at the inn for the night.

No longer showing any signs of grumpiness, Dash followed Matty into the room and closed the door behind them. She took both his hands and backed toward the bed, pulling him with her as she went, watching him. His eyes darkened in anticipation with every step.

She stopped in front of the bed and he closed the distance, his arms wrapping around her.

"Now, about that smile thing," she said.

ACKNOWLEDGEMENTS

I FEEL LIKE A BROKEN record now that I am lucky enough to be writing my third acknowledgements page. On the other hand, it's good to be repetitive, since to me it means I have good people and good relationships in my life, the kind that will stick. I thank my former publisher, Booktrope, and marketing manager, Sophie Weeks, for their trust and belief in me as well as all their efforts to get my stories out there. And Julie Molinari, my editor, who is the book world equivalent of that borderline-sadistic personal trainer we all know—the one that smiles and then somehow gets you to workout until you want to barf. Or shove a pencil in your eye. But in the end I get a book that's in much better shape than before; it's toned, put together, and works the way it's supposed to. You should thank her, too.

Thanks also always goes to my ladies, Sarah A, Jere, Lisa, Megs, and Sian (my friend and designer!) and to my mountain movers, Sarah C and Angeli—we may see each other less these days, but distance is inconsequential (and we tend to make up for it when we do see each other).

And last, special thanks to the family—all of it. I'm glad we're back in California.

Keep reading for a preview of Tamsen Schultz's

WHAT ECHOES RENDER
WINDSOR SERIES BOOK 3

Betrayal was something Jesse Baker thought she already knew too much about. But when her dead husband's past comes back to haunt her, both the life she's built for herself and her sons and the story she's told herself to make it through threaten to crumble into ashes.

Fire and ashes are David Hathaway's life. Since sending his daughter to college, his time is his own and the arson investigator intends to make the most of having no one to look after but himself. That is, until he meets Jesse and an explosion nearly takes her life, changing his forever.

Echoes from their pasts follow them both. And they know those memories, like fire, can give life just as easily as they can destroy it. But before Jesse and David can decide for themselves how their histories will influence their future, they must first stop a killer intent on making Jesse burn for the sins of others.

CHAPTER 1

ALERTED BY THE CLICK OF her heels on the industrial floor, several heads raised from behind nurses' stations as Jesse Baker walked down the hall of Riverside Hospital's intensive care unit. Housing the sickest of the sick, this floor was, naturally, one of the quietest in the hospital. But even so, as Jesse made her way from the sixth floor elevators toward the east wing, the silence seemed to have seeped into everything around her, dampening movements and slowing time; the people, the lights, the machines, all seemed to be moving in their own worlds.

But then again, it had been a somewhat surreal day altogether.

Rounding the corner to her destination, Jesse came upon a man standing with his back to her. Wearing cargo pants, work boots, and a navy blue t-shirt emblazoned with the firefighters' emblem and "AFD," he stood with his hands in his pockets, as still, as contained, as everything else around him. From the back, he looked youngish. And fit, judging by his shape. He wasn't what Jesse had been expecting. But her surprise was only of the curious kind that happens when one isn't actually aware of one's expectations until presented with something that doesn't meet them.

His head turned at the sound of her approach and she caught a glimpse of his profile. His brown hair, streaked with gold, touched the top of his ears. His nose was straight and his skin the color of a man who spent time outdoors. When he turned toward her, she noted the emblem over his pectoral, a miniature of that on the back of his shirt.

"You must be the investigator from the state," Jesse said, striding toward him with her hand outstretched, her voice sure.

She didn't miss the way his eyes took her in—taking stock, not judging—as his hand closed around hers. His fingers and palm were rough, the hand of a man who did more than just type on a keyboard.

"I'm Jesse Baker," she said. "The Hospital Administrator."

"David Hathaway, Arson Investigator."

"And Albany Firefighter, if your shirt is anything to go by?" she asked. The official who had called to alert her about the visit had only mentioned the investigator's arson credentials.

He nodded. "The state called, I assume?" he asked.

She confirmed with a nod then glanced around the hallway, wondering if maybe they should go somewhere else to talk. She'd never been in this kind of situation before. But he resolved her indecision by taking control of the conversation.

"You run the show then, Ms. Baker?" he asked with a vague gesture of his hand meant to encompass the facility.

She inclined her head, going along.

"Such as it is. And please, call me Jesse," she added.

"It's a nice place," he responded, his eyes sweeping the area. He looked about her age, mid-to-late thirties. And though his attempts to put her at ease weren't subtle, she appreciated them nonetheless.

"Have you been here long?" he asked, returning his gaze to her.

Despite everything, she let herself smile a bit at that. She looked young, always had. She wasn't young, in any sense of the word, but people always thought she was a good ten years younger than she was. Including, apparently, David Hathaway.

"I've been the administrator for six years, but I've been at Riverside Hospital for over twelve," she answered.

His brows shot up in surprise and then he seemed to catch himself.

"Then I can't imagine much surprises you these days," he said, his voice indicating that his mind had returned to the reason for his visit.

Again, she dipped her head.

"Generally, that's true. But this, well, this situation *is* new to me, Mr. Hathaway."

"Please, call me David."

She nodded then looked down the empty hallway again. What she'd gleaned from the first responders, and the news, was that the house that had gone up in flames earlier in the day. It was so rural that, while the neighbors eventually saw the smoke, no one had heard anything. And based on what the state official had told her, the cause of the fire which had brought Aaron Greene to her hospital was still, officially, undetermined. But he had also told her, confidentially, that there had been an explosion. What kind, she assumed, was the investigator's—David's—job to figure out, but the man from the state had intimated that it might not have been accidental and may not have been meant for the house. Which left her thinking what he'd no doubt intended her to think: Aaron had been involved, somehow, with a bomb.

The thought made her sick, and knowing what it might do to the community, if in fact Aaron had been planning to detonate a bomb somewhere in the area, she had every intention of keeping it quiet until the state made an official ruling. So, even though she and David weren't talking about anything confidential—yet—she didn't particularly want prying eyes and ears nearby. Especially since it was still possible that the explosion wasn't anything intentional.

"I've never met an arson investigator investigating this kind of thing," she continued as she stepped to the side of the hall, toward an empty room. He followed and seemed to sense her desire to keep things quiet as he moved close enough for her to lower her voice as she spoke. "And while we have our fair share of kids doing stupid things, I can safely say, Aaron Greene and his father are our first…" She let her voice trail off, not wanting to say "bomb victims."

A frown touched his lips and she knew that he heard the concern in her voice. Concern about the explosive that had ripped through the Greenes' rural farmhouse, to be sure, but also concern for those involved and what it all might mean. But he didn't know the community the way she did, didn't know how its people would react or respond, and wisely, she thought, he held his tongue, handing her a folded piece of paper instead.

"The warrant for Aaron's medical records?" she asked.

He nodded and she gave it a cursory glance before refolding it.

"How is he?" David asked.

"He's in serious condition," she answered. "It was a toss-up as to whether we should transport him to Albany or not. But he seemed to stabilize here so we've kept him. They have a better burn unit there, but he'll get more individualized care here since we're a bit smaller."

"And he's part of the community," David suggested but didn't seem to be judging.

"There is that part of it, yes," Jesse answered then gestured for him to follow her. "Aaron and my son Matt are in the same class," she explained as they began to walk toward Aaron's room. "As is Danielle Martinez, the daughter of the doctor who worked on him." They turned the corner and headed toward the end of another hall. "But believe me," she added, "if we thought he'd have had a better chance up there, we would have sent him."

And they would have, but it had been a judgment call, like so many decisions in hospitals were. And thankfully, it looked like it was a decision that was going to work out okay. Aaron *was* in serious condition, but he was stable.

David didn't seem to feel the need to comment, so, with the exception of the click of Jesse's heels, they made their way down the hall to Aaron's room in silence. She stopped in front of the large glass window that separated the hallway from the room where Aaron lay. For a moment, they observed the young man—his body, bandaged and unmoving, hooked to machines that monitored the life still fighting for a chance within him.

The smell of burnt clothes and flesh had been awful when he'd first come in over seven hours earlier. Even now, there were still hints of it lingering in the hall, although it had mostly been suppressed by the antiseptics used to clean every surface in the ICU and by the glass wall dividing the patient from the hall. There was also the plastic containment unit Dr. Martinez had ordered constructed around Aaron as an additional layer of protection.

"Did they know him?" David asked, presumably referring to her son, Matt, and Dr. Martinez's daughter, Danielle.

"Not well." She shook her head. "But while Riverside is a small town, Windsor, where we're from, where Aaron is from, is even smaller. And it's an even smaller high school."

"Everyone-knows-everyone kind of place?" he asked.

She nodded. They stood, not speaking for a moment, and she wondered just what an arson investigator would be thinking about what he was seeing in front of him.

"So, what do you think?" he asked, surprising her.

"About?" she responded, not entirely sure what he was asking her.

"About Aaron," he clarified, keeping his voice low. "Do you think he was the kind of kid to build an explosive device?" he asked, confirming her assumptions about just what he was investigating.

She glanced at David, caught a little off guard by the question, before letting her gaze fall back on the boy. He was eighteen, so not legally a child anymore. But lying there alone, he looked small and helpless.

"I think that, whether he constructed a bomb that killed his father or he was the victim of it, it's going to be a tragic story," she said, her voice soft.

She could feel David's gaze on her as she stared at Aaron for a moment longer. As a mother, her heart broke for the young man. She knew enough about his life to know it hadn't been easy for him these past few years. Not that she thought that would be an acceptable excuse if he did end up being responsible for building a bomb that ruined his home and killed his father, but she believed what she'd just said. Whichever way things turned out, it was going to be a tragedy.

Not wanting to sink too far into maudlin thoughts, Jesse straightened and turned away from the glass window to face the investigator. "I'll take you to my office and we can pull the files. I'll also call Dr. Martinez so that she can come up and answer any of your questions," she said. "Once you have what you need from us up here, we can head down to the morgue where Dr. DeMarco is finishing up the autopsy of Brent Greene, Aaron's father."

David recognized her comment for what it was, more of a plan than a request, and he gestured with his hand for her to precede him. She led him back down to the elevators and to her office located on the first floor. When they arrived outside her office, Kayla, her assistant, looked up from her desk.

"Here is the official warrant for the records for Aaron Greene," Jesse said, handing the paper to Kayla, who took it from her without a word. She had no doubt Kayla would know exactly what to do with the document. Kayla was one of the brightest, most detail-oriented people Jesse knew, despite the fact that, unlike herself, her assistant actually *was* young, very young.

Leaving Kayla to her task, they entered Jesse's office where she offered David a seat. He declined, opting instead to take a slow tour around the room, checking out her pictures and books while she sat down at her desk to make a quick call to Abigail Martinez and bring up the electronic medical records. Hitting the print button she sat back and waited for the documents to spit themselves out.

"Is that your boy Matt?" David asked, pointing to a picture. It was one of her favorites of her oldest son. Matt was sweaty and his hair was sticking out all over the place, but the grin he wore, along with the medal from the track championships, reminded her of the little boy he'd once been.

"Yes, it was at the all-state track meet last year," she answered. "He came home with several medals," she added, not bothering to hide the hint of parental pride. Her printer stopped and she walked to a file cabinet to retrieve a folder from the bottom drawer for David to take the papers in. Straightening away from the cabinet, she turned to find him watching her. She held his gaze for a split second, then he looked away.

"You must be very proud," he said, turning back to the picture. For just a beat, Jesse felt a touch off balance. That he was an attractive man hadn't escaped her notice, but she was so used to being heads-down working during her time at the hospital that recognizing a person as anything other than a colleague was a skill she had long ago lost. Or maybe not. Because that look had felt like more than just a collegial exchange.

Deciding she'd imagined it, she turned back to the printer to pick up the documents as she answered. "I'm proud of both my boys. They're good kids."

She handed him the file and he looked about to ask another question when a knock sounded at the door.

"Are you ready for me?" Abigail Martinez asked as she popped her head through the doorway. At more than a decade older than Jesse, Abigail's short, dark hair was streaked with gray and her face held hints of her age. But her deep brown eyes danced with almost childlike humor just as often as they reflected the strain of her job.

Jesse offered her friend a smile and welcomed her in, thankful for the break in the conversation that was turning a bit too much toward her family. It's not that she had anything to hide, but no matter how good-looking David Hathaway was, he was still a virtual stranger.

After making the introductions, they agreed that Abigail would bring David back to Jesse's office when the two had finished going over Aaron's injuries and medical condition. After that, Jesse would take him down to the morgue where the autopsy on Brent Greene would be finishing up. In the meantime, she had paperwork to finish, reports to review, and a newsletter to write. Good times.

Jesse watched the two leave as an errant thought filtered into her head. David Hathaway might be an interesting distraction, but, like most parents, she already had more on her plate than she could handle. Really.

• • •

David walked through the hospital with Dr. Martinez as his mind stayed in the office with Jesse Baker. He had watched her lean over to pull a folder out of a cabinet drawer and for a moment his mind had gone blank. She had more than caught his attention as she'd come striding toward him in the hallway earlier—with her long blonde hair pulled back into a ponytail, she wore a fitted V-necked sweater the same color as her brown eyes and a not-quite demure skirt that hit just below her knees, but hugged every curve. A pair of four-inch heels that he was sure were an attempt to disguise her petite stature were the coup de grâce. He'd thought her too young to run Riverside Hospital and had initially thought maybe the administrator had sent an assistant to handle the inquiry into Aaron Greene. And to say he was surprised when she said she'd been there for twelve years was an understatement. He vaguely remembered thinking it put her closer to his own age if she had started right out of graduate school.

But then when she'd bent over in her office, pure male instinct had taken over and the only thought that had flitted through, and stuck, in David's mind was that he saw no panty lines under that nicely formed skirt—that and the short list of reasons why he saw no panty lines. All very nice thoughts, in his opinion.

Then she'd straightened and looked at him. The shape of her standing before him, slightly turned at the hip and glancing over her shoulder, had reminded him of the bombshells from the fifties. She wasn't tall, maybe five foot four in her heels, but she looked like someone had taken Marilyn Monroe, blonde hair and all, and just shrunk her down without changing any of the proportions.

David had never been very attracted to skinny women and, for good or for bad, Jesse Baker had reminded him of that with every move she made, from her confident walk, to the way she slid into her chair, to the way she held his gaze for just a moment after she'd straightened away from the file cabinet.

But then she'd handed him the file. And he had reminded himself that he wasn't there to flirt, a skill that was so rusty he was pretty sure he'd lost the ability altogether anyway. No, he was there to figure out if eighteen-year-old Aaron Greene had built a bomb that had gone off earlier in the day, destroying the peaceful spring morning as well as Aaron's home, his body, and his father's life.

David gave an internal sigh as he followed Dr. Martinez and begrudgingly admitted to himself that it was probably a good thing she had arrived when she did. He had no business digging into Jesse's life, asking about her sons. His own life was finally, after years and years of effort, becoming less complicated. He didn't need to fuck that up by flirting with a woman he'd just met. A woman he knew nothing about and who was, most likely, married. So, dutifully, he wrenched his brain away from the tempting curves of the hospital administrator and focused on the horror that Dr. Martinez was about to lay before him.

Forty-five minutes later, he had the gist of what he needed to know. Aaron had suffered third-degree burns on 10 percent of his body and had another 20 percent affected by first- and second-degree burns. The bulk of the serious injuries were centered around his right palm, left forearm, and down the left side of his torso. The majority of the second-degree burns impacted the left side of his body—his leg, shoulder, and that side of his face. He was in shock, unconscious, and would likely remain so for at least another day or two. If he didn't come to in that timeframe, Dr. Martinez indicated that his chances of survival would drop significantly.

She and her team were competent, more so than he'd expected walking into the hospital of a relatively small town. But while Windsor, where the explosion had happened, with its mix of wealthy weekenders and hard-working, blue-collar full-time residents was a town with a low crime rate, Riverside was a different story. David knew it was gentrifying, but he also knew from his chief that, for decades, Riverside had seen more than its share of crime, violence, drugs, and poverty. And the hospital, by necessity, had responded accordingly.

After going over everything and peppering Dr. Martinez with a number of questions, David followed her back to Jesse's office where they found her sitting behind her computer screen, leaning back in her chair, chewing on her lip. She looked up at them from under her eyelashes with a decidedly irritated expression.

Dr. Martinez laughed, the first laughter he'd heard from anyone since he'd walked into the hospital. "Let me guess, the monthly newsletter?" she asked.

Jesse let out a huff. "I hate this thing," she responded. She stared at her computer for a moment more before sitting forward and shutting it off.

"I foolishly started it three years ago and now everyone expects it," she explained, looking at David as she stood and began gathering her things.

Beside him, Dr. Martinez chuckled. "It's true, everyone does expect it. But only because you have a way with words."

"Ha, anyone who manages a facility filled with two hundred doctors better have a way with words," Jesse countered. "Anyway, I'll figure it out later." She closed her laptop and slid it into her bag. "Will I see you at the meet later?" she asked Dr. Martinez, pulling the bag's strap over her shoulder. "Matt and Danielle are both on the track team. We only have a couple of meets left before they both graduate," she added as an aside to David. A hint of parental sadness tinged her voice. He knew the feeling.

The two women made plans to meet at the high school and when it was clear they were finished, he thanked the doctor. She'd agreed to keep him updated and it was all he could ask for at the moment.

"Ready?" Jesse asked, once Dr. Martinez had left. He nodded and followed her out.

"You seem to have a good staff here," he said, making small talk as they left her office.

"I know, not what you'd expect from a small-town hospital, but you're right, we do," she answered. "Don't get me wrong," she added as she hit the down button outside the elevator. "We're not nearly as equipped as Albany or even Pittsfield, Massachusetts, but we're pretty good for our size and location. You must not be from around here?"

They stepped into the elevator and he was surprised to catch a delicate whiff of her perfume. It was hard to smell much of anything not industrial or biological in a hospital, but he definitely caught her scent. With a shake of his head, he answered.

"No, I moved here about ten months ago from Northern California."

"What brought you here? I love it, but it's not a well-known area."

David shrugged. "I like it, too. Colder than where I'm from, but I wanted to be on the East Coast and Albany offered me the chance to be both a firefighter and an arson investigator. I've done both, but in the past several years, I've mostly done the investigation part. I like it, but I missed being part of a team." That was part of the story—all true, just not all of the story.

"And how does that work?" she asked. The elevator dinged and the doors slid open, revealing a basement hallway. Stepping out, she directed him to the right as she clarified, "Being a firefighter and an investigator, I mean."

"In big cities they're usually different roles," he said, following her through the dim corridor. "But in areas like this, with lots of rural municipalities, towns and counties that don't have the need or funds to keep someone like me on staff full time rely on the state. So I'm employed by the State of New York as a part-time investigator and the rest of the time I work for the Albany FD."

He finished explaining just as Jesse stopped at a pair of closed doors. As she looked up at him, he noted that she had the longest eyelashes ringing her eyes, which he now realized were more hazel than brown.

"Sounds like a reasonable compromise," she said, her hand on the swinging door.

He shrugged.

She studied him for a moment, then took a deep breath. "You ready?".

After his sharp nod, they pushed into the morgue, a serviceable room containing a single table, a desk, and a woman washing up at the sink. On the table lay a form under a white sheet. The woman turned and looked at them over her shoulder as the door clicked shut behind them.

"Jesse," she smiled. "I'm glad you came down, I wasn't sure if you were going to." She finished rinsing her hands and grabbed a couple of paper towels before turning all the way around.

Presumably this was the medical examiner. She was another attractive woman, but in a very different way than Jesse. Even in her scrubs, it was easy to see she had an athletic build, though she looked like she'd either put on weight recently or was in the early stages of pregnancy. She was a lot taller than Jesse and had dark hair and Mediterranean skin. In looks, about the only thing the two women had in common was the way they wore their hair. As his eyes met the woman's, he recognized a look of idle curiosity in her expression.

"I wanted to make sure we were still on for tonight?" Jesse asked.

The other woman's eyes swung back to her friend.

"And by the way, this is David Hathaway, the arson investigator," Jesse said. "David, this is Dr. Vivienne DeMarco. She is, among many things, our medical examiner. She's also a professor at the university in Boston and an FBI consultant."

The introduction was meant to impress him and it did. He wondered how such a small town had landed such a person.

"She's also pregnant and shouldn't be working so hard."

David turned at the new voice and saw a man in a sheriff's uniform stride into the room with a resigned expression on his face. The officer walked up to Dr. DeMarco and gave her a swift kiss.

"You shouldn't be standing so much." The man's voice was soft with affection.

"I'm pregnant, Ian, not ill. Now, don't be rude," Dr. DeMarco responded as she gestured toward David with her head. The sheriff ignored her statement for a moment and stared at her with a look of repressed exasperation. When she arched a brow at him, he rolled his eyes and turned toward David.

"Sheriff Ian MacAllister. Also Vivienne's husband. But call me Ian, please," he said, holding out his hand.

"David Hathaway," he responded, taking the proffered hand. The assessment the sheriff subjected him to was swift, but David didn't doubt it was complete. Something in the man's bearing screamed competence. Probably military-trained competence.

"It's nice to meet you. Can't say I'm a fan of the circumstances, but what can we do?" Ian said with a shrug.

David couldn't agree more and said so.

"So, is there a reason you called me here?" Ian asked his wife, who elbowed him in response.

"Yes, now don't be pushy," she answered. "Let me just finish up with Jesse and I'll be right with you both."

The two women walked toward the door. It was obvious they were good friends and they seemed to be making plans to meet later that night for dinner. It was amazing to him that they could be talking about such a thing considering where they were. Oh, he was used to it. Sort of. He'd been around enough burned bodies that the smell didn't completely turn his stomach anymore. And, well, Dr. DeMarco—he understood that, given her job, she probably had a cast-iron stomach.

But it said a lot about Jesse that she hadn't flinched a bit when they'd walked into the room. He didn't get the sense that she spent a lot of time in the morgue or saw all that much violent death, but she just seemed strong. Able to take what life put in front of her. Today it happened to be a body burned to nearly nothing. He had to admire her for that.

"So what's the public story?" Ian asked, pulling David's attention back to the situation at hand.

"About?" David countered, feeling a little slow.

Ian lifted a shoulder. "I haven't heard much of the news today, but if they suspected a bomb was the origin of the fire, it'd be all over the media. We wouldn't be hearing about anything else. So even if that's what you are investigating, the public story must be something else."

David studied the sheriff, taking in the man's matter-of-fact assumption that what was being made public might not be the real, or entire story. It made David wonder about Ian's background. Not that it mattered one way or another.

"Officially undetermined, but we're mentioning a possible gas explosion," was all he said, figuring that as law enforcement, Ian should probably know the company line, so to speak.

Ian raised his shoulders in an "it'll do" gesture and they fell back into silence. David didn't miss the fact that he wasn't the only one whose eyes seemed to gravitate to the two women.

"They might be talking about you," Ian said, out of the blue.

David turned at Ian's voice. "I beg your pardon?"

"My wife is steadfastly trying not to look in my direction. That usually means she's up to something," he said. "And my guess is, given the way Jesse is shaking her head and rolling her eyes, Vivienne is probably trying to suss out whether or not she's interested in you."

David wasn't quite sure what to say to that. At least Ian had answered the question of whether or not Jesse was married. But still, even knowing small towns had lots of small-town gossip, being sucked into it after knowing a man for less than five minutes left David with very little to say. And he must have looked it because Ian let out a big laugh.

"Don't worry. If there's a single guy within a forty-mile radius, my wife is trying to set Jesse up with him. I try not to get involved. But there it is."

"There what is?" Dr. DeMarco asked, returning to their side of the room. David watched as Jesse gave him one last look before pushing the morgue door open and leaving him alone with the couple.

"You, trying to set Jesse up," Ian responded as he crossed his arms over his chest, all but daring his wife to argue. She opened her mouth, then shut it, then opened it again before pursing her lips and glaring at her husband—like a puppy caught in the act.

"I have no idea what you're talking about," she finally retorted. "Now, if you'd both like to turn your attention to Brent Greene, I will present you with my findings."

"Please," Ian said, making a grand gesture toward the table. David encountered a lot of people in his line of work. Some earned his respect, some he enjoyed working with. But it seemed that everyone he'd met in just the last few hours during his visit to Riverside were people he might actually like. Not just as colleagues, but possibly as friends.

They were genuine in the way they worked together and treated each other as professionals. But they also seemed to somehow cross over and have real relationships outside of work—meeting for dinner, cheering their kids on together—or, in the case of Dr. DeMarco and Ian, working and living together. Maybe there was something to be said for small towns.

"Now, Mr. Hathaway—" Dr. DeMarco began.

"David," he interrupted.

She acknowledged his interjection with a nod then continued. "You might be wondering why I called Ian here. Aside from being my husband, of course." She cast a smile at Ian over her shoulder and her husband's lips lifted in return.

"I assumed it was because arson, of any sort, is a criminal investigation and him being the sheriff and all," David responded, his curiosity piqued. If Dr. DeMarco had found something to indicate it was more than arson, this could get interesting.

"It is, of course. But let me direct your attention here." She led both men over to a large computer screen and pulled up a couple of x-ray images. Both showed a skull. "Now, Mr. Greene's ultimate cause of death is smoke inhalation," she said.

"He wasn't killed by the fire? Or the explosion?" David clarified.

"No," she shook her head. "He was dead before the fire got to him and the injuries that I did find that resulted from the explosion wouldn't have killed him."

"But you did find evidence of an explosion?" David asked.

Dr. Demarco nodded. "Most definitely. But I found those injuries mostly on the lower part of his body and not severe enough to be the cause of death. So, as I was saying," she continued, "the smoke is what ultimately caused his death, but I want to draw your attention here." She pointed to the forehead area of the x-ray. David stepped closer and peered at the area. At his side, he felt Ian do the same.

"Is that a series of fractures I see?" David asked, frowning.

"It is," she answered.

"He was hit on the head before he died from the smoke?" Ian clarified.

"He was. And whatever it was he was hit on the head with, or by, was powerful. This bone here," she circled the area of the forehead, "is a very strong bone. As you can see from the x-rays, there are several small radiating fractures. It would take a hard instrument and a strong person to do that."

"And not something that would happen if he fell and hit his head?" David asked.

"Definitely not. Not enough force," she answered.

"Can you tell if it happened before or after the injuries he got from the explosion?" David asked.

Dr. DeMarco shook her head. "Not by the injuries themselves. The best I can tell from the remains is that they happened either close together or at the same time."

"But?" Ian pressed, obviously hearing something in his wife's voice.

She cast him a glance, then spoke. "But if we look at the placement of the injuries, not the injuries themselves, I would posit that he was hit on the head, fell down, and *then* the explosion went off, sending debris and such into his legs, particularly the lower portions which were probably closest to the origin."

Ian bobbed his head. "Okay, so a forceful hit to the head knocked him out."

"So, what would do that?" David asked.

"And who?" Ian added.

"As to who, that's your job, babe," she said with a grin. Out of the corner of his eye, David saw Ian roll his eyes at his wife's dry tone.

"As to what," she continued, "I'd say something thick and hard."

"Like a baseball bat?" David offered.

She shook her head. "Not round, something flat. Like a two-by-four or the like."

"Like something that would have burned up in the fire." The sheriff's voice wasn't thrilled and David could sympathize.

"You think a third person might have been involved? Someone who whacked the dad?" David asked.

"That's not my territory," she answered.

"It *is* her territory, Hathaway. Maybe not officially, but by experience. And don't let her fool you into thinking otherwise," Ian interjected, clarifying for David. For a moment the sheriff's eyes narrowed on his wife, as if trying to figure her out, then he shrugged.

"For some reason, she's trying to stay out of it, though. Not sure why, since she never has before, but I'll figure that out later. Officially, an assault like this would be my case," he said, studying the image. "Unless of course the state or the feds take over, depending on what you find, Hathaway," he added, taking a step away from the computer screen.

"But if someone were to ask me," Dr. DeMarco continued, ignoring her previous statement with a sly smile directed at her husband, who shot David a look as if to say "I told you so." "I'd say you should look into the possibility of a third person, but my guess is you'll find that Aaron did it," she pronounced as she placed her hands on the small of her back and stretched, displaying her growing belly.

"You need to sit down, Vivienne," Ian said, noticing his wife's movements with concern.

"I'm fine," she waved him off.

"Why?" David asked, cutting off the protest that was no doubt forming on Ian's lips.

"Maybe to stop his father," she offered, her head tilted as she studied the images.

"Stop his father from setting off the bomb or stop his father from stopping *him* from setting off the bomb?" he pressed.

She took a moment to answer. "You'll have to figure that out," she finally said. But it was clear from the way her gaze slid to the side that the good doctor definitely had her opinions.

David frowned and mentally went through what Dr. Martinez had told him about Aaron's condition. "Aaron's injuries might be consistent with an attempt to diffuse a bomb," he posited, thinking out loud more than anything. He hadn't really formed any opinions yet, didn't have enough information. But he wanted to throw it out there and see what this couple did with that option.

"Or they might be consistent with someone who was attempting to build one and accidentally set it off," Ian suggested, though his tone was more pragmatic than persuasive or argumentative.

"Would this injury have killed him, Dr. DeMarco, if the smoke hadn't?" David asked, pointing to the x-ray images.

"Call me Vivi, please, and yes, it probably would have if he didn't seek treatment for it. The force of the blow was strong enough that the impact of the fractures would have caused damage and bleeding of the brain. Left untreated, his brain would likely have swollen, eventually killing him."

"So if it was Aaron who hit his father and then set off the bomb, he's probably responsible for his father's death either way," David said.

"But if he hit his father and tried to diffuse the bomb, he was likely acting in some form of self-defense," Ian countered.

David had to admit that, even though he would track the evidence where it took him, the idea of Aaron Greene being involved in this debacle as a hero rather than a killer appealed to him. He knew it was possible for a kid to be cold-blooded, to build bombs and set fires that killed people. But he preferred to give the young man the benefit of the doubt. And though everyone he'd met so far at Riverside had maintained professional detachment and no one had raved about Aaron being innocent, it was clear from how they talked about him, how they talked about the situation, that everyone was having a hard time buying he was the bad guy in all this.

Printed in the USA
CPSIA information can be obtained
at www.ICGtesting.com
JSHW031706140824
68134JS00038B/3542